"Everyone has secrets, d
they share with those th
prefer to keep to themse

Wyatt was quiet for a long mo.......
that if you ever want to share yours, you can trust me."

Rosa trusted very few people. And she certainly wasn't
going to trust Wyatt, who was only a temporary tenant
and would be out of her life in a few short weeks.

"If I had any secrets, I might do that. But I don't. I'm a
completely open book."

She tried for a breezy smile but could tell he wasn't at all
convinced. In fact, he looked slightly disappointed.

She tried to ignore her guilt and opted to change the
subject instead. "The lightning seems to have stopped
for now. I am sure the power will be back on soon."

"No doubt."

"Thank you again for coming to my rescue. Good night.
Be careful going back down the stairs."

"I will do that. Good night."

He studied her, his features unreadable in the dim
light of her flashlight. He looked as if he wanted to say
something else. Instead, he shook his head slightly.

"Good night."

As he turned to go back down the stairs, the masculine
scent of him swirled to her. She felt again that sudden
wild urge to kiss him but ignored it. Instead, she went
into her darkened apartment, her dog at her heels,
and firmly closed the door behind her. If only she
could close the door to her thoughts as easily.

The Women of Brambleberry House

New York Times, USA TODAY, and #1 *Publishers Weekly* bestselling author **RaeAnne Thayne** finds inspiration in the beautiful northern Utah mountains, where she lives with her family. Her stories have been described as "poignant and sweet," with "beautiful honest storytelling that goes straight to the heart." She loves to hear from readers and can be reached through her website at raeannethayne.com.

RaeAnne Thayne

A BRAMBLEBERRY SUMMER

HARLEQUIN

SPECIAL
EDITION

Recycling programs
for this product may
not exist in your area.

ISBN-13: 978-1-335-91778-2

A Brambleberry Summer

Copyright © 2021 by Harlequin Books S.A.

The publisher acknowledges the copyright holder of the individual works as follows:

A Brambleberry Summer
Copyright © 2021 by RaeAnne Thayne LLC

A Cold Creek Reunion
Copyright © 2012 by Raeanne Thayne

This edition published by arrangement with Harlequin Books S.A.

For questions and comments about the quality of this book, please contact us at CustomerService@Harlequin.com.

Harlequin Enterprises ULC
22 Adelaide St. West, 40th Floor
Toronto, Ontario M5H 4E3, Canada
www.Harlequin.com

Printed in Lithuania

MIX
Paper from
responsible sources
FSC® C021394

CONTENTS

A BRAMBLEBERRY SUMMER   7

A COLD CREEK REUNION   217

A BRAMBLEBERRY SUMMER

To all the readers who have asked me
to write Rosa's story over the years.

Chapter 1

Summer Saturdays in a busy tourist town like Cannon Beach, Oregon, were not for the faint of heart.

As always, the sidewalk outside Rosa Galvez's gift shop, By-The-Wind, was packed with tourists. Kids in swimming suits. Parents with sunburned noses, their arms loaded with buckets and towels and umbrellas. And, her favorite, older people arm in arm, enjoying an afternoon of browsing through the local stores.

The long, wide stretch of beach that gave the town its name was only a half block from her store, which meant she had a nonstop view of the action, both in front of her store and farther down the beach.

One could never grow bored watching the kites, the recumbent bicycles, the children building sandcastles.

Some hardy souls were even swimming in the shallows, though Rosa always considered it entirely too cold. Maybe her childhood in Honduras had left her too warm-blooded.

Instead, she was busy working the cash register at her gift shop while her newest employee and dear friend, Jen Ryan, rearranged a display of tiny hand-carved lighthouses an artist in Lincoln City had crafted for her.

Nearby, Jen's six-year-old daughter, Addie, giggled at something in the small children's area Rosa had created, complete with a miniature kitchen and dollhouse. The children's area worked beautifully to keep little hands away from the more breakable items in the store while their parents browsed.

While she finished ringing up a cute handmade teapot for her customer, she kept a watchful eye on Jen. This was only her second day working in the store, though she and Addie had been in town for a few weeks. She still seemed anxious, and was constantly looking toward the door as if she expected something horrible to burst through at any moment.

Rosa hoped that with time her friend would lose that skittish air, the impression she gave off that at the slightest provocation, she would grab her child and bolt out the door of the shop.

How could Rosa blame her, after everything Jen had been through? It was a wonder she could even go out in public. All things considered, she was doing remarkably well and seemed to be settling into life here in Cannon Beach. Having her living at Brambleberry House was a joy.

She finished carefully wrapping the customer's teapot in bubble wrap so it would be safe in whatever corner of luggage it was stuffed into.

"There you are," Rosa said, handing over the bag. "Thank you for shopping at By-The-Wind."

"Thank *you*. This is such an adorable shop. We've been to every store in town and you have the best merchandise.

Authentic and charming souvenirs. I'll definitely be back before we leave town."

"I am very glad to hear this." She smiled and waved the woman and her husband on their way. She was replenishing her supply of bubble wrap under the counter when the front-door chimes rang out again.

She happened to be looking in Jen's direction and didn't miss the way her friend's features tensed with fear and then visibly relaxed when a woman came in, trailed by a young teenager.

Rosa's day, already good, immediately brightened even further, as if the sun had just come out from behind the clouds.

"Look who it is," she exclaimed. "Two of my favorite people!"

"*Hola*, Rosa," the girl said, beaming brightly at her with a mouth full of braces.

"Hello, my dear." Her friend Carrie Abbott brushed her cheek against Rosa's.

"What a wonderful surprise. How may I help you? Are you looking for a gift for someone? I have some gorgeous new purses in and also some fantastic jewelry from an artisan in Yachats you might like."

"Where's the jewelry?" Like a little magpie, Bella was instantly drawn to anything shiny.

Rosa showed her the new display and they spent a moment looking over the hand-beaded pieces.

"Ooh. Those turquoise starburst earrings are gorgeous! How much are they?"

She named an amount that had the girl's shoulders slumping. "I better not. I'm saving for an electric scooter."

"You know, that's the markup amount. I can probably drop the price by ten dollars."

Bella looked tempted. "I'm babysitting this weekend. If they're still for sale, I'll come back and get them."

"I'll set them aside until you can get back in," Rosa promised, which earned her another braces-filled smile.

"You're too tempting!" Carrie said, shaking her head. "I could blow my entire mad-money budget in here. Believe it or not, we didn't come in to buy earrings, no matter how lovely they are."

"Is there something else I can help you find? You should try the new soaps from Astrid Larsen."

Carrie laughed. "Stop. We're not supposed to be shopping! I came in because I need to talk to you."

Against her will, Rosa's gaze shifted to Bella and then back to the girl's mother. "Oh?" she said, hoping her voice sounded casual.

Carrie leaned against the counter. "Yes. How are you, first of all? I haven't talked to you in forever."

Carrie did not usually drop in just to chat. What was this about? She looked back toward Bella, who was holding the turquoise earrings up to her ears and looking in the mirror of the display.

"I have been good." She smiled. "Summer is always such a busy time here but I am glad for the tourists. Otherwise, I would not be able to keep the store open. And how are you?"

"Good. Busy, too. Bella is going in a hundred different directions, between babysitting and softball and her music lessons."

Such a normal, happy childhood. It warmed her heart. "Oh, that is nice."

"Did I tell you, we have tickets to the theater in Portland next month?" Bella said. "It's a traveling Broadway production of *Hamilton*. And then we're driving down the coast to San Francisco. I cannot *wait*!"

Rosa hid a smile. Bella had only mentioned the upcoming trip about a hundred times since spring, when she and her parents had first started talking about it. "That will be wonderful for you."

"Other than that, everything is pretty good," Carrie said. "Well, okay. I do have one small problem I was hoping you might be able to help us out with."

"Of course. What can I do?"

"Don't answer so quickly. It's a huge favor."

Carrie had to know Rosa would do anything for her. Theirs was that kind of friendship.

"I was wondering if you've found a tenant to sublease your empty apartment until fall, when your renters come back."

Rosa lived on the top floor of a sprawling old Victorian, Brambleberry House. She managed the property for her aunt and her aunt's friend, Sage Benedetto Spencer.

Right now, Jen lived in the second-floor apartment, but the older couple who had been renting the furnished ground-floor apartment for the past year had moved to Texas temporarily to help with an ill family member.

"It is still empty for now."

She didn't have the energy to go the vacation-rental route, with new people constantly coming in and out.

Carrie's features brightened. "Oh, yay! Would you consider renting it for the next month or so?"

Rosa frowned. "Why would you need a place to rent? Are you doing something to your house?"

Carrie and her husband lived in a very nice cottage about a mile from Brambleberry House. She had recently remodeled the kitchen but perhaps she was thinking about doing the bathrooms.

"Not for me," Carrie assured her. "For Wyatt and Logan."

Rosa tensed at the mention of Carrie's brother and his young son. While the boy was adorable, seven years old and cheerful as could be, his father was another matter.

Wyatt Townsend was a detective for the Cannon Beach Police Department and always seemed to look at her as if she was up to something illegal.

That was surely her imagination. She had done nothing to make him suspicious of her.

"I thought he was staying with you while his home is being repaired."

"He is. And I would be fine with him living with us until the work is done, but everything is taking so much longer than he expected. It has been a nightmare of wrangling with the insurance and trying to find subcontractors to do the work."

Wyatt's small bungalow had been damaged in a fire about a month earlier, believed to have been caused by faulty wiring. It had been a small miracle that neither he nor his son had been home at the time and that a neighbor had smelled the smoke and called the fire department before widespread damage.

Rosa knew from Carrie that the fire damage still meant he had to renovate several rooms and had been living with his sister and her husband while the work was being completed.

"That must be hard for Wyatt."

"I know. And after everything they have both been through the past three years, they didn't need one more thing. But he's doing his best to rebuild."

Rosa certainly knew what it mean to rebuild a life.

"The work will take at least another month."

"That long?"

"Yes. And to be honest, I think Wyatt is a little tired of sleeping on the sofa in my family room with his leg hanging over the edge. Since the insurance company will cover rent for the next few months, he said last night he was thinking about looking around for somewhere to stay temporarily. He even brought up the idea of renting a camp trailer and parking it in his driveway until the repairs are done. I immediately thought of your empty apartment and thought that would be so much better for him and Logan, if it's still available."

The apartment was available. But did she really want Wyatt Townsend there? Rosa glanced over at Jen, who was talking to Addie in a low voice.

She could not forget about Jen. In the other woman's situation, how would she feel about having a police detective moving downstairs?

"I know it's a huge ask. You probably have a waiting list as long as my arm for an apartment in that great location."

Rosa shook her head. "I have not really put it on the market, to be honest. I have been too busy and also I know the Smiths want to move back if they can at the end of the summer, after June's mother heals from her broken hip."

That still did not mean she wanted to rent it to Wyatt and his son. She could not even say she had a compelling reason not to, other than her own unease.

The man made her so nervous. It did not help that he was extraordinarily good-looking.

He always seemed to be looking at her as if he knew she had secrets and wouldn't rest until he figured them out.

That wouldn't bother her, as she did not usually have much to do with him. Except she *did* have secrets. So many secrets. And he was the last man in town she wanted to figure them out.

She should just say no. She could tell Carrie she had decided to paint it while it was empty or put in new flooring or something.

That wasn't completely a lie. She had talked to Anna and Sage about making a few cosmetic improvements to the apartment over the summer, but had not made any solid plans. Even if she had, none of them was urgent.

The apartment was in good condition and would be an ideal solution for Wyatt and his son while repairs continued on their house.

She had to let him stay there. How could she possibly say no to Carrie? She owed her so very much.

What would Jen think? Maybe she would find comfort in knowing a big, strong police detective lived downstairs. Their own built-in security.

"Yes. Okay. He can stay there, if he wants to."

"He will," Carrie assured her, looking thrilled. "I should mention that he has a dog. He's the cutest little thing and no trouble at all."

Rosa was not so sure about that. She had seen Wyatt and Logan walking the dog on the beach a few times when she had been walking her own dog, Fiona. Their beagle mix, while adorable, seemed as energetic as Logan.

"It should be fine. The Smiths had a little dog, too. The ground-floor apartment has a dog door out to the fenced area of the lawn. Fiona will enjoy the company."

"Oh, how perfect. It's even better than I thought. I can't thank you enough!"

"He probably will want to take a look at it before he makes any decisions. And we need to talk about rent."

She told her what the Smiths had been paying per month and Carrie's eyes widened.

"Are you kidding? That's totally a bargain around here, especially in the summer. I know the insurance company was going to pay much more than that. I'm sure it will be fantastic. You are the best."

Carrie and Bella left the store a few moments later, with Bella promising to come back so she could pay for the earrings.

As soon as the door closed behind them, Rosa slumped against the jewelry counter. What had she done?

She did *not* want Wyatt Townsend living anywhere close to her. The man looked too deeply, saw too much.

Ah, well. She would simply work a little harder to hide her secrets. She had plenty of practice.

"Sorry. Run that by me again. You did what?"

Wyatt gazed at his sister in shock. She lifted her chin, somehow managing to look embarrassed and defiant at the same time. "You heard me. I talked to Rosa Galvez about you moving into her empty apartment at Brambleberry House."

He adored his older sister and owed her more than he could ever repay for the help she had given him the last three years, since Tori had died. But she had a bad habit of trying to run his life for him.

It was his own fault. He knew what Carrie was like, how she jumped on a single comment and ran with it. He should never have mentioned to her that he was thinking about renting an apartment until the fire renovations were done. He should have simply found one and told her about it later.

"When I mentioned I was thinking about moving out,

I didn't mean for you to go apartment hunting right away for me."

"I know. When you said that, I remembered Rosa had an empty apartment. As far as I'm concerned, you can stay on my family-room couch forever, but I thought a three-bedroom apartment would be better than a little camp trailer for a grown man and an active seven-year-old."

Wyatt could not disagree. In truth, he had made a few inquiries himself that day, and had discovered most of the available rental homes were unavailable all summer and those that were left were out of his price range.

What else did he expect? Cannon Beach was a popular tourist destination. Some of the short-term rentals had been booked out years in advance.

He did not mind living with his sister, brother-in-law and niece. He loved Carrie's family and Logan did, as well. But as the battle with his insurance company dragged on about doing repairs to his bungalow, he had been feeling increasingly intrusive in their lives.

Carrie was already helping him with his son. She didn't need to have them taking up every available inch of her living space with their stuff.

"The apartment at Brambleberry House is perfect! You can move in right now, it's fully furnished and available all summer."

"Why? I would have thought Rosa would want to rent it out on a longer lease."

"The couple who have been living there are supposed to be coming back in a few months. I don't think Rosa is very thrilled about having vacation renters in and out all summer."

"What makes you think having Logan and me downstairs would be better for her?"

"She knows you two. You're friends."

He was not sure he would go that far. Rosa hardly talked to him whenever they were at any kind of social event around town. He almost thought she went out of her way to avoid him, though he was not sure what he might have done to offend her.

"She said it was fine and that you can move in anytime. Today, if you want to. Isn't that wonderful?"

Again, Wyatt wasn't sure *wonderful* was the word he would use. This would only be a temporary resting place until the repairs were completed on their house.

On the other hand, it would be better for Logan than Wyatt's crazy camp-trailer idea. He couldn't deny that.

Poor kid. His world had been nothing but upheaval the past three years, though Wyatt had tried to do his best to give him a stable home life after Tori died.

Wyatt had been working as a police officer in Seattle when his wife went into cardiac arrest from a congenital heart condition none of them had known about. Logan had been four.

Numb with shock at losing his thirty-year-old, athletic, otherwise healthy wife, he had come home to Cannon Beach, where his sister lived, and taken a job with the local police department.

He hadn't known what else to do. His parents had wanted to help but both were busy professionals with demanding careers and little free time to devote to a grieving boy. Carrie had love and time in abundance, and she had urged him to move here, with a slower pace and fewer major crimes than the big city.

The move had been good for both of them. Wyatt liked his job as a detective on the Cannon Beach police force.

He was busy enough that he was never bored but he was also not totally overwhelmed.

He worked on a couple of drug task forces and the SWAT team, which had only been called out a handful of times during his tenure here, all for domestic situations.

The move had been even better for Logan. He loved spending time with his aunt, uncle and older cousin, Bella. He had a wide circle of friends and a budding interest in marine biology.

Wyatt loved seeing his son thrive and knew Carrie and her family were a huge part of that. Logan spent as much time at her house as he did their own.

During the past month, both of them had spent more than enough time with Carrie and her family, since they were living there.

Another month and they could move back to his house, he hoped.

Wyatt counted his blessings that his bungalow hadn't been a complete loss. Fire crews had responded quickly and had been able to save most of the house except the kitchen, where the fire had started, probably from old, faulty wiring. The main living area had also been burned. Even so, all the rooms had suffered water and smoke damage.

Dealing with the renovations was a tedious job, filled with paperwork, phone calls and aggravation, but Wyatt could definitely see the light at the end of the tunnel.

"What do you think?" Carrie looked apprehensive but excited. "Don't you think it's a fabulous idea? Brambleberry House is so close, you can easily drop off Logan when you need me to watch him."

Location definitely was a plus. Carrie's house and Rosa's were only a few blocks apart. Brambleberry House was also positioned about halfway between his house and his sister's, which would be convenient when he was over-seeing the repairs.

Wyatt knew there were many advantages to moving into an apartment at Brambleberry House. Wouldn't it be good to have their own space again? Somewhere he could walk around in his underwear once in a while if he needed to grab a pair of jeans out of the dryer, without having to worry about his sister or his niece walking in on him?

"It could work," he said, not quite willing to jump a hundred percent behind the idea. "Are you sure Rosa is okay with it?"

"Totally great." Carrie gave a bright smile that somehow had a tinge of falseness to it. What wasn't she telling him? Did Rosa Galvez really want to rent the apartment or had Carrie somehow manipulated her into doing it?

He wouldn't put it past his sister. She had a way of per-suading people to her way of thinking.

Wyatt's cop instincts told him there was more to Rosa Galvez than one could see on the surface. She had secrets, but then most people did.

The bottom line was, he was not interested in digging into her secrets. She could keep them.

As long as she obeyed the law, he was not going to pry into her business. Rosa could have all the secrets she wanted. It was nothing to him.

So why, then, was he so apprehensive about moving into Brambleberry House?

He did not have a rational reason to say no. It really did make sense to have their own place. It would be better for Logan, which was the only thing that mattered, really.

It was only a month, maybe two at the most. Wyatt would survive his unease around her.

"Are you sure the apartment is affordable?"

"Absolutely. She told me how much she's charging and you won't find anything else nearly as nice in that price range. It's well within your budget. And I forgot to mention, the apartment already has a dog door for Hank and a fenced area in the yard."

That would be another plus. Logan's beagle mix was gregarious, energetic and usually adorable, but Carrie's two ragdoll cats were not fans of the dog. They would be more than glad to have Hank out of their territory.

"It sounds ideal," he said, finally surrendering to the inevitable. "Thanks for looking into it for us."

"As I said, the apartment is ready immediately. You can stay there tonight, if you want."

He blinked. How had things progressed so quickly from him merely mentioning the night before that he was thinking about moving out to his sister handling all the details and basically shoving him out the door today?

He could think of no good reason to wait and forced a smile. "Great. I'll start packing everything up and we can head over as soon as Logan gets home from day camp."

Carrie's face lit up. "You can at least wait for dinner. I imagine Rosa is probably working until six or seven, anyway."

"Right."

"I think you're going to love it. Rosa is so nice and she has a new tenant, Jen Ryan, who has a little girl who is a bit younger than Logan. Rosa has a wonderful dog, Fiona, who is more human than dog, if you ask me. I'm sure Hank will love her."

At the sound of his name, Wyatt's beagle mix jumped up from the floor, grabbed a ball and plopped it at Wyatt's feet. He picked it up and tossed it down the hall. Hank scrambled after it, much to the disdain of one of the ragdolls, who was sprawled out in a patch of sunlight.

He had seen Rosa on the beach, walking a gorgeous Irish setter. They were hard to miss, the lovely woman and her elegant dog.

Rosa was hard to miss anywhere. She was the sort of woman who drew attention, only in part because of her beautiful features and warm dark eyes.

She exuded warmth and friendliness, at least with everyone else in town. With Wyatt, she seemed watchful and reserved.

That didn't matter, he supposed. She was kind enough to let him live in her apartment for the next month. He didn't need her to be his best friend.

Chapter 2

Now that the deed was done, Rosa was having second, third and fourth thoughts about Wyatt Townsend moving in downstairs.

Why had she ever thought this would work?

That evening as she pulled weeds in the backyard after leaving the store, she had to fight all her instincts that were urging her to call up Carrie right now and tell her she had made a mistake. The apartment was no longer available.

"There is no law against changing your mind, is there?" she asked out loud to Fiona, who was lying in the grass nearby, watching butterflies dance amid the climbing roses.

The dog gave her a curious look then turned back to her business, leaving Rosa to sigh. She yanked harder at a stubborn weed that had driven deep roots into the ground.

She would do nothing. She had given her word and could not back out now. Integrity, keeping her word, was important. She had learned that first from her own mother and then from her adopted parents.

Lauren and Daniel Galvez were two of the most honorable people she knew. They would never think of reneging on a promise and she couldn't, either.

Yes, Wyatt made her extremely nervous. She did not want him moving in downstairs. But she had given her word to his sister. End of story.

Because of that, she would be gracious and welcoming to him and to his sweet son.

Thinking about Logan left her feeling a little bit better about the decision. He was a very adorable boy, with good manners and a ready smile.

It was not the boy's fault that Wyatt made her so nervous.

She had almost talked herself into at least accepting the new status quo, when an SUV pulled up to the house a half hour later.

Fiona lifted her head to sniff the air, then rose and hurried over to the vehicle to greet the newcomers.

Rosa climbed to her feet a little more slowly, pulled off her gloves and swiped at her hair before she headed for the vehicle. She might be accepting of her new tenants, but summoning the same kind of enthusiasm her dog showed so readily would be a stretch.

When Rosa reached the vehicle, Logan was opening the back door and jumping to the ground, his little dog close behind.

Fiona barked a greeting, then leaned in to sniff the newcomer, tail wagging. The Townsends' dog sniffed back, and a moment later, the two were circling each other with joy.

At least Fiona was happy to have them here.

"Hello, Logan," Rosa said.

"Hi." The boy beamed at her, showing off a gap in his teeth that she found adorable.

"Guess what?" he said. "We're moving into your house! Dad says we can stay here until our house is done and I'll have my own bedroom and won't have to sleep in Aunt Carrie's sewing room anymore."

"This is so wonderful, no?" She smiled down at him, trying not to pay any attention to his father walking around the vehicle, looking big and serious and intimidating.

"What is the name of your dog?"

"This is Hank. Don't worry. He's nice."

"I never doubted it for a minute," she assured him. "Hello, Hank."

She reached down to pet the dog, who responded by rolling over to have his belly scratched. Rosa loved him immediately.

"This is Fiona. She is also very nice."

Logan grinned and petted Fiona's long red coat.

Wouldn't it be lovely if she only had to deal with the boy and the dog? Unfortunately, the boy had a father. She had to say something to Wyatt, at least. Bracing herself, she lifted her attention from the two dogs and the boy, and faced the man who always looked as if he could see through her skin and bones into her heart, and was not convinced he liked what he saw.

She drew in a deep breath and forced a smile. "Hello. Welcome to Brambleberry House."

He nodded, always so serious. "Thank you for allowing us to stay here until our house is repaired. It's very kind of you."

She shrugged. "The apartment was empty. Houses are meant to be lived in. Brambleberry House in particular seems a little sad without people, especially children."

She immediately regretted her words, especially when Wyatt raised a skeptical eyebrow.

"Your house seems sad."

Logan giggled. "Houses can't be sad. They're just houses."

She shrugged. "This is no ordinary house. I think you will find that after you have been here a few nights. Come. I will show you your apartment."

She did not wait for a response, but simply walked up the front steps and into the entryway.

"There are three levels of the house with three apartments, one taking up each level. We share the foyer. We try to keep the outside door locked for the security of our residents. I will give you the code, as well as the key."

She was even more vigilant about that right now for Jen's sake.

Wyatt nodded. "Makes sense."

"Your apartment has a separate key. It is on the ground floor. I live on the top floor. If you have any questions or problems, you can find me there or at the store."

"My sister told me you have another new tenant on the second floor."

Rosa's protective instincts flared. "This is true. Her name is Jen Ryan. She lives there with her daughter, Addie, who is six."

"I don't believe I know her."

It was one thing for Wyatt to look at *her* with suspicion. She could not let him turn his police detective's scrutiny toward Jen.

"Jen and Addie only moved here a short time ago from Utah. She is a friend of mine from university."

"Ah. That must be why her name doesn't ring a bell. What brought her to Cannon Beach?"

Rosa's hackles rose. Jen did not need all these questions. It would not do for Wyatt to become too curious. "She works for me. She was looking for a change and I needed someone to help me at the gift store."

He nodded. "Guess I haven't been in for a while or I might have met her already."

He hadn't been in ever, as far as she could remember. But then, Wyatt Townsend was not the sort to buy shell wind chimes or lighthouse-shaped knickknacks.

"I can introduce you after I show you your apartment, if you would like."

"Sure."

Better to get their introduction out of the way. With luck, Wyatt could then forget about Jen.

She would have to send a text to Jen to warn her before showing up at her door with a police detective.

She had already told the other woman about the new tenant moving in. As she had expected, Jen had been both apprehensive and relieved, for a complex mix of reasons.

"This house is big," Logan exclaimed, looking up at the grand entry stairway, one of Rosa's favorite parts of Brambleberry House.

She smiled, in full agreement. "Yes. Each apartment has at least two bedrooms and two bathrooms. And each has a lovely view of the ocean."

She unlocked the first-floor apartment and swung open the door. Immediately, the sweet scent of freesia drifted through the air.

It wasn't unusual to smell flowers at random places in the house. She knew her aunt Anna and Sage Spencer believed the ghost of the previous owner still walked the halls.

Abigail Dandridge had died a decade ago and left the house jointly to Anna and Sage. She had been dear friends to them and also had left Anna By-The-Wind, the gift shop in town that Rosa was a part owner of and now running.

All the old-timers in town still remembered Abigail with fondness. Hardly a week went by when someone did not come into the shop with a memory of Abigail.

Rosa wished she could have known her. She also wanted to be the sort of person whom people remembered with such fondness.

She wasn't sure she believed the stories that Abigail still lingered in the home she had loved and she was also quite certain a no-nonsense police officer like Wyatt Townsend would never believe a benevolent spirit drifted through the place.

She couldn't deny that scent of freesia, though, which had no logical explanation.

Ignoring it for now, she let them inside the apartment.

"This apartment is the largest in the house. It has three bedrooms and a very nice sunroom. The master bedroom and the kitchen face the ocean. The other two bedrooms each have a view of the garden."

"Oh, I like this place." Logan ran into the sunroom, which had an entire wall made of glass.

"That looks like a great place to read a book on a stormy afternoon."

"Yeah. Maybe you can read me more of *The Hobbit*," Logan said.

"Sure thing."

Wyatt smiled down at his son with a softness Rosa had not seen before. Instead of looking stern and foreboding, he looked younger and far more handsome.

A little shiver of awareness blossomed in her stomach. She swallowed, taken completely off guard.

No. No, no, *no*. She did not want to be attracted to this

man. It was nothing personal against Wyatt Townsend. She wasn't interested in romance at all. Okay, it was a *little* personal. She especially didn't want to suddenly find herself attracted to a police detective who was trained to be suspicious of people.

She let out a slow breath. This was ridiculous. He was her tenant and her friend's brother. That was all. She was not attracted to him. She would simply not allow it.

She had too much to worry about right now, keeping Jen safe. She did not have time to be distracted by a gruff detective, no matter how sweetly he smiled at his adorable son.

"The laundry room is off the kitchen there. You can control the temperature of your apartment independently of the other two units in the house. The control is in the hallway. The garbage trucks, they come on Monday. This apartment has a dog door so that Hank can go out into the fenced area of the yard during the day if he needs."

"That will be handy."

"The garden is for all the guests to use at any time. We have a swing in the tree that Logan might enjoy. I know that Addie does. We also have direct access to the beach, but I ask that you keep the gate locked for security reasons. It is the same code as the front door, which I have written on the paper for you, and your key will also open it."

"Got it."

"Do you have any questions?"

"I have a question," Logan said. "Can Hank and me play with your dog sometime?"

She smiled. "Of course. Anytime. She comes to the store with me most of the time during the day, but when we are home, she would love to play with you."

She looked up to find Wyatt watching her with an expression she could not read. It still made her nervous.

"If you think of any other questions, my phone number is there on the desk."

"Got it. Thank you again. We'll try not to be any trouble for you."

His features were stern once more, making her wish suddenly that he would smile at her as he smiled at his son.

"Yes. We don't like trouble here at Brambleberry House. I would hate to have to call the *policia* on you."

Logan's eyes went big. "My dad is the *policia*!"

She smiled at him. "I know. I was only teasing. Do you have things I could help you carry in?"

"Not much. A couple of suitcases. Logan and I can get them."

"Only that?"

"We're traveling pretty light these days. A lot of our things were damaged in the fire by the smoke and by the water from the fire hoses."

She needed the reminder that they had been through difficult things the past few months. It was a small sacrifice to offer a home to them, which she could easily do.

She could also be kind and gracious to them, despite her personal misgivings about having Wyatt in her space.

"I am sorry for that. If there is anything else you need, please let me know."

"Carrie said you have dishes and pots and pans and things."

"Yes. The apartment is fully furnished."

"That will be handy. Thanks."

His poor little boy. First, he lost his mother, then he lost his house to a fire. She wanted to cuddle him close and make everything all better.

"What about food? You will need to get groceries."

"Carrie sent along some meals I only have to thaw and

heat for the first few days. We'll head to the grocery store this evening to pick up some staples after we unload our things. Most of the time, we eat pretty simply, don't we, Logan?"

The boy nodded. "Except Aunt Carrie says we go out to eat too much and I need more vegetables." He gave Rosa a conspiratorial look. "I don't really like vegetables."

"Yes, but you must eat them, anyway, if you want to be strong and healthy when you grow up. My mother used to tell me 'Rosa, if you eat enough vegetables, soon they will taste like candy.' They never did, but I still like vegetables."

He laughed, as she'd hoped, and Rosa felt a little pang. She loved children but didn't expect she would ever have any of her own, for a wide variety of reasons.

"Your mother sounds funny."

"She was. She always tried to make me laugh, even when things sometimes felt very dark."

She missed her mother deeply. The older she got, the more Rosa realized how many sacrifices Maria Elena made on her behalf. She had never been hungry, even though she knew her mother barely made a living cleaning homes for some of the more well-off people in their village. Her mother had always insisted she work hard at school so she could have a brighter future.

She pushed away the memories of her childhood. Her first fifteen years sometimes seemed a lifetime ago, as if they had happened to someone else.

"Oh," she said, suddenly remembering. "I wanted you to meet Jen and Addie, who live upstairs from you."

"All right."

"Let me check if she can meet you."

She quickly sent a text to her friend. After a longer-than-usual pause, Jen replied that she and Addie would come down to the foyer.

"She said she would meet us outside your door," she explained to Wyatt.

"Okay."

"You will like Addie, Logan. Maybe you will make a new friend."

"Maybe."

Life could be filled with so much pain sometimes, Rosa thought as they walked out into the hall to wait for Jen. Each of the inhabitants of Brambleberry House had walked a hard road.

At least for now, they had a safe place to rest, a beautiful home set on the seashore surrounded by flowers, one that might contain a friendly spirit who could not seem to leave.

As Wyatt waited for his upstairs neighbor to come down to meet him and Logan, he couldn't shake the feeling that this was too good to be true.

The apartment was perfect for their needs, with a good-size bedroom for Logan and a very nice en suite for him, as well as an extra room he could use for an office if he needed.

It was actually bigger than their little house and certainly had a bigger yard for Logan to play in.

Brambleberry House would be an ideal temporary home for them while the construction crew repaired the fire damage at his place.

He still had misgivings but Rosa had been welcoming enough. She was certainly kind to Logan, if still distant toward Wyatt.

He followed her into the foyer, with its sweeping staircase and elegant chandelier, to find a woman walking down with a young girl's hand clutched tightly in hers.

She had brown hair pulled back into a tight ponytail and quite striking blue eyes with shadows under them.

"Jen, here are the new tenants I was telling you about," Rosa said in her melodious, accented voice. "This is Wyatt Townsend and his son, Logan. Wyatt is a police officer in Cannon Beach and Logan is seven years old, starting second grade when the summer is over."

"Hello."

She was soft-spoken and didn't meet his gaze directly.

Just what he needed. Another woman here who had secrets.

"Pleasure to meet you." He purposely kept his voice calm, neutral, as he did when he walked into a situation where a witness or a suspect might be prone to bolt.

He didn't miss the way Rosa placed her body slightly in front of her friend's, as if to protect her. He had a feeling Jen didn't miss it, either.

From him? Did Rosa really think he posed a threat to either of them?

The little girl seemed to have none of her mother's skittishness. She stepped forward with a big smile. "Hi. My name is Addie and I'm six years old."

"Hi, Addie." Wyatt was happy to see she seemed well-adjusted and friendly. Whatever was going on with her mother hadn't impacted her yet.

"Hi," she said to Logan, who hadn't said anything yet. "My name is Addie."

"I know. I heard you before."

"What's your name?"

"Logan. I'm seven." His son spoke with a tinge of superiority over his advanced age that made Wyatt hide a smile.

He caught Rosa's gaze and didn't miss her surprised look. What? Did she think he never smiled?

Addie pointed behind them. "Is that your dog?"

Wyatt turned to find Hank plopped in the doorway as if he owned the place.

"Yep," Logan answered. "His name is Hank."

"Will he bite?"

"Only if you bite him first," Logan said, which made Addie giggle.

"I'm not going to bite a dog! That would be gross."

"You can pet him, if you want."

She plopped onto the ground and Hank, predictably, rolled over to have his belly scratched. The dog was shameless for affection.

"I don't have a dog, I have a cat. Her name is Lucy. She's old," Addie explained. "Sometimes I pretend that Fi is my dog."

"Who is Fi?" Logan looked confused.

"Fiona," Rosa explained. "My dog, remember? Sometimes we call her Fi. And you can pretend all you want, darling."

"I will," the girl said cheerfully.

"How are you enjoying Cannon Beach so far?" Wyatt asked Jen Ryan.

She focused her attention somewhere over his shoulder, still not meeting his gaze.

"I like it here. The people are friendly, for the most part, and the scenery is amazing."

"Rosa said you came from Utah. I've got friends there. What part?"

He wasn't surprised when his innocent-seeming question made both Rosa and Jen tense. As he suspected, she was in some kind of trouble. Was she running from an abusive relationship or a custody problem? Or something else?

The two women looked at each other for a moment then Jen gave a smile that looked forced. "A small town in Utah, near the Idaho border. No one has ever heard of it."

She answered in such an offhand manner, he knew she was being deliberately evasive.

He wanted to ask her what town in Utah, but suspected she would shut down fast if he asked.

He also didn't want to raise the wrath of Rosa Galvez. Not when she was doing him a big favor by letting him stay here.

Anyway, Jen Ryan was only a neighbor. Not a suspect.

She probably had very legit reasons to be cautious of strangers.

Sometimes he needed to remind himself to separate the detective from the man. They would be sharing this house for the next month, but likely would not see much of each other, anyway. Did he really need to know the poor woman's life story?

"Rosa says you are a police detective."

"Yes."

"I see."

She didn't sound thrilled at the confirmation. He couldn't help feeling a little defensive. He was passionate about his job, protecting and serving, and tried to do it with compassion and dedication toward all.

"It was nice to meet you," she said, though he suspected she was lying. "I hope you're comfortable here."

"Thank you."

"Come on, Addie."

The girl protested a little but still took her mother's hand and the two of them went back up the stairs again. Addie sent a smile over her shoulder all the way up the stairs at Logan and Hank and her pretend dog, Fiona.

That one would be a little heartbreaker when she grew up. He could tell she already knew how to charm people.

He turned back to Rosa in time to see her watching Jen with a worried expression. When she felt his gaze, she quickly wiped it away.

"There. Now everyone knows everyone else living in the house."

"Yes." One big not-so-happy family. "We'll just grab our things and settle in."

She nodded. "Be sure to contact me if you have any questions."

"Thank you."

"Good night, then. Come on, Fiona. We have tools to put away."

She walked outside in the fading sunlight and he and Logan followed her to grab their suitcases and the few boxes of belongings he had brought from his sister's house.

When they returned from the last trip outside, Logan collapsed onto the comfortable-looking couch. "I like this place. It feels nice."

Logan was the reason he was here. Wyatt was grateful for the reminder. He and his son needed their own place until the house was ready. It was only a short time, and then they could get back to their real life.

Yes, he might be uncomfortably attracted to Rosa Galvez, but he wasn't about to make the mistake of acting on that attraction.

No matter how tempting.

Chapter 3

The busy summer season and her responsibilities at By-The-Wind, combined with her volunteer activities, meant Rosa only saw her new tenants in passing for several days after they moved in.

Even when she didn't actively see them, she was aware of them. Knowing that Wyatt was living two floors below her, she couldn't seem to stop imagining him walking around the house at night. Taking a shower, sprawling out on the big king-size bed wearing next to nothing...

Her entirely too vivid imagination annoyed her severely. When she would catch her mind dwelling on him, she would quickly jerk away her attention and make herself think about something boring, like taking inventory or meeting with her tax accountant. Anything to keep her mind off the attractive man who lived downstairs.

She wasn't sure how she would make it through an entire month or more of this.

Rosa was trying hard to remember that Wyatt and Logan were guests in the house. A month wasn't long, especially during the busy tourist season, when the store was so busy she didn't have much free time, anyway.

She could endure having them there, even if their stay dragged into two months, especially as it was one small way she could work on repaying her vast debt to his sister.

Nearly a week after Wyatt and Logan moved in, Rosa sat in her spare bedroom at the desk she had pulled beneath the window overlooking the Pacific, wishing for rain. For the last few days, the weather seemed as unsettled as she felt. The days had been overcast, brooding like a petulant teenager.

Outside, the ocean seethed and churned, restless in the random moonbeams that found their way through the gathering clouds.

Perhaps a storm would blow through and wash away the unseasonable heat that seemed to have settled over the area.

Brambleberry House did not have air conditioning, as summers here along the coast were mild. The nights usually turned cooler, but until the sun went down, her apartment on the third floor of the old house could be stultifying.

Rosa spent most of her evenings working in the garden. She missed Sonia Davis, the woman who had lived on the second floor until two Christmases earlier, when her estranged husband had come to fetch her, and Rosa had learned her tenant had been living under an assumed name.

Rosa's thumb wasn't nearly as green as Sonia's, and her friend now lived happily with her husband in Haven Point, Idaho. The gardens didn't look as good as they had under Sonia's care, but Rosa did her best.

To her delight, Jen and Addie joined her most evenings. She enjoyed both the company and the help, and was thrilled to see Jen becoming more at ease here in Cannon Beach.

Her friend was settling in. She seemed more comfortable at the gift shop, as well, no longer looking as if she wanted to escape every time a man walked in.

Rosa felt good about her progress. She had wondered if encouraging Jen and her daughter to leave behind their life in Utah was the best decision. Seeing her friend begin to relax into her new life gave her hope that she had been right.

Rain suddenly clicked against the window and she looked up from her laptop. Finally! Perhaps a storm would at last blow away the heat.

Unable to resist, she opened the window more and leaned down to watch the storm roll in.

Lightning arced across the sky, followed closely by a low rumble of thunder. In the blast of light, she could see the sea, dark and tumultuous.

Rosa loved a good storm. They probably should frighten her, especially after some of the intense storms she had experienced in Honduras, but she always found them invigorating. Refreshing in their own way.

She gave up work and decided to relax with a book. The only thing better than a storm was curling up with a good book while she enjoyed it from a safe shelter.

Books had saved her when she first came to the United States. She had always loved to read, but the book selection had been limited in their village.

Once she had moved in with Daniel and Lauren, she had free rein at the town library in Moose Springs and at the school library. Books helped her learn English. Like most other girls her age, she had fallen in love with Harry Potter. Lauren had been wise enough to buy her both the Spanish and the English versions. Rosa would read both at the same time, comparing the words and the sentences to help with her word fluency and her grammar construction.

She still reread the books often. Once in a while she would read the Spanish version so that she didn't lose touch with the language of her heart, but mostly she read in English.

She was currently reading a cozy mystery by one of her favorite authors. She settled into her favorite reading spot, a wide armchair in the corner of her bedroom, and was deep into the story when she was distracted by a sudden banging from outside.

The sound stopped as abruptly as it started. She sank back down and picked up her book again, then she heard it once more.

With a sigh, she set aside the book. If only she had a landlord she could call. Unfortunately, things that banged in the night were *her* responsibility.

She had a feeling she knew what the trouble was. The door on the garden shed wasn't latching tightly. She had noticed it the last time she had mowed the lawn.

If she wasn't mistaken, that was the door to the shed blowing open, then banging shut.

Lightning flashed again, and in that burst of light, she could see she was right. The garden shed door was wide open.

As much as she didn't want to go out into the rain, she couldn't let the banging continue all night, for her tenants' sake, as well as to protect the contents of the shed.

Rosa threw on her rain boots and coat and found a flashlight, then hurried down the stairs.

When she reached the bottom step, the door to the ground-floor apartment swung open suddenly. Startled, she almost stumbled but caught herself just in time.

Wyatt stood there, silhouetted by the light coming from inside the apartment. He looked rumbled and gorgeous, his hair messy as if he had been dozing.

He was wearing jeans and a T-shirt, and was barefoot. Through the open doorway, she could see a television on inside with a baseball game playing.

Logan was nowhere in sight, which led her to believe he must be sleeping.

Her mouth felt dry suddenly and Rosa had to grip the railing of the stairs to keep her balance.

Ridiculous. What was *wrong* with her?

"Sounds like trouble out there."

She nodded. "Nothing major. I believe it is the door to the garden shed. It is not latching the way it should."

"You're not going out in that, are you? Some of those lightning strikes seem close. That's nothing to mess around with."

"I know. But I cannot let it bang all night to disturb everyone."

He gave her a long look, then nodded. "Give me a moment to throw on some shoes, then I'll come with you."

"That is not necessary," she protested. "I can wedge it closed with a rock if I can't fix it."

"Wait. I'll only be a minute."

She really could handle it by herself, but didn't want to be rude so she waited. A few moments later, he returned wearing tennis shoes and a raincoat with a Cannon Beach Police Department logo.

Together they walked out of the house. The temperature had cooled down considerably. Rosa shivered a little at the wet wind that blew through the porch.

Her eagle-eyed neighbor didn't miss her reaction. "I can

handle this, if you want to stay here on the porch, where it's dry."

She shook her head. "*You* should stay here where it's dry. Taking care of the house is my responsibility."

"Fine. We'll both go."

She pulled up her hood and hurried down the steps toward the garden shed.

When they reached it, she was grateful for his help. The door was heavy and the wind made it hard to move. She wasn't sure she could have wrestled it on her own.

"I don't think you're going to be able to fix the latch tonight. Where's the rock you were talking about so we can keep it closed until the weather is a little better?"

"I will have to find something."

Lightning flashed again, followed almost immediately by thunder. It was one thing to enjoy the storm from the comfort of her easy chair. It was something else to be out in the middle of it, with the wind whipping raindrops hard at her face.

She fumbled to turn on the light inside the shed. Wyatt joined her in the small space and she was instantly aware of him. He smelled delicious, some sort of masculine scent that reminded her of the mountains around Moose Gulch, covered in sagebrush and pine.

His gaze landed on a heavy concrete block. "That should do it for now."

He reached down to pick it up and brushed against her. Rosa quickly took a step back, though there wasn't much room to escape.

He didn't appear to notice, much to her relief.

He left the shed again. She took a moment to draw a steadying breath, then turned to follow him. As she reached to turn the light off, her hand caught on something sharp inside.

Pain sliced through her and she couldn't help her gasp.

"What is it?"

"Nothing," she said. "Only a scratch. I am fine."

In another lightning flash, she saw he looked doubtful but he didn't argue with her.

He muscled the door shut, then wedged the concrete block in front of it.

"That should do it, barring a hurricane tonight." He raised his voice to be heard over the storm.

"Let us hope we do not have a hurricane. I had enough of those when I was a girl."

He gave her an interested look but didn't ask questions. Another lightning bolt lit up the sky, followed by the loudest thunder yet, a rumble that seemed to shake the little garden shed.

"That one was too close." Wyatt frowned. "We need to get to shelter. We're too exposed here."

He led the way to the closest entry to the house, the door to his sunroom.

This was one of her favorite parts about Brambleberry House. If she was ever tempted to leave her third-floor sanctuary, it would be to move to this floor so that she could have the sunroom, with the glorious view of the ocean.

Rosa could spend all day every day here. She would probably put in a bed so she could sleep here on long summer nights with the sound of the sea and the breeze blowing through.

She liked the idea of it but the reality probably would not be as appealing. She would feel too exposed here. Anyone could walk up from the beach, climb over the beach gate and break a window to get in.

She would have no defenses.

That was the reason she had not given this apartment to Jen, though both had come vacant at the same time and this apartment was larger. Jen needed to feel safe, above all else.

Security wasn't an issue for Wyatt. Something told Rosa the man could take care of himself in all situations.

"Now," he said when they were inside, "let's take a look at your hand."

Rosa tensed, suddenly aware of how cozy this sunroom was in the middle of a storm.

She should not have come in here with him. Not when she was fighting this unwanted attraction.

"It is fine. I only need to put a bandage on it. I can take care of it upstairs."

Wyatt frowned. "It's your right hand, which is always harder to bandage for someone who is right-handed. Let me take a look."

How had he noticed she was right-handed? Something told her Wyatt was a man who did not miss much.

He flipped on the light inside the sunroom and held out his hand. Unless she wanted to run through the apartment and up two flights of stairs in her awkward rain boots, she had no choice but to show him the wound.

The cut on her palm was about two inches long, shallow but bloody.

Rosa felt her knees go weak at the sight of those streaks of red. To her great embarrassment, the sight of blood always left her feeling as if she would faint.

Her mother used to be a healer of sorts and people would come to their small house for care. Maria Elena had even delivered a few babies.

Rosa had never liked seeing blood or having to help her

mother clean it up. It was a weakness she despised in herself, but one she couldn't seem to help.

"Sit down and I'll go grab my first-aid kit. Normally, I
keep one in the kitchen but it burned up in the fire. Lucky
for you, I've got another one out in my vehicle."

Was she lucky? Rosa would have liked to argue but she
was trying too hard not to look at the blood dripping off
her hand.

After he left, she tried to focus instead on the storm still
rumbling around them.

He and Logan had already left a mark on this room. It
was obviously well-used. A couple of children's chapter
books were stacked on the table and she could see some
small trucks on the floor.

Wyatt returned a moment later with a red case. "Come
into the kitchen, where we can wash off the blood. I should
have had you do that while I was getting the first-aid kit.
Sorry. I wasn't thinking."

She followed him, trying to come up with the words to
tell him again that she could take care of her very minor
injury on her own.

No words would come to her other than the truth—that
she was afraid to let him touch her.

Since she couldn't tell him that, of course, she followed
him into the kitchen.

Here, again, he and Logan had made the space their
own. A couple of art-class projects had been stuck with
magnets to the refrigerator and homework was spread out
on the table.

Hank, his cute little dog, wandered into the room and
stretched in a dog-yoga pose as Wyatt pulled a few paper
towels off the roll.

"Come over here by the sink."

Keeping her gaze fixed away from the cut, she followed him. He turned on the sink and ran his hand under it for a few moments to gauge the temperature, then carefully gripped her hand and guided it under.

Rosa held her breath. Why did he have to smell so good?

He turned her hand this way and that to rinse off the blood. "I don't think you need stitches. It's fairly shallow."

"That is what I thought also."

"We can clean it off pretty well and I think I have a bandage big enough to cover it."

She didn't see any point in arguing with him when he was trying to help her. "Thank you."

Why did her voice sound so breathy and soft? She had to hope he did not notice.

Lightning flashed again outside, followed almost immediately by a loud clap of thunder. She managed to swallow her instinctive gasp.

"How does Logan sleep through such a noise?"

He smiled softly and she felt those nerves sizzle inside her again.

"He can sleep through just about anything. It's a talent I wish I shared."

"I, as well." She was unable to resist smiling back. He seemed a different person when talking about his son, much more open and approachable.

He looked at her for a moment, then seemed to jerk his attention back to her hand.

He patted it dry with a bit of gauze from the first-aid kit. "I didn't see what you scratched your hand on out there."

"A nail, I think. I am not sure. I will have to look more closely in the daylight."

He nodded. "Any idea when your last tetanus shot was?

If it was a nail, it might be rusty. This is the coast, after all. Everything rusts."

"I had the shot only a few years ago after I stepped on a rock at the beach and needed a few stitches."

It was a good thing she had been with friends that time. Her foot had bled so much, she probably would have been too light-headed to walk to her car.

"Good news, then. You shouldn't need a second shot. I'm just going to put a little first-aid cream on it. If it doesn't start to heal in a few days, you will probably want to see your doctor."

"Yes. I will do that."

She missed having Melissa Fielding living in this apartment. Melissa was a nurse and was great at patching up scrapes and cuts. Now she was happily married to Eli Sanderson, who was a doctor in town. Eli was a wonderful stepfather to Melissa's daughter, Skye, and they had a new baby of their own, Thomas.

Wyatt squeezed out the antibiotic cream on the bandage before sticking it onto her skin.

"That is smart."

"A little trick my mother taught me."

"She sounds like a very wise woman."

He smiled a little and she again had to order her nerves to behave. "She is. She's a judge in Portland. That's where Carrie and I grew up."

"I thought your mother was friends with Abigail." She frowned a little, trying to make the connection.

"She was, sort of. It was really our grandmother who was best friends with Abigail. My mother grew up here, in a house not far from Brambleberry House. Her parents lived there until they died several years ago. I can remember visiting Abigail a few times, back in the days when the house was all one unit, with no apartments."

The curtains suddenly fluttered and Hank, who had just settled down on the kitchen rug, rose again to sniff at the air. Rosa could swear she suddenly smelled freesia.

"Do you smell that?"

He sniffed. "What?"

"Flowers."

He raised an eyebrow. "I smell vanilla and berries. It's making me hungry."

She could feel herself flush and was grateful he probably could not tell with her brown skin. That was her shampoo, probably.

"I thought I smelled freesia. That was Abigail's signature scent."

"Why would it still smell like her?"

"My aunt and her friend who own the house think Abigail still wanders through the house. Do not worry. If she is here, she is a kind spirit, I think."

"Do you buy that?"

"Not really. Sometimes I must wonder, though."

He seemed to take the news of a ghost in stride. "I suppose I'm a big skeptic. I haven't noticed anything in the time we've been living here."

"Did you not see Hank standing in the corner, looking at nothing? Fiona sometimes does that. She makes me wonder what she can see that I cannot."

"I hadn't really noticed."

She studied him. "Would you mind if Abigail were still hanging about?"

"Not really. I remember her as being very kind when I was a boy. She always gave me butterscotch candy."

He smiled a little at the memory.

"As long as she doesn't watch me while I sleep, we should get along fine."

Rosa had a hard enough time not thinking about him sleeping a few floors below her. She didn't need another reason to picture it.

"I do not know if you can tell a ghost she is not welcome in your bedroom."

He smiled. It wasn't a huge smile and certainly not anything as overt as laughter. She still found it enormously appealing.

She wanted to stare at his mouth, will his lips to lift again into a smile as heat soaked through her.

After an awkward moment, she forced herself to look away. She slid her hand back and pressed it into her stomach against the silly butterflies dancing there.

"I should go," she said. "Thank you for your help with the door and with this."

She raised her hand and, as if she had waved a magic wand, another bolt of lightning lit up the kitchen and an instant later the lights flickered and went out.

"Oh, dear," she exclaimed. "I was afraid of this happening."

"It would not be a storm along the coast without some kind of power outage."

He went to the window of the living area that faced out to the street. "I don't see any lights on in the whole neighborhood. It looks like the power is out everywhere."

Rosa knew that was not unusual. Electricity often went out during big storms in the area.

She knew there was nothing to fear. Still, she could feel herself begin to panic. Full darkness always did that to her. It reminded her too much of hiding in the back of a pickup truck, afraid she would not see another day.

"Where is my flashlight? Did I leave it in your sunroom?" She looked around the dark kitchen, as if she could summon it with her will, and tried not to panic.

He must have sensed some of her unease. Wyatt reached out a comforting hand and rested it briefly on her arm. Heat radiated from where he touched her and she wanted to lean into his warmth and solid strength.

"I'll find it. Stay here. I don't want you to hurt yourself again."

She leaned against the kitchen sink, breathing deeply and ordering herself to be calm.

A moment later, he returned with her flashlight on, pointed to the ground so he didn't shine it in her eyes.

"Here you are."

"Thank you."

She felt silly at her overreaction, wishing for a different past that wasn't filled with moments of fear and pain.

"Thank you again for your help. Good night."

She turned to leave and somehow wasn't surprised when he followed closely behind her.

"I'll walk you up the stairs to your place."

She shook her head slightly. "That is really not necessary. I can find my way. I am up and down these stairs all the time."

"Maybe so. But not in the dark. I would hate for you to fall on my watch."

She didn't want to argue with him. Not when he was being so helpful. She gave an inward sigh as she headed for the apartment door and out to the main foyer.

Wyatt followed her up one flight of stairs. When she saw Jen's door, Rosa immediately felt guilty. She had been so busy trying not to become stupid over Wyatt Townsend, she had not given a thought to her friend and how nervous Jen and Addie might be in the dark.

She was a terrible friend. The worst.

She paused outside the door and turned to face him. "I should probably check on Jen and Addie."

"They might be asleep."

"I do not believe so. I saw lights on inside earlier, when we were out by the shed. She might be nervous with the power outage."

"Good idea."

She knocked softly on the door. "Jen? This is Rosa. Are you all right?"

A moment later the door opened. Jen held a candle in one hand and a flashlight in the other.

Rosa couldn't see her face well, but her blue eyes seemed huge in the dim light.

"Everything is fine here," Jen said. "Thank you for checking." She suddenly noticed Wyatt and seemed to freeze. "Oh. I thought you were alone."

Rosa shook her head. "Wyatt helped me fix the banging door on the garden shed and now he seems to think I need his help or I will fall down the stairs."

"How nice of him to help you." Jen smiled a little, though her anxiety still seemed palpable. "Quite a storm, isn't it?"

"Yes. But do not worry. The power should be back on soon. I see you have a flashlight. Do you need anything else?"

"Only for the power to come back on." Jen's gaze shifted down the stairs behind them, as if she expected someone else to come racing up any moment.

Oh, the poor thing. She had been through so very much. Rosa's heart broke all over again for her.

She knew very well what it felt like to be so afraid of what might be lurking around every dark corner. Rosa had seen plenty of real boogeymen in her life and knew that reality could be worse than any horror movie.

That was a long time ago, she reminded herself. A world away from this beautiful house, which might or might not contain a friendly spirit who smelled like flowers.

She tried to give Jen a reassuring smile. "It should not be long," she repeated. "But if you need anything at all— even company—you know where to find me. In fact, if you would like, you and Addie could sleep in my guestroom."

Jen looked up the stairs as if tempted by the idea, then shook her head. "We should be all right. It's only a storm. But thank you."

Impulsively, Rosa reached out and hugged the other woman, sensing Jen needed reassurance as much as Rosa did.

"Good night, my friend. Everything will be better in the morning. That is what my mother always told me."

"I might have to hold you to that."

Jen waved at them both then closed the door. Rosa could hear the sound of the dead bolt locking. Good. Jen could not be too careful.

She and Wyatt continued up the final flight of stairs. She had not locked her door when she'd left in such a hurry. Behind it, she could hear Fiona whining.

She hurried to open it and was met with a warm, worried dog, who came bounding out to lick her hand.

"I'm here. Safe and sound, darling. Were you worried about me? I am so sorry I left you."

She rubbed her dog until Fi settled down enough to go over to investigate Wyatt.

He reached an absent hand down to pet her. Here on her apartment landing in the dim light of the flashlight, a quiet intimacy seemed to swirl between them.

She wanted to kiss him.

The urge came over her, fiercely undeniable.

She *had* to deny it. She should get that crazy thought out of her head immediately. Wyatt wasn't the man for her and he never would be.

It was hard to remember that now, here in this cozy nook with the rain pounding against the glass and his scent swirling around her.

"What is your neighbor downstairs running from?"

Rosa tensed, all thought of kissing him gone in her instant defensiveness over Jen.

"What makes you say that?"

"I've been in law enforcement for a long time. I can tell when someone is scared of something. Jen is frightened, isn't she?"

She could not betray her friend's confidence. If Jen wanted Wyatt to know what had happened to her over the past year, she would have to be the one to tell him.

"I cannot tell you this."

"Can't? Or won't?"

"What is the difference? She is my friend. Her business is her business."

"Just like your secrets are your own?"

What did he know about her secrets? Rosa felt panic flare. Carrie would not have told him what she knew, would she?

No. She could not believe that. Carrie had agreed never to tell anyone the things she knew about Rosa's past and she trusted her friend completely.

"Everyone has secrets, do they not? Some they share with those they trust, some they prefer to keep to themselves."

He was quiet for a long moment. "I hope you know that if you ever want to share yours, you can trust me."

She trusted very few people. And she certainly wasn't going to trust Wyatt, who was only a temporary tenant.

"If I had any secrets, I might do that. But I don't. I'm a completely open book."

She tried for a breezy smile but could tell he wasn't at all convinced. In fact, he looked slightly disappointed.

She tried to ignore her guilt and opted to change the subject instead. "The lightning seems to have stopped for now. I am sure the power will be back on soon."

"No doubt."

"Thank you again for coming to my rescue. Good night. Be careful going back down the stairs."

"I will do that. Good night."

He studied her, his features unreadable in the dim light of her flashlight. He looked as if he wanted to say something else. Instead, he shook his head slightly.

"Good night."

As he turned to go back down the stairs, the masculine scent of him swirled toward her. She felt that sudden wild urge to kiss him again but ignored it. Instead, she went into her darkened apartment, her dog at her heels, and firmly closed the door behind her, wishing she could close the door to her thoughts as easily.

Chapter 4

He didn't want this.

As Wyatt returned down the stairs at Brambleberry House, his own flashlight illuminating the way ahead of him, his thoughts were tangled and dark.

He didn't want to be attracted to Rosa but couldn't seem to shake her image. The high cheekbones, the warm, dark eyes, the mouth that looked soft and delicious.

He had wanted to taste that mouth, with a hunger he hadn't known for a long time.

He didn't want it. He wasn't ready. He didn't know if he ever would be.

Tori had been the love of his life. His childhood sweetheart. He had loved her fiercely and wholeheartedly.

She had been funny and smart, a little acerbic sometimes but kind. A dedicated school guidance counselor, she had loved her students, their home, their family.

He had fully expected they would have a lifetime together. Her death, especially coming out of nowhere, had shattered Wyatt's entire world. For the last three years, he had done his best to glue back together the pieces, for Logan's sake.

He thought he had done a pretty good job for his son. He knew Logan missed his mother. How could he not? Tori left a huge hole to fill. But by moving to Cannon Beach, Wyatt had made sure Logan had his aunt Carrie to fill in some of those gaps. She was there with hugs at the end of the school day, she baked him cookies and she helped him with his homework.

His son was happy. That was the most important thing.

As for Wyatt, he knew he couldn't stay in this odd limbo forever.

For the first two years, he had been in a daze just trying to survive with work and being a single father. About six months ago, he had started dating a little here and there, mostly going out to lunch or coffee while Logan was in school.

Those experiences had been such a bust that he had decided he wasn't ready to move on.

Maybe he would never be ready.

He would be okay with that, though he knew Tori wouldn't have wanted him to be alone forever.

He kept recalling a conversation between them when they were driving home from some event or other, just a month before her death. Almost as if she'd had some instinctive premonition, Tori had brought up what should happen if one of them died.

He worked in law enforcement, was at much higher risk for a premature death, so he had assumed she had been thinking about what she would do if *he* died.

They both said they wanted the other one to move on

and find happiness again. She had been insistent about it, actually, saying she would hate thinking about him being lonely and would haunt him forever if he didn't find another woman.

Maybe she and Abigail were in cahoots. The thought made him smile a little, imagining a couple of ghostly matchmakers, scheming in the background.

Now that the raw pain of losing Tori had faded to a quiet, steady ache, Wyatt knew he should probably start thinking about the rest of his life.

He wasn't ready, though. The past three years had been so hard, he didn't know if he could ever risk his heart again—and there was no point in even thinking about it in connection to someone like Rosa Galvez, who didn't seem to like him very much.

Rosa had secrets. He had known that for some time. She always seemed evasive and tense whenever he was around, especially on the rare occasions he was wearing his badge.

Maybe she didn't like the police. He knew there were plenty of people in that camp, for some very justifiable reasons.

She could keep her secrets. They were none of his business. He was living in her house for only a short time and then he and Logan would be back in their own home, away from a woman who smelled like vanilla and berries and made him ache for things he wasn't ready to want again.

A major fraud investigation kept him busy over the next week and Wyatt didn't see much of his lovely landlady or his intriguing, skittish neighbor on the second floor. He was grateful, he told himself. At least about the former. He didn't need any more temptation in the form of Rosa Galvez.

He had decided it was easier all around to pretend his attraction to her was only a figment of his imagination.

By the Friday of the week after the storm, Fourth of July weekend, he was looking forward to extended time with Logan. He had the weekend off and he and his son had a whole list of fun things to do before he had to go back to work on Monday—fishing, going for a bike ride and picking out new furniture for Logan's room in their house.

Right now, his focus was dinner. Wyatt hadn't given any thought to what to fix and Hank was running around in circles after spending all day cooped up.

He decided to solve both problems at the same time. "Why don't we take him for a walk down the beach and grab some dinner at the taco truck?"

"Tacos!" Logan exclaimed joyfully, setting down the controller of his device.

After Wyatt changed out of his shirt and tie and into casual weekend attire, they hooked up Hank's leash—a tricky undertaking while the dog jumped around with excitement.

Neither Rosa nor Jen and her daughter were out in the large yard of Brambleberry House as he and Logan walked through the garden toward the beach gate at the back of the property.

The early evening was beautiful, the air scented with the flowers blooming all around them.

Though it was still a few hours from sunset, the sun had begun to slide toward the water, coloring the clouds orange as it went.

The beach was crowded with weekend visitors. Everybody seemed in a good mood, which was one of the benefits of working in a town frequented by tourists.

"What did you do at camp today?" he asked Logan as they walked across the sand. With Carrie's help, Wyatt had been lucky enough to find a place for his son in one of the most popular science day camps in town.

"Tons of stuff. We went tide pooling and I saw about a zillion starfish and a cool purple anemone. And when we had free time, I played on the slide with my friend Carlos, mostly."

"Do I know Carlos?"

"He just moved here and he's my age. He likes *Star Wars*, just like me."

Logan went on to enumerate the many wonderful qualities of his new friend as they walked a few blocks along the packed sand toward the parking lot just above the beach, where their favorite taco truck usually parked.

"And after lunch and free time, we did another art project, the one I showed you. And then you came to get me to go home."

"Sounds like a fun-packed day."

"Yeah," Logan said cheerfully just as they turned up toward the taco truck.

"There it is. Yay. I'm starving!"

Seven-year-old boys always seemed to be starving. "Are you going to get the usual? A soft chicken taco and a churro?"

"Yes!"

The taco truck was busy, as usual. The food here was fresh and invariably delicious. He and Logan joined the queue and were talking about some of the things they planned to do that weekend when Logan's face suddenly brightened.

"Look who's here! Hi, Rosa. Hi, Fiona. Hank, look. It's your friend Fiona!"

Hank sidled up to greet Fiona with enthusiastic sniffing,

as if they hadn't seen each other for months, while Wyatt tried to calm the ridiculous acceleration of his heartbeat.

He had not been able to stop thinking about Rosa since the night of the storm.

She beamed at his son but avoided meeting his gaze. Was it deliberate or accidental?

"*¡Buenas, Logan! ¿Cómo estás?*"

"I don't know what that means."

"It means 'good evening. How are you?'"

"How do I say I'm good?"

"You can say *soy bueno* or just *bueno*."

"*Bueno*," Logan said, parroting her. "*¿Cómo estás?*"

She smiled. "*Soy buena.*"

Wyatt had to again fight the urge to kiss her, right there in front of everyone in line.

"This is our favorite taco truck," Logan told her. "Do you like tacos, too? Oh, yeah. You probably do because you speak Spanish."

He winced at his son's cultural misassumption but Rosa didn't seem offended. "Except I am from a country called Honduras and these are tacos from Mexico. I like them very much, though. The owner is also my friend."

They reached the order window at that moment and the owner in question, Jose Herrera, ignored Wyatt for a moment to greet Rosa in Spanish.

Wyatt had taken high-school Spanish and had tried to work on his language skills over the years. Unfortunately, he still understood best when Spanish speakers spoke slowly, which didn't happen often in general conversation.

He had no idea what the guy said. Whatever it was, it made Rosa laugh. She answered him in rapid-fire Spanish, which sparked a belly laugh in Herrera.

"Go ahead and order," Wyatt said to her.

"You were here first."

"We're still trying to decide," he lied.

She gave her order then stepped aside for him and Logan to do the same.

"Don't forget my churro," Logan instructed.

"How could I?" Wyatt smiled at his son.

When he finished, the three of them moved together to one of the open picnic tables set around the truck that overlooked the beach.

"And how are you, Señor Logan?" Rosa asked.

"Señor means 'mister.' We learned that in school."

"You are correct."

"I am fine. I like living in your house. It's friendly."

She smiled with warm delight. "I am so happy you think so. Some houses, they are cold. Brambleberry House is not that way. When you step inside, you feel like you are home."

"And it always smells good, too. Like flowers," Logan said.

Rosa met Wyatt's gaze with an expressive eyebrow, as if to say *See? I told you.*

"Aren't we lucky to live in such a nice place with beautiful flower gardens that smell so good?" Wyatt replied blandly.

"How is your house coming along?"

Was she in a hurry to get rid of them? No. Rosa had been nothing but accommodating.

"We're making progress. They're painting soon, then we need to do the finish carpentry."

"That *is* progress. You will be home before you know it, back in your own bedroom. Your dog will like that, yes?"

He loved listening to her talk, completely entranced by her slight accent and unique phrasing. Okay, the truth was, he was completely entranced by *her*. She could read a lawn-mower instruction manual and he would find her fascinating.

"I think so far he's having fun being friends with Fiona," Logan said.

The two dogs did seem pretty enamored of each other. Hank hadn't been around a lot of other dogs and it was good to see him getting along well with the Irish setter.

Rosa smiled at his son. "Fiona can be a charmer. She is quite hard to resist."

That made two of them. Wyatt sighed. This had to stop. He didn't want this attraction. Even after a short time, he still hadn't come to terms with his growing interest in his landlady.

Seeing her again here in the July sunshine, bright and vibrant and lovely, only intensified the ache that had been growing since the night of the storm.

He pursed his lips, determined not to think about that. "How is Jen settling in, living in Cannon Beach?"

He had only seen the second-floor tenant in passing a few times. She still seemed as anxious and uncomfortable around him as before.

"Good, as far as I know. She and Addie seem content for now."

Something told him that was a new state of affairs. He didn't know what the woman was going through but was glad at least that she was finding peace here.

"We bumped into Addie and Jen at the grocery store the other night. Jen seems a little uncomfortable around me."

If he hoped Rosa might take the bait and tell him what was going on with Jen, he was doomed to disappointment. She quickly changed the subject away from her friend.

"I'm sure I don't know why. Logan, did I see you walking past my store window today with a bucket?"

"I don't know. Maybe. My day camp went tide-pooling."

"Oh, I love doing that at low tide. What did you see?"

"About a zillion sea stars and some anemone and a sea cucumber. Only it's not the kind you can eat."

"How wonderful. Is it not fun to see what can be found beneath the water?"

"Yeah. It's like another whole world," Logan said. He started regaling Rosa with a few stories of interesting things he had seen during previous tide-pooling trips.

"My teacher said you can sometimes go snorkeling and be right in the water looking at some different habitats. That would be fun, don't you think?"

"Yes. Very fun. Maybe your father should take you to Hawaii. Or to my country, Honduras."

Logan's face lit up. "Can we go, Dad? And can Rosa come with us?"

Wyatt cleared his throat, his mind suddenly full of images of warm tropical nights and soft, flower-scented breezes.

"That would be fun. But Rosa has a busy job here. She probably wouldn't have time."

Logan seemed unconcerned. "Maybe we could go with Aunt Carrie, Uncle Joe and Bella. That would be fun, too."

Not as fun as Hawaii or Honduras with Rosa, but, of course, Wyatt couldn't say that. To his relief, a moment later Logan's attention was diverted from snorkeling and travel when he saw another friend from school ride up to the taco truck along with her parents on bikes.

"There's my friend Sadie," he announced. "I need to tell her something."

He handed the leash to Wyatt and hurried over to talk to his friend. Wyatt realized that left him alone at the table to make conversation with Rosa.

"What part of Honduras are you from?"

He didn't miss the way she tensed a little, then seemed to force herself to relax. "A small fishing village near the coast. I left when I was a teenager."

"How did you go from a small village in Honduras to living at Brambleberry House and running a gift shop on the Oregon coast?"

She shrugged. "A long story. The short version is that *mi Tia* Anna is part owner of the house, along with her friend Sage. Anna and her husband live in Portland while Sage and her family spend most of their time in California. Anna needed someone to run the gift shop for her. I have a retail marketing degree and was working a job I didn't enjoy that much in Park City."

"Utah?"

"Yes. Have you been there?"

"No. I'm not much of a skier. My parents used to take us to Mount Hood when I was a kid. I never really enjoyed it."

She smiled a little. "I do not ski, either. It seems a silly pastime to me."

"I guess some people like the thrill. You're not an adrenaline junkie?"

"No. Not me. I have had enough adventure for a lifetime, thank you."

He wanted to pursue that line of questioning but didn't have a chance as Logan and their food arrived at the picnic table at the same time.

They had never really made a conscious decision to eat together, but it somehow felt natural, especially as their dogs were nestled together and had become fast friends.

What happened to Hank's restlessness? Wyatt wondered. Right now, the dog did not look like he wanted to move.

The food was as good as always, the chicken flavorful and the salsa spicy.

He spent a moment helping Logan get situated, then turned his attention back to Rosa. "So you were saying you lived in Utah but you don't like to ski. And that you have had enough adventure and aren't an adrenaline junkie."

She took a drink of the *horchata* she had ordered. "Utah is beautiful year-round. In the summertime, I do like to hike in the mountains and mountain-bike with my parents and *primos*. Cousins," she explained at Logan's quizzical look."

"I have one *primo*. Cousin. Her name is Bella."

Rosa smiled at him. "I know your cousin very well."

"You sound like you are close to your family," Wyatt said.

"Oh, yes. Very. My family is wonderful. My parents, Daniel and Lauren Galvez, are the most kind people you will ever meet. Daniel is in law enforcement, as well. He is the sheriff of our county."

"Is that right?" He found the information rather disheartening. If she had law-enforcement members in her own family, his occupation wasn't likely to be the reason she was so distrustful of Wyatt.

"Yes. Everyone loves him in Moose Springs and the towns nearby. And my mother, she is the doctor in town."

"The only one?"

"It is not a very big town. Some people go to Park City when they need specialists, but Lauren is the best doctor in the whole world."

She spoke of her parents by their first names, which made him wonder at the relationship.

"Is she also from Honduras?"

He wasn't surprised when her jaw tensed at the question.

"No. She is from Moose Springs. Daniel, as well. They adopted me when I came to this country."

He wanted to pursue that line of questioning but reminded himself this was a casual encounter over tacos, not an interrogation. She had the right to her privacy. This was obviously a touchy subject for her and he didn't want to make her uncomfortable.

"So. What do you think of your taco?" she asked Logan.

"Muy delicioso," he said with a grin. "That means 'very delicious.' I learned that from my friend Carlos. That's what he says every day at lunch."

"That is the perfect thing to say about the tacos here. They are definitely *muy delicioso.*"

She and Logan spent a few more minutes comparing ways to gush about their meals, leaving Wyatt to wonder what made Rosa so uncomfortable when she talked about her past.

What was she hiding? She did not like to talk about herself, which he found unusual. In his line of work, he had learned that most law-abiding people loved talking about themselves and their lives. With a few well-aimed questions, Wyatt usually could find out anything he wanted to know.

People who had things to hide, however, learned techniques to evade those kinds of questions.

Her secrets were not his business, he reminded himself. She was a private person and there was certainly no law against that.

He would be smart to remember that her history was her own. He wasn't entitled to know, especially when their only relationship was that of landlady and tenant.

Chapter 5

The man was entirely too curious.

It didn't help that she couldn't seem to keep her usual defensive techniques in place when he looked at her out of those blue eyes. She forgot about protecting herself, about concealing the parts of her life she preferred to forget. She forgot everything, lost in the totally ridiculous urge to lean across the picnic table and press her mouth against his. Anything to stop his questions.

Wouldn't that go over well? She could just imagine how he would react. It almost made her wish she had the nerve to try it.

To her relief, he seemed to give up his interrogation as they finished dinner. He sat back and let her and Logan chatter about Logan's friends, his day camp and the very cool dinosaur bones he saw at a museum in Portland with his aunt Carrie.

He was really an adorable boy, filled with life and energy. He loved *Star Wars*, Legos, his dog and his father, not necessarily in that order.

She enjoyed their company immensely, especially once Wyatt stopped digging into her life.

"Good choice on dinner, kiddo," he said with a warm smile to his son.

Seeing him with Logan was like glimpsing a different person. He was more lighthearted, and certainly more approachable. He had smiled more during dinner than she had seen in all the time she had known him.

The Townsend men were both extremely hard to resist.

"That was so yummy," Logan said as he balled up the wrapper of his taco and returned it to the tray. "Thanks, Dad."

"I didn't do much except pay for it, but you're welcome. You should tell Jose how much you enjoyed it."

At that moment, the taco-truck owner was delivering another tray to a nearby table so Logan jumped up and hurried over to him.

"*Gracias* for the taco. It was *muy delicioso*."

Jose, bald head gleaming in the fading sunlight, beamed down at the boy with delight. "You are welcome. You come back anytime."

He fist-bumped Logan, who skipped as he hurried back to their table.

"That was very nice of you," Rosa said. "People like to feel appreciated."

"My dad taught me we should always tell people thank you for things they do. Sometimes we might be the only ones all day who say it to them."

Rosa had to smile at that. Her gaze met Wyatt's and she found him watching her out of those unreadable blue eyes again.

"That is probably true. Then I must say thank you for sharing dinner with me. I enjoyed it very much."

"So did I," Logan said.

"As did I," Wyatt said to her surprise.

He rose and took her trash and his to the garbage can and dumped it, then returned to the table. "Are you walking back to Brambleberry House?"

"Yes."

"We're headed that way, too. We can walk together, if you want."

Did she? A smart woman would tell him she only just remembered an errand she needed to run at one of the little shops close to the taco truck. Spending more time with Wyatt and Logan was definitely dangerous to her peace of mind.

She couldn't think of anything she needed at any of the touristy places in this area of town, anyway.

"Sure. It makes sense as we are going the same place."

Fiona jumped up from her spot beside Hank, almost as if she had been following the conversation and knew it was time to go.

Sometimes Rosa thought the dog had to be the smartest animal in the world.

As if on cue, Hank jumped up as well, then sat on his haunches and looked pointedly at his owner, as if to tell him he was ready to leave, too.

"I'll take Hank," Logan said and picked up the leash. He led the way, still chattering, as they headed along the sand toward Brambleberry House.

"Looks like it's going to be another gorgeous sunset." Wyatt looked out across the water at the clouds fanning out across the sky in shades of apricot and plum.

"Lovely."

It was the sort of beautiful, vibrant summer evening meant to be spent with a special someone.

Too bad she didn't have a special someone.

Rosa sighed. She hadn't dated anyone seriously since she moved to Cannon Beach four years earlier.

She really should go out on a date or two. All of her friends were constantly trying to set her up, but lately it all seemed like so much bother. Maybe that would distract her from this unwanted and inconvenient attraction to Wyatt.

Rosa was not a nun or anything. She dated, when she found someone worthy of her time, though it was rather depressing to realize she hadn't dated anyone seriously in a long time. Not since college, really?

For two years, she had been very close to a fellow business major whose parents had emigrated from Peru. She and Santos had talked about returning to South America to open a string of restaurants.

As far as she knew, he might have even done that. They had lost track of each other after graduation and she rarely thought of him anymore.

Santos and the few other serious relationships she'd had had taught her that sex could be beautiful and meaningful with someone she cared about.

She was happy with her life. She was running a successful business, she lived in a beautiful home and she loved the surroundings in Cannon Beach. She had good friends here and back in Utah and loved her volunteer work for the local women's shelter.

Okay, maybe she was sometimes lonely at night. Maybe she sometimes wished she could have someone to cuddle with, to talk to at the end of the day, to share her hopes and dreams.

Fiona was lovely but talking to her had its limitations since she couldn't respond.

At the same time, she was not sure she was ready for the inherent risks of trusting her heart to someone.

She had told no one else about the things that had happened to her. Not even Santos or the few other men she had dated seriously had known the entire truth. She had told them bits and pieces, but not everything.

Maybe that was why those relationships had withered and died without progressing to the next level, because she had never completely trusted them to know.

She certainly wasn't about to spill her life story to Wyatt, as much as she enjoyed the company of him and his son.

The walk back to the house passed quickly, mostly because Logan dominated the conversation. He pointed out a kite he liked, told her about riding a bike along the hard-packed sand near the water, went into a long story about the time he and his dad took a charter out to see whales up near Astoria.

"Sorry about Logan," Wyatt said in a low voice when the boy was distracted by something he saw on the sand and ran ahead with Hank to investigate. "He's in a chatty mood tonight. Some days I wish I could find a pause button for a minute."

She smiled. "I do not mind. I love listening to him. Your son is terrific."

"Agreed," he said gruffly. "He's the best seven-year-old I know, even if he does tend to show off a little in front of pretty women."

Rosa felt flustered and didn't know how to answer that. Fortunately, they had reached the beach gate at Brambleberry House.

She punched in the code and the door swung open. As

they walked through the back garden, she suddenly saw a strange car in the driveway, a small late-model bright red SUV she didn't recognize.

Rosa tensed, worrying instantly for Jen. She was reaching for her phone to check in with the woman when two females hurried around the side of the house. She recognized them instantly—Carrie and Bella—and shoved her phone back into her pocket.

She smiled and waved, happy at the unexpected visit even as she could feel the usual mix of joy and tension settle over her.

"Hi!" Bella called out to all of them, waving vigorously.

"Hi, Bella," Logan shouted, then beamed toward Rosa. "That's my cousin, Bella, and her mom."

"It is good to see them," Rosa said.

As they moved toward each other, she thought she saw Carrie look between her and Wyatt with a surprised sort of look, as if she wouldn't have expected to see them walking up from the beach together.

"There you are! We rang both your doorbells but nobody answered."

"We bumped into each other while we were grabbing dinner and walked back together," Rosa said quickly, so that his sister didn't get the wrong idea about the two of them. "We got tacos at the food truck."

"Oh, I love that place," Bella gushed. "My friends and I like to stop there after school. I love their churros."

"Me, too," Logan declared, as if the cinnamon and sugar still dusting his clothes wasn't enough of a giveaway.

Rosa had to smile. She thought she saw Carrie give her a speculative sort of look but couldn't be certain.

"I came by to show off my new wheels," her friend said. "What do you think?"

"Let's take a look," Wyatt said.

They moved toward the driveway and the small red SUV.

"Nice," Wyatt said, walking around the vehicle to check it out.

"I like your new car," Logan said. "It's pretty."

"Thank you, dear." Carrie beamed at him.

"And guess what?" Bella's voice vibrated with excitement. "We're keeping Mom's old car and when I start learning how to drive, I get to practice in that one."

Driving. Bella would be driving in only a few more years. How was it possible that she had grown so much?

"There's plenty of time for that," Wyatt said, looking alarmed.

"Not really. In less than two years, I'll be old enough to get my learner's permit. I'll be driving around town before you know it."

"Good luck with that," Wyatt said to his sister.

"I know. I remember Dad teaching me how to drive. It was a nightmare. And I believe you wrecked a car or two in your day."

"You wrecked cars, Uncle Wyatt?" Bella looked at him wide-eyed and so did his son.

Wyatt gave his sister a rueful look. "One. And it wasn't my fault. A guy T-boned me in an intersection. He got the citation."

"In that case, I'm sorry I impugned your driving credentials," Carrie said.

He shrugged. "I will confess that in the past, I might have had a propensity to drive too fast. Good thing I can do that legally now, with lights and sirens going."

He tapped Bella lightly on the head. "But remember, I'm a highly trained officer of the law. You should always stay within the legal speed limit."

Bella giggled. "What about you, Rosa. Where did you learn to drive? Here or in Honduras?"

She always felt strange talking about her childhood life with Bella and Carrie. "Here. My father taught me when I was in high school. He and my mother were tired of driving me to after-school activities all the time. We had many ranch roads in Utah, where they live, so we practiced for hours until I could feel comfortable behind the wheel."

That was one more gift Lauren and Daniel had given her. Independence. They had wanted her to have all the skills she would need to make a success of her life. She knew they were proud of what she had done and how far she had come. At the same time, she knew Lauren especially worried about her love life.

What would Lauren think about Wyatt? Rosa could guess. She would probably adore him—first because he was in law enforcement like Daniel and second because he was a good man who loved his child.

She would be over the moon if she had any idea how Rosa couldn't seem to stop thinking about him.

She didn't plan to tell either of them about her new tenant. Her parents and siblings were coming to town just before Labor Day, but Logan and Wyatt would be back in their own home by then. She would have to tell them nothing.

Oddly, the thought of the Townsends moving out left her feeling slightly depressed.

"When I get my learner's permit," Bella said, "I'm going to need a lot of practice time. Rosa, maybe you and Uncle Wyatt can help and give my mom and dad a break so they don't always have to ride with me."

Rosa couldn't find words for a few seconds, she was so honored that Bella would even consider allowing her to help her learn how to drive.

"I would enjoy that," she said, her voice a little ragged.

"It's a deal," Wyatt said. "It will be good practice for when I have to teach this kiddo how to drive."

Would she be here when Bella was learning how to drive? Rosa wasn't sure. She had never intended to stay in Cannon Beach for long, but once she had moved here, it had been hard to drag herself away. Now that she was a part owner of the gift store, it became even more difficult.

She didn't like thinking about leaving all the friends she had made here, but perhaps she would one day find it inevitable.

"Showing off my car wasn't the only reason we dropped by. I know you have the weekend off. Joe and I were thinking of grilling steaks and then watching the fireworks on Sunday. We would love to have you. Rosa, you're invited as well. And your friend Jen, if she would like to come."

Rosa wasn't sure if she was ready to have another social outing with the irresistible Townsend men. On the other hand, how could she refuse an invitation from Carrie?

At her hesitation, Carrie made a face. "I know it's rude to just drop in with an invitation two days beforehand. I should have planned better. Please don't worry if you already have plans. But if you can come, we will eat at about seven thirty."

"I do not have plans," she said. In truth, she had been so busy at work, she had not given the holiday weekend much thought.

She could handle a few hours in Wyatt's company. She would simply spend the evening talking with Carrie and Bella.

"Dinner would be nice. What should I bring?"

"Yourself. That's the main thing. But if you want to bring a salad or a fruit plate, that's always good."

She nodded. "Yes. I can do that."

"Oh, lovely. We will see you Sunday, then. Now we're off to take this beauty for a drive down the coast. With me behind the wheel, of course," she assured them, which made Bella moan in mock disappointment.

A moment later, she stood beside Wyatt and watched the little red SUV back out of the driveway.

"Your sister. She is wonderful."

Rosa could not even put into words her deep gratitude toward Carrie.

"She is pretty terrific. Our mom had breast cancer when I was in high school and Carrie basically stepped in to take care of all of us while Mom was having treatment. She was a young bride herself but that didn't stop her."

"That is wonderful. My mother died of breast cancer when I was fourteen."

She wasn't sure why she told him that. It was another part of her past she didn't usually share.

He gave her a sympathetic look. "I'm sorry. That's a hard loss for a teenager."

She had been so frightened after her mother died. She had no one to share her pain except a few of her mother's friends.

They had been as poor as Rosa and her mother and couldn't help her survive when they were barely subsisting. She had known she was on her own from the moment her mother had died.

That cold truth had led her to making some terrible decisions, with consequences she could never have imagined.

"Hey, Dad, can I show Rosa what I built out of Legos this week?"

Wyatt shook his head. "We've taken up her whole evening. I'm sure she has things to do."

Rosa did have things to do, always. Most small-business owners never really stopped working, even if it was only the constantly turning wheels of their subconscious.

But at the disappointed look on Logan's face, she smiled at the boy. "I do have things to do tonight but I would love to see your creation first."

She could tell Wyatt wasn't particularly pleased at her answer. Why not? Was he in a hurry to get rid of her? Too bad. He could survive a few more moments of her company, for his son's sake.

Wyatt unlocked the front door. As she stood in the entryway waiting for him to open his apartment, Rosa smelled the distinctive scent of flowers that had no logical reason to be there.

Hank sniffed the air and so did Fiona. They both went to the bottom of the stairs, wagging their tails.

Apparently, Abigail was active tonight. Rosa rolled her eyes at her own imagination. She did not believe in ghosts, benevolent or otherwise. If she did, she would never be able to sleep for all the ghosts haunting her.

The dogs followed them as they went into the ground-floor apartment.

"My room is back here," Logan said. He grabbed Rosa's hand and tugged her in the direction of his space.

A *Star Wars* blanket covered the bed and toys were scattered around the room. It made her happy to see the signs a child lived there, and somehow she had the feeling it would have made Abigail happy, too.

"It's over here. This was the biggest set I've ever made. It had over two hundred pieces! I wasn't sure I could do it but my dad helped me."

He showed her a complicated-looking brick master-piece, which she recognized as a spacecraft from one of the *Star Wars* movies, though she couldn't have said for sure which one.

It warmed her heart to think about the boy and his father working together on the project.

"How wonderful. It must have taken you a long time."

"Not really. It's not that hard if you follow the picture directions. My friend Carlos got one, too, and he was able to put it together and Carlos can't even read in English very much."

"Can't he?"

"He's getting better." Logan looked as if he didn't want to disrespect his friend. "Anyway, he hasn't been here very long, only a few months. He told me he speaks Spanish at home all the time. I want to learn Spanish so I can talk to him better but I don't know very many words."

His eyes suddenly grew wide. "Hey. You speak Spanish *and* English. You could teach me."

"Me?" Rosa was so shocked at the suggestion that she didn't quite know how to respond.

"Rosa is very busy with her store," Wyatt said from the doorway. "We don't need to bother her. You and I can keep reading the books and practicing with the language app on my phone."

How could she be anything but charmed at the idea of Wyatt and his son trying to learn Spanish together so Logan could talk to his friend?

"I would not mind practicing with you when I can," she said quickly. "I should tell you that I have been speaking mostly English almost as long as I spoke only Spanish, so some of my vocabulary might be a little rusty."

"Oh, yay! Thanks, Rosa. *Gracias.*"

"*De nada.* I am usually home after six most nights. You can come knock on my door and if I'm home, we can practice a little in the evening."

"Cool! Thanks!"

To her shock, her gave her a quick, impulsive hug. Her arms went around him and she closed her eyes for a moment, grateful for this tender mercy.

When she opened her eyes, she found Wyatt watching her with a strange look in his eyes.

"Okay. Bath time. Tell Rosa good-night, then go find your pajamas and underwear. The clean ones are still in the dryer."

"How do I say 'good night' again?"

"*Buenas noches*. Or sometimes just *buenas*."

He repeated the words, then hurried off to find his pajamas.

"Thanks for your patience with us," Wyatt said in a low voice after the boy had left.

"I do not mind. He is a sweet boy. I enjoy his company."

And yours, she wanted to add. *Even when I know I should not*.

"If you don't really have time to practice Spanish with him, don't worry about it. He'll probably forget by tomorrow morning."

She frowned. "I will not forget. I promised to help him and I would not make a promise I did not intend to keep."

He looked down at her, that odd light in his eyes again. "An admirable quality in a person."

She was not admirable. At all. If he knew her better, he would know that.

"I meant what I said. I will be happy to help him. Send him up any evening he is free or even outside when I am working in the yard. I do not know if I would be a good teacher, but I will do my best."

"I'm sure you will be great," he said. "I just don't want my son to bother you."

"He is never a bother. I will enjoy it."

"Thank you, then. He will probably learn faster from a native speaker than any app could teach him."

"I will do my best," she said again. "Now if you will excuse me, I must go."

She really needed to leave soon, before she did something foolish like throw herself into his arms.

"Good night," she said, edging toward the door.

"Buenas noches," he replied, with a credible pronunciation. "I guess I'll see you on Sunday at Carrie's house."

Oh. Right. She had almost forgotten the invitation. "Yes. I guess so."

"We could always walk over together."

What would Carrie think if the two of them came together to her dinner party? Rosa suspected his sister was already getting the wrong idea about them after seeing them together tonight.

Still, it made sense. It would be silly to drive when the house was so close. "All right. Come, Fiona," she called.

Her dog rose from the rug, where she was cuddled with Hank, and gave the little dog a sorrowful look, then followed Rosa up the stairs to her apartment.

Something seemed to have shifted between her and Wyatt during this evening spent together, but she couldn't have said exactly what.

He was attracted to her.

She wasn't sure how she knew that but she did. Maybe that look in his eyes as he had watched his son hug her... Touched, surprised...hungry.

She was imagining things. Wyatt Townsend was certainly not hungry for her.

If he was, it was only because he didn't know the truth. All the secrets of her past, which she had pushed into the deep corners of herself, where no one else could see.

Chapter 6

Summer evenings along the Oregon coast could be magical, especially when they were clear, with no sign of coastal fog.

As they walked the short distance between Brambleberry House and his sister's place on Sunday, the air smelled of the sea, mingled with pine and cedar and the flowers that seemed to grow in abundance this time of year, spilling out of flower baskets and brightening gardens.

Independence Day turned out to be perfect. He and Logan had spent the morning fishing in their favorite spot along the nearby river. Even though the fishing was a bust and they didn't catch anything big enough to keep, Logan still had a great time.

Afterward, they had gone on a hike at one of their favorite trails in Ecola State Park and then had spent the afternoon playing in the sand.

He wouldn't be surprised if Logan fell asleep early.

Of course, he wasn't anywhere close to sleeping now. He was having too much fun quizzing Rosa about the Spanish word for everything they passed.

"How do you say *mailbox*?" Logan asked, pointing to a row of them across the road.

"Buzón."

"And *house* is *casa*, right?"

"Yes. Very good. And we are walking. *Estamos caminando.*"

"Yes. To my aunt Carrie's *casa.*"

She smiled down at him, looking bright and lovely in the golden evening light. To himself, Wyatt could admit that the main reason the evening seemed particularly beautiful had to do with the woman he was walking beside.

"Excellent," she said. "You and Carlos will be jabbering up a storm in Spanish before you know it."

"I think his English will always be better than my Spanish."

"But you are trying to learn for your friend. That is the important thing. It was very hard for me when I came to this country and could not always find the words I wanted. I am grateful I had very patient family and friends to help me."

He had to wonder again at her story. She had said her mother died when she was fourteen, which meant she had probably come here by herself. But what were the circumstances that had led to her being adopted by a family in Utah?

None of his business, he reminded himself. She was his landlady, nothing more, though it was hard to remember that on an evening like this, especially when his son slipped his hand in hers, as if it was the most natural thing in the world.

Rosa looked down at Logan and their joined hands with

an expression of astonishment, and then one of wonder, that touched Wyatt deeply.

"How do you say *whale*?" Logan asked when they passed a house that had a little whale-shaped bench out front.

"Ballena."

"What about *tree*?"

"Arborio."

"How about *library*?"

"Biblioteca."

Rosa never seemed to lose her patience with the constant barrage of questions. He could only guess how relieved she must have been when they reached Carrie and Joe's house a short time later.

"Now you tell me. What was *door* again?" she asked him as they approached the porch.

"Puerta."

"No. *Puerto. Puerta* means *port*."

"It's so confusing!"

"English is far more confusing," she said with a laugh. "Try figuring out the difference between *there*, *they're* and *their*."

"I guess."

"You are doing great. We will keep practicing."

His son was already enamored with Rosa. They had practiced together the night before while Rosa was working in the small vegetable garden at the house. Wyatt had come out ahead in the arrangement, as she had sent Logan back to their apartment with a bowl of fresh green beans and another of raspberries, his favorite.

He always felt a little weird just walking into his sister's house, even though he had been living there only a few weeks earlier. He usually preferred to ring the doorbell, but this time he didn't have to. Bella opened the door before they could and grinned at them. "I saw you all walking up. *Hola.*"

"Hola." Rosa's features softened. "That's a very cute shirt. Is it new?"

Bella twirled around to show off her patriotic red, white and blue polka-dotted T-shirt. "Yeah. I picked it up this afternoon on clearance. It was super cheap."

"I like it very much," Rosa said.

"I'm going with some friends to watch the fireworks in Manzanita."

He thought he saw disappointment flash in Rosa's dark eyes before she quickly concealed it. "Oh. That will be fun for you."

"I'm going to go play on the swings," Logan announced, then headed out to the elaborate play area in the backyard.

"I'll take these into the kitchen," Wyatt said, lifting the woven bag that contained the bowl of Rosa's salad, the one he had insisted on taking from her when they met up outside Brambleberry House for the walk here.

He found his sister in the kitchen slicing tomatoes. He kissed her cheek and she smiled. "You're here. Oh, and Rosa's here, too. You came together."

"Yes," Rosa said. "It was such a beautiful evening for a walk. I made a fruit salad with strawberries from my garden."

"Oh, yum. How is your garden this year? I've had so much trouble with my flowers. I think I have some kind of bug."

"They are good," Rosa replied. "Not as lovely as when Sonia was here to take care of them but I do my best with it."

"I miss Sonia," Carrie said. "I guess we should call her Elizabeth now."

Rosa nodded. "I will always think of her as Sonia, I am afraid."

Wyatt knew the story of Rosa's previous tenant. For several years, she had lived in Cannon Beach as Sonia Davis but a year earlier, she had admitted her real name was Elizabeth Hamilton. For many complicated reasons, she had been living under a different name during her time here, until her husband showed up out of the blue one day to take her back to their hometown. It had been the talk of Cannon Beach for weeks.

Rosa had been good friends with her tenant and Carrie had told him how astonished she had been at the revelation that the woman she thought she knew had so many secrets.

"How is Sonia Elizabeth?" Carrie asked, the name some of the woman's friends had taken to calling her. "Do you ever talk to her?"

"Oh, yes. We speak often," Rosa said. "I texted her the other day to ask her a question about a plant I didn't recognize and we did a video call so she could take a better look at it. She seemed happy. Her children are happy. She said she isn't having seizures much anymore and she and her husband are even talking about taking in a foster child with the idea of adopting."

Carrie looked thrilled at the news. "Oh, that's lovely. Do you know, I was thinking about Sonia the other day. I bumped into Melissa and Eli and Skye at the grocery store. Do you see them much?"

Melissa Fielding Sanderson had been another tenant of Brambleberry House. She had married a doctor, Eli Sanderson, whom Wyatt had known when he used to visit his grandmother here during his childhood.

"Oh, yes," Rosa answered. "We still meet for lunch or

dinner about once a month. She's very busy with the new baby."

"Thomas is such a sweetheart," Bella said. "I watched him last week when Melissa had a test."

Melissa, a registered nurse, was studying to be a nurse practitioner and juggled school with being a mother and working at the clinic with her husband and father-in-law. Somehow she made it all work.

"What time is Jaycee's mom picking you up?" Carrie asked her daughter.

"Not until eight."

"Then you probably have time to eat with us. Why don't you and Rosa start carrying things out to the patio? We thought it would be nice to eat outside and take advantage of the gorgeous weather. Bell, you can take the plates and silverware and Rosa can take these salads."

Rosa looked delighted, which Wyatt thought was odd. Maybe she was just happy to have a task.

"Yes. That is a wonderful idea. I am happy to help."

She picked up the fruit salad she had brought and the green salad Carrie had just finished preparing, then carried them through the back door to the patio. Bella joined her, arms laden with plates and the little basket full of silverware Carrie used for outdoor entertaining. As they opened the door, Wyatt caught the delicious scent of sizzling steak.

"What can I do?"

"I think that is it for now." Carrie paused, then gave him a meaningful look. "Rosa is lovely, isn't she?"

Oh, no. He knew where this was going. Carrie seemed to think it was her job now to find him dates. She was always trying to set him up with women she knew, despite his repeated attempts to convince her he was perfectly happy and not interested in dating right now.

He gave her a stern look, though he feared it would do no good. Carrie wasn't great at taking hints.

"Yes. She's lovely."

"Inside and out," his sister said, then gave a careful look to make sure she and Bella were busy setting the patio table.

"You know, so many people could have let what she has been through turn them bitter and angry. Not Rosa. I think it's only made her stronger and more empathetic to everyone."

Wyatt frowned. "What has she been through?"

Carrie gave him a vague look. "Oh, you know. Life in general. Coming here when she was young. Losing her mother when she was just a girl."

What else did she know about Rosa's background? He wanted to push, but then had to remind himself that he was already becoming too entangled in her world. The more he learned about her, the harder it was becoming to fight off this attraction.

Bella came back into the kitchen as he was wrestling against his curiosity to know everything he could about the intriguing Rosa Galvez.

"What else can we take out?" she asked. "Also, Dad is asking for a platter for the steaks."

Carrie pulled one out of the cabinet above the refrigerator and handed it to Bella, who immediately headed back outside with it.

"I only meant to say that Rosa is a lovely woman," she said when they were alone again. "When you're ready to start thinking about dating again, she would be an excellent choice."

Wyatt shifted, vowing to do his best that evening to keep his sister from figuring out that he was already fiercely drawn to Rosa. Once she realized that, Carrie would never give up trying to push them together.

"What if I'm never ready?"

"Oh, don't say that." His sister looked anguished. "You are a young, healthy man. You can't spend the rest of your life alone, for your sake or for Logan's. You know Tori would never have wanted that."

Yes. He knew. That conversation with her had been running through his head more and more often. But a hypothetical discussion with his wife when he still thought they would have the rest of their lives together was one thing. The reality of letting someone else into his heart was something else entirely.

He was tired of being alone, though. Maybe there had been a few nights lately when he had thought it might be lovely to have someone in his life again. Someone to make him laugh, to help him not take himself so seriously, to remind him that life was a beautiful, complex mix of joy and hardship.

Even if he was ready to move on, he sensed that Rosa wasn't that person. She was wonderful with Logan but it was clear she didn't trust *him*.

Just as well. Since he *wasn't* ready, there was no point in dwelling on the issue, especially on a sweet summer night.

Rosa always loved spending time with the Abbotts. Joe and Carrie were deeply in love, even after being married more than twenty years. They held hands often, they touched all the time and they kissed at random moments.

And Bella. Being around the girl was a unique experience, like constantly walking a razor wire between joy and pain.

At dinner, Bella wanted to tell Rosa all about a boy she

liked named Charlie, who might or might not be going to the same place in the nearby town to watch the fireworks.

"I really like him but I'm not allowed to date until I'm sixteen. That's not fair, is it?"

Rosa looked over to where Carrie was talking to Joe and Wyatt. She did *not* want to interject herself into a dispute between Bella and her parents over rules.

"I think that your parents have your best interests at heart. You should listen to them."

Bella clearly did not welcome that answer. "It's not like we're going to go somewhere and make out. We're watching fireworks with about a billion other people."

Rosa did not want to come across as a boring old woman but she also felt compelled to offer some advice. Bella looked on her as an older sister of sorts, just the person who *should* be giving counsel.

"You should stay with your friend and her parents, especially since they are giving you a ride."

"I know. I would never ditch my friends over a boy, no matter how cute he is."

"What cute boy are you talking about?" Carrie asked, overhearing her daughter's words.

Bella looked as if she didn't want to answer her mother but she finally sighed. "Charlie. He texted me to tell me he might be going to the fireworks."

Carrie looked vaguely alarmed. "You didn't tell me that."

"Because I knew you would blow everything out of proportion. We're not going together. I might not even see him there."

She gave Rosa an annoyed look, as if it was *her* fault Carrie had overheard their conversation.

"I don't even know if I like him that much," Bella said. "You don't have to make a big deal about it."

"I just want you to be careful. You have plenty of time for boyfriends," her mother said.

"I know. I told you he's not my boyfriend. I like him a little but that's all. I need to go find my portable phone charger. Jaycee's going to be here any minute."

"Don't forget to take a hoodie. It's going to be much colder once the sun goes all the way down."

"I know." Bella hurried off to her room and Rosa had to fight the urge to go after her and warn her again not to leave her friends.

"I hope I can make it through these teenage years," Carrie said, shaking her head.

"You can."

"All this talk of boys and learning to drive. She's growing up, isn't she?"

Rosa nodded, that bittersweet joy a heavy weight in her heart.

Chapter 7

The barbecue was one of the most delightful evenings Wyatt had experienced in a while. He always enjoyed hanging out with his sister and considered his brother-in-law one of his closest friends. But having Rosa there, listening to her laugh with Carrie and Bella, tease Joe and trade corny jokes with Logan, somehow turned the night magical.

He tried to tell himself he was simply savoring the delight of good food and family. That didn't explain how the stars seemed to sparkle more brightly and the air smelled more sweet.

"Everything was delicious," he said to Carrie. "That cherry pie was divine. Did you try a new recipe?"

She shook her head. "No. I'm using the same one Grandma always made. She got it from Abigail Dandridge, actually. The cherries are just extra delicious this year, I think."

"That must be it."

"Looks like somebody is out for the count," Joe said, gesturing to their outdoor sofa, where Logan had curled up a little while ago.

Wyatt followed his gaze and found his son sound asleep under the blanket Carrie had brought out for him earlier, after the sun had gone down and the evening had turned chilly.

He wasn't completely surprised. Their day had been filled with activity and fun.

Love for his son washed over him. Logan was the greatest gift.

"Good thing he can sleep anywhere."

"He is very lucky," Rosa said. "Some nights, I cannot even sleep in my comfortable bed with cool sheets and soft music playing."

What was keeping her up at night? Did she also ache for something she didn't have?

"We're watching Logan for you tomorrow and you said you're going into work early, right?" Carrie asked.

He made a face. "Yeah. Sorry about that."

"You know it's no problem at all. But I've got a great idea. Why don't you just let Logan stay over here for the night? He can sleep in and so can we, since tomorrow is the official holiday and we don't have a single thing planned."

That did make sense, though Wyatt didn't like spending even a night away from his son.

"Are you sure?"

"Yes. If you want the truth, I would rather sleep in tomorrow, since I imagine we will be up late worrying until Bella gets home safely."

Rosa looked concerned. "I am sure she will be fine. Bella is a smart girl and she is with her friend Jaycee and

Jaycee's parents. They will make sure she does not get into any trouble."

"Parents always worry. It's what we do." Carrie shrugged. "Intellectually, I know Bella will be fine. I'll still probably stay up, which means I'll be doubly glad not to have to get up at six a.m., when you come to drop off Logan."

"I didn't bring any clothes for him."

"He has as many clothes here as he probably does at Brambleberry House. We have everything he should need. Swimsuits, shorts and sweatshirts. Even extra socks. It will be great."

Seriously, what would he have done without his sister and her family over the last three years, when they had stepped in after Tori died to help him raise his son?

"That does seem like a good solution, then. I'll carry him into the guest room."

"Afraid we're going to leave him out here on the patio to sleep?" Joe teased.

Wyatt smiled. "He probably wouldn't care. The thing is, Logan would never even notice if it started raining."

Only after he and Rosa had helped clean up and he had carried a still-sleeping Logan and tucked him into the sewing room daybed did Wyatt realize one significant issue he had overlooked.

If his son stayed here, that meant he and Rosa would be walking home alone together.

He frowned, suddenly suspicious. Carrie had been awfully quick to suggest that Logan stay the night, hadn't she? Were her reasons really about convenience and sleeping in the next day, or was she trying to do some behind-the-scenes matchmaking again?

He gave his sister a swift look, remembering that conversation in the kitchen.

Her reasons didn't matter. The deed was done. He and Rosa were walking back to Brambleberry House together and he could do nothing about it.

A short time later, they left the house, with Rosa carrying the bag with the bowl she had brought, now empty and washed.

Why had he thought it was a good idea to walk here earlier? If he had driven, they could have been home in two minutes.

The walk wasn't far, only a few blocks, but there was an intimacy to walking alone with Rosa that left him uncomfortable.

He hadn't noticed it at all on the walk to Carrie's house, probably because Logan had kept up a constant chatter. His son had provided a much-needed buffer.

"The night turned a little cooler, didn't it? That came on suddenly."

She had brought a sweater, which she had put on earlier. Even so, she shivered a little.

"Yes. And it looks as if the fog they've been talking about is finally moving in."

Tendrils of coastal fog stretched up from the beach, winding through the houses. It added to the strange, restless mood stealing over him like the fog creeping up the street.

He put it down to leaving his son back at his sister's house. Surely that's what it was, not anything to do with his growing feelings for Rosa.

"You were right—Logan can sleep through anything. I would not have believed it but he did not even open his eyes when you carried him to bed. Will he wake up confused in a strange place?"

"I don't think so. He's spent the better part of the past two months sleeping there, except for the few weeks we've been at Brambleberry House. He's probably as comfortable there as he is in his own bed. I, on the other hand, probably won't sleep at all."

She gave him a sideways look. "Why is that?"

He shrugged, wishing he hadn't said anything. "When I don't have Logan nearby, I feel like part of me is missing."

She looked touched. "He is a very sweet boy."

"You've been very kind to help him learn Spanish for his friend. I know you're busy. Please let me know if it becomes too much of a burden."

"Impossible," she declared. "I am always happy to speak Spanish with someone. Sometimes I worry I will forget the language of my birth."

He suddenly remembered the conversation he'd had with his sister about her. What had she been through, the reasons Carrie said she deserved to be happy?

"That fog is growing more thick. I hope it goes out again in the morning so the weather stays good for the rest of the holiday weekend. It is a busy time for my store."

"Don't you have better business if it starts to rain? I would have thought fewer people would want to sit at the beach when it's raining, so they're more inclined to go shopping instead."

"Sometimes. Or sometimes they decide since it's raining to take a drive down the coast to Lincoln City, or even farther down to some of the other lighthouses like Heceta Head."

"The police department is busy whether it's raining or not. It seems like holiday weekends always bring out the worst in people."

"Do you like your job as a detective?" she asked as they turned onto the Brambleberry House road.

The question took him by surprise. Not many people

asked him that. He pondered for a moment before answering, wanting to be as honest as possible.

"I like when I have the chance to help people. That doesn't always happen. The past few years have made me question my job choices. I've seen a lot of injustice and been frustrated by it. Attitudes are changing, I think. It's just taking longer than it should. At the end of the day, I hope I can say I've worked for victims and for justice."

She said nothing for several long moments. When she spoke, her voice was low. "I will always be grateful for the *policia*. My father is the sheriff and he saved my life and the lives of my friends."

She turned onto the walk of Brambleberry House as if her words hadn't landed between them like an errant firework.

After his first moment of shock, he quickly caught up with her. "How did he do that?"

In the moonlight, she looked as if she regretted saying anything at all. "It is a long story, and not a very nice one. I do not like to talk about it."

Wyatt wanted to point out that she had been the one to bring it up. He had the odd feeling Rosa wanted to tell him about her past, but was afraid of his reaction.

"Well, if you ever decide you're willing to share your story with me, I like to think I'm a pretty good listener."

"I have noticed this. That is probably a help in your line of work, when you are fighting crime."

"I hope so."

He knew he had to get up early for his shift the next morning, yet he didn't want the evening to end.

To his vast relief, she didn't seem in a hurry to go to inside, either. She stood looking at the big, graceful old house in the moonlight. It was mostly in darkness except for a light in the shared entry and two lights glowing on the second floor.

In the wispy coastal fog, it looked mysterious, intriguing, though not nearly as interesting as the people who lived inside.

"Looks like our neighbor is home."

Wyatt didn't miss the way Rosa looked protectively toward the second floor, where a shadow moved across the closed curtain.

"Yes. I think she and Addie planned a quiet evening."

"She doesn't go out much, I've noticed."

"Have you?"

As he expected, she didn't take the bait, so he came right out and asked the question he had been wondering since he moved in.

"What is Jen's story? You can tell me, you know."

In the moonlight, he saw Rosa's features tighten. "I don't know what you mean."

She did. She knew perfectly well. "Why does she seem so nervous around me?"

"Nervous?"

"Yeah. She has allowed her little girl to play with Logan a few times, but Jen herself clearly goes out of her way to avoid me. I'm not sure she's ever looked me in the eye."

Rosa looked away herself. "Maybe she does not like policemen."

"Is she in some kind of trouble? Do you know?"

"Why would you ask that?" Her innocent-sounding question didn't fool him at all. She knew exactly what was going on with Jen.

"I can't help her if nobody will tell me what's going on," he pointed out mildly. He didn't want to intrude, but he was

an officer of the law and his job was to protect and serve.
That included those who shared the same house with him.

"She has work at the store and she has a safe place to
live. That is good for now." She paused. "But thank you for
being concerned for her."

"I'm here to help, if you or she ever want to tell me
what's going on."

She nodded slowly. "I will tell her this."

"You know I'm one of the good guys, right? At least I
try to be."

She gave him a long look in the moonlight. "Yes. I know.
I would not have let you move in if I did not think that."

Her words made him feel as if he had passed some kind
of test he had no idea he'd been taking.

He was suddenly glad that Carrie had encouraged him
to take this apartment for the month, grateful for summer
nights and lovely women.

Again, he felt an overwhelming urge to kiss her, this
woman with secrets who was filled with so much compassion for those around her.

She didn't trust him. He looked at the house, hating the
idea of his empty apartment and his empty bed and the loneliness that had been such a part of his life since Tori died.

"I should probably go in."

"Yes. You are working early tomorrow."

He nodded. "Thank you for the lovely evening. I enjoyed
the walk home. I think maybe I've forgotten how much I
enjoy talking with a woman."

She gazed at him, eyes wide. In the dim light of the
moon, he saw her swallow and her gaze seemed to slide
to his mouth.

The scent of her, sweet and feminine, with hints of vanilla and berries, drifted to him. He wanted to close his eyes and inhale her inside him.

"I am glad I could remind you of this," she finally said.

He knew he should walk away, turn around and go into the house, to that empty apartment and the even emptier bed. He couldn't seem to make his muscles cooperate. The pull of her was too strong and he had no tools to withstand this slow, aching desire churning through his blood.

"I would like to kiss you right now."

As soon as he heard the words, he wanted to call them back, but it was far too late. They danced between them like petals on the breeze.

He thought she would turn and walk away since he couldn't seem to do it. Instead, she only gazed up at him out of those soft brown eyes he wanted to sink into.

"Would you?" she finally asked, her voice soft and her accent more pronounced than usual.

"Yes. Would you mind?"

After a brief hesitation, as if she was debating with herself, she shook her head slightly.

That was all the encouragement he needed. He lowered his mouth to hers, his heart beating so loudly in his ears it almost drowned out the ever-present sound of the ocean.

If he had forgotten how much peace he could find talking with a woman, he had *really* forgotten how much he loved to kiss a woman in the moonlight.

Her mouth tasted of strawberries and cream, and her lips trembled slightly. She must have set down the bag she had been carrying because one hand grasped his shirtfront and the other slid around his neck.

It was the perfect moment, the perfect kiss. He had no other way to describe it. A light breeze stirred the air around them, the ocean murmured nearby and the moonlight played on her features.

He wanted to stay right here, with his heart pounding and her mouth soft and sweet and generously responding to his kiss.

Here, he could focus only on the perfection of this moment. Not on the pain of the past or the mysteries that surrounded her or all the reasons they could never have anything but this kiss.

Chapter 8

In her secret dreams, Rosa had wondered before what it would be like to kiss Wyatt. Having him live downstairs from her these last few weeks had only increased her attraction to the man, so, of course, she would wonder.

She had suspected kissing him would be an unforgettable experience.

She had not expected it to knock her legs out from under her.

Rosa closed her eyes, her heart pounding as his mouth explored hers.

Now, as he kissed her, she could admit that she had been attracted to him for a long time. Long before he had moved to Brambleberry House, she had been nervous around him. She had told herself it was because of his position with the police department. Now she could admit it was because of the man himself.

His kiss staggered her.

Why? She had kissed other men, of course. Not counting the awful time in her youth that she didn't like to think about, she had had boyfriends.

She wanted to think she had a healthy relationship now with men, with sex, especially after the counseling her parents had insisted on.

She didn't blame all men for what had happened to her.

Even so, Rosa was fully aware that she usually gravitated toward a different sort of man. Someone who was not as masculine as Wyatt.

Those kind of men were the safer bet, she realized now. They didn't threaten her. She always had held most of the control in every other situation.

Not with Wyatt. Kissing him felt like being caught in a riptide, as if she were whirling and spinning from forces beyond her control.

Sometimes when she saw the intensity between Lauren and Daniel, or her aunt Anna and Harry, Rosa wondered if she had something fundamental broken inside her.

She had assumed that the scars she bore so deeply inside made it impossible for her to feel that kind of passion.

Kissing Wyatt in this moment made her question every single one of those foolish assumptions.

She could want, with a searing intensity that left her breathless.

She wanted to drag him to the dewy grass and kiss him for hours. And more. She wanted more with him.

And then what?

Cold, hard reality seemed to push through the dreamy haze that surrounded her.

After this kiss, then what? Try as she might, she couldn't envision a scenario where she and Wyatt could have anything but a few wild kisses. Where they could live happily ever after.

He was a police detective and she was…herself. A product of what had happened to her and the choices that had led her here to this moment.

They could never be together, so what was the point in setting herself up for more pain?

She drew in a breath, willing her hunger to subside. When she thought she had herself under control enough that she could think straight again, she slid her mouth away, cooled by the night air that swirled around them. After another inhalation, she made herself take a slight step back.

She couldn't see him clearly, but she could tell he had been as caught up in the kiss as she was.

He gazed down at her, his eyes slightly unfocused and his hair messy from her fingers. He looked so delicious, she had a hard time not stepping straight back into his arms.

She had to say something, but all the words seemed tangled up inside her like fishing line discarded on the beach, a jumble of Spanish and English that made no sense, even to her.

She finally swallowed hard and forced a smile.

"That was a surprise."

He continued to look down at her, his face so close she could see each distinct long eyelash and the fine network of lines etched into the corners of his eyes.

He released a long breath. "Yes. It was."

"I thought you meant a little good-night kiss like a friend would give a friend."

"That was substantially more, wasn't it?"

She could feel the imprint of his mouth on hers, could still taste him on her tongue—the wine and mint, the strawberries and cream from the dessert his sister had made. She shivered a little, wishing she could lean in for another kiss.

"Indeed." She hated this awkwardness between them, especially after the closeness they had shared on the walk from his sister's house. She shook her head.

"I'm sorry if I turned the kiss into more than you wanted."

"You didn't. That is the problem. I want, though I know I should not."

He gave a slightly raw-sounding laugh, as if startled by her honesty. "Same. I want. And I know I should not. What are we going to do about that?"

Rosa spent a delicious moment imagining what she would like to do. She wanted to drag him up two flights of stairs to her cozy bedroom under the eaves and spend the entire night exploring all his muscles and hard edges.

That was impossible, for a hundred reasons. The biggest one was right now at the house they had come from.

"I don't know what you will do, but I will go inside, take a soak in the tub and try to focus on something else."

A muscle worked along his jawline as if he was trying to keep himself from responding. He finally nodded. "I suppose that's for the best."

Rosa managed a smile, trying to pretend she wasn't fighting with everything inside her to keep from doing what she longed to do—tug him back into her arms and kiss him again until they both forgot all the shoulds and should nots.

"Good night to you, Wyatt. I enjoyed the evening…and the kiss."

"Rosa…" he began, but she didn't wait to hear what he said. She hurried up the steps, unlocked the front door with hands that trembled and rushed up to her apartment.

As she took the stairs quickly, she thought she felt an

odd cold spot on the stairs and had the strangest feeling that the house or its inhabitants were disappointed in her.

She and Wyatt had decided not to take the dogs with them because of Carrie's spoiled and rather unfriendly cats. Inside the apartment, Fiona rose to greet her, giving her an unblinking stare, as if she knew exactly what Rosa had just been doing in the moonlight with their downstairs neighbor.

"Not you, too."

Fi snorted as if she had plenty to say but only regretted that she did not have the words.

"What do you want me to do?" she said aloud to her dog. "You know I cannot invite the man up. He is a police officer. He would not be interested in me, if he knew the truth."

Fiona whined. She needed to go out, but Rosa wasn't eager to go down the stairs again and risk meeting up with Wyatt. Her dog's needs came first, though.

"Don't be like that," she said as she hooked up Fi's leash. "You know it is true. I have too many secrets I cannot tell him."

The dog didn't look convinced.

"I cannot," Rosa insisted. "You know I cannot. They are not only my secrets. I cannot tell him."

Wyatt was a good man, A decent, honorable man, she thought as she walked down the stairs again and outside into the moonlight. To her relief, she didn't see any sign of him.

He reminded her so much of Daniel, who would always be her hero for rescuing her in her darkest moment.

She loved her adopted father dearly so she supposed it was only natural that she would be so fiercely drawn to a man who had all of Daniel's best qualities.

"It doesn't matter," she said. She didn't feel foolish carrying on this conversation with her dog. Fiona was the best possible confidante, who listened to all her inner thoughts and only judged a little.

She didn't tell the dog that she suspected she might be falling for Wyatt, though she knew he would never feel the same. Not if he knew the truth.

She knew he was still grieving for his wife. Even if the two of them shared a few kisses, she knew Wyatt wasn't in a good place for anything more.

She wanted things to be different. If only they were both free of their pasts and had met under other circumstances. But she knew she wouldn't have been the same person without all that had happened to her and she thought the same of Wyatt.

She would not kiss him again. What would be the point? Nothing could come of it and she would only end up with more pain.

With the Oregon coast in full tourist season, Rosa didn't have time to think about that kiss more than about two or three dozen times a day at random moments.

Over the next week, she made several day trips out of town to the central coast and to Portland to pick up inventory from some of their vendors.

Today she was busy revamping her window display a week after Independence Day, adding in the new products she had collected to feature, while Jen worked the cash register and assisted customers.

Rosa was thrilled at the change in her friend. Jen had come so far over the past few weeks. She was far more relaxed with the customers. She smiled and chatted easily and seemed to have lost that haunted look she used to wear at random moments.

"Thank you. Come back again. We have new inventory

all the time," she told the final customer at her register. A few other browsers were looking at their selection of T-shirts, but they didn't seem in any hurry so Rosa left the window to walk over to Jen and check on her.

"How are things going?" she asked.

"Great. Really good." Jen smiled, looking far more like the woman Rosa remembered from their college days together. "It's hard to be in a bad mood when the weather is so glorious, isn't it?"

They really had been blessed with unusually sunny weather. It was good now, but made her worry about forest fires later in the season.

"You seem to be more comfortable with the customers."

"I am enjoying the work, but to tell you the truth, I'm starting to miss teaching. This is the time of year when I would usually start thinking about my classroom decorations for the next school year and working on lesson plans."

Jen had been a third-grade teacher in Utah and had loved her career. That was one of the things that angered Rosa the most, that her friend had been forced to leave all that she loved in order to escape.

"I can understand that."

"I was actually wondering if I could take a day off tomorrow. I know it's short notice."

"Of course," Rosa said immediately. "I can rearrange the schedule. If I cannot find anyone to cover for you, I will work myself. That should not be a problem, especially now that the holiday weekend is over."

"Thank you. You won't believe this but I already have a job interview lined up!"

"Oh, that's wonderful!"

Rosa knew Jen had recently finished the process to certify her Utah teaching license in Oregon and that she had started applying in the area.

"The first school I contacted called me today and want to talk to me tomorrow. It's at Addie's school, which would be ideal."

"Oh, that is so exciting. Of course, you can have the day off. Or more than that, if you need it."

"To be honest, I'm not sure if I should apply. If I found a job, I would have to quit working here before the tourist season is over in September."

Rosa waved a hand. "Don't worry about that for a moment. I have temporary seasonal workers who have asked for more hours, so I can give them your shifts if you get a new teaching contract. I'm just happy that you like it enough here in Oregon to think about staying for a while."

Jen hugged her and Rosa was happy to note that she had started to gain weight again and seemed to have lost that frail, hunted look.

"It's all because of you," Jen said. "I can't thank you enough for all you've done since I moved here. Giving me this job, a place to live. You have been amazing."

Rosa was only happy she had been in a position to offer help.

"I have been grateful to have you and Addie here. You would have a job here at the store as long as you want, but it would be wonderful for you to return to teaching. You were made to be a teacher."

The T-shirt customers came over to ask a question, distracting them from further conversation. The door opened and more customers entered, so Rosa moved to help them.

A constant flow of traffic moved in and out of the store over the next few hours and she was too busy to have another chance to talk to her friend about her interview.

Finally, things seemed to slow near the end of Jen's shift. One of the other seasonal workers, Carol Hardesty, came in a little early for her own shift and Rosa was about to tell Jen to take off for the day when she suddenly heard a loud crash.

Rosa jerked up her head, instantly alert, to find Jen staring out the window, the shards of a broken coaster scattered at her feet.

Fortunately, it was a fairly inexpensive one in a design that hadn't been particularly attractive, anyway.

"Is everything okay?" she asked, when Jen continued to stare out the window.

Her words seemed to jolt the woman back to her senses. Jen looked down at the mess, a dawning look of horror on her features.

"Oh, no. I'm so sorry."

Rosa moved quickly to her. "You look frightened. Are you all right? Has something happened?"

"Yes. No. I don't know. I just… I thought I saw…"

"A ghost?" Carol hurried up with a broom and dustpan and started sweeping in her no-nonsense way. "We get those here in Cannon Beach. Once, I swear I saw a man all wrapped up in bandages walking around the side of Highway 101. When I slowed down to see if he needed help, he was completely gone. Spooky!"

"Yes. It must have been…something like that."

Jen looked like a ghost herself with her suddenly pale features.

"And the really creepy part is," Carol went on, "when I mentioned it to a few people, I found out Bandage Man is kind of a legend around here. There was even a stretch of the old highway called Bandage Man Road. Weird, right?"

Jen hardly seemed to hear her, still staring out the window.

"You need to sit down for a minute."

"Yes," Carol urged. "I've got this mess and I'll handle any customers. Don't worry about a thing."

Rosa guided a numb Jen to the back room she used as an office, which was also where most of the employees took their breaks. Jen sagged into a chair and Rosa crouched beside her, holding her hand.

"Who did you see? Was it the man you fear?"

Jen shook her head. "Not him. But maybe a friend of his. I can't be sure. I only caught a glimpse of him through the window, but I think he was looking at me as if he knew me."

Her panic was only too familiar to Rosa. She knew just how it felt to be hunted. The memories crowded into her mind but she pushed him away.

This was not about her. This was about Jen and her fear and the man who had made her life hell for months.

Rosa did not offer platitudes because she knew how useless they could be.

"What do you need? Do you want me to call the police? You know you can trust Wyatt. Detective Townsend. He is a good man."

For a moment, Jen looked as if she would consider doing just that, then she shook her head. "What would I say? That I think I might have seen a man who might be friends with a man who scares me but who has never actually touched me? He will think I'm crazy."

"He will not think you are crazy." Rosa did not know how she knew this so completely, but she had no doubt that Wyatt would take Jen's concerns seriously. "Stalking is against the law in Oregon, just as it was in Utah. I believe Wyatt will help you. He will want to know what you think you saw."

Again, Jen looked tempted. Rosa even pulled out her

phone, but her friend finally shook her head firmly. "I'm imagining things. I'm sure of it. It was only a man who looked like someone from our town. I don't want to bring Wyatt in."

"You know he will help."

"Yes. If there was anything he could do, but there's not. I cannot run from shadows for the rest of my life. Aaron would have no reason to know I'm here. He doesn't know one of my dearest friends lives here. I never mentioned you to him. And if it was his friend, he couldn't possibly recognize me. I don't look the same. I've lost thirty pounds, my hair is shorter and a different color. I have contacts now instead of glasses. He would have no reason to even connect Jen Ryan with the woman he knew as Jenna Haynes."

Rosa was still not convinced. She had heard the fear, the sheer terror in Jenna's voice when Rosa had called her. She thought it would just be a regular phone call to wish her a happy birthday. Instead, Jenna had spewed out such a story of horror that Rosa had been physically sick to her stomach.

"You must come here," she had told her college friend firmly in that phone call. "I have an empty apartment right now. Just bring Addie and come tonight."

"I can't drag you into this," Jen had replied through her tears. "You've been through enough."

"That is why I have to help you. You are my friend. I cannot let you live in fear if you do not have to. Come to Oregon, where this man does not know anyone. You will be safe here."

Jen had been desperate enough to escape her situation that she had finally agreed, leaving in the middle of the night with only their clothes.

She was finally beginning to relax and enjoy her life again. Rosa hated to think of her living in fear again.

"Please. Consider talking to Wyatt," she said now. "He

knows something is wrong. He asked me about it the other night. You know he is a good man. He will do what he can to keep you safe."

"I'll think about it," Jen finally said. Color had returned and she seemed to be breathing more easily, Rosa was glad to see.

"Give me a moment and I will give you a ride home."

Worried that the man stalking her had put a trace on her vehicle, Jen had traded her car in the Boise area for an older model sedan that had seen better days. It was currently in the shop, where it had been for several days.

Jen shook her head. "No. Thank you, though. I would rather walk."

"Are you sure?"

"It's less than a mile and I can pick up Addie on the way. The walk will clear my head."

"Are you sure?"

Jen nodded. Her features grew soft. "I meant what I said earlier. I cannot thank you enough for all you've done for me. You've given me hope that someday soon I will stop looking over my shoulder. I wish there was some way I could repay you."

"You have, a hundred times. I love seeing you take back your life. You and Addie deserve everything wonderful I know is in store for you."

Jen smiled, though traces of panic still lingered in her eyes. As soon as she left, Rosa almost picked up her phone and called Wyatt herself, but she decided against it. Jenna's story was her own. She had her reasons for keeping it to herself.

Rosa, who had plenty of secrets of her own, could not fault her for that, even though she knew Wyatt was the kind of man who would do everything he could to keep Jenna and Addie safe.

Chapter 9

After leaving Carol and another of her part-time workers to close the store, Rosa returned to Brambleberry House tired, but in a strange, restless mood. She needed to bake something. The urge did not hit her very often, but when it did, she tried to go with it.

Baking reminded her of her mother. Maria Elena had been an amazing baker who used to make delicious delicacies she would sometimes sell in the market. Anything to make a few lempiras.

Rosa still liked making the treats of her childhood, but today she was feeling more like good old-fashioned chocolate-chip cookies, a treat she had come to love as a teenager.

She was just taking the first batch out of the oven when her phone rang. For a moment, she thought about ignoring it. Hardly anyone ever reached out to her with a phone call anymore, unless there was some kind of trouble. It might be Lauren, though, who still liked to have long chats on the phone since they couldn't connect as often in person.

Without looking at the caller ID, she tapped her earbud to answer the call as she slid the tray of cookies onto the cooling rack and put the next tray into the oven.

"Buenas," she said, distracted.

"Hello?" a male voice replied. "Is this Rosa Galvez?"

Her heartbeat accelerated as she recognized Wyatt.

Oh, this was so stupid. They had shared one kiss. Granted, it had been earthshaking for her, but that did not explain why she became weak in the knees, simply knowing he was on the other end of a telephone call.

She was tempted for a moment to tell him "no, wrong number," and disconnect the call. That would be childish, though. What was the point of hiding from the reality that she was falling for a completely inappropriate man?

"Si. Yes. This is Rosa."

"Hola, Rosa. This is Wyatt Townsend. From downstairs."

As if she knew any other Wyatt Townsends who could make her head spin. "Yes. I know. Is everything all right?"

He sighed. "Not really. I have a little problem and was wondering if I could ask for your help."

The word shocked her. Wyatt was not the sort of man who could ask for help easily. "Of course. What do you need?"

"I just got called to cover an emergency and Carrie, Joe and Bella have gone to Portland. They're leaving for San Francisco from there. I'm in a bind and need someone to watch Logan for a few hours."

"Of course," she said instantly. "Fiona and I would be glad to help you. I can be down in ten minutes, as soon as I take some cookies out of the oven."

"You don't have to come down. I can bring him upstairs to you. He's used to sleeping on the couch."

"Don't be silly. He would be more comfortable in his own bed. We will be there in ten minutes."

She had more dough, but decided she could put it in the refrigerator for now and later freeze it for another day.

"Thank you. I appreciate that. Hopefully I won't be gone past midnight."

"Even if you are, I won't mind," she assured him. "I'll be down soon."

While she waited for the timer, she gathered her laptop and a small knitting project she had been working on. She also waited for the first batch of cookies to cool enough before transferring them to a plate to take downstairs with her. As soon as the timer went off, she turned off her oven, pulled out the cookie tray and transferred the cookies to another cooling rack, then headed down the stairs with Fiona following close behind her.

Wyatt opened the door before she could knock, as if he had been watching for her.

"I'm really sorry about this."

"Please do not apologize. I'm happy to do it."

"Logan is already in bed. He'll be sorry he missed you."

She was disappointed that she wouldn't have a chance to hang out with the sweet boy and teach him more Spanish words. She would have enjoyed reading him a story and tucking him in.

"Too bad. I brought him some cookies. Ah, well. He can have one when he wakes up."

"If I don't eat them all first. They look delicious."

He smiled and she had to remind herself she was here to watch his child, not to moon over the boy's father.

She did her best to ignore how fiercely she wanted to

kiss him again. It helped to focus on the gleaming badge he was wearing over the pocket of his sports coat, which reminded her of all the differences between them.

"Anything special I need to know or do?"

"Not really. Since the fire, Logan does have the occasional nightmare. If he has one, you only have to stay close and help talk him through it until he falls back asleep."

"Oh, *pobrecito*," she exclaimed.

His eyes seemed to soften. "Yeah. He's been through a few things. The nightmares are not as frequent as they were right after the fire. He probably won't even wake up but I wanted to warn you, just in case."

"Got it."

"Thank you again."

"Do not worry about things here. Go take care of what you have to do. I will be here. And take a cookie with you."

He grabbed one with a smile that left her feeling slightly light-headed. She told herself it was because she had only eaten a warm cookie for dinner.

After he left, she was again struck by how Wyatt and Logan had settled into the space. A video-game controller sat on the coffee table, along with a trio of plastic dinosaurs and several early-reader chapter books.

The house smelled like Wyatt, that combination of scents she couldn't pinpoint. She only knew it reminded her of walking through a forest after a rainstorm.

A light was on next to the easy chair in the sunroom. She wandered in and found a mystery novel with a bookmark halfway through on the side table. A small bowl of popcorn sat next to it.

Rosa's own limited detective skills told her he must have been reading and enjoying a snack when he got the call from work. She liked thinking about him here, enjoying the sound of the ocean in the night through the screens.

While Fiona found a comfortable spot on the rug next to Hank, Rosa continued on her tour. She briefly went to the room she knew Logan used and opened the door a crack to check on him.

The boy was sleeping soundly, sprawled across the bed with a shoebox that looked like it contained treasures tucked nearby.

She fought the urge to go to him, to smooth away the hair falling into his eyes.

The night of the storm, Wyatt had said Logan was a sound sleeper, but she still didn't want to run the risk of waking him and having him be confused at finding her here and not his father.

She did, however, take a moment to adjust the blanket more solidly over his shoulders.

Oh, he was dear boy. Just looking at him made her smile. He looked a great deal like his father, but his lighter coloring and the shape of his nose must have come from his mother's side.

Rosa had to wonder about the woman. She had seen a picture of them all together at Carrie and Joe's house. She had been pretty, blonde, delicate-looking.

Carrie had told her Tori Townsend had been a talented artist and writer, in addition to a school guidance counselor. Though she had been a runner who regularly worked out, she had tragically died of a previously undiagnosed heart condition at a shockingly young age.

Logan must grieve for her terribly, she thought. *Both of them must.* It made her heart ache, thinking of this sweet boy growing up without his mother.

At least he had a father who doted on him and an aunt,

uncle and cousin who showered love and affection on him, as well.

After she had assured herself Logan was sleeping comfortably, she returned to the living area. It felt strange to be here in Wyatt's space without him. She wasn't quite sure what to do with herself.

She finally turned on the audiobook she was listening to through her ear pods and picked up her knitting. While the dogs slept tangled together at her feet, she worked and listened to the audiobook above the sound of the wind in the trees and the ever-present song of the ocean.

The chair was comfortable and her day had been long. Soon she gave in to the inevitable and closed her eyes, thinking she would only doze for a moment.

She had a dream she was running. It was cold, bitterly cold, and she was barefoot. She was so afraid, not only for herself. She had nowhere to go and the winter snow blew past her and through her. So cold. Always so cold. She had been used to sunshine and heat and could never seem to warm up here.

Everything hurt. Her face, her arms, her stomach where she had been kicked and beaten. She needed help but didn't know where to go.

And then she saw him. A police officer. She thought at first it was Daniel but as he came closer she saw it was Wyatt, looking down at her with concern.

"What happened? Why are you running?"

She shook her head, too afraid to tell him. What would he think if he knew? He would never look at her the same way.

"It does not matter," she told the dream Wyatt. "I must keep running. If I don't, they will find me."

"Who?"

"The ghosts," she told him. Tears were running down her face. She could feel them dripping down her cheeks and reached to brush one away but it dried before she could touch it.

"I will protect you. I'm with the *policia*. Just like Daniel. Trust me, Rosa. Trust me. Trust me."

As she watched, the fear still coursing through her with every heartbeat, his image grew more and more faint until he completely disappeared, leaving her alone again.

She awoke with gritty eyes, a dry mouth and the unsettling sensation that she was not alone.

Rosa blinked for a moment in the darkness, not sure exactly where she was. Not her bedroom in Brambleberry House. She would remember that. Not her room at her parents' home in Utah, either.

A man was there, she suddenly realized. She could see the outline of him in the darkness. She struggled up, tangled in yarn, as instinctive fear and dark memories crowded through her, leaving little room for rational thought.

She had to escape. Run. Hide.

A hand was suddenly on her arm. "Easy. It's okay. It's me."

The voice, calm and measured, seemed to pierce her sudden panic. She knew that voice. Wyatt Townsend.

Was this still part of her nightmare?

Not a nightmare. She blinked a little more as the room came into focus and her consciousness seemed to calibrate again. Right. She had been watching his son for him while he went out to a crime scene and she must have fallen asleep.

Rosa drew in a deep, shuddering breath, embarrassed that she had given in to unreasonable panic for a moment. She thought she had come too far for that.

"You startled me."

"I'm sorry. I didn't mean to. I was just debating if you would be more annoyed with me for waking you or for letting you sleep here until the morning."

"I am not annoyed with you," she assured him. "I was having a bad dream. I am glad you woke me from it."

"Do you mind if I turn on the lamp?"

She probably looked horrible, with her hair tangled and her eyes shadowed. She carefully reached a hand up to her cheek and was relieved when she didn't feel any moisture. The tears must have only been in her dream.

"It's fine. Go ahead."

He did, and that's when she saw the fatigue in his eyes. This was more than physical, she realized instinctively. Something was very wrong. She wasn't sure how she knew but there was an energy that seemed to be seething around him. Something dark and sad.

"What is it?" She could not resist asking, though she wasn't sure she wanted to know the answer. "What has happened?"

He released a sigh that sounded heavy and tired. "It was a long, difficult night. That's all."

Whatever he had been dealing with seemed to have impacted him deeply.

She had seen that look before on her adopted father's face when he would return from a bad crime scene or accident. He would walk in the door and go immediately to Lauren, wherever she was, and would hold her tightly, as if she was his only safe haven in a terrible storm. She would hold him, comfort him, help him put the pieces of his soul back together before she sent him out again to help someone else.

She could not do that for Wyatt and it made her sad, suddenly. She was no one's safe haven.

"How can I help? Can I make you some tea?"

As soon as she made the offer, she thought it was silly to have even suggested it, but for some reason she thought something warm and comforting might be exactly what he needed to ease the turmoil.

He gave a ragged sound that wasn't quite a laugh. "I don't have any tea. And before you say you've got some upstairs and it will only take you a moment to run and get it, I'll tell you thank you but no. I probably need sleep more than anything. And maybe one of your cookies, but I might save those for breakfast."

"Are you certain? I don't mind going to get tea."

He shook his head. "No. You have done more than enough. I'm sorry I kept you so late."

"What time is it?"

"Nearly two. I thought I would be back long before now but the case was…more complicated than I expected."

"I do not mind. I was glad to help."

"I'm deeply grateful to you for staying with Logan. Let's get you back home so you can at least spend a few hours in your own bed."

She rose, again fighting the urge to go to him, wrap her arms around his waist and let him lean on her for a moment.

"Did everything go okay with Logan?" he asked. "No nightmares?"

She'd had one but hadn't heard a peep out of the boy. "Yes. Just fine. I checked on him when I first arrived and he was sleeping soundly. He doesn't keep the blanket on, though, does he?"

"Not usually. Sometimes I go in three or four times a night to fix it. He rolls around like he's doing gymnastics in his sleep. Once when we went camping, I actually woke up with bruises on my rib cage from him kicking me in his sleep."

He was a good father who adored his child. She could picture him checking on the boy and making sure he was warm in the night. It touched her heart.

"I cannot think you enough for coming down at the last minute and helping out. None of our usual babysitters were available. With Carrie and Joe out of town, I didn't know what else to do."

"I really did not mind. I was honored that you would ask. Please do not hesitate to ask me again."

"If I do, I'll try not to keep you up until the early hours of the morning."

She shrugged and slung her bag over her shoulder. "I slept more soundly here than I probably would have at home. Please do not worry."

He smiled a little at that, but she could tell his eyes were still hollowed. What had happened?

"Do you have everything? Can I carry something?"

She wanted to roll her eyes when she realized he really did intend to walk her upstairs. "I have told you before, it is only two flights of stairs. I think I will be fine by myself. Get some rest."

"I need to move a little bit after tonight."

She nodded, understanding that sentiment. After that terrible time, she had needed to take long walks with Lauren, finding peace and comfort and a sort of meditation in the rhythm and the movement.

"Do you...want to talk about what happened tonight?" she finally asked.

"You don't want to hear. It was ugly."

She couldn't help it. She rested a hand on his arm. "I

am sorry, whatever it was," she said quietly. "I can tell you are upset. If you were not, if you did not care and did not let the ugly touch you, then you would not be the good man you are."

He gazed down at her hand, his features tortured. After a moment, he made a sound of distress, then he folded her into his arms and held on tight.

"Why are people so horrible to each other?" he said, his voice sounding raw and strained.

She had no answer. What could she say? It was the question that had haunted her for fifteen years. One she was quite certain she would never be able to answer.

She only held him tightly, as she had seen Lauren do for Daniel, and tried to give him a little of her strength. She wanted to whisper that she would not let him go, no matter what, but, of course, she could not say that. How foolish to think that she, Rosa Vallejo Galvez, could protect anyone from the storm.

"Sometimes they are horrible," she agreed finally. "I do not know why. I wish I did. But more often people are good. They try to help where they can. I try to focus on the helpers instead."

They stood in the front room of his apartment, holding each other as emotions seemed to pour out of him. He didn't make a sound, but every once in a while, she could feel his shoulders shake as if it was taking everything inside him to keep from breaking down.

"Most of the time, I'm fine," he finally said, his voice still strained. "I like to think I can handle just about anything. But this one was hard. So hard."

"Tell me," she murmured.

"It was a murder-suicide. A domestic. A father who had lost a custody fight because of drug use and mental illness.

Instead of accepting the court ruling or trying to fix his problems so he could have visitation, he decided that if he couldn't have his son, the mother wouldn't, either. He shot the boy and then shot himself. The kid was only five. A kindergartener. Younger than Logan."

At the despair in his voice, her heart cracked apart. She could only imagine how excruciating it must have been for Wyatt, who did everything possible to make his son's world better, to witness this kind of a crime scene.

Aching for him, she could do nothing but tighten her arms around him. "I'm so very, very sorry," she murmured.

He clung to her for a long time, there in the apartment, and she felt invisible threads between them tighten. Finally, he eased away, looking embarrassed.

"I'm sorry. I didn't mean to lose it like that. I'm…not sure why I did."

She suspected he had no one to share this kind of pain with since his wife died, which made her heart ache all over again.

"You hold too much inside," she said softly. "It cannot be easy, what you deal with every day."

"Yeah. Sometimes." He studied her, his expression intense. "This helped. More than I can ever tell you."

"I am glad. So glad. If you have another bad night, you know where to find me. Everyone needs someone to hold them when the world seems dark and hard."

"Thank you."

"You are welcome, Wyatt."

Something flashed in his gaze, something hungry and fierce. "I love the way you say my name."

All of the breath seemed to leave her in a whoosh. She swallowed as an answering heat prickled across her skin. "I do not say it in any way that is special."

"It is. It's unlike the way anyone else says it. Don't get me wrong. You speak beautiful, fluent English. I wish I could speak Spanish as well as you speak English. But sometimes your native language comes through on certain words."

The heat seemed to spread across her chest and down her arms. "I am sorry."

"No. Don't ever apologize. I like it."

He looked embarrassed that he had said anything, even as the first hint of a smile lifted the edges of his mouth.

He liked the way she said his name. She couldn't hear anything different in her pronunciation, but she wasn't going to argue.

"Wyatt," she repeated with a smile. "If it makes some of the sadness leave from your eyes a little, I will say it again. Wyatt. Wyatt. Wyatt."

His smile widened, becoming almost full-fledged for a brief moment, and Rosa could feel those invisible threads go taut.

After a moment, his smile faded. "What am I going to do about you?" he murmured.

She swallowed again. A smart woman would leave this apartment right now, would turn and hurry up the stairs to the safety of her own place. "There is nothing to do. We are friends. Friends help each other. They lean on each other when they need help."

He gazed down at her, his expression one of both hunger and need. "Do friends think about kissing each other all the damn time?"

Chapter 10

Wyatt knew he shouldn't have said the words.

As soon as they were out, he wanted a do-over. Not because they weren't true. God knows, they were. He thought about Rosa Galvez constantly. Since the last time they had kissed, thoughts of her seemed to pop into his head all the time. She was like a bright, beautiful flower bringing happiness to everyone around her.

He was no exception. Thinking about her made him smile. Since he was thinking about her all the time, he was also smiling more than he had done in years. He knew it was becoming a problem when even other police officers had remarked on it.

Not that he really had anything to smile about. He and Rosa could not be together. Yeah, they had shared a brief, intense embrace. But that was the end of it.

If he could only get his brain to get with the program, he would be fine. But every single time he thought about her, he thought about kissing her. And every time he thought about kissing her, he tried to remind himself of all the reasons why it was not a good idea for him to kiss her again.

None of that stopped him from yearning. He wanted Rosa Galvez in his arms, in his bed, in his life.

In some ways, Wyatt felt as if he had been living in a state of suspended animation for the past three years, as if he had been frozen, like some glitch on one of Logan's video games, while the world went on around him.

It wasn't a good place, but it wasn't really terrible, either. He could still enjoy time with his son, with his sister and her family, with his friends.

He handled his day-to-day responsibilities, cared for Logan, managed to do a good job of clearing his caseload. But whenever he thought about what the future might hold for him, all he could see was a vast, empty void.

Nothing had been able to yank him out of that emptiness. Even when his house caught fire, he hadn't really been devastated, only annoyed at the inconvenience.

His own reaction had begun to trouble him. People had told him that a house fire was one of the most traumatic things that could happen to a person, but Wyatt had merely shrugged and moved into problem-solving mode. Where they would live, what he might change about the house as he was having crews work on the renovations.

Even something as dramatic as being displaced hadn't really bothered him.

He could see now that his reaction had been a self-protective mechanism. After Tori's shocking death and the vast grief that had consumed him, he had slipped into some kind of place where he did not let anything touch him deeply.

Now he felt as if kissing Rosa had somehow kicked him in the gut, jolting him off his axis—that safe, bland existence—and into a world where everything seemed more intense.

A few months ago, he would have felt sad about the crime scene he had dealt with earlier, but it wouldn't have left him feeling shattered.

He was beginning to feel things more deeply and wasn't at all sure he liked it. A big part of him wanted to go back to the safety of his inertia.

If kissing her once could jerk him into this weird place, maybe kissing her a second time would help set things back the way they were before.

Even as he thought it, he knew kissing her again was a stupid idea. That did not stop him from reaching for her, pulling her into his arms again and lowering his mouth to hers.

She made a small, surprised sound, but didn't pull away. If she had, he would have stopped instantly. Instead, her arms went around his neck again and she pressed against him. She kissed him back, her mouth soft, sweet, delicious.

As she parted her lips and touched him tentatively with her tongue, he went a little crazy, all the raw emotions of the evening consolidating into one, his wild need for Rosa Galvez.

He deepened the kiss, his mouth firm and demanding on hers. He had to be closer to her. To touch her, to feel her against him.

She said his name again with that sweet little accented pronunciation, this time in a voice that was throaty and aroused.

He wanted to absorb it inside him.

He wanted to lose himself inside *her*.

His body ached with it, suddenly, the need he had shoved down for so long. He wanted to make love to Rosa Galvez right here in his living room. To capture her gasps and sighs with his mouth, to see her shatter apart in his arms.

Her breasts were pressed against him and he wanted more. He wanted to see her, to taste her. He reached beneath the hem of her shirt, to the warm, sweet-smelling skin beneath.

She shivered. The movement rippled over his fingers and brought him to his senses.

What the hell was wrong with him?

This woman had just spent hours sleeping in his easy chair to help him with his son and he repaid her by groping her in his front room?

He couldn't seem to catch his breath, but he did his best as he dropped his arms from around her.

She was breathing hard, too, her hair loose from the messy bun she had been wearing. She gazed at him out of eyes that looked huge and impossibly dark.

She had been so sweet to him, so comforting and warm when he needed it most. He had been at the lowest point he could remember in a long time and she had held him and lifted him out of it. In return, he had let his hunger for her overwhelm all his common sense.

"I'm sorry," he said, his voice ragged. "I don't know what happened there."

"Do not apologize." Her voice wobbled a little bit.

"Are you…okay? I didn't hurt you, did I?"

Her gaze narrowed, as if he had offended her somehow. "You only kissed me. I am not like some glass figure in my store falling off the shelf. I cannot be broken by a kiss, Wyatt."

There was his name again. It seemed to slide under his skin, burrowing somewhere in his chest.

What was he going to do about her?

Nothing, he told himself again. He just had to suck it up and forget about the way her kisses made him feel alive for the first time in years.

"I'll walk you upstairs."

She didn't argue, much to his relief. She only turned away, gathered her things and called to Fiona, then she and her dog hurried up the stairs.

Wyatt caught up with them on the second landing. The dog seemed to give him a baleful look, but he thought maybe that was just a trick of the low lighting out here in the stairway.

At her apartment, Rosa unlocked the door and opened it. "Good night."

Before he could thank her again for helping him out with Logan, she slipped inside and closed the door firmly behind her.

Wyatt stood for a moment, staring at the beautiful woodwork on the door, a match to his own two floors below.

That was as clear a dismissal as he could imagine. She had literally shut the door in his face.

He couldn't blame her. It was now nearly three and he knew she had to open the store early the next day, just as he had another shift.

He turned and headed down the stairs. He gripped the railing and told himself the shakiness in his legs was only exhaustion.

Something told him it was more than that. That kiss had just about knocked his legs right out from under him.

He was falling for her.

The reality of it seemed to hit him out of nowhere and he nearly stumbled down the last few steps as if the fabled ghost of Brambleberry House had given him a hard shove.

No. He couldn't be falling for Rosa. Or for anyone else, for that matter.

He didn't *want* to fall in love again. He had been through that with Tori. Once was enough, thanks all the same. These feelings growing inside him were only attraction, not love. Big difference.

Yes, he liked her. She was sweet, compassionate, kind. And, okay, he thought about her all the time. That wasn't love. Infatuation, maybe.

He wouldn't let it be love.

The next day, Rosa was deadheading flowers in one of the gardens when Jen drove up in her rickety car, now running but not exactly smoothly. It shimmied a little as it idled, then she turned off the engine.

Rosa waved and Jen and Addie walked over.

"Hello, there," Rosa said. "How did the interviews go?"

"Good. Great, actually. The school offered me a job on the spot."

"Oh, that's terrific! We should celebrate. Have you eaten?"

"Yes. Sorry. Addie wanted a Happy Meal today."

"No problem. Maybe we can celebrate later. I have a bottle I've been saving for something special."

"It's a deal, as long as it goes with your famous chocolate-chip cookies."

Rosa had to smile. She had taken a plate down before she headed to the store and left them outside Jen's front door.

"Can we help you with the gardening?"

"Yes. Of course. That would be great. Thank you."

Addie frowned. "Why are you pulling all the flowers, Rosa? That's naughty. My mommy says I can't pick the flowers or they die."

She smiled, charmed by the girl even as she felt a little ache in her heart. "I am not picking *all* the flowers. Only the ones that have finished blooming and have started to die. This way the flower plant has more energy to make new blossoms. You can help, if you want to. You just pop off the flower if it's brown or the petals have come off and put it in the bucket there."

"I can do that!"

Addie began the task, humming a little as she worked, which made Rosa smile.

"I have a confession," Jen said after a few moments. "After my interview, I probably could have come in and worked this afternoon. Instead, I picked up Addie from day care early and we played hooky for most of the afternoon."

"Good for you," Rosa said, feeling a twinge of envy. "Did you do something fun?"

"Yes. It was wonderful. We made a huge sandcastle and then played in the water a bit, then took a hike around the state park near Arch Cape."

"Oh, I love that area. It is so beautiful and green, like walking through a movie, with all the ferns and moss."

"Yes. Addie thought it looked like a fairy land."

Oh, Addie was cute. She had such an innocent sweetness about her. Rosa hoped she could keep it forever.

"So," Jen said after a moment. "You and Detective Gorgeous. Is that a thing now?"

Rosa, yanking out a nasty weed that had dug its roots in deep, almost lost her balance.

She could feel her face grow hot. "Why would you say such a thing?"

"I *might* have heard two people going up the stairs together in the early hours of the morning."

Rosa could only be grateful they had kissed in his apartment and not in the stairway for her friend to overhear.

"So are you two...dating or something?"

She had a sudden fervent wish that she could say yes. The idea of doing something as ordinary and sweet as dating Wyatt seemed wonderful but completely out of reach.

"No. We are not dating. Only friends." *Who kiss each other as if we can't get enough,* she wanted to add, but, of course, she couldn't say that to Jen.

"He needed someone to watch his son last night while he went out on an emergency police call. His sister is out of town and he did not have anyone else to ask. It was an easy thing for me to help him."

Jen made a face. "Too bad. I was thinking how cute you two would be together. And it's obvious his son likes you."

Rosa could feel herself flush. She was coming to adore both Townsend males, entirely too much. "I am not interested in dating anyone right now." *No matter how gorgeous.*

Jen nodded and carefully plucked away at a rose that had bloomed past its prime. "I totally understand that and feel the same way. I'm not sure I'll ever date again."

Her emphatic tone made Rosa sad. Jen had so much love inside her to give. It was a shame that one bad experience had soured her so much on men.

"Your husband, he was a good man, yes?" Jen and her husband had met after college and Rosa had only met him at their wedding, and the few times they had socialized afterward, before she moved to Oregon.

"Oh, yes," Jen said softly. "Ryan was wonderful. After he died, I never thought I would find anyone again."

She plucked harder at the rose bush. "I wish I hadn't ever entertained the idea of dating again. I obviously don't pick well."

Rosa frowned. "You did well with your husband. Nothing else that happened to you is your fault. I wish I could help you see that. You had no way of knowing things would turn out like they have."

"That's what I tell myself," Jen said quietly. "Most of the time I believe it. In the middle of the night when I think about everything, it's harder to convince myself."

"You did nothing wrong," Rosa repeated in a low voice so that Addie didn't overhear. "You went on three dates with this man then tried to stop dating him when you began to see warning signs. You had no way of knowing he would become obsessive."

Jen sighed. "I still wish I could go back and do everything over again. I wish I had said no the very first time he asked me out."

"I know. I am sorry."

Rosa became angry all over again every time she thought about how one man's arrogance and refusal to accept rejection had forced Jen to flee her life and live in fear.

She was so glad her friend seemed to be trying to put the past behind her and make plans for the future.

"And while I don't think I am the best judge of character right now and don't seem to pick well for myself, I do like Detective Townsend. He seems very kind and he is a wonderful father."

Rosa could not disagree. She felt a little ache in her heart at the reminder that she and Wyatt could not be together. Soon, he and his son would be moving out of Brambleberry House.

"He is a good man and, I think, cares very much about helping people."

She paused, compelled to press the situation. "He would help you, you know. You should tell him what is going on."

"I don't know about that."

"I do. Wyatt is a man you can trust. While he is living here, he can look around for anything unusual. Like having security on site."

"I suppose it is a little like that."

Rosa nodded. "That is one of the reasons I agreed to let him move in. I was worried about you and thought it might make you more comfortable to know he is only downstairs."

Jen gave her a sidelong look. "You mean it wasn't because of those beautiful blue eyes?" she teased.

Rosa flushed and tried to pretend she was inordinately fascinated with clipping back a climbing vine. "Does he have blue eyes? I do not believe I had noticed."

Jen snorted a little, which made Rosa smile. She was happy to be a subject of teasing if it could bring a smile to Jen's face.

"You said you're not interested in dating. Why is that?"

"I date," Rosa protested. "I went out three weeks ago to a concert down in Lincoln City."

"With a seventy-five-year-old widower who had an extra ticket."

"Mr. Harris is very sweet. And also lonely, since he lost his wife."

"You know you don't have to take care of everyone else in town. You should save a little of your energy for going after what you want."

If only it could be that easy. She knew what she wanted. She also knew she could not have it.

She didn't have a chance to answer before a vehicle pulled into the driveway. She stood up, suddenly breathless when she recognized Wyatt's SUV. She had not seen him since that emotional, passionate kiss the night before and wasn't sure how to act around him.

He climbed out, and a moment later opened the back door for his son, who hopped out and raced over to them.

"Logan! Hi, Logan!" Addie made a beeline for the boy, who waved at her.

"Hi, Addie. Your hands are muddy."

"I'm picking flowers. Rosa said I could, to help the other flowers grow better."

"Remember, you should only pick the flowers when a grown-up tells you it's okay," Jen said.

She looked momentarily worried, as if afraid Addie would wander through the entire beautiful gardens of the house pulling up the flowers willy-nilly.

"I want to help pick flowers. Can I?" Logan asked Rosa.

"You will have to ask your father if he does not mind."

The father in question drew nearer and she felt tension and awareness stretch between them. He gave her a wary smile, as if he didn't quite know how to act this evening, either. Seeing his unease helped her relax a little.

Yes, they had shared an intense, emotional kiss. That didn't mean things had to be awkward between them.

"Can I pick flowers?" Logan asked Wyatt. "Rosa said it's okay."

"We are taking away the dead and dying flowers to make room for new growth," she told him.

"I want to help, too," Logan said.

"Fine with me. As long as you do what Rosa says."

"Not a bad philosophy for life in general," Jen said, which made Rosa roll her eyes. She wasn't handling her own life so perfectly right now. Not when she was in danger of making a fool of herself over Wyatt.

"Is there something I can do to help?" Wyatt asked. "Were you trying to hang this bird feeder?"

She followed his gaze to the feeder she had left near the sidewalk.

"Yes. It fell down during the wind we had the other night. I was going to get the ladder and hang it back up."

"That would be a good job for Logan and me. Let me put our groceries away and I'll be right back out to do that for you."

"I'm sure you have enough to do at your house. You don't need to help me with my chores."

"Hanging a birdhouse is the least I can do after you pinch-hit for me last night with Logan."

To Rosa's dismay, she felt her face heat again. Oh, she was grateful her blushes were not very noticeable. She felt as red as those roses.

She couldn't seem to help it, especially when all she could think about was being in his arms the night before, his mouth on hers, and the way he had clung to her.

Something seemed to have shifted between them, as if they had crossed some sort of emotional line.

She, Jen and the children continued clearing out the flower garden and moved to another one outside the bay window of Logan's room.

A few moments later, Wyatt came out of the house. He had changed out of his work slacks, jacket and tie into jeans and a T-shirt that seemed to highlight his strong chest and broad shoulders.

"Is the ladder in the shed?" he asked.

"Yes. It should be open."

"Come help me, Logan. You, too, Addie. This might be a job for three of us."

She watched them go to the shed and a moment later Wyatt emerged carrying the ladder mostly by himself, with each of the children holding tightly to it as if they were actually bearing some of the weight, which she knew they were not.

"He's really great with kids," Jen murmured.

Maybe so. That didn't make him great for *Rosa*.

It did not take him long to rehang the birdhouse in the tree she pointed out. While she would have liked to hang it higher up on the tree, on a more stable branch, she knew she would not be able to refill the feeder easily without pulling out a ladder each time.

After Wyatt and his little crew returned the ladder to the shed, they came back out and she set them to work helping her clear out the rest of the weeds and dead blossoms in the garden.

Her back was beginning to ache from the repetitive motion, but Rosa would not have traded this moment for anything. There was something so peaceful in working together on a summer evening with the air sweet from the scent of flowers and the sun beginning to slide into the ocean.

"So how did you two meet?" Wyatt asked them.

"College," Jen replied promptly. "We were assigned as roommates our very first day and became best friends after that."

Both of them had been apprehensive first-year college students. Rosa had been quite certain she was in over her head. She had only been speaking English for three years. She hadn't known how she would make it through college classes. But Jen had instantly taken her under her wing with kindness and support.

She owed her a huge debt that she knew she could never repay.

"Here you are, living as roommates again, of a sort," Wyatt said casually.

"Yes," Jen answered. "Isn't it funny how life works

sometimes? I was looking for a change and Rosa had an empty apartment. It worked out for both of us."

Wyatt looked at the children, now playing happily on the tree swing. "What about Addie's father? Is he in the picture?"

Jen gazed down at the flowers, grief washing across her features. "Unfortunately, no. He died two years ago of cancer. Melanoma."

"I'm sorry," Wyatt said gently.

He knew what it was to lose someone, too, Rosa thought. In fact, the two of them would be perfect for each other. So why did the idea of them together make her heart hurt?

Jen sighed and rose to face him. "I might as well tell you, Jen Ryan is not really my name."

Rosa held her breath, shocked that her friend had blurted the truth out of nowhere like that. She could tell Wyatt was shocked, as well, though he did his best to hide it.

"Isn't it?"

"Well, it's not wholly a lie. My name is Jenna Michelle Haynes. Ryan was my late husband's name."

He studied her. "Are you using his name for your surname now as some kind of homage?"

"No." She looked at Rosa as if asking for help, then straightened her shoulders and faced Wyatt. Rosa could see her hands clenching and unclenching with nerves. "Actually, if you want the truth, I'm hiding from a man."

Chapter 11

Wyatt stared, shocked that she had told him, though not really by what she said.

He had suspected as much, judging by her nervous behavior and the way Rosa was so protective of her. He just didn't know the details.

He suddenly felt as protective of her as Rosa did. Who would want to hurt this fragile woman and her darling little girl?

He immediately went into police mode. "Who is he? Can you tell me? And what did he do to make you so afraid?"

She sighed and looked at the children, who were laughing in the fading sunshine as Logan pushed Addie on the swings. The scene seemed innocent and sweet, completely incongruous to anything ugly and terrifying.

She swallowed hard and couldn't seem to find the words until Rosa moved closer, placing a supportive arm through hers. Jen gave her a look of gratitude before facing him again.

"His name is Aaron Barker. He's also a police officer in the small Utah town where I was living after my husband died. He... We went out three times. Three dates. That's all."

Rosa squeezed her arm and Jen gripped her hand. One of the hardest parts of his job was making people relive their worst moments. It never seemed to get easier. He didn't want to make her rehash all the details, but he couldn't help her if he didn't know what had happened.

She seemed to sense that because after a moment, she went on. "Aaron was very nice at first. Showering me with affection, gifts, food. Sending flowers to the school where I taught. I was flattered. I was lonely and—and I liked him. But then he started pushing me too hard, already talking about marriage. After three dates."

She shook her head. "I finally had to tell him he was moving too fast for me and that I didn't think I was ready to start dating again."

Her voice seemed to trail off and she shivered a little, though the evening was warm. He didn't like the direction this story was taking. It had to be grim to send her fleeing from her home to Oregon.

"What happened?"

"He wouldn't take no for an answer. He kept asking me out, kept bringing me gifts. I finally had to be firm and tell him we weren't a good match and I wasn't going to change my mind. I thought he understood, but then he started driving past in his squad car at all hours of the day and night. He kept calling and texting, sometimes dozens of times a day. I had to turn my phone off. I went out to dinner one day with another teacher, a coworker and friend who happens to be a man. Nothing romantic, just friends, but that night Aaron sent me a long, vitriolic email, calling me a whore, saying if he couldn't have me, no one could, and all kinds of other terrifying things. I knew he must have been watching me."

"Why didn't you report him to the police?"

"I tried but this was a small town. The police chief was his uncle, who wouldn't listen to me. He wouldn't even take my complaint. I tried to go to the county sheriff's department but they said it was a personnel issue for our town's police department. I think they just didn't want to bother and didn't want to upset Aaron's uncle."

Again, Wyatt had to fight down his anger. He knew how insular small-town police departments and their surrounding jurisdictions sometimes could be. Often, police officers for one agency didn't want to get other agency police officers in trouble.

He had also been involved in stalking investigations and knew just how difficult the perpetrators could be to prosecute. Most laws were weak and ineffective, leaving the victim virtually powerless to stop what could be years of torture.

"This went on for months," Jen said. "I can't explain how emotionally draining it was to be always afraid."

Rosa made a small sound, her features distressed. He sensed she was upset for her friend but had to wonder if there was something else behind her reaction. Why wouldn't she tell him her secrets, like Jen was finally doing?

"I understand," Wyatt said quietly. "I have worked these kinds of cases before. I know how tough they can be on the victims."

"Aaron was relentless. Completely relentless. I changed my number, my email, closed down my social-media accounts, but he would find a new way to reach me. He… started making threats. Veiled at first and then more overt.

When he mentioned Addie in one of his messages, I quit my teaching job and moved closer to my sister, about an hour away, but the night after I moved, my tires were slashed. Somehow he found me anyway."

So things had taken an even uglier turn. Wyatt wasn't surprised.

"How did you end up here?"

"Rosa happened to reach out to me out of the blue, right in the middle of everything. We hadn't talked in a while and she was just checking up on me. Calling to wish me a happy birthday. I didn't want to tell her, but everything just gushed out and I finally told her everything that had been going on."

She squeezed Rosa's arm. "I don't know what I would have done without her. I was telling her that tonight. She invited me to come stay with her here for a while. She offered me a job and an apartment. It seemed perfect, and honestly, I didn't know what else to do."

"I only wish I had known earlier what was happening to you," Rosa said, looking guilty. "I should have called you sooner."

"Don't ever think that. You reached out right when I was at my lowest point and offered me a chance to escape."

Jen turned back to Wyatt. "I packed up what we had and drove as far as Boise. Maybe I watch too much *Dateline*, but I traded my car on the spot at a used-car lot, in case Aaron had put some kind of tracker on my vehicle, then I drove here."

"That was smart."

"I don't know about that. I had a nice little late-model SUV with four-wheel drive that was great for the Utah winters. Now I've got a junker. It was probably the best swap the dealer ever made. But it got us here to Brambleberry House, where I have felt safe for the first time in months."

"I am so glad," Rosa said.

"I can't tell you how nice it has been not to constantly look over my shoulder."

"Do you think he's given up?" Wyatt hated to ask but didn't have a choice.

Her expression twisted with distress. "I want to think so. I hope so. But I don't know. I don't know how to find out without possibly revealing my new location."

"He was obsessed," Rosa said, placing a protective arm around her friend. "Jenna is only telling you a small portion of the things this man has done to her."

Wyatt hoped the man had given up, though he worried that by fleeing, she had only stoked his unhealthy obsession.

Moving several states away might not be enough to escape a determined stalker, especially not one with law-enforcement experience.

"Thank you for telling me this. I know it wasn't easy, but you've done the right thing. I'll do what I can to help you. You said his name is Aaron Barker?"

"That's right."

"Do you have a picture or description?"

"Yes. I can email you a picture and also link you to his social media."

"Texting me is better. He might have hacked into your email."

"He's done that before but I changed my account and password."

That might not be the deterrent she hoped. Someone determined enough could find ways around just about anything.

"Once you get me a picture of him and a description, I'll

pass it around to other officers in the local PD and sheriff's department so we can be on the lookout. You're in Cannon Beach now and we take care of our own."

"Thank you." Jen looked overwhelmed to have someone else on her side. He understood. Victims of stalking could feel so isolated and alone, certain no one else would understand or even believe them and that their ordeal would never end.

"You're welcome."

He glanced at Rosa and found her looking at him with such warmth and approval that he couldn't seem to look away.

Addie came running over, with Logan close behind.

"Mommy," she said, tugging on Jen's shirt, "I have to go to the bathroom."

Jen gave her a distracted look then seemed to sharpen her focus on her child. "Right. The door is locked. I'll get it for you."

She turned back to Wyatt. "Thank you," she said again. "I'll get you that picture."

"That's the best thing you can do right now."

"I'm glad I told you. Rosa was right."

She gave Rosa a look he couldn't quite interpret, but one that left him feeling as if he had missed something significant, and then Jen grabbed her daughter's hand and hurried for the house.

After she left, Wyatt turned to Rosa and found her looking at him with that same expression of warmth and approval.

"What were you right about?" he asked.

She shrugged. "I told her she could trust you. That you would help her if you could."

If she believed that, why wouldn't she trust him herself?

He could not ask. "I don't know how much I can do. I hope she's right, that he has lost interest."

"But you do not think so."

He couldn't lie. "If the man was willing to break the law to hack into her emails and completely disrupt her life to that extent, I can't see him giving up easily. I think he will keep searching until he finds her."

"What can we do?"

"Not a great deal unless he does something overt. I'm sorry."

"I feel so helpless."

"I know. It's a terrible feeling. I'll do a little internet sleuthing and see what I can dig up on the guy without coming right out and contacting his department. I don't want to run the risk of him getting wind that a detective in Oregon is looking into him, or that will certainly clue him in that she's here. Meanwhile, I'll circulate the picture around here when she gives me one and we will keep our eyes open."

It didn't sound like much, even to Wyatt. He hated that he couldn't do more. If this Aaron Barker was obsessed enough about Jenna and Addie, he would figure out a way to find them.

"Why can't some men take no for an answer?" she asked quietly.

He gave her a searching look but she quickly shifted her gaze away.

"It usually has to do with power and control. And some men just can't accept rejection."

"She has already been through so much, losing the man she loved with all her heart. It is not fair."

"No. It's not. I hate when any man hurts or threatens a woman, but I especially hate when he's in law enforcement."

"Thank you for believing her. That was the most important thing. Everyone else she told thought she was making it up to get attention or to get this man in trouble."

"You believed her."

"I know fear when I see it," Rosa said simply. "She is afraid or she would not have taken her daughter away from her family and her friends."

Something told him Rosa knew plenty about fear, as well. He wanted to press her to tell him but held his tongue.

"Have you had dinner?" he asked instead. "We were about to order takeout from the Thai place in town. Buying you dinner is the least I can do for your help last night."

She looked shocked by the invitation. For a moment, he thought she was about to say yes. She looked at Logan, who was now digging in the dirt nearby, with a softness in her eyes that touched him deeply.

After a moment, she looked back at Wyatt, her expression shielded again.

"No, thank you."

He wasn't expecting the outright rejection and didn't know what to say for a few seconds. "If you don't like Thai food, there's a good Indian place with fabulous curry that just opened on the other side of town. I've heard they deliver, too. Or we can hit up the trusty taco truck down the beach."

"I like Thai food," she said, her voice low.

He gazed at her, confused. Was it *him* she didn't like? "Have you already eaten, then?"

She shook her head. "No. I'm not really hungry and I have much work to do tonight."

"We can help you after we grab dinner," he suggested.

After a moment, she sighed, looking distressed again. "I...think it is best if we do not spend a great deal of time together."

"Why not?" He was either being particularly dense or

she was being obtuse. "I thought we were friends. That's what you said last night."

"Yes. And then you kissed me and I forgot about being friends and…wanted more."

He felt his face heat up. He could be such an idiot sometimes. Did he really think they could go back to a casual friendship after he had basically had a breakdown in her arms the night before, and then kissed her with all the pent-up loneliness and need inside him?

"Neither of us is looking for romance right now," Rosa went on, deliberately looking away from him. "I know this. But when you kiss me, I forget."

He did, too. When he kissed her, when he felt her arms around him and her soft mouth under his and the curves he longed to explore, Wyatt wanted to forget everything and get lost in the wonder and magic of holding her.

Rosa was right. Neither of them was looking for romance. The more time they spent together, the harder it was becoming for him to remember that.

It would be better to keep their distance until his house was fixed, when he and Logan would move out. Once things were back to normal and he didn't run the risk of bumping into her every time he came home, they would be able to go back to their regular lives.

No more moonlit kisses on the stairway, no more quiet talks on the front porch of Brambleberry House.

Just him and his son and his work.

The future seemed to stretch out ahead of him, gray as a January day.

What if he was beginning to want more?

Chapter 12

A week later, he stood at his sister's kitchen sink, helping Carrie thread vegetables onto skewers for the grill.

"Thanks for having us for dinner. I've been so busy, I haven't had much time to cook and I think Logan is getting a little tired of the taco truck for dinner."

Carrie laughed. "Surely not. Who could be tired of that?"

He impaled a yellow squash on the metal skewer, followed by a mushroom and then a slice of onion. "I feel like I haven't seen you since the Fourth. Tell me all about your trip."

After taking Bella to the concert in Portland a week earlier, Joe and Carrie had driven down to San Francisco for a few days with her.

"It was fun. We did all the touristy things. Alcatraz, riding a cable car, going to Fisherman's Wharf. And, of course, shopping. You can't visit San Francisco without spending too much money. We bought some cute school clothes for the new year."

He needed to start thinking about the new school year. Logan would be starting second grade. Wyatt still had a hard time believing he was that old.

He was finishing the last of the skewers while Carrie did some shrimp and some chicken when the doorbell rang.

"Are you expecting someone else?"

His sister somehow managed to look coy. "Sounds like Bella is getting it. That will be Rosa."

He nearly impaled his finger instead of a mushroom. "Rosa is coming to dinner, as well?"

He had been trying to stay away from her the past week, at her request. How the hell was he supposed to do that when his sister invited them both over for dinner?

"Yes. I happened to drop into her store today and mentioned Joe was going to grill tonight, and we had plenty. She seemed a little down and I thought it might cheer her up a bit. I hope you don't mind."

Why was she down? He wanted to rush out and ask if she was all right but made himself stay put.

"And you didn't think to tell me until now that she was coming?"

"Does it matter?"

Yes. Most certainly. He would have refused Carrie's last-minute invitation if he had known the dinner party included a woman who had specifically told him they should avoid spending more time together.

"I just wish you had told me."

Carrie made a face. "I'm sorry. I just thought one more person for dinner wouldn't make a difference."

He frowned. This was the second time in only a few weeks that Carrie had invited them both over for a meal at the same time. That couldn't be a coincidence, could it?

She had already mentioned she thought he should think about dating her friend.

Did his sister suspect he was beginning to have feelings for Rosa?

If Carrie had any idea about the attraction that simmered between them, Wyatt knew she wouldn't hesitate to do whatever she could to push them together as much as possible. She wouldn't be subtle about it, either.

He wanted to say something but before he could, Rosa and Bella came into the kitchen, Bella chattering a mile a minute about their trip.

Rosa didn't seem to notice him at first. She was listening intently to Bella's story about the ghost tour they went on, and smiling at the girl's animation.

The two of them shared similar coloring. The same dark hair and dark eyes. With their heads together like that, they looked as if they could be sisters, catching up after a long time away.

He frowned suddenly as a crazy thought flitted across his brain. No. Impossible. He pushed it away just as Rosa lifted her head and caught sight of him.

Her eyes widened with shock. "Oh. Wyatt. Hello. I did not know you would be here."

If she had known, he had a feeling she would have refused his sister's invitation. Well, they were both here. Might as well make the best of it.

"Hi," he answered, just as Logan came in from the family room, where he had been playing a video game with Joe.

He, at least, looked thrilled about the other dinner guest.

"Rosa! Hi, Rosa!" he exclaimed. He rushed to her and wrapped his arms around her waist as if he hadn't seen her for months.

It had only been a few nights ago when he had gone up

to her apartment for another Spanish lesson and had come back down naming every single kind of fruit they had in their house in Spanish.

"Buenas," she said to him. "How are you tonight?"

"I'm good. Guess what? We're having *piña* and *fresas* tonight."

"Delicious. Pineapple and strawberries. My favorite."

"I didn't know strawberries were *fresas*. I don't think I learned that in Spanish class last year. How did you know?" Bella asked.

"Rosa's teaching me Spanish so I can talk better to my friend Carlos."

Carrie beamed at them and gave Wyatt a significant look. Yeah. She was definitely matchmaking, despite the way he had basically told her to stand down the last time.

He was going to have to do whatever he could to deflect any of Carrie's efforts in that department.

To his relief, his sister was not overtly obvious over dinner, though she did suggest he and Rosa take a look at how her climbing roses were growing, something they both managed to avoid by changing the subject.

Having his sister and her family there, along with Logan, helped make things a little less awkward between them, but he still couldn't help remembering his hurt when she had told him they should avoid being together.

The food was good, at least. Carrie had a great marinade he always enjoyed and Joe was a whiz at the grill. Really, any time Wyatt didn't have to cook, he was happy.

Rosa was too busy talking to Bella and Logan to seem bothered by his presence.

After they ate, Rosa was the first to stand up. "Thank you for dinner, but things were so chaotic as I was leaving work that I am afraid I was not thinking. I just remem-

bered I left some invoices I need to pay tonight on my desk.
I would not want to leave them there overnight. Will you
excuse me?"

Carrie made a face. "You're not staying for dessert? It's
homemade vanilla ice cream that Bella helped me make
this afternoon."

Rosa gave a vague smile. "It sounds very good but I really do need to go. Thank you, though."

She hugged both females and Logan, then waved to
Wyatt and Joe before hurrying away.

After she left, some of the sparkle seemed to go out of
the evening. Wyatt knew he wasn't the only one who felt it.

She was definitely trying to avoid him. He could only
hope that everyone else didn't guess that her reasons for
leaving so abruptly had anything to do with him.

"I'll have ice cream," Logan said.

"Same here," Bella said. "It's delicious."

He had to agree. It *was* delicious. But all that frozen,
creamy sweetness still couldn't remove the sour taste in
his mouth.

"Dinner was great," he said after everyone had finished
dessert. "Logan, let's help with dishes."

His son groaned a little but stood up to help clear away
plates and carry them back inside the house.

When the dishwasher was loaded, Bella asked if she and
Logan could take Hank for a walk before Wyatt left with
the dog for home. He almost said no but was in no hurry
to return to the tension of Brambleberry House.

"Sure. I can wait a little longer."

Logan was staying the night again with his aunt and
uncle because Wyatt had an early meeting.

Joe got a phone call from his parents, who lived in Arizona, and excused himself to talk to them for a few moments, leaving Wyatt alone with Carrie.

"How's the house coming?" Carrie asked after her husband left the room.

"Almost there, I'm happy to report. We should be able to move back in another few weeks."

"That seems fast. But living at Brambleberry House worked out well, didn't it?"

A week ago, he would have said yes. "It's been fine. Logan has enjoyed having his own room again. It's a lovely old house and our apartment is roomier than our actual house."

"I'm glad. And your neighbors are nice, both of them. I like Jen and Rosa."

That was another area of frustration. He hadn't been able to make much progress in Jen's situation, other than to alert the department and do a little online sleuthing. Aaron Barker seemed to be a good cop, from what he could find out. He had no black marks on his reputation that Wyatt could find after a cursory search.

At least nothing suspicious seemed to have happened since Jen had told him about her stalker. He had been extra vigilant but hadn't learned anything new.

"Rosa is lovely, isn't she?" Carrie said in a casual voice that did not fool him for an instant.

He finally voiced the suspicion that had been nagging at him since he discovered Rosa had also been invited to dinner.

"I don't suppose there's any chance you're trying to push Rosa and me together, even after I told you not to, is there?"

"Me? Would I do that? Don't be silly." She gave him a shocked sort of look but he knew his sister well enough to see past it easily. She would do that kind of thing in a heartbeat, if she thought he might have the slightest interest in Rosa.

"Are you sure? This is the second time you've invited us both to dinner. Come to think of it, you seemed pretty determined that I move into her empty apartment at Brambleberry House."

"Only because it was the perfect solution when you yourself talked about moving out! I was only trying to help. As for dinner, it just so happens she is my dear friend and you are my brother. I like spending time visiting with each of you. I can't help it if sometimes those visits overlap."

"Can't you?"

"I didn't realize it would be a problem," she said rather stiffly. "I thought you and Rosa were friends. Logan is always talking about how she's teaching him Spanish and how much he loves her dog and how you go out for tacos together."

He frowned. "That was one time, when we bumped into each other at the taco stand. Rosa and I are friends. That's all. Neither one of us is in the market for a relationship right now. I told you that."

"But you two are perfect for each other!"

Wyatt felt that little tug on his heart again, remembering how Rosa had held him during his moment of despair over the ugly crime scene he had just left, generously offering him a comfort and peace he had desperately needed.

He was beginning to think Carrie was right, at least on one side of the equation. Rosa was perfect for him. Smart, sweet, kind. He loved how warm she was with Logan and how compassionate and protective she was for her friend.

None of that mattered. Not when she had made it clear she wanted nothing to do with him except friendship.

"It's not going to happen. Get it out of your head, please. I would hate for you to make things awkward between us."

Carrie looked deeply disappointed. "It's just that I love her, you know? I want her to be happy. I want *you* to be happy. Why shouldn't you be happy together? I guess I just thought…after everything she's been through, she deserved a wonderful guy like you."

He frowned. "That's the second time you've made reference to something in her past. What do you know? What has she been through?"

Carrie immediately looked away, but not before he saw guilt flash in her eyes. "Life can be hard for people trying to make it in a new country. She came here with nothing. She didn't even speak the language well. How fortunate she was to find her adoptive family, Anna Galvez's brother and his wife."

There was something else here. Something he couldn't quite put his finger on. A suspicion had begun to take root but it was one he didn't even dare ask his sister.

What if he was wrong?

Meantime, he had to do what he could to divert Carrie's attention and prevent her from meddling further between the two of them.

"Rosa is an extraordinary woman. I agree. But I'm not looking for anybody, no matter how extraordinary. Got that?"

She looked as if she wanted to argue, but to his relief, she finally sighed. "Fine. I won't invite you both to dinner, unless it's a party that includes a bunch of other people."

Would he be able to handle even that much? Right now, he wasn't sure. At least he would be moving away from

Brambleberry House within the next few weeks. When he wasn't living downstairs from her, perhaps he could stop dreaming about her and wishing he could hold her again.

Chapter 13

It was fully dark when Rosa returned to Brambleberry House after stopping at By-The-Wind and running the bills to the post-office drop box.

She hadn't been lying about the invoices. She really had forgotten them, though mailing them certainly could have waited until the next day. That had been sheer fiction, an excuse to escape the tension between her and Wyatt.

She always loved spending time with the Abbotts. Carrie was invariably warm and kind and Joe treated her like a beloved younger sister.

And then there was Bella, full of energy and fun and enthusiasm for life. Her mood always seemed to rub off on Rosa, leaving her happier than when she had arrived.

This time, though, Rosa couldn't shake a deep sense of melancholy.

She knew the reason. Because Wyatt and Logan had

been there. Spending time with them was beginning to make her ache deep inside.

She knew she was setting herself up for heartbreak. She could sense it hovering, just out of sight.

She was falling for them. Both of them.

Logan was impossible to resist. His sweet personality and eagerness to learn touched something deep inside of her. She would be so sad when he was no longer a regular part of her life.

And Wyatt. She brushed a lock of hair from her eyes. It was very possible that Wyatt was the most wonderful man she had ever met. She wanted to wrap her arms around him and not let go.

She could not, though. Rosa knew she could not have what she wanted.

She knew people who spent their entire lives wanting something other than what they had. Rosa tried not to be that person.

As a girl growing up with little in the way of material things, she had become used to that feeling of lack. Mostly, she had learned to ignore it, instead finding happiness with what she *did* have.

She was part owner in a business she loved running, she lived in a beautiful house at the seaside, she had cherished friends and a loving family. Most of the time, those things were enough.

Once in a while, though, like on moonlit summer nights, she caught glimpses of the future she might have had if not for a few foolish choices, and it made her heart ache.

Rosa sighed, a sad sound that seemed to echo in the emptiness of her apartment. Fiona nudged at her leg, resting her chin on Rosa's knee and gazing at her out of eyes that seemed filled with empathy.

Sometimes the dog seemed to sense her emotions keenly and offered exactly the right thing to lift her mood.

"You want to go for a walk, don't you?"

Fiona wagged her tail wildly in agreement. Rosa sighed again. She had let her dog out when she first came home a short time earlier, but apparently that was not enough for her, especially when the work day had been so hectic and she hadn't had time to take her on a walk.

Rosa was tired and not really in the mood for a nighttime walk. Part of being a responsible pet owner, though, was doing what she didn't always feel like doing when it was in the best interest of her beloved Fi.

"Okay. Let's find your leash."

Fiona scampered to the hook by the door of the apartment, where Rosa kept all the tools necessary for a walk. A hoodie, Fi's leash, a flashlight, treats and waste bags.

A few moments later, she headed down the steps. They had just reached the bottom when the door to Wyatt's apartment suddenly opened.

She gave a little gasp of surprise when he and Hank came out, the cute little dog all but straining on the leash.

"Oh," Rosa exclaimed. "You startled me."

Wyatt made a face. "Sorry. Hank was in a mood and nothing seemed to be settling him down. I was just going to take him on a quick walk. Are you coming or going?"

"Going. Fiona was in the same mood as Hank."

"Maybe they're talking to each other through the pipes."

Despite her lingering melancholy, Rosa had to smile a little at that idea. Fiona was smart enough that she could probably figure out a way to communicate to other dogs inside the house.

She looked behind him. "Where is Logan?"

"He's sleeping over at Carrie's again. I've got an early

meeting tomorrow so they offered to keep him after dinner so I don't have to drag him out of bed so early."

"That is nice of them. Your sister is very kind."

"Truth. She is the best. I would have been lost without her after Tori died. Totally lost. She and Joe have been amazing, basically stepping in to help me parent Logan."

The dogs seemed delighted to see each other, sniffing like crazy with their tails wagging a hundred miles an hour.

She knew it was impossible, but Rosa still could not shake the suspicion that somehow her dog had manipulated events exactly this way, so that she and Wyatt would meet in the entryway of the house.

He opened the door and they both walked out into the evening, lit by a full moon that made her flashlight superfluous.

"Want to walk together?" he asked after a moment.

His suggestion surprised her so much that she did not know how to answer for a moment. Intellectually, she knew she was supposed to be maintaining a careful distance between them. She did not want to fall any harder for him.

How could she say no, though? Especially when she knew her time with him was so fleeting?

"That makes sense, doesn't it?"

"Which direction were you going? To the beach?"

Usually she liked to stick to the paths with streetlights and some traffic when she was walking late at night. Since Wyatt was with her, that wasn't necessary.

"Yes. Let's walk on the beach. The water always calls me."

They walked through the gardens, the air sweet with the scent of flowers and herbs. He opened the gate for her and she and Fiona went first down the path to the sand.

The moon was bright and full, casting a pearly blue light on everything. She certainly did not need her flashlight.

They walked mostly in silence for the first few moments, content to let the sounds of the waves fill the void. Despite everything between them, it was a comfortable silence.

She was the first to break it. "You said at dinner that your house is almost finished. Is everything going the way you like?"

"Yes. We had a few issues early on. It's an old house with electrical issues, which is what started the fire in the first place. I want to make sure everything is exactly right. I think I have been getting on the electrician's nerves a little, but we're getting there."

He gave her a sidelong look. "I'm sure you'll be glad when everything is finished so we can get out of your way."

"You are not in my way," she protested. It wasn't exactly the truth. He was very much in the way of her thoughts constantly. "You know you can stay as long as you need."

"I know. Thank you for that."

"I am sure you are more than ready to be back in your house."

He shrugged. "I suppose."

"You do not sound convinced."

"It's just a house, you know? I bought it after Tori died, when I knew I needed help and the best thing would be to move near Carrie and Joe. That one was available and it was close but it's never really felt like a home."

She had not been to his house and couldn't offer an opinion, but she had to wonder if the house needed a woman's touch.

She did not want to think about any other woman going in and decorating his house with warm, comfortable touches. She wanted to be the one turning his house into a home.

She pushed away the thought.

"You had many changes in a short time. That can be hard for anyone."

"I guess."

They walked in silence for a few more moments, stopping only when Hank lifted his leg against a tuft of grass.

"Carrie said something tonight that made me curious." He spoke slowly, as if choosing his words with care.

"Oh?"

"Something about you. She implied you had a tough time after you came to the United States. It made me wonder again how you came to be adopted after you arrived. That seems unusual. You were a teenager, right?"

Rosa tensed, remembering that horrible time in her life, full of fear and darkness and things she did not like to think about.

"Yes. Fifteen."

"And you didn't have family here or back in Honduras who could have helped you?"

Her heart seemed to squeeze at the memory of her dear mother, who had tried so hard to give Rosa a better life. She gripped Fiona's leash. The dog, who had been cavorting with Hank, suddenly returned to her side as if sensing Rosa's distress.

"No."

"How did you get here?"

That was a long and twisted story.

"I told you my mother died. I had no money and no family. A friend of my mother's told me I could find work at a factory in the city. She helped me find a place to live with some other girls and gave me a little money."

"That's nice."

"Yes. But then some men came to the factory telling us they knew of many jobs we could do across the border. I was afraid and didn't want to, but other girls, my friends, said yes. Then I…had some trouble with my boss at the factory and he fired me."

She thought of how innocent she had been in those days. Her mother had tried to shelter her when she was alive. As a result, Rosa knew little about the world or how to protect herself from men who wanted to take advantage of her. First her boss, then those offering riches and jobs in a new world. She had been monumentally naive, had thought maybe she would be working in another factory in the United States, one that paid better.

She had been so very wrong.

She was not going to tell any of that to Wyatt.

"What did you do then?"

"I came here and shortly after, I met Daniel and Lauren and they took me in and helped me go to school and then become a citizen," she said quickly.

He gave her a searching look through the darkness, as if he knew full well there had to be more to her story. She lifted her chin and continued walking, pretending that Fiona had led her a little ahead of him and Hank.

She didn't want him to press her about this. If he did, she would have to turn around and go back to the house without him. To her relief, he seemed to know she had told him all she was going to about that time.

"They must be very kind people."

She seized gratefully on his words. "The best. I told you Daniel is a sheriff in Utah and Lauren is a doctor. I was very lucky they found me."

She knew it was more than luck. It was a miracle. She

had prayed to the Virgin and to her own mother that someone would help her, that she could find some light in the
darkness. And then, literally, a light had found her hiding
in the back of a pickup truck in the middle of a January
storm. She had been beaten and bloodied, and had been
semiconscious when Daniel and Lauren had found her.
They had pulled her from that pickup truck and had saved
her. An answer to her prayers.

They had stood by her then as she had spoken out against
those who had hurt her. And they had stood by her later
when she had to make the most difficult decision of her life.

"Carrie talked about how much courage it must have
taken you to make your way in a new country."

Rosa loved her country and her people. People from
Honduras called themselves and each other *Catrachos*, a
name that had come to mean resilience and solidarity.

She would always consider herself part *Catracha* but
this was her home now.

If her mother had not died, she might have stayed and
built a happy life there. She probably would have married
young and would have had several children by now.

After Daniel and Lauren rescued her, she had been able
to get an education that would have been completely out of
reach to her in that small, poor village.

"Courage? No. I had nothing there after my mother died.
And here I had a family. People who loved me and wanted
the best for me. That was everything to me. It still is."

Wyatt could not doubt the quiet sincerity in her voice.
She loved the people who had taken her in.

He was suddenly deeply grateful for them, too. He would
have loved the chance to have met them in person to tell
them so.

They walked in silence for a few more moments, heading back toward Brambleberry House, which stood like a beacon above the beach a short distance away.

He could tell Rosa did not like talking about this. Her body language conveyed tension. He should let it go now. Her secrets were none of his business, but since she had told him this much, perhaps she would trust him and tell him the rest of it.

"You said you were fifteen when you came here?"

"Yes," she said, her voice clipped.

How had she even made it across several borders? And what about the men who had promised her work in the United States?

He wasn't stupid. He could guess what kind of work they wanted from her and it made him sick to his stomach. Sex trafficking was a huge problem, especially among young girls smuggled in from other countries.

Was that what Daniel and Lauren had rescued her from?

He couldn't seem to find the words to ask. Or to ask her how she had escaped. He was quite sure he would not like the answer.

How was it possible? She was the most loving and giving person he knew, kind to everyone. How could she have emerged from something so ugly to become the person he was falling for?

Maybe he was wrong. He truly hoped he was wrong.

"You could have found yourself in all kinds of danger at that young age."

"Yes."

She said nothing more, only looked ahead at her dog and at the house, now only a hundred feet away.

He thought again of his suspicions earlier that evening

at dinner. He was beginning to think they might not be far-fetched, after all.

"I think my sister is right," he said quietly when they reached the beach gate to the house. "You are a remarkable person, Rosa Galvez."

Her face was a blur in the moonlight as she gazed at him, her eyes dark shadows. She shook her head. "I am not. Lauren and Daniel, who reached out to me when I was afraid and vulnerable, they are the remarkable ones."

Tenderness swirled through him. She was amazing and he was falling hard for her. Learning more details about what she had endured and overcome, including the things she hadn't yet shared with him, only intensified his growing feelings.

"We will have to agree to disagree on that one," he finally said. "Every time I'm with you, I find something else to admire."

"Don't," she said sharply. "You don't know."

"I know I think about you all the time. I can't seem to stop."

"You shouldn't."

"I know that. Believe me, I know. But you're in my head now."

And in my heart, he thought, but wasn't quite ready to share that with her yet.

"May I kiss you again?"

Because of what he suspected had happened to her, it became more important than ever to ask permission first and not just take what he wanted.

He thought she would refuse at first, that she would turn into the house. After a long moment, she lifted her face to his.

"Yes," she murmured, almost as if she couldn't help herself.

This kiss was tender, gentle, a mere brush of his mouth against hers.

All the feelings he had been fighting seemed to shimmer to the surface. He could tell himself all he wanted that he was not ready to care for someone again. He could tell everyone else the same story. That did not make it true.

He had already fallen. Somehow Rosa Galvez, with her kindness and her empathy and her determination to do the right thing, had reached into the bleak darkness where he had been existing and ripped away the heavy curtains to let sunshine flood in again.

He was not sure yet how he felt about that. Some part of him wanted to stay frozen in his sadness. He had loved Tori with all his heart. Their marriage had not been perfect—he wasn't sure any healthy marriage could be completely without differences—but she had been a great mother and a wonderful wife.

Wyatt wasn't sure he was ready to risk his heart again.

But maybe he didn't have a choice. Maybe he had already fallen.

He wrapped his arms around her tightly, wanting to protect her from all the darkness in the world. She made a small sound and nestled against him, as if searching for warmth and safety.

"I lied to my sister," he said, long moments later.

He felt her smile against his mouth. "For shame, Detective Townsend. How did you lie to Carrie?"

He brushed a strand of hair away from her face. "She admitted after you left that she invited us both to dinner because she has some wild idea of matchmaking."

Instead of continuing to smile, as he thought she would, Rosa suddenly looked distressed.

Her eyes widened and her hands slipped away from around his neck. "Oh, no."

He nodded. "I told her to get that idea out of her head. I told her we were only friends and would never be anything more than that."

She stepped away. "You told her the truth. That is not a lie. We *are* friends."

"But we're more than that, aren't we?"

She folded her hands together, her mouth trembling a little. "No. What you said to her is the truth. We are friends. Only that."

"You can really say that after that kiss?"

"Sharing a few kisses does not make us lovers, Wyatt. Surely you see this."

He wasn't sure why she was so upset but she was all but wringing her hands.

"This thing between us is not exactly your average friendship, either. You have to admit that. I have lots of friends and I don't stay up nights thinking about kissing them."

She made a small, upset sound and reached for her dog's leash.

"We cannot do this anymore, Wyatt. You must see that. I was wrong to let you kiss me. To—to kiss you back. I should have stopped you."

She started moving toward the house. He gazed after her, hurt at her abrupt dismissal of what had felt like an emotional, beautiful moment between them.

He knew she had felt it, as well. Rosa was not the sort of woman who would kiss someone with so much sweetness and eagerness without at least some feeling behind it.

He quickly caught up with her just as she pushed open the beach gate and walked into the Brambleberry House gardens.

"Why are you so determined to push me away? What aren't you telling me?"

"Nothing. I told you before—I am not looking for this in my life right now."

"I wasn't, either, but I think it's found us. I care about you, Rosa. Very much. For the first time since Tori died, I want to spend time with a woman. And I might be crazy but I suspect you wouldn't kiss me if you didn't have similar feelings for me. Am I wrong?"

She was silent for a moment. When she faced him, her chin was up again and her eyes seemed without expression.

"Yes. You are wrong," she said, her voice muted. "I do not have feelings for you. It is impossible. You are the brother of my friend and you are my tenant who will be leaving soon. That is all you are to me, Wyatt. I… You must not kiss me again. Ever. Do you understand this? No matter what, you must not."

She turned and hurried for the house, leaving him staring after her, hurt and confusion and rejection tumbling through him.

She sounded so very certain that he could not question her conviction. Apparently he had misunderstood everything. All this time, he had been falling for her, but the feeling apparently was not mutual.

She had told him they should stay away from each other. Why had he not listened?

He knew the answer to that. His feelings were growing so strong that he couldn't believe they could possibly be one-sided.

Lord, he was an idiot. No different than Jenna's cop, who couldn't accept rejection even after it slapped him in the face.

He should have kept his mouth shut. She had told him

over and over that she was not interested in a relationship with him, but he'd been too stubborn to listen.

Now he just had to figure out how he was going to go on without her.

Rosa sat in her darkened apartment a short time later, window open to the ocean and Fiona at her feet. Usually she found solace in the sound of the waves but not now.

This night, it seemed to echo through Brambleberry House, accentuating how very alone she felt.

What had she done? With all her heart, she wished she could go downstairs, knock on his door and tell Wyatt *she* was the one lying now.

I do not have feelings for you. It is impossible. You are the brother of my friend and you are my tenant who will be leaving soon. That is all you are to me, Wyatt.

None of those words were true, of course. Or at least not the whole truth. She cared about Wyatt, more than any man she had ever known. She was falling in love with him. Here in the quiet solitude of her apartment, she could admit the truth.

She realized now that she had started to fall for him the first time she met Carrie's brother with the sad eyes and the adorable little boy.

How could she not love him? He was everything good and kind she admired in a man. He was a loving father, a loyal brother, a dedicated detective. An honorable man.

That was the very reason she had no choice but to push him away. Wyatt deserved a woman with no demons. Someone courageous and good.

If he knew the truth about her and her choices, he would quickly see how wrong he was about her.

The walls of the house did not embrace her with comfort, as they usually did.

Somehow, it felt cold and even sad. For some ridiculous reason, Rosa felt as if she had faced some sort of test and she had failed spectacularly.

It was a silly feeling, she knew. Houses could not be sad.

Fiona lifted her head suddenly and gazed off at nothing, then whimpered for no reason. Rosa frowned. There was no such thing as ghosts, either. And absolutely no reason for her to feel guilty, as if she had failed Abigail somehow.

"I had to push him away," she said aloud, though she wasn't sure just who she was trying to convince. Fiona, Abigail or herself. "Someday he will see that I was right. He will be glad I at least could see that we cannot be together."

Fiona huffed out a breath while Abigail said nothing, of course.

As for Rosa, her heart felt as if it was going to crack apart. She knew it would not. She had been through hard things before—she would figure out a way to survive this.

In a short time, he and his son would be moving out of Brambleberry House and back to their own home. As before, she would only see them occasionally. Maybe on the street, maybe at some town celebration. Maybe even at a party with Joe and Carrie. She could be polite and even friendly.

Wyatt did not ever need to know about these cracks in her heart, or how hard she found it to think about moving forward with her life without him, and without Logan.

Chapter 14

Somehow, she wasn't sure exactly how, Rosa made it through most of the next week without seeing either Logan or Wyatt.

They seemed to leave early in the morning and come back late at night. She could only guess they were hard at work on the part of renovations Wyatt was handling on their house and getting it ready for their move back.

This guess was confirmed when she came home for lunch one day and found a note tucked into her door.

Repairs to the house are done, the note said in bold, scrawling handwriting. *We will be moving out tomorrow. Wyatt.*

Rosa had to catch her breath as pain sliced through her at the brusque, clipped note and at the message it contained.

Tomorrow. A week earlier than he had planned. He must have spent every available moment trying to finish things in his eagerness to get out of her house and her life.

She returned to the store with a heavy heart but a sense

of relief, as well. She could not begin to put back together the pieces of her life when he was living two floors below her.

Even when she did not see him or Logan, she was still constantly aware they were both so close and yet completely out of her reach.

When she walked into the store, she found Jen laughing at something with a customer. The change in her friend was remarkable. She looked bright and pretty and happy, a far cry from the withdrawn, frightened woman she had been when she first came to Cannon Beach.

Jen finished ringing up the customer with a genuine smile Rosa once had feared she would not see again.

"You are in a good mood," she said.

"Yes. I heard from the online graduate program I've been in touch with. I've been accepted for fall semester and they're offering a financial-aid package that will cover almost the whole tuition."

"That's terrific! Oh, Jen. I'm so happy for you. How will you juggle teaching, graduate school and Addie at the same time?"

"It's going to be tricky but I think I can handle it, especially now that she's starting first grade. I can do the coursework at night after she's in bed. It will take me a few years, but when I'm done, it will open up other career doors for me."

"Oh, I am so happy for you."

Jen beamed at her. "It's all because of you. I never would have had the courage to even apply if you hadn't been in my corner, pushing me out of my comfort zone."

Rosa might not have a happily-ever-after with the man she was falling in love with. But she had good friends and wanted to think she was making a difference in their lives, a little bit at a time.

"We should celebrate tonight," Rosa said.

"You don't have a hot date?"

She made a face. "Not me. I have no date, hot or otherwise."

"What about our sexy neighbor?" Jen teased.

That terse note of his flashed through her mind again and her chest gave a sharp spasm.

"He will not be our neighbor long. Wyatt and Logan are moving out in the morning."

Jen's smile slid away. "Oh, no! Addie will miss having them around. She has really enjoyed playing with Logan in the evenings. I thought they wouldn't be moving for a few more weeks."

"Apparently, their house is finished. Wyatt left me a note on the door when I went home for lunch and to bring back Fiona."

Jen gave her a sharp look that Rosa pretended not to see.

"My evening is totally free," she said, "and I would love nothing more than to celebrate with you. Do you want to go somewhere?"

Jen gazed out the window. "It looks like it's going to be another beautiful night. I would be just as happy taking Fiona for a walk on the beach and then grabbing dinner at the taco truck. I think Addie would be all over that, too."

Rosa was not sure she would ever be able to eat at the taco truck without remembering that delightful evening with Logan and Wyatt, but for the sake of her friend, she would do her best.

"Done."

The store was busy with customers the rest of the afternoon. Rosa preferred it that way. Having something to do gave her less time to think.

Jen's shift was supposed to end at five, but during a lull in the hectic pace about a half hour before that, Rosa pulled her aside. "Your shift is almost over and Paula and Juan will be here soon for the evening shift. Why don't you go pick up Addie from her day care and I will meet you at home?"

"Sounds great."

Jen took off her apron, then hung it on the hook in the back room and quickly left.

Rosa was going to miss having her around when school started, not just because she was a good worker, but Rosa enjoyed her company. They made a good team.

She finished ringing up two more customers, then spent a few more moments talking to the married older couple who helped her out a few nights a week during busy summer months.

Finally, she and Fiona walked out into a lovely July evening. The dog was eager for a walk and Rosa was, too. She was looking forward to the evening with Addie and Jen. Tacos and good friends. What was not to enjoy?

When she neared the house, she didn't see Wyatt's SUV. Rosa told herself she was glad.

Perhaps she wouldn't have to see him at all before he moved out the next day.

Fiona went immediately to the backyard. When Rosa followed her, she found Jen and Addie on the tree swing. Addie's legs were stretched out as she tried to pump and she looked so filled with joy, Rosa had to smile.

"Look at me!" Addie called. "I'm flying!"

"You are doing so well at swinging," Rosa exclaimed.

"I know. I never went so high before."

She almost told her to be careful but caught herself. She wanted all little girls to soar as high as they dared.

"We got home about a half hour ago and haven't even been inside yet," Jen said with a laugh. "Addie insisted she had to swing first."

"It is very fun," Rosa agreed. Addie's excitement and Jen's good mood went a long way to cheering her up.

She might not have everything she wanted but her life could still be rich and beautiful. She had to remember that.

"I noticed the handsome detective isn't home yet. I was going to see if he wanted to come with us to the taco truck."

Jen spoke so casually that Rosa almost missed the mischievous look in her eyes.

Rosa avoided her gaze. "He is probably at his house making sure things are ready for him and Logan to return home tomorrow."

"I'll miss them."

Rosa wasn't sure she liked that pensive note in her friend's voice. Was Jen interested in Wyatt, as well?

Why wouldn't she be? He was a wonderful man and Jen was exactly the sort of woman who could make him happy. The two of them would be very good together, even though the idea of it made Rosa's chest hurt.

"When you are ready to date again, maybe you should think about dating Wyatt. You both have a lot in common."

Jen gave her a shocked, rather appalled look that Rosa thought was out of proportion to her mild suggestion. "Besides being single parents, I don't think so."

"He's a widower, you're a widow," she pointed out.

"True. And that's the only thing we have in common. Don't get me wrong. I like Wyatt a lot. He seems very nice. But I don't think he would be interested in me. His interests appear to lie...elsewhere."

Jen gave her such a significant look that Rosa could feel her face heat.

I care about you, Rosa. Very much. For the first time since Tori died, I want to spend time with a woman. And I might be crazy but I suspect you wouldn't kiss me if you didn't have similar feelings for me.

Wyatt would soon forget her and any wild idea he had that he might have feelings for her.

Before she could answer, she heard a noise and saw someone walk around the side of the house to where they were.

For a moment, with the setting sun shining on his face, she thought it might be Wyatt. Her heart skipped a beat and she felt foolish, hoping he hadn't heard their conversation.

Jen suddenly gasped, her features going instantly pale, and Rosa realized her mistake.

This was not Wyatt. It was a man she didn't recognize.

This man was big, solid, with wide shoulders and a rather thick neck. He had close-cropped brown hair and blue eyes that should have been attractive but were somehow cold.

Fiona, at her feet, instantly rose and growled a little, moving protectively in front of the two of them. That didn't seem to stop the man, who continued walking until he was only a few feet away.

"Jenna," he said, gazing at her friend with an odd, intense, almost possessive look. "Here you are. It is you. It took me forever to track you down."

Rosa knew instantly who this was. Who else could it be? Aaron Barker, the police officer who was stalking Jen and had driven her from her Utah home to Cannon Beach. She should have realized it the moment the color leached away from Jen's features.

Jenna stood frozen for a moment as if she couldn't remember how to move, then she quickly moved to the side and stopped the swing, pulling Addie off and into her arms.

"Hey!" the girl exclaimed. "I'm not done swinging."

Addie started to complain but something of her mother's tension seemed to trickle to the girl. She fell silent, eying the adults around her with sudden wariness.

"What do you want?" Jen asked. Her voice shook slightly.

"I've missed you so much, baby. Aren't you happy to see me?" He took another step forward as if to embrace her. Jen quickly stepped back.

Rosa didn't know what to do. They were on the side of the house without an entrance. The only way to get inside to safety was through the front door. To get there, they would have to go around this man.

Aaron Barker was dangerous. She recognized the fierce, violent look in his eyes. She had seen that before…

Old, long-suppressed panic started to bubble up inside her, those demons she thought she had vanquished long ago.

Rosa drew in a harsh breath and then another, suddenly desperate to escape.

No. She had to protect her friend. She wouldn't let her be hurt again.

"What do you want?" Jen asked again. She took a sideways step, Addie in her arms, and Rosa realized she was edging closer to the front door.

"Just to talk. That's all."

Jenna shuffled to the side another step and Rosa moved, as well, hoping he hadn't noticed.

"I don't want to talk to you. I tried that before and you wouldn't listen. Please. Just leave me alone."

He moved as if to come closer but Fiona growled. She

wasn't particularly fierce-looking with her long, soft fur and her sweet eyes, but she did have sharp teeth.

The dog's show of courage gave Rosa strength to draw upon her own.

"You heard her."

Jen took another sideways step and Rosa did, too. The front porch was still so very far away.

"This is private property," she went on. "You are trespassing. Please leave."

"I'm not leaving without talking to Jenna." When he spoke, she caught a definite whiff of alcohol on his breath. He had been drinking and he already had to be unstable to put Jenna through long months of torture. Rosa knew this was not a good combination.

"She clearly does not want to talk to you."

"She has to."

"No. She does not." Hoping to distract him further from realizing she and Jenna had maneuvered so that they were now closer to the door than he was, Rosa reached into her pocket for her cell phone. "I must ask you again to leave or I will have to call nine-one-one."

"You think that worries me? I'm a police officer."

"Not here," she said firmly. "The police here do not stand by while someone hurts a woman, even if he is also a police officer."

She had to hope that was true of all officers in the Cannon Beach Police Department and not only Wyatt.

"Now. I am asking you for the final time to leave or I will call the police."

Now Jenna was backing toward the door and Rosa did the same, with Fiona still standing protectively in front of them.

He frowned. "I'm not leaving without Jenna. We love each other."

He took another step closer and from behind Rosa, Jen made a small sound of panic.

"Jenna. Go inside. Call nine-one-one."

She must have made a move toward the house because several things happened at once. Aaron Barker growled out a sound of frustration and lunged for her. Fiona jumped into protective mode and latched on to his leg and he kicked out at the dog, who whimpered and fell to the ground.

"No! Fi!" Rosa cried out. The coward pulled his leg back as if to kick again and Rosa instantly dropped to the ground, her body over the dog's.

Seconds later, she felt crushing pain in her back and realized he had kicked *her* instead of the dog.

This was the first time in fifteen years someone had struck out at her in anger. Instantly, she was transported to another time, another place. The past broke free of the prison where she kept it, the memories pouring over her like acid.

Other boots. Other fists. Again and again until she was in agony as vicious words in Spanish called her horrible names and told her she was going to die.

Something whimpered beneath her and the past suddenly receded—she was back in the present with her back throbbing and her dog wriggling beneath her.

Fiona was alive, and was just winded like Rosa. Thank God.

She could not just lie here trying to catch her breath. She had to protect her friend. Already, the man was making his way past Rosa and the dog toward the porch, where Jenna was desperately trying to punch in the code to unlock the door.

"I'm sorry, baby," Rosa said to Fi, then rose shakily to her feet. Her amazing dog was right behind her and she realized Fi had been whimpering for her to get up so they could both keep fighting.

Rosa ignored her pain as she limped after him.

"Stop. Right now," she said. He had almost reached the porch and Rosa did the only thing she could think of to slow him down. Though her back groaned with pain, she jumped on him, her arms around his neck as she had been taught in the self-defense classes Daniel had insisted she take.

He cried out in frustration and swung his elbows back, trying to get her off. One elbow caught her mouth and she tasted blood but still she clung tightly.

"Stupid dog!" he cried out again and she realized Fiona must have bitten him again to protect them.

She was so busy hanging on for dear life, she almost missed the sound of the door opening as Jenna finally managed to unlock it. She could see the other woman looked undecided whether to go inside to safety or come to Rosa's aid.

"Go," she yelled to Jenna. "Call nine-one-one."

An instant later, she heard the sound of the dead bolt. She was so relieved, she relaxed her hold slightly, but it was enough for him to shake her off as Fiona would with a sand fly.

She fell to the grass, barely missing the walkway, and rolled out of the way of his kicking boots. Fiona was still growling but had retreated also, and now came to stand in front of her.

"You bitch," he growled. "You stupid bitch. This is none of your damn business."

She could hardly breathe, but she managed to squeeze out a few words. "My friend. My house. My business."

He started for the door and she grabbed the closest weapon she could find, a rock from the flower garden. Rosa stood up and held it tightly.

"I will not let you hurt her," she gasped out.

He appeared genuinely shocked by that. "I would never hurt Jenna. Never. I love her and she loves me."

He ran a hand through his hair. The man was definitely unhinged, whether from his obsession or from alcohol, she did not know. What did it matter? She only knew there was no point in arguing with him. She longed for the safety of the house, but didn't know how she could get inside without him following her and having access to Jenna.

"How can you say you love her? She ran away from you."

"I've been out of my head, worried about her. She disappeared in the middle of the night and no one would tell me where she went."

He sounded so plaintive that she would have felt sorry for him if she didn't know the torture he had put Jenna through these past few months.

"How did you...find her?" She was so afraid and in pain, she could barely breathe enough to get the question out, but had some wild thought that if she could keep him talking, perhaps the police would arrive before he killed her.

"Luck," he growled. "Sheer luck. A friend who knew how broke up I was about her leaving said he thought he saw someone who looked like her working in a gift shop when he was here on vacation with his family."

Rosa closed her eyes, remembering that day Jen had thought she saw someone she recognized. She had been right. Completely right.

"How did you know it was Jenna?"

He shrugged. "I'm a cop. I've got connections. I traced her Social Security number and found an employment record here at some shop in town. I figured they wouldn't tell me where she lived so I asked at the shop next door."

All their efforts to protect her hadn't been enough. Rosa

had never thought of putting their neighboring stores on alert. She felt stupid for not thinking of it.

"As soon as I heard she might be here, I had to see if it was her." His face darkened. "I have to talk to her. Make sure she's okay."

"You have seen her. Jenna is fine. She wants you now to leave her alone."

"I'm not going to do that. We love each other. She's just being stubborn."

Rosa stood in front of him on the porch, Fiona growling at her side. "You cannot see her now."

She could see his talkative mood shift to anger again.

"Get out of my way," he said slowly and deliberately, and moved a step closer.

"No," she said, gripping the rock more tightly.

"You think I'm going to let some stupid little bitch keep me away from the woman I love after I've come all this way?"

Always, it was about him. Not about the woman or the child he had displaced from their home, forced to flee his unwanted obsession.

Rosa was shaking and she realized it was a combination of fear, pain and anger.

"Get out of my way. If you think I'm leaving, you don't know a damn thing about me."

Rosa lifted her chin. "I know all I need to know about you, Aaron Barker. I know you are a coward, a bully, a despicable human being. You have terrorized Jenna, one of the kindest women I know, who has already been through enough, because you refuse to believe a woman is not interested in you."

"Shut up. Jenna loves me."

"Then why did she move eight hundred miles to get away from you?"

His face turned red with anger. "Move. Last warning."

"I am not going anywhere."

He reached to shove her aside and Fiona lunged again. He kicked out at the dog, but she would not let her sweet canine protector be hurt again.

Rosa lifted the rock with both hands and, with every ounce of strength she had left, she slammed it into the side of his head. He stared at her in shock, dazed, then staggered backward, stumbling off the porch.

Rosa stared at him for only a second before she rushed to the door. She was fumbling to punch in the code when she heard sirens and a door slam, then a voice yelled out, "Don't move!"

Wyatt!

He had come.

Vast relief poured over her and Rosa, shaking violently now, sagged to the ground, her back pressed against the door and her arms wrapped around her brave, wonderful dog.

Chapter 15

Wyatt restrained the son of a bitch, who seemed groggy and incoherent, and was mumbling about how much he loved Jen and how she had to talk to him.

It took every ounce of control he had not to bash the man's head against the porch steps, especially when he saw blood trickling out of Rosa's mouth.

This man had hurt Rosa. And not just physically. She looked...shattered. He wanted to go to her, but he needed to secure the scene first before he could comfort her.

"Where are Jen and Addie?" he asked. He had been at his sister's house when Jen had called, her voice frantic. He hadn't been able to understand her at first, but had quickly surmised through her distress that her stalker was there and he was hurting Rosa and Fiona.

She had hung up before he could ask any questions and he had assumed she was calling 911 as he heard the call go out of an assault while he was en route, screaming through town with lights and sirens blazing.

The door opened. "I'm here," Jenna said. "I sent Addie into our apartment. Oh, Rosa. You saved us."

She wrapped her arms around her friend and Wyatt didn't miss the way Rosa winced. She had more aches and pains than just the bloody lip he could see.

The bastard was bleeding, too, from what looked like a nasty contusion. Wyatt looked around and found a large rock with blood on it. Had Rosa hit him with that? Good for her.

He finished handcuffing Barker and read him his rights, all while the man kept babbling about being a police officer and how this was all a big mistake.

"Tell them, Jenna. Tell them you love me."

The woman looked down at the man who had so tormented her, driving her away from her home with his obsession.

"I despise you," she said clearly. "I hope you rot in hell."

Barker made a move toward her but Wyatt yanked the restraint.

"We can straighten everything out down at the station," Wyatt said, just as backup officers arrived to help him secure the scene.

Only after they had taken custody of the man and another officer started taking Jenna's statement about the incident and the months of torment preceding it could Wyatt finally go to Rosa, who was now sitting on the porch steps.

She forced a smile when he approached and he saw her lip was cracked and swollen.

"He hurt you." He reached a hand out and tenderly caressed her face.

She let out a little sob and sagged into his arms. He held

her, burying his face in her hair as he tried not to think about what might have happened to her.

How would he have endured it? He had already lost one woman he loved. He couldn't stand the idea of losing another.

"I am all right," she murmured. "Jenna is safe. That is the important thing. But I have to take Fiona to the vet. That man kicked her. She was so brave."

They both were incredibly brave. He looked over her shoulder, where Fiona's tail was wagging. She almost looked like she was smiling as the two of them embraced. "She seems okay to me."

Rosa drew away a little and he instantly wanted to pull her back into his arms.

"I would still like to have her checked out. The veterinarian is my friend. I will call her."

An ambulance pulled up, followed by a fire truck. The whole town was coming to her rescue, which was only proof about how well-regarded Rosa was in town.

Right behind them, a couple he recognized came racing up the driveway.

"Rosa!" Melissa Sanderson exclaimed. "What happened? We saw all the police racing past and hurried right over."

"I am fine," Rosa said. "A man came to hurt Jen but she and Addie were able to get to safety."

"Because of you," Jenna said as she approached with her daughter in her arms. "You saved us."

She hugged her friend again and Wyatt could see Rosa was trying not to wince.

"You look like you've gone a few rounds with a heavyweight champion." Melissa's husband, Eli, a physician in town, looked concerned. "You should let me have a look."

Rosa, his battered warrior, glowered at them all. "This is all too much fuss for a sore lip."

"He kicked her in the back, too," Jenna said. "At least once. Maybe more. I don't know. I was so scared."

"You need to go to the ER," Wyatt said.

She shook her head. "Not until Fiona sees the veterinarian."

"You can at least let Eli and the paramedics check you out while I call the veterinarian," Wyatt said.

She gave him a grateful look. "Yes. I will do that. Thank you."

Chapter 16

To his deep regret, that was the last chance he had to talk to her for the next few hours. He didn't want to leave, but as the on-scene arresting officer, he had paperwork and an investigation to deal with.

He had tried to interrogate Barker but the man was sleeping off what appeared to be a large quantity of alcohol, as well as a concussion delivered by Rosa and her trusty rock and several dog bites from Fiona.

By the time he left the station, the sun was beginning to set.

He knew from the other officers on scene that Rosa had refused transport to the hospital, though she had allowed Eli to clean and bandage her cuts.

Stubborn woman.

Only now, as he walked up the front steps to the house hours later, did Wyatt feel his own adrenaline crash.

He had never been so scared as the moment when Jenna

had called him, her voice thready with panic. All he had registered were her words that Rosa was being hurt.

It seemed odd to be here without either Hank or Logan, but Carrie had offered to keep both of them overnight.

"You do what you need to for Jen and Rosa," she had told him when he called from the station. She had been half out of her mind with worry for her friend and only his repeated assurances that Rosa's injuries appeared to be minor had kept Carrie from rushing to the house herself.

He half expected to find Rosa in the flower gardens around Brambleberry House, seeking peace and solace amid the blossoms and the birds, as she so often did. But from what he could see, the gardens were empty except for a few hummingbirds at the bright red feeder. They immediately flitted away.

The big house also seemed quiet when he let himself inside. He walked to the third floor and knocked, but Rosa didn't answer. He couldn't hear Fiona inside, either.

He frowned, not sure what to do.

As he headed back down the stairs, the door on the second-floor landing opened. Jenna peeked out. "I thought I heard you come in."

"Yeah. How are you?"

"I've had better days."

"It has to help to know that Barker is in custody, doesn't it?"

She shrugged and he could see she wasn't entirely convinced her nightmare was over. He couldn't blame her for the doubt after the way the system had already treated her, but Wyatt was quick to reassure her.

"You should know that Barker won't be going anywhere for a long time. He's facing extensive state and federal charges. And we haven't even started on the stalking charges. That will only add to his sentence. He won't bother you again."

"I hope not."

He knew it would probably take time for that reality to sink in.

"Is Rosa with you?"

"No. I heard her take Fiona out about a half hour ago."

She paused. "I never wanted her to get hurt. I hope you know that. I thought we would be safe here. If I had for a moment dreamed he would find me and would come here and hurt Rosa and Fiona, I never would have come."

"I know that and I'm sure Rosa doesn't blame you for a second."

Jenna didn't look convinced about this, either. "She was amazing. I wish you could have seen her. She was so fierce. Aaron was twice as big, but that didn't stop her. She's an incredible woman."

"Agreed," he said, his voice gruff.

"She risked her life to protect me and Addie." Jenna's voice took on an edge and she gave him a hard stare. "For the record, I will do the same for her. Anybody who hurts her in any possible way will live to regret it."

Was that a threat? It certainly sounded like one. He couldn't decide whether to be offended that she could ever think he would hurt Rosa, or touched at her loyalty to her friend. He settled on the latter.

"You and I are the same in that sentiment, then," he said quietly.

She studied his features for a moment, then nodded. "I saw her from my window as I was putting Addie to bed. She and Fiona appeared to be heading for the beach."

He smiled and on impulse reached out and hugged her. After a surprised moment, Jenna hugged him back.

He headed for the beach gate, his heart pounding. As he went, he carried on a fierce debate with himself.

Rosa had basically ordered him to keep his distance and told him she wasn't interested in a relationship. He had tried his best. For a week, he had worked long hours at his house so that he and Logan could move out as soon as possible. The whole time, he had done his best to push her out of his head and his heart.

It hadn't worked.

The moment Jenna had called him in a panic, the moment he knew they were in danger, Wyatt had realized nothing had changed. He was in love with Rosa and would move heaven and earth to keep her safe.

He pushed open the beach gate and found her there, just beyond the house. She was sitting on a blanket on the sand, her arm around Fiona and her back to him as she watched the sun slipping down into the water in a blaze of color.

She didn't hear him come out at first. Fiona did. The dog turned to look at him, but apparently decided he was no threat because she nestled closer to her human.

He moved across the sand, still not sure what he would say to her, only knowing he had to be close to her, too.

He saw the moment she registered his presence. Her spine stiffened and she turned her head. He couldn't see her expression behind her sunglasses.

"Oh. Hello."

"Here you are. I was worried about you."

"Yes. We are here. The sunset seems especially beautiful tonight."

He had to agree. Streaks of pink and purple and orange spilled out in glorious Technicolor. "May I join you?"

She hesitated. He could see her jaw flex, as if she wanted

to say no, but she finally gestured to the empty spot on the blanket, which happened to be on the other side of her dog.

He would have liked to be next to Rosa, but this would do, he supposed.

"Where are Logan and Hank?"

"They were both with Carrie when Jenna called me. After Carrie heard what happened to you and found out I was part of the investigation, she insisted they stay the night with her."

"Ah."

He reached out and rubbed her brave, amazing dog behind the ear. His hand brushed against Rosa's and it hurt a little when she pulled her hand away.

"How's Fiona?"

"Fine. Dr. Williams said she might be a little bruised, but nothing appears to be broken. I am to watch her appetite and her energy over the next few days and tell her if I see anything unusual."

"You're a good, brave girl, aren't you?" He scratched Fi under the chin and the dog rested her head on his leg.

All the emotions he had put away in the heat of the moment as he did his duty and stood for justice seemed to come rushing over him again, all at once.

"What you did—protecting your friend. It was incredibly brave."

She gave a short laugh. "I think you mean to say stupid."

"I would never say that. Never. You were amazing."

He reached for her hand, unable to help himself. He thought she would pull away again, but she didn't. Her fingers were cool and seemed to be trembling a little, but he couldn't say whether that was from the cool coastal air or from the trauma of earlier.

She drew in a breath that sounded ragged, and before he quite realized it, she let out a sob and then another.

Oh, Rosa.

His poor, fierce Rosa.

Fiona, blessed Fiona, moved out of the way so that Wyatt could pull Rosa into his arms. He held her while she cried silently against his chest, not making a sound except the occasional whimper.

His heart ached for her, both for the fear she must have felt and for everything else she had endured.

"I am sorry," she finally said, sounding mortified. "I think I have been holding that in all afternoon."

"Or longer."

She shifted her face to meet his gaze. Somehow, she had lost her sunglasses and he could see her now, her eyes dark and shadowed in her lovely face. Instead of answering his unspoken question, she focused on the events of the day.

"I was so frightened. I thought this man, he was going to kill me, then get to Jenna and Addie. I could not let him."

"He won't get to Jenna now. He is in custody and will be charged with assault, trespassing, drunk driving, driving across state lines with the intent to commit a felony and a whole host of other charges related to whatever stalking charges we can prove. He's not going to get out for a long time."

"I hope that is the case."

"It is," he promised. He would do whatever necessary to make sure of it.

"I suppose I should be relieved I did not kill him with that rock."

"You were pretty fierce."

"I could not help it. I could only think about protecting Jenna and Addie from someone who wanted to hurt them.

Something seemed to take over me. Maybe some part of my brain that was fifteen years old again, focused only on surviving another day."

As soon as she said the words, she looked as if she wished she hadn't. She closed her eyes. He thought she would pull away from him but she didn't. She continued to nestle against him as if he was providing safe shelter in a sandstorm.

With his thumb, he brushed away a tear that trickled down her cheek, his heart a heavy ache. "Tell me what happened when you were fifteen."

"I have already told you too much. I don't talk about that time in my life, Wyatt. It is the past and has nothing to do with who I am now."

"You don't have to tell me. I understand if you prefer to keep it to yourself. But I hope you know you can trust me, if you ever change your mind."

She eased away from him and sat once more on the blanket beside him. Fiona moved to her other side and plopped next to her. Rosa wrapped her arms around her knees and gazed out at the water, a pale blue in the twilight.

She was silent for a long time, so long that he thought she wasn't going to answer. But then she looked at him out of the corner of her gaze and he fell in love with her all over again.

"Sometimes it feels like it all happened to someone else. Something I read about in a terribly tragic novel."

He did not want to hear what was coming next, but somehow Wyatt sensed it was important to both of them that she tell him. This was the reason she had pushed him away. He was suddenly certain of it.

That moment when he had rushed onto the porch earlier, he had seen raw emotion in her expression. That was the image he couldn't get out of his head. She had looked at him with relief, with gratitude and with something else, too.

She thought her past was a barrier between them. If he could show her it wasn't, that together they could face whatever demons she fought, perhaps she would stop pushing him away.

"I told you about the men who offered me a job in this country and who...brought me here."

"Yes."

"It was not a factory job they were bringing me to, as I thought. I was so stupid."

"I didn't think it was."

She closed her eyes. "You are a detective. I am sure you can guess what happened next."

"I've imagined a few possible scenarios since the night you told me."

"Pick the worst one and you might be close enough."

He gripped her hand tightly, not wanting to ever let go. "Human trafficking."

She made a small sound. "Yes. That is a polite phrase for it. I was brought here to work in the sex trade. Me, an innocent girl from a small town who had never even kissed a boy. I barely knew what sex was."

Everything inside him went cold as he thought about what she must have endured. "Oh, sweetheart. I'm so sorry."

"I refused at first. The men who brought me here, they did not care whether I was willing or not."

How was it possible for his heart to break again and again? "You were raped."

She looked at him, stark pain in her eyes. "Now you know why I don't like thinking about the past. Yes. I was raped. At first by the men who wanted to use me to make money for them. Then by some of their customers. I did not cooperate. Not one single time. They threatened me, hurt me, tried to make me take drugs like the other girls, so I would be quiet and do what they said. I would not. I only cried. All the time."

"That couldn't have been good for business."

She gave a short, humorless laugh. "No. Not at all. Finally, they left me alone. I still do not know why they did not kill me. It would have been easy for them. But then one of the girls died of too much drugs. She was...not well, so they had let her do all the cooking and cleaning for the other girls. They let me take her place. At least I no longer had to let strangers touch me."

He squeezed her fingers. How had she possibly emerged from that hell still able to smile and laugh and find joy in the world, with a gentle spirit and a kind heart? Most people would have curled up and withered away in the midst of so much trauma.

"This went on for a few months and then I made a mistake. I knew I had to do something to change my situation. I could not stay. I tried to escape but they...caught me. They would have killed me that night. They knew I could tell the police who they were. I expected to die. I thought I would. But somehow, I did not. I do not know why. I only knew I had to do all I could to survive. Mine was not the only life at risk that night."

"One of your friends?"

She gave a tiny shake of her head and gazed out at the undulating waves. He waited for her to explain. When she did not, suddenly all his suspicions came together and he knew. He didn't know how. He just did.

"You were pregnant."

She met his gaze, her expression filled with sadness and pain. "No one else knew. I did not even know myself until I was too far along to—to do anything. I told you I was innocent."

"How did you get away?"

She shrugged. "A miracle from God. That is the only thing it could have been."

He had never heard her being particularly religious but the conviction in her voice seemed unswerving. He would take her word for it, since he hadn't been there.

"We were kept above a restaurant in a tourist town in Utah. They left me to die in a room there, but I did not. I had only pretended. After they left, I saw they had not locked the door, like usual. They thought I was dead. Why should they?"

How badly had she been hurt? Wyatt didn't even want to contemplate. And she'd only been a child. Not much older than his niece. How had she endured it?

"Somehow, I found strength to stand and managed to go out, stumbling down the back stairs. I still cannot believe they did not hear me. Once I was out, I did not know what to do. Where to go. I knew no one. I was certain I only had moments before they found me and finished what they had started, so I… I somehow climbed into the back of a truck."

"With a stranger?"

He thought of all the things that could have happened to her by putting her trust in someone she did not know. On the other hand, she was escaping certain death so she probably thought anything was better than the place she was leaving.

"I was lucky. There was a blanket there for the horses and I was able to pull it over me so I did not freeze. The man was a rancher. He did not spot me until we were away from town, when he had a flat tire and found me sleeping."

"What did he do?" Wyatt was again almost afraid to ask.

"He called the police and a kind sheriff and a doctor came to my rescue. Daniel and Lauren. My parents."

Chapter 17

Rosa could feel herself trembling, though the night was pleasant. She knew it was probably a delayed reaction from the attack earlier and from the emotional trauma of reliving the darkest time in her life.

When Wyatt wrapped his arm around her and pulled her close to his heat, she wanted to sink into him. He was big, safe and comforting, and offered immeasurable strength.

She could not tell by his expression what he thought about what she had told him. She thought maybe that wasn't such a bad thing. Did she want to know what he was thinking about her?

"They took you in."

"They were not married at the time. Not even together. I like to think I helped them find each other. But, yes. Lauren took me home with her. I was still in danger. I had information about the men who took me. I knew who they were, where they were, so I—I stayed with Lauren until all the men were caught."

"All of them?" Wyatt's voice had a hard note she had not heard before, as if he wanted to go to Utah right now and find justice for her.

Oh, he was a dear man. A little more warmth seeped into her heart. How was she supposed to resist him?

"Yes. Some were deported. Others are still in jail here in this country. Daniel made sure all the girls were rescued and the men were punished."

"I would like to meet Sheriff Galvez," he said gruffly.

"You two are similar. I think you would be friends. That is one reason why I…" Her voice trailed off and she felt her face heat, as she was unable to complete the sentence. *Why I fell in love with you.*

"Why you what?"

"Nothing," she said quickly. "I only wanted to tell you, after Daniel and Lauren married, they gave me a home and then legally adopted me."

"They sound wonderful."

"The best. Though they can be too protective of me."

"That's understandable, don't you think?"

She nodded. "Yes. I do understand but this is one reason I think I had to move somewhere else. Somewhere I would not be poor Rosa Galvez."

"What about your baby?" he asked.

Ah. Here was the most difficult part. The other things that had happened—the abuse, the beatings. Even the rapes. Those scars had healed. She hardly thought of them anymore.

Her child. That was a wound that would never close completely.

She chose her words carefully, wishing she did not have

to tell him this part. "I had a baby girl ten weeks later and... she was adopted."

There. The words still burned her throat.

He was quiet for a long time. Was he recoiling now from her? She could not blame him. It had been a terrible choice for someone who had been little more than a child to have to make.

"It's Bella, isn't it? Your daughter?"

That was the last thing she expected him to say. In horror, she jerked away and scrambled to her feet. Fiona immediately moved to her side, as if sensing more danger.

"No! Bella? How ridiculous! Do not say this. You are crazy."

He rose, as well, gazing at her across the sand. The rising moon lit up one side of his face, leaving the other in shadow. "I'm not crazy though, am I?" he said quietly. "I'm right."

She didn't know what to say. How could she convince him he had made a terrible mistake? She had no words to undo this.

"No. This is not true," she said, but even she could hear her words lacked conviction. "I do not know how... Why did you think of this?"

"The time frame lines up. Bella is the right age and she was adopted through your aunt Anna. You're her birth mother." If her own words lacked conviction, his did not. He spoke with a growing confidence she had no way to combat.

"I don't know why I didn't see the resemblance before. Maybe I didn't want to see it. Does she know?"

Rosa stared at him, not sure what to say. All of her instincts were shouting at her to go inside the safety of the house, but she couldn't leave. She had started this by telling him her history. It was her fault. He was a police detective.

How could she blame him for connecting all the pieces of the jigsaw and coming up with the correct picture?

This was the part of the story she did not want him to know. The part she had been trying to protect him from. What must he think of her now? She had abandoned his niece, a girl he loved. She had given birth and handed her over to another woman to be her mother, then went on with her life. Learning English. Finishing school. Dating boys. Going to college.

Why did he not seem angry? Why was he looking at her like that, with a tender light in his eyes? Did he not understand what she had done?

She could not think about that now. For this moment, she had to focus on controlling the damage she had done. She should not have told him anything. Since she had, now she had to make sure he did not ruin all the care she had taken during the years she had lived in Cannon Beach, so close to her daughter but still far enough away.

"No. She does not know," she finally said. "And you cannot tell her. Oh, please. Do not tell her."

"I would never, if you don't want me to."

"You must promise me. Swear it."

He seemed to blink at her vehemence, but then nodded. "I swear. I won't tell her. This is not my secret to tell, Rosa. Again, please trust me enough to know I would never betray you."

Oh, she wanted to trust him. The urge to step back into his arms was so overpowering, she had to wrap her own arms around herself to keep from doing it. "I thank you. She might have come from an ugly time in my life but none of that was her fault. She is the most beautiful, precious girl. From the moment I felt her move inside me, I loved her. I wanted so much to keep her but it was… It was impossible."

"You were only a child yourself."

"Yes. What would I do with a baby? I had no way to take care of her myself, though I wanted to."

"It's obvious you love her. Whether she knows the truth or not, there is a bond between you."

"How could anyone not love her? Bella is wonderful. Smart and pretty, always kind. She reminds me of my mother."

"That's funny. She reminds me of *her* mother, now that I know who she is."

She blushed at the intensity in her voice. "Carrie is her mother. She has loved her and cared for her far better than I ever could."

"Do Joe and Carrie know?"

"Yes. Of course. I would not have come here without telling them. When Anna asked me to come to help her with the store, I knew I must tell Carrie and Joe first. I called them to see how they might feel if I moved to town. I did not want to cause them any tension or discomfort."

"What did they say?"

"They welcomed me. They have always been so kind to me. Always. From the day we met in the hospital. They never once made me feel as if I had…done something wrong."

"Because you hadn't!"

She sighed. It was easy for others to say that. They had not lived her journey. "I know that most of the time but sometimes I do wonder. I made foolish choices. Dangerous choices. And because of that, an innocent child was born."

He reached for her hands again and curled his fingers around hers. To Rosa's shock, he lifted her hands and pressed first one hand to his mouth and then the other.

"You did nothing wrong, Rosa. *Nothing*. You were an

innocent child yourself, looking for a brighter future. You couldn't have known what would happen to you."

Tears spilled out again at his words and the healing balm they offered. He was not disgusted by her story. She did not know why. It seemed the second miracle of her life.

He pulled her back into his arms. She knew she should try to be strong but she couldn't. Not right now. She would try to find the strength later to restore distance between them but right now she needed the heat and comfort of him. She wrapped her arms around his waist and rested her head against his chest again, wishing she could stay here forever.

"If Carrie and Joe know the truth, why doesn't Bella?"

Thinking about it made her stomach hurt. This was her greatest fear. Every day, she worried Bella would learn the truth and would come to hate her.

"They wanted to tell her but I—I begged them not to. I thought it would be better for her if I could be in her life only as a friend. Maybe like a sort of…older sister or cousin."

"Why would that be better?"

She shrugged against him. "How do I tell her that she was created through an act of violence at a time in my life I wish I could forget?"

"You wouldn't have to tell her that part."

"What do I say when she asks me about her father? I did not know how I could answer that. I still do not know. How can I tell her I do not even know his name? No. It is better that she not know the truth."

His silence told her he didn't agree.

"When I came here, I did not want to intrude in her life," she said. "Carrie and Joe are her parents in every way that matters and they have been wonderful to her. I only wanted to…see her. Make sure she was happy. Healthy. I thought

I would only be here a short time but then I came to love her and to love Cannon Beach and Brambleberry House. Anna offered me a partnership in the store and it became harder to think about leaving."

"I am glad you stayed. So glad," he said. And before she realized what he intended, he lowered his mouth and kissed her with a sweetness and gentleness that took her breath.

Her mouth still burned where she had been hit, but she ignored it, lost in the peace and wonder of kissing the man she loved on a moonswept beach.

He still wanted to kiss her, after everything she told him. All this time, she had been so afraid for him to learn the truth. He now knew the ugliest part of her past and yet he kissed her anyway with a tenderness that made her feel... cherished.

"Thank you for coming to my rescue." She realized in that moment she had not really told him that yet. And while she was speaking about earlier, with Aaron Barker, her words held layers of meaning.

He smiled against her mouth. "I don't think you needed help from me. You were doing just fine. You're pretty ferocious, Rosita."

The endearment—Little Rosa—made her smile, too. Her mother had always called her that and Daniel still did.

"Ow. Smiling still hurts."

"Oh. I forgot about your mouth. I shouldn't have kissed you. I'm sorry."

"I am glad you did." To prove it, she pressed her mouth, sore lip and all, to his.

All of the emotions she could not say were contained in that kiss. All the love and yearning she had been fighting for so long.

When he lifted his head, Wyatt was breathing hard and

Rosa realized they were once more on the sand, sitting on the blanket she had brought.

"I have to tell you something," Wyatt said after a long moment. He gripped her hands again, and even through the darkness, she could see the intense light in his eyes.

"I was scared to death when Jenna called me and said you were in trouble. I made all kinds of deals with God on my way to Brambleberry House, begging Him to keep you safe until I could get here."

"You…did?" She didn't know what to say, shaken to her core by the emotion in his voice. Her heart, already beating hard from the kiss, seemed to race even faster.

"Yes. Though I suppose I should have known you could take care of yourself," he said with a little smile. "You're amazing, Rosa. One of the most amazing women I have ever met."

She could not seem to wrap her mind around this man speaking such tender, wonderful words.

"I do not understand," she finally asked. "How can you say that after—after everything I have told you about my past? About what I had to do? About…about giving my baby to someone else?"

"All of those things only make me love you more."

She thought she must have misheard him.

"Love me. You cannot love me." She stared through the darkness, wishing she could see him better. She wanted to drag him back to the house so she could look at him in the light to read the truth.

"Yet I do," he said, his voice ringing with so much truth she had to believe him. "What you did was remarkable. Even more so because of what you have been through. You were scared to death but you still risked your life to protect your friend. You make me ashamed of myself."

"Ashamed? Why? You came as soon as you heard we were in danger."

"I don't have your kind of courage. I have been fighting falling in love with you for a long time. I think long before I moved to Brambleberry House."

"Why?" She was still not sure she could believe it but she wanted to. Oh, she wanted to.

"I loved my wife," he said simply. "When she died, I thought I had nothing else to give. I did not want to love someone else. Love brought too much pain and sadness and it was easier, safer, to keep my heart locked away."

He kissed her gently, on the side of her mouth that had not been hurt. "I am not brave like a certain woman I know who has endured horrible things but still manages to be kind and cheerful and loving."

His words soaked through her, more comforting than she could ever tell him.

"This woman. She sounds very annoying. Too good to be true."

He laughed. "She isn't. She's amazing. Did I tell you that she also reaches out to those in need and is willing to protect them with every fierce ounce of her being?"

She was not the perfect woman he was describing. But hearing how he saw her made her want to be.

Wasn't that what love should be? A window that allowed you to discover the best in yourself because someone else saw you that way?

She didn't know. She only knew she loved Wyatt with all her heart and wanted a future with him, as she had never wanted anything in her life.

"I know something about this woman that you might not," she said.

"What's that?"

The words seemed to catch in her throat as those demons of self-doubt whispered in her ear. No. She would not listen to them. This was too important.

"This woman. She very much loves a certain police detective. She has loved him for a long time, too. Probably since he moved to town with his sad eyes and his beautiful little boy."

He gazed down at her, those eyes no longer sad but blazing with light, joy and wonder. "Well. That works out then, doesn't it?"

He kissed her again, his arms wrapped tightly around her. Her entire journey had been leading her to this moment, she realized. This moment and this man who knew all her secrets and loved her despite them. Or maybe a little because of them.

She loved Wyatt. She wanted a future with him and with Logan. Thinking about that boy who already held such a big part of her heart only added to her happiness.

She could clearly picture that future together, filled with laughter and joy. Kisses and Spanish lessons and walks along the beach with their dogs.

She had no doubt that it would be rich and beautiful, full and joyous and rewarding. The scent of freesia drifted across the sand and Rosa smiled, happy to know that Abigail approved.

Epilogue

One year later

What a glorious day for a wedding.

Rosa woke just as the sun was beginning to creep over the horizon in her third-floor apartment of Brambleberry House.

She stayed in bed for a moment, anticipation shivering through her. For a few disoriented moments, she wasn't sure why, then she caught sight of Fiona's head on the bed, the dog watching her intently, and she remembered.

Today was the day. This day, she was marrying Wyatt and becoming Logan's stepmother.

In a few short hours, they would stand in the gardens of Brambleberry House and exchange their vows.

Everyone was in town. Her parents, Anna and Harry, Sonia Elizabeth and her husband, Luke.

Fiona made the little sound she did when she wanted to go for a walk and Rosa had to smile.

"I am not even out of bed yet. You really want a walk now?"

The dog continued to give her a steady look she could not ignore.

With a sigh, she slipped out of bed, threw on sweats and a baseball cap and then put on Fiona's leash. A moment later, they headed down the stairs of Brambleberry House.

This was her last morning in this apartment and her last morning as Rosa Vallejo Galvez. Tonight she would be Rosa Vallejo Galvez Townsend.

A wife and a mother.

After their honeymoon, she and Wyatt would be returning to the ground-floor apartment of Brambleberry House. They had decided to stay here for now.

He was going to rent out his small bungalow and they would move to the larger apartment, with its sunroom and extra bedroom. It was larger than his house, plus had extensive grounds where Logan could play, as well as his best friend, Addie, living upstairs.

She knew it wouldn't last. At some point, they would probably want to find a house of their own. For now, she was glad she did not have to leave the house completely.

She knew it was silly but Rosa felt like Brambleberry House was excited about the upcoming wedding and all the coming changes. She seemed to smell flowers all the time and wondered if Abigail was flitting through the house, watching all the preparations.

The summer morning was beautiful, with wisps of sea mist curling up through the trees. It was cool now but she knew the afternoon would be perfect for a garden wedding overlooking the sea.

The decorations were already in place and she admired them as she walked through with Fi toward the beach gate.

Fiona, usually well-behaved, was tugging on the leash

as Rosa walked onto the sand. She lunged toward a few other early-morning beach walkers, which was completely not like her.

It looked like a man and a child walking a little dog, but they were too far away for her to see them clearly. Suddenly Fiona broke free of Rosa's hold and raced toward them, dragging her leash behind her.

The boy, who Rosa was now close enough to recognize as a nearly eight-year-old boy with a blond cowlick and his father's blue eyes, caught Fiona's leash and came hurrying toward Rosa.

"Rosa! *Buenos*, Rosa!"

"Buenos, mijo." When he reached her, he hugged her hard and Rosa's simmering joy seemed to bubble over.

A few more hours and they would be a family.

A year ago, she never could have imagined this day for herself. She expected she would be content going to other people's weddings. She would dance, laugh, enjoy the refreshments and then go home trying to ignore the pang of loneliness.

Destined to be alone. That is what she had always thought.

She could not have been happier to be so very wrong.

"I don't think I'm supposed to see you today. Isn't it bad luck?" Wyatt's voice was gruff but his eyes blazed with so much tenderness and love, she felt tears of happiness gather in hers. He always made her feel so cherished.

"I think you are not supposed to see me in the wedding dress. I do not think the superstition means you cannot see me in my old sweatpants, when I have barely combed my hair and look terrible. Anyway, I do not care about such things. We make our own luck, right?"

He laughed and reached for her. "Yes. I guess we do. To be safe, I won't tell Carrie and Bella we bumped in to you on our walk. They *do* care about that kind of thing."

Rosa smiled and her heart seemed to sigh when he kissed her, his mouth warm and firm against the morning chill.

"You do not have to tell me. I have heard every superstition about weddings from them since the day we became engaged."

"I don't know how it's possible, but I think Bella is even more excited about this wedding than we are."

Rosa smiled, adding even more happiness to her overflowing cup when she thought of his niece. Her niece, after today.

And her daughter.

After talking with Joe and Carrie several months earlier, she had decided she must tell Bella the truth.

They had all sat down together and, gathering her courage and without giving all the grim details, Rosa had told Bella she was her birth mother.

To her shock, Bella had simply shrugged. "And?" she had said. "I've only known that, like, forever."

"You have not!" Rosa had said, shocked nearly speechless. "How?"

"It wasn't exactly hard to figure out. You just have to look at a selfie of us together. We look enough alike to be sisters."

"Why didn't you say anything?" Carrie had looked and sounded as shocked as Rosa.

"I figured you all would say something eventually when you wanted me to know. What's the big deal? You're like one of my best friends, anyway."

Rosa had burst into tears at that and so had Carrie.

Nothing seemed to have changed between them. Bella still confided in her about boys she liked, and Rosa still tried to be like a wise older sister.

In that time, Bella had never asked about her father. Maybe some day, when she was older, Rosa would figure out a way to tell her something. For now, she was grateful every day for the bright, beautiful daughter who seemed happy to let her into her life.

"She has done a great job of helping me plan the wedding. I would have been lost without her," she said now to Wyatt.

Bella was one of her bridesmaids and could not have been more excited to help her work out every detail of the wedding, from the cake to the dresses to the food at the reception. In fact, Rosa thought she might have a good future as a wedding planner, if she wanted.

"I'm sure she's done a great job," he said. "It's going to be a beautiful day. But not nearly as gorgeous as you."

She smiled as he kissed her again. A loud sigh finally distracted them both. "Can we be done kissing now? You guys are gross."

"Sorry, kid." Wyatt smiled down at his son but made no move to release her. "We both kind of like it."

That was an understatement. They were magic together. She loved his kiss, his touch, and could not wait until she could wake up each morning in his arms.

"Fiona and Hank want to take a walk," Logan informed them. "So do I."

Wyatt kissed Rosa firmly one more time then drew away. "Fine," he said. "But you'd better get used to the kissing, kid."

He reached for Rosa's hand and the three of them and their dogs walked down the beach while gulls cried and the waves washed against the shore.

The perfect day and the perfect life seemed to stretch out ahead of them and Rosa knew she had everything she could ever need, right here.

* * * * *

A COLD CREEK REUNION

To romance readers who, like me,
love happily ever afters.

Chapter 1

He loved these guys like his own brothers, but sometimes Taft Bowman wanted to take a fire hose to his whole blasted volunteer fire department.

This was their second swift-water rescue training in a month—not to mention that he had been holding these regularly since he became battalion chief five years earlier—and they still struggled to toss a throw bag anywhere close to one of the three "victims" floating down Cold Creek in wet suits and helmets.

"You've got to keep in mind the flow of the water and toss it downstream enough that they ride the current to the rope," he instructed for about the six-hundredth time. One by one, the floaters—in reality, other volunteer firefighters on his thirty-person crew—stopped at the catch line strung across the creek and began working their way hand over hand to the bank.

Fortunately, even though the waters were plenty frigid

this time of year, they were about a month away from the real intensity of spring runoff, which was why he was training his firefighters for water rescues now.

With its twists and turns and spectacular surroundings on the west slope of the Tetons, Cold Creek had started gaining popularity with kayakers. He enjoyed floating the river himself. But between the sometimes-inexperienced outdoor-fun seekers and the occasional Pine Gulch citizen who strayed too close to the edge of the fast-moving water, his department was called out on at least a handful of rescues each season and he wanted them to be ready.

"Okay, let's try it one more time. Terry, Charlie, Bates, you three take turns with the throw bag. Luke, Cody, Tom, stagger your jumps by about five minutes this time around to give us enough time on this end to rescue whoever is ahead of you."

He set the team in position and watched upstream as Luke Orosco, his second in command, took a running leap into the water, angling his body feetfirst into the current. "Okay, Terry. He's coming. Are you ready? Time it just right. One, two, three. Now!"

This time, the rope sailed into the water just downstream of the diver and Taft grinned. "That's it, that's it. Perfect. Now instruct him to attach the rope."

For once, the rescue went smoothly. He was watching for Cody Shepherd to jump in when the radio clipped to his belt suddenly crackled with static.

"Chief Bowman, copy."

The dispatcher sounded unusually flustered and Taft's instincts borne of fifteen years of firefighting and paramedic work instantly kicked in. "Yeah, I copy. What's up, Kelly?"

"I've got a report of a small structure fire at the inn, three hundred twenty Cold Creek Road."

He stared as the second rescue went off without a hitch. "Come again?" he couldn't help asking, adrenaline pulsing through him. Structure fires were a rarity in the quiet town of Pine Gulch. Really a rarity. The last time had been a creosote chimney fire four months ago that a single ladder-truck unit had put out in about five minutes.

"Yes, sir. The hotel is evacuating at this time."

He muttered an oath. Half his crew was currently in wet suits, but at least they were only a few hundred yards away from the station house, with the engines and the turnout gear.

"Shut it down," he roared through his megaphone. "We've got a structure fire at the Cold Creek Inn. Grab your gear. This is not a drill."

To their credit, his crew immediately caught the gravity of the situation. The last floater was quickly grabbed out of the water and everybody else rushed to the new fire station the town had finally voted to bond for two years earlier.

Less than four minutes later—still too long in his book but not bad for volunteers—he had a full crew headed toward the Cold Creek Inn on a ladder truck and more trained volunteers pouring in to hurriedly don their turnout gear.

The inn, a rambling wood structure with two single-story wings leading off a main two-story building, was on the edge of Pine Gulch's small downtown, about a mile away from the station. He quickly assessed the situation as they approached. He couldn't see flames yet, but he did see a thin plume of black smoke coming from a window on the far end of the building's east wing.

He noted a few guests milling around on the lawn and had just an instant to feel a pang of sympathy for the owner.

Poor Mrs. Pendleton had enough trouble finding guests for her gracefully historic but undeniably run-down inn.

A fire and forced evacuation probably wouldn't do much to increase the appeal of the place.

"Luke, you take Pete and make sure everybody's out. Shep, come with me for the assessment. You all know the drill."

He and Cody Shepherd, a young guy in the last stages of his fire and paramedic training, headed into the door closest to where he had seen the smoke.

Somebody had already been in here with a fire extinguisher, he saw. The fire was mostly out but the charred curtains were still smoking, sending out that inky-black plume.

The room looked to be under renovation. It didn't have a bed and the carpet had been pulled up. Everything was wet and he realized the ancient sprinkler system must have come on and finished the job the fire extinguisher had started.

"Is that it?" Shep asked with a disgruntled look.

"Sorry, should have let you have the honors." He held the fire extinguisher out to the trainee. "Want a turn?"

Shep snorted but grabbed the fire extinguisher and sprayed another layer of completely unnecessary foam on the curtains.

"Not much excitement—but at least nobody was hurt. It's a wonder this place didn't go up years ago. We'll have to get the curtains out of here and have Engine Twenty come inside and check for hot spots."

He called in over his radio that the fire had been contained to one room and ordered in the team whose specialty was making sure the flames hadn't traveled inside the walls to silently spread to other rooms.

When he walked back outside, Luke headed over to him. "Not much going on, huh? Guess some of us should have stayed in the water."

"We'll do more swift-water work next week during training," he said. "Everybody else but Engine Twenty can go back to the station."

As he spoke to Luke, he spotted Jan Pendleton standing some distance away from the building. Even from here, he could see the distress on her plump, wrinkled features. She was holding a little dark-haired girl in her arms, probably a traumatized guest. Poor thing.

A younger woman stood beside her and from this distance he had only a strange impression, as if she was somehow standing on an island of calm amid the chaos of the scene, the flashing lights of the emergency vehicles, shouts between his crew members, the excited buzz of the crowd.

And then the woman turned and he just about tripped over a snaking fire hose somebody shouldn't have left there.

Laura.

He froze and for the first time in fifteen years as a firefighter, he forgot about the incident, his mission, just what the hell he was doing here.

Laura.

Ten years. He hadn't seen her in all that time, since the week before their wedding when she had given him back his ring and left town. Not just town. She had left the whole damn country, as if she couldn't run far enough to get away from him.

Some part of him desperately wanted to think he had made some kind of mistake. It couldn't be her. That was just some other slender woman with a long sweep of honey-blond hair and big blue, unforgettable eyes. But no, it was definitely Laura, standing next to her mother. Sweet and lovely.

Not his.

"Chief, we're not finding any hot spots." Luke approached him. Just like somebody turned back up the volume on his flat-screen, he jerked away from memories of pain and loss and aching regret.

"You're certain?"

"So far. The sprinkler system took a while to kick in and somebody with a fire extinguisher took care of the rest. Tom and Nate are still checking the integrity of the internal walls."

"Good. That's good. Excellent work."

His assistant chief gave him a wary look. "You okay, Chief? You look upset."

He huffed out a breath. "It's a fire, Luke. It could have been potentially disastrous. With the ancient wiring in this old building, it's a wonder the whole thing didn't go up."

"I was thinking the same thing," Luke said.

He was going to have to go over there and talk to Mrs. Pendleton—and by default, Laura. He didn't want to. He wanted to stand here and pretend he hadn't seen her. But he was the fire chief. He couldn't hide out just because he had a painful history with the daughter of the property owner.

Sometimes he hated his job.

He made his way toward the women, grimly aware of his heart pounding in his chest as if he had been the one diving into Cold Creek for training.

Laura stiffened as he approached but she didn't meet his gaze. Her mother looked at him out of wide, frightened eyes and her arms tightened around the girl in her arms.

Despite everything, his most important job was calming her fears. "Mrs. Pendleton, you'll be happy to know the fire is under control."

"Of course it's under control." Laura finally faced him, her lovely features cool and impassive. "It was under control before your trucks ever showed up—ten minutes after we called the fire in, by the way."

Despite all the things he might have wanted to say to her, he had to first bristle at any implication that their response time might be less than adequate. "Seven, by my calculations. Would have been half that except we were in the middle of water rescue training when the call from dispatch came in."

"I guess you would have been ready, then, if any of our guests had decided to jump into Cold Creek to avoid the flames."

Funny, he didn't remember her being this tart when they had been engaged. He remembered sweetness and joy and light. Until he had destroyed all that.

"Chief Bowman, when will we be able to allow our guests to return to their rooms?" Jan Pendleton spoke up, her voice wobbling a little. The little girl in her arms—who shared Laura's eye color, he realized now, along with the distinctive features of someone born with Down syndrome—patted her cheek.

"Gram, don't cry."

Jan visibly collected herself and gave the girl a tired smile.

"They can return to get their belongings as long as they're not staying in the rooms adjacent to where the fire started. I'll have my guys stick around about an hour or so to keep an eye on some hot spots." He paused, wishing he didn't have to be the bearer of this particular bad news. "I'm going to leave the final decision up to you about your guests staying here overnight, but to be honest, I'm not sure it's completely safe for guests to stay here tonight. No matter how careful we are, sometimes embers can flare up again hours later."

"We have a dozen guests right now." Laura looked at him directly and he was almost sure he saw a hint of hostility there. Annoyance crawled under his skin. *She* dumped him, a week before their wedding. If anybody here had the right to be hostile, he ought to be the first one in line. "What are we supposed to do with them?"

Their past didn't matter right now, not when people in his town needed his help. "We can talk to the Red Cross about setting up a shelter, or we can check with some of the other lodgings in town, maybe the Cavazos' guest cabins, and see if they might have room to take a few."

Mrs. Pendleton closed her eyes. "This is a disaster."

"But a fixable one, Mom. We'll figure something out." She squeezed her mother's arm.

"Any idea what might have started the fire?" He had to ask.

Laura frowned and something that looked oddly like guilt shifted across her lovely features. "Not the *what* exactly, but most likely the *who*."

"Oh?"

"Alexandro Santiago. Come here, young man."

He followed her gaze and for the first time, he noticed a young dark-haired boy of about six or seven sitting on the curb, watching the activity at the scene with a sort of avid fascination in his huge dark brown eyes. The boy didn't have her blond, blue-eyed coloring, but he shared her wide, mobile mouth, slender nose and high cheekbones, and was undoubtedly her child.

The kid didn't budge from the curb for a long, drawn-out moment, but he finally rose slowly to his feet and headed toward them as if he were on his way to bury his dog in the backyard.

"Alex, tell the fireman what started the fire."

The boy shifted his stance, avoiding the gazes of both his mother and Taft. "Do I have to?"

"Yes," Laura said sternly.

The kid fidgeted a little more and finally sighed. "Okay. I found a lighter in one of the empty rooms. The ones being fixed up." He spoke with a very slight, barely discernible accent. "I never saw one before and I only wanted to see how it worked. I didn't mean to start a fire, *es la verdad*. But the curtains caught fire and I yelled and then *mi madre* came in with the fire extinguisher."

Under other circumstances he might have been amused at the no-nonsense way the kid told the story and how he manipulated events to make it seem as if everything had just sort of happened without any direct involvement on his part.

But this could have been a potentially serious situation, a crumbling old fire hazard like the inn.

He hated to come off hard-nosed and mean, but he had to make the kid understand the gravity. Education was a huge part of his job and a responsibility he took very seriously. "That was a very dangerous thing to do. People could have been seriously hurt. If your mother hadn't been able to get to the room fast enough with the fire extinguisher, the flames could have spread from room to room and burned down the whole hotel and everything in it."

To his credit, the boy met his gaze. Embarrassment and shame warred on his features. "I know. It was stupid. I'm really, really sorry."

"The worst part of it is, I have told you again and again not to play with matches or lighters or anything else that can cause a fire. We've talked about the dangers." Laura glowered at her son, who squirmed.

"I just wanted to see how it worked," he said, his voice small.

"You won't do it again, will you?" Taft said.

"Never. Never, ever."

"Good, because we're pretty strict about this kind of thing around here. Next time you'll have to go to jail."

The boy gave him a wide-eyed look, but then sighed with relief when he noticed Taft's half grin. "I won't do it again, I swear. Pinky promise."

"Excellent."

"Hey, Chief," Lee Randall called from the engine. "We're having a little trouble with the hose retractor again. Can you give us a hand?"

"Yeah. Be there in a sec," he called back, grateful for any excuse to escape the awkwardness of seeing her again.

"Excuse me, won't you?" he said to the Pendleton women and the children.

"Of course." Jan Pendleton gave him an earnest look. "Please tell your firefighters how very much we appreciate them, don't we, Laura?"

"Absolutely," she answered with a dutiful tone, but he noticed she pointedly avoided meeting his gaze.

"Bye, Chief." The darling little girl in Jan's arm gave him a generous smile. Oh, she was a charmer, he thought.

"See you later."

The girl beamed at him and waved as he headed away, feeling as if somebody had wrapped a fire hose around his neck for the past ten minutes.

She was here. Really here. Blue eyes, cute kids and all.

Laura Pendleton, Santiago now. He had loved her with

every bit of his young heart and she had walked away from him without a second glance.

Now she was here and he had no way to avoid her, not living in a small town like Pine Gulch that had only one grocery store, a couple of gas stations and a fire station only a few blocks from her family's hotel.

He was swamped with memories suddenly, memories he didn't want and didn't know what to do with.

She was back. And here he had been thinking lately how lucky he was to be fire chief of a small town with only six thousand people that rarely saw any disasters.

Taft Bowman.

Laura watched him head back into the action—which, really, wasn't much action at all, given that the fire had been extinguished before any of them arrived. He paused here and there in the parking lot to talk to his crew, snap out orders, adjust some kind of mechanical thing on the sleek red fire truck.

Seeing him in action was nothing new. When they had been dating, she sometimes went on ride-alongs, mostly because she couldn't bear to be separated from him. She remembered now how Taft had always seemed comfortable and in control of any situation, whether responding to a medical emergency or dealing with a grass fire.

Apparently that hadn't changed in the decade since she had seen him. He also still had that very sexy, lean-hipped walk, even under the layers of turnout gear. She watched him for just a moment, then forced herself to look away. This little tingle of remembered desire inside her was wrong on so many levels, completely twisted and messed up.

After all these years and all the pain, all those shards of crushed dreams she finally had to sweep up and throw away, how could he still have the power to affect her at all? She should be cool and impervious to him, completely untouched.

When she finally made the decision to come home after Javier's death, she had known she would inevitably run into Taft. Pine Gulch was a small town after all. No matter how much a person might wish to, it was generally tough to avoid someone forever.

When she thought about it—and she would be lying to herself if she said she *hadn't* thought about it—she had foolishly imagined she could greet him with only a polite smile and a *Nice to see you again,* remaining completely impervious to the man.

Their shared history was a long time ago. Another lifetime, it seemed. She had made the only possible choice back then and had completely moved on with her life, had married someone else, given birth to two children and put Pine Gulch far in her past.

As much as she had loved him once, Taft was really just a small chapter in her life. Or so she told herself anyway. She had been naively certain she had dealt with the hurt and betrayal and the deep sense of loss long ago.

Maybe she should have put a little more energy and effort into making certain of all that before she packed up her children and moved thousands of miles from the only home they had ever known.

If she'd had a little energy to spare, she might have given it more thought, but the past six months seemed like a whirlwind, first trying to deal with Javier's estate and the vast debts he had left behind, then that desperate scramble to juggle her dwindling bank account and two hungry children in expensive Madrid, and finally the grim realization that she couldn't do it by herself and had no choice but to move her little family across the world and back to her mother.

She had been focused on survival, on doing what she thought was right for her children. She supposed she really hadn't wanted to face the reality that moving back also meant dealing with Taft again—until it smacked her upside the head, thanks to her rascal of a son and his predilection for finding trouble wherever he could.

"What are we going to do?" Her mother fretted beside her. She set Maya down on the concrete sidewalk, and the girl immediately scampered beside Alex and stood holding her brother's hand while they watched the firefighters now cleaning up the scene and driving away. "This is going to ruin us!"

Laura put an arm around her mother's plump shoulders, guilt slicing through her. She should have been watching her son more carefully; she certainly knew better than to give him any free rein. She had allowed herself to become distracted checking in some guests—the young married couple on spring break from graduate school in Washington who had found more excitement than they had probably anticipated when their hotel caught fire before they had even seen their room.

While she was busy with them, Alex must have slipped out of the office and wandered to the wing of the hotel they were currently renovating. She still couldn't believe he had found a lighter somewhere. Maybe a previous guest had left it or one of the subcontractors who had been coming in and out the past week or so.

It really *was* a miracle her son hadn't been injured or burned the whole place down.

"You heard Chief Bowman. The fire and smoke damage was contained to only one room, so that's good news."

"How is any of this good news?" In the flash of the emergency vehicles as they pulled away, her mother's features looked older somehow and her hands shook as she pushed a stray lock of carefully colored hair away.

Despite Taft and all the memories that had suddenly been dredged up simply by exchanging a few words with the man, she didn't regret coming back to Pine Gulch. The irony was, she thought she was coming home because she needed her mother's help only to discover how very much Jan needed hers.

Care and upkeep on this crumbling twenty-room inn were obviously wearing on her mother. Jan had been deeply grateful to turn some of those responsibilities over to her only daughter.

"It could be much worse, Mom. We have to focus on that. No one was hurt. That's the important thing. And outdated as it is, the sprinkler system worked better than we might have expected. That's another plus. Besides, look at it this way—now insurance will cover some of the repairs we already planned."

"I suppose. But what are we going to do with the guests?" Her mother seemed defeated, overwhelmed, all but wringing her hands.

Laura hugged her again. "Don't worry about anything. In fact, why don't you take the children back to the house? I think they've had enough excitement for one afternoon."

"Do you think Chief Bowman will consider it safe?"

Laura glanced over at the three-bedroom cottage behind the inn where she had spent her childhood. "It's far enough from the action. I can't see why it would be a problem. Meantime, I'll start making phone calls. We'll find places for everyone and for our reservations for the next few nights while the smoke damage clears out. We'll get through this just like everything else."

"I'm so glad you're here, my dear. I don't know what I would do without you."

If she *hadn't* been here—along with her daughter and her little firebug of a son—none of this would have happened.

"So am I, Mom," she answered. It was the truth, despite having to confront a certain very sexy fire chief with whom she shared a tangled history.

"Oh, I should go talk to poor Mr. Baktiri. He probably doesn't quite understand what's going on."

One of their long-term guests stood in the middle of the lawn, looking at the hectic scene with confusion. She remembered Mr. Baktiri from when she was a girl. He and his wife used to run the drive-in on the outskirts of town. Mrs. Baktiri had passed away and Mr. Baktiri had moved with his son to Idaho Falls, but he apparently hated it there. Once a month or so, he would escape back to Pine Gulch to visit his wife's graveside.

Her mother gave him substantially reduced rates on their smallest room, where he stayed for a week or two at a time until his son would come down from Idaho Falls to take him back home. It wasn't a very economically feasible operating procedure, but she couldn't fault her mother for her kindness.

She had the impression Mr. Baktiri might be suffering from mild dementia and she supposed familiar surroundings were a comfort to him.

"Mommy. Lights." Maya hugged her legs and looked up, the flashing emergency lights reflecting in her thick glasses.

"I know, sweetie. They're bright, aren't they?"

"Pretty."

"I suppose they are, in a way."

Trust Maya to find joy in any situation. It was her child's particular skill and she was deeply grateful for it.

She had a million things to do, most pressing to find somewhere for their guests to spend the night, but for now she gathered this precious child in her arms.

Out of the corner of her gaze, she saw Alex edge toward them somewhat warily.

"Come here, *niño,*" she murmured.

He sank into her embrace and she held both children close. This was the important thing. As she had told her mother, they would get through this minor setback. She was a survivor. She had survived a broken heart and broken engagement and then a disaster of a marriage.

She could get through a little thing like a minor fire with no problem.

Chapter 2

"Guess who I saw in town the other day."

Taft grabbed one of his sister's delicious dinner rolls from the basket being passed around his family's dining-room table and winked at Caidy. "Me, doing something awesome and heroic, probably. Fighting a fire. Saving someone's life. I don't know. Could be anything."

His niece, Destry, and Gabrielle Parsons, whose older sister was marrying Taft's twin brother, Trace, in a few months, both giggled—just as he had intended—but Caidy only rolled her eyes. "News flash. Not everything is about you, Taft. But oddly, in a way, this is."

"Who did you see?" he asked, though he was aware of a glimmer of uneasy trepidation, already expecting what was coming next.

"I didn't have a chance to talk to her. I just happened to see her while I was driving," Caidy said.

"Who?" he asked again, teetering on the brink of annoyance.

"Laura Pendleton," Caidy announced.

"Not Pendleton anymore," Ridge, their older brother and Destry's father, corrected.

"That's right," Trace chimed in from the other side of the table, where he was holding hands with Becca. How the heck did they manage to eat when they couldn't seem to keep their hands off each other? Taft wondered.

"She got married to some guy while she was living in Spain and they had a couple of kids," Trace went on. "I hear one of them was involved in all the excitement the other day at the inn."

Taft pictured her kid solemnly promising he wouldn't play with matches again. He'd picked up the definite vibe that the kid was a mischievous little rascal, but for all that, his sincerity had rung true.

"Yeah. Apparently her older kid, Alex, was a little too curious about a lighter he found in an empty room and caught some curtains on fire."

"And you had to ride to her rescue?" Caidy gave him a wide-eyed look. "Gosh, that must have been awkward for both of you."

Taft reached for more mashed potatoes, hoping the heat on his face could be attributed to the steaming bowl.

"Why would it be? Everything was fine," he muttered.

Okay, that was a lie, but his family didn't necessarily need to know he hadn't been able to stop thinking about Laura for the past few days. Every time he had a quiet moment, her blue eyes and delicate features would pop into his head and some other half-forgotten memory of their time together would emerge like the Tetons rising out of a low fog bank.

That he couldn't seem to stop them annoyed him. He had worked damn hard to forget her after she walked away. What was he supposed to do now that she was back in town and he couldn't escape her or her kids or the weight of all his mistakes?

"You'll have to catch me up here." Becca, Trace's fiancée, looked confused as she reached for her glass. "Who's Laura Pendleton? I'm taking a wild guess here that she must be related to Mrs. Pendleton at the inn somehow—a client of mine, by the way—but why would it be awkward to have Taft put out a fire at the inn?"

"No reason really." Caidy flashed him a quick look. "Just that Taft and Laura were engaged once."

He fidgeted with his mashed potatoes, drawing his fork in a neat little firebreak to keep the gravy from spreading while he avoided the collective gaze of his beloved family. Why, again, had he once enjoyed these Sunday dinners?

"Engaged? Taft?" He didn't need to look at his future sister-in-law to hear the surprise in her voice.

"I know," his twin brother said. "Hard to believe, right?"

He looked up just in time to see Becca quickly try to hide her shocked gaze. She was too kindhearted to let him see how stunning she found the news, which somehow bothered him even more.

Okay, maybe he had a bit of a reputation in town—most of it greatly exaggerated—as a bit of a player. Becca knew him by now. She should know how silly it all was.

"When was this?" she asked with interest. "Recently?"

"Years ago," Ridge said. "He and Laura dated just out of high school—"

"College," he muttered. "She was in college." Okay, she had been a freshman in college. But she wasn't in high school, damn it. That point seemed important somehow.

"They were inseparable," Trace interjected.

Ridge picked up where he'd left off. "And Taft proposed right around the time Laura graduated from the Montana State."

"What happened?" Becca asked.

He really didn't want to talk about this. What he wouldn't give for a good emergency call right now. Nothing big. No serious personal injury or major property damage. How about a shed fire or a kid stuck in a well or something?

"We called things off."

"The week before the wedding," Caidy added.

Oh, yes. Don't forget to add that little salacious detail.

"It was a mutual decision," he lied, repeating the blatant fiction that Laura had begged him to uphold. Mutual decision. Right. If by *mutual* he meant *Laura* and if by *decision* he meant *crush-the-life-out-of-a-guy blow.*

Laura had dumped him. That was the cold, hard truth. A week before their wedding, after all the plans and deposits and dress fittings, she had given him back his ring and told him she couldn't marry him.

"Why are we talking about ancient history?" he asked.

"Not so ancient anymore," Trace said. "Not if Laura's back in town."

He was very much afraid his brother was right. Whether he liked it or not, with her once more residing in Pine Gulch, their past together would be dredged up again—and not by just his family.

Questions would swirl around them. Everybody had to remember that they had been just a few days away from walking down the aisle of the little church in town when things ended and Laura and her mother sent out those regrets and made phone calls announcing the big celebration wasn't happening—while he had gone down to the Bandito and gotten drunk and stayed that way until about a month or two after the wedding day that didn't happen.

She was back now, which meant that, like it or not, he would have to deal with everything he had shoved down ten years ago, all the emotions he had pretended weren't important in order to get through the deep, aching loss of her.

He couldn't blame his family for their curiosity—not even Trace, his twin and best friend, knew the full story about everything that had happened between him and Laura. He had always considered it his private business.

His family had loved her. Who didn't? Laura had a knack for drawing people toward her, finding commonalities. She and his mother used to love discussing the art world and painting techniques. His mother had been an artist, only becoming renowned around the time of her murder. While Laura hadn't any particular skill in that direction, she had shared a genuine appreciation for his parents' extensive art collection.

His father had adored her, too, and had often told Taft that Laura was the best thing that would ever happen to him.

He looked up from the memory to find Becca's eyes filled with a compassion that made him squirm and lose whatever appetite he might have had left.

"I'm sorry," she murmured in that kind way she had. "Mutual decision or not, it still must have been painful. Is it hard for you to see her again?"

He faked a nonchalant look. "Hard? Why would it be hard? It was all a decade ago. She's moved on. I've moved on. No big deal."

Ridge gave what sounded like a fake cough and Trace had the same skeptical expression on his face he always wore when Taft was trying to talk him into living a little, doing something wild and adventurous for a change.

How was it possible to love his siblings and at the same time want to throw a few punches around the table, just on general principles?

Becca eyed him and then his brothers warily as if sensing his discomfort, then she quickly changed the subject. "How's the house coming?" she asked.

His brother wasn't nearly good enough for her, he decided, seizing the diversion. "Good. I've got only a couple more rooms to drywall. Should be done soon. After six months, the place is starting to look like a real house inside now."

"I stopped by the other day and peeked in the windows," Caidy confessed. "It's looking great."

"Give me a call next time and I can swing by and give you the tour, even if I'm at the fire station. You haven't been by in a month or so. You'll be surprised at how far along it is these days."

After years of renting a convenient but small apartment near the fire station, he had finally decided it was time to build a real house. The two-story log house was set on five acres near the mouth of Cold Creek Canyon.

"How about the barn and the pasture?" Ridge asked, rather predictably. Over the years, Taft had bred a couple mares to a stallion with excellent lines he had picked up for a steal from a rancher down on his luck up near Wood River. He had traded and sold the colts until he now had about six horses he'd been keeping at his family's ranch.

"The fence is in. I'd like to get the barn up before I move the horses over, if you don't mind keeping them a little longer."

"That's not what I meant. You know we've got plenty of room here. You can keep them here forever if you want."

Maybe if he had his horses closer he might actually ride them once in a while instead of only stopping by to visit when he came for these Sunday dinners.

"When do you think all the work will be done?" Becca asked.

"I'm hoping by mid-May. Depends on how much free time I can find to finish things up inside."

"If you need a hand, let me know," Ridge offered quietly.

"Same goes," Trace added.

Both of them had crazy-busy lives: Ridge running the ranch and raising Destry on his own and Trace as the over-worked chief of police for an understaffed small-town force—in addition to planning his future together with Becca and Gabi. Their sincere offers to help touched him.

"I should be okay," he answered. "The hard work is done now and I only have the fun stuff to finish."

"I always thought there was something just a little crazy about you." Caidy shook her head. "I must be right, especially if you think finish work and painting are fun."

"I like to paint stuff," Destry said. "I can help you, Uncle Taft."

"Me, too!" Gabrielle exclaimed. "Oh, can we?"

Trouble followed the two of these girls around like one of Caidy's rescue dogs. He had visions of paint spread all over the woodwork he had been slaving over the past month. "Thanks, girls. That's really sweet of you. I'm sure Ridge can find something for you to touch up around here. That fence down by the creek was looking like it needed a new coat."

"There's always something that needs painting around here," Ridge answered. "As soon as the weather warms up a little at night, I can put you both to work."

"Will you pay us?" Gabrielle asked, always the opportunist.

Ridge chuckled. "We can negotiate terms with your attorney."

Caidy asked Becca—said attorney—a question about their upcoming June wedding and attention shifted away from Taft, much to his relief. He listened to the conversation of his family, aware of this low simmer of restlessness that had become a familiar companion.

Ever since Trace and Becca found each other and fell in love, he had been filled with this vague unease, as if something about his world had shifted a little. He loved his brother. More than that, he respected him. Trace was his best friend and Taft could never begrudge him the happiness he had found with Becca and Gabi, but ever since they announced their engagement, he felt weird and more than a little off-balance.

Seeing Laura and her kids the other day had only intensified that odd feeling.

He had never been a saint—he would be the first to admit that and his family would probably stand in line right behind him—but he tried to live a decent life. His general philosophy about the world ran parallel to the premier motto of every emergency medical worker as well as others in the medical field: Primum Non Nocere. First, Do No Harm.

He did his best. He was a firefighter and paramedic and he enjoyed helping people of his community and protecting property. If he didn't find great satisfaction in it, he would find something else to do. Maybe pounding nails for a living because he enjoyed that, too.

Despite his best efforts in the whole *do no harm* arena, he remembered each and every failure.

He had two big regrets in his life, and Laura Pendleton was involved in both of them.

He had hurt her. Those months leading up to her ultimate decision to break things off had been filled with one wound after another. He knew it. Hell, he had known it at the time, but that dark, angry man he had become after his parents' murder seemed like another creature who had emerged out of his skin to destroy everything good and right in his life.

He couldn't blame Laura for calling off their wedding. Not really. Even though it had hurt like the devil.

She had warned him she couldn't marry him unless he made serious changes, and he had stubbornly refused, giving her no choice but to stay true to her word. She had moved on, taken some exotic job in hotel management in Spain somewhere and a few years later married a man she met there.

The reminder of her marriage left him feeling petty and small. Yeah, he had hurt her, but his betrayal probably didn't hold a candle to everything else she had lost—her husband and the father of her children, whom he'd heard had drowned about six months earlier.

"Are you planning on eating any of that or just pushing it around your plate?"

He glanced up and, much to his shock, discovered Ridge was the only one left at the table. Everybody else had cleared off while he had been lost in thought, and he hadn't even noticed.

"Sorry. Been a long couple of days." He hoped his brother didn't notice the heat he could feel crawling over his features.

Ridge gave him a long look and Taft sighed, waiting for the inevitable words of advice from his brother.

As the oldest Bowman sibling left after their parents

died, Ridge had taken custody of Caidy, who had been a teenager at the time. Even though Taft and Trace had both been in their early twenties, Ridge still tried to take over the role of father figure to them, too, whether they liked it or not—which they usually didn't.

Instead of a lecture, Ridge only sipped at his drink. "I was thinking about taking the girls for a ride up to check the fence line on the high pasture. Want to come along? A little mountain air might help clear your head."

He did love being on the back of a horse amid the pine and sage of the mountains overlooking the ranch, but he wasn't in the mood for more questions or sympathy from his family about Laura.

"To tell you the truth, I'm itching to get my hands dirty. I think I'll head over to the house and put in a window frame or something."

Ridge nodded. "I know you've got plenty to do on your own place, but I figured this was worth mentioning, too. I heard the other day at the hardware store that Jan Pendleton is looking to hire somebody to help her with some renovations to the inn."

He snorted. As if Laura would ever let her mother hire him. He figured Ridge was joking but he didn't see any hint of humor in his brother's expression.

"Just saying. I thought you might be interested in helping Laura and her mother out a little."

Ah. Without actually offering a lecture, this must be Ridge's way of reminding Taft he owed Laura something. None of the rest of the family knew what had happened all those years ago, but he was pretty sure all of them blamed him.

And they were right.

Without answering, he shoved away from the table and

grabbed his plate to carry it into the kitchen. First, do no harm. But once the harm had been done, a stand-up guy found some way to make it right. No matter how difficult.

Chapter 3

Laura stared at her mother, shock buzzing through her as if she had just bent down and licked an electrical outlet.

"Sorry, say that again. You did *what?*"

"I didn't think you'd mind, darling," her mother said, with a vague sort of smile as she continued stirring the chicken she was cooking for their dinner.

Are you completely mental? she wanted to yell. *How could you possibly think I wouldn't mind?*

She drew a deep, cleansing breath, clamping down on the words she wanted to blurt out. The children were, for once, staying out of trouble, driving cars around the floor of the living room and she watched them interact for a moment to calm herself.

Her mother was under a great deal of strain right now, financially and otherwise. She had to keep that in mind—not that stress alone could explain her mother making such an incomprehensible decision.

"Really, it was all your idea," Jan said calmly.

"*My* idea?" Impossible. Even in her most tangled nightmare, she never would have come up with this possible scenario.

"Yes. Weren't you just saying the other day how much it would help to have a carpenter on the staff to help with the repairs, especially now that we totally have to start from the ground up in the fire-damaged room?"

"I say a lot of things, Mom." *That doesn't mean I want you to rush out and enter into a deal with a particular devil named Taft Bowman.*

"I just thought you would appreciate the help, that's all. I know how much the fire has complicated your timeline for the renovation."

"Not really. Only one room was damaged and it was already on my schedule for renovations."

"Well, when Chief Bowman stopped by this morning to check on things after the excitement we had the other day—which I thought was a perfectly lovely gesture, by the way—he mentioned he could lend us a hand with any repairs in his free time. Honestly, darling, it seemed like the perfect solution."

Really? Having her daughter's ex-fiancé take an empty room at the inn for the next two weeks in exchange for a little skill with a miter saw was *perfect* in what possible alternative universe?

Her mother was as sharp as the proverbial tack. Jan Pendleton had been running the inn on her own since Laura's father died five years ago. While she didn't always agree with her mother's methods and might have run things differently if she had been home, Laura knew Jan had tried hard to keep the inn functioning all those years she had been living in Madrid.

But she still couldn't wrap her head around this one. "In theory, it is a good idea. A resident carpenter would come in very handy. But not Taft, for heaven's sake, Mom!"

Jan frowned in what appeared to be genuine confusion. "You mean because of your history together?"

"For a start. Seeing him again after all these years is more than a little awkward," she admitted.

Her mother continued to frown. "I'm sorry but I don't understand. What am I missing? You always insisted your breakup was a mutual decision. I distinctly remember you telling me over and over again you had both decided you were better off as friends."

Had she said that? She didn't remember much about that dark time other than her deep despair.

"You were so cool and calm after your engagement ended, making all those terrible phone calls, returning all those wedding presents. You acted like you didn't care at all. Honey, I honestly thought you wouldn't mind having Taft here now or I never would have taken him up on his suggestion."

Ah. Her lying little chickens were now coming home to roost. Laura fought the urge to bang her head on the old pine kitchen table a few dozen times.

Ten years ago, she had worked so hard to convince everyone involved that nobody's heart had been shattered by the implosion of their engagement. To her parents, she had put on a bright, happy face and pretended to be excited about the adventures awaiting her, knowing how crushed they would have been if they caught even a tiny glimmer of the truth—that inside her heart felt like a vast, empty wasteland.

How could she blame her mother for not seeing through her carefully constructed act to the stark and painful reality, especially when only a few years later, Laura was married to someone else and expecting Jan's first grandchild? It was unfair to be hurt, to wish Jan had somehow glimpsed the depth of her hidden heartache.

This, then, was her own fault. Well, hers and a certain opportunistic male who had always been very good at charming her mother—and every other female within a dozen miles of Pine Gulch.

"Okay, the carpentry work. I get that. Yes, we certainly need the help and Taft is very good with his hands." She refused to remember just *how* good those hands could be. "But did you have to offer him a room?"

Jan shrugged, adding a lemony sauce to the chicken that instantly started to burble, filling the kitchen with a delicious aroma. "That was his idea."

Oh, Laura was quite sure it *was* Taft's idea. The bigger question was *why?* What possible reason could he have for this sudden wish to stay at the inn? By the stunned look he had worn when he spotted her at the fire scene, she would have assumed he wanted to stay as far away from her as possible.

He had to find this whole situation as awkward and, yes, painful as she did.

Maybe it was all some twisted revenge plot. She had spurned him after all. Maybe he wanted to somehow punish her all these years later with shoddy carpentry work that would end up costing an arm and a leg to repair....

She sighed at her own ridiculous imaginings. Taft didn't work that way. Whatever his motive for making this arrangement with her mother, she had no doubt he would put his best effort into the job.

"Apparently his lease was up on the apartment where he's been living," Jan went on. "He's building a house in

Cold Creek Canyon—which I've heard is perfectly lovely, by the way—but it won't be finished for a few more weeks. Think of how much you can save on paying for a carpenter, all in exchange only for letting him stay in a room that was likely to be empty anyway, the way our vacancy rate will be during the shoulder season until the summer tourist activity heats up. I honestly thought you would be happy about this. When Taft suggested it, the whole thing seemed like a good solution all the way around."

A good solution for everyone except *her!* How would she survive having him underfoot all the time, smiling at her out of those green eyes she had once adored so much, talking to her out of that delicious mouth she had tasted so many times?

She gave a tiny sigh and her mother sent her a careful look. "I can still tell him no. He was planning on bringing some of his things over in the morning, but I'll just give him a ring and tell him never mind. We can find someone else, honey, if having Taft here will make you too uncomfortable."

Her mother was completely sincere, she knew. Jan would call him in immediately if she had any idea how much Laura had grieved for the dreams they had once spun together.

For an instant, she was tempted to have her mother do exactly that, call and tell him the deal was off.

How could she, though? She knew just what Taft would think. He would guess, quite accurately, that she was the one who didn't want him here and would know she had dissuaded her mother from the plan.

Her shoulder blades itched at the thought. She didn't want him thinking she was uncomfortable having him around. Better that he continue to believe she was completely indifferent to the ramifications of being back in Pine Gulch with him.

She had done her very best to strike the proper tone the day of the fire, polite but cool, as if they were distant acquaintances instead of once having shared everything.

If she told her mother she didn't want to have Taft here, he would know her demeanor was all an act.

She was trapped. Well and truly trussed, just like one of the calves he used to rope in the high-school rodeo. It was a helpless, miserable feeling, one that felt all too familiar. She had lived with it every day of the past seven years, since her marriage to Javier Santiago. But unlike those calves in the rodeo ring, she had wandered willingly into the ropes that bound her to a man she didn't love.

Well, she hadn't been completely willing, she supposed. From the beginning she had known marrying him was a mistake and had tried every way she could think short of jilting him also to escape the ties binding them together. But unlike with Taft, this time she'd had a third life to consider. She had been four months pregnant with Alexandro. Javier—strangely old-fashioned about this, at least—wouldn't consider any other option but marriage.

She had tried hard to convince herself she was in love with him. He was handsome and seductively charming and made her laugh with his extravagant pursuit of her, which had been the reason she had finally given in and begun to date him while she was working at the small, exclusive boutique hotel he owned in Madrid.

She had tried to be a good wife and had worked hard to convince herself she loved him, but it hadn't been enough. Not for him and not for her—but by then she had been thoroughly entangled in the piggin' rope, so to speak, by

Alex and then by Maya, her sweet-natured and vulnerable daughter.

This, though, with Taft. She couldn't control what her mother had done, but she could certainly control her own response to it. She wouldn't allow herself to care if the man had suddenly invaded every inch of her personal space by moving into the hotel. It was only temporary and then he would be out of her life again.

"Do you want me to call him?" her mother asked again.

She forced herself to smile. "Not at all, Mama. I'm sorry. I was just…surprised, that's all. Everything should be fine. You're right—it's probably a great idea. Free labor is always a good thing, and like you said, the only thing we're giving up is a room that probably wouldn't have been booked anyway."

Maya wandered into the kitchen, apparently tired of playing, and gave her mother one of those generous hugs Laura had come to depend upon like oxygen and water. "Hungry, Mama."

"Gram is fixing us something delicious for dinner. Aren't we lucky to have her?"

Maya nodded with a broad smile to her grandmother. "Love you, Gram."

"I love you, too, sweetheart." Jan beamed back at her.

This—her daughter and Alex—was more important than her discomfort about Taft. She was trying her best to turn the hotel into something that could actually turn a profit instead of just provide a subsistence for her mother and now her and her children.

She had her chance to live her lifelong dream now and make the Cold Creek Inn into the warm and gracious facility she had always imagined, a place where families could feel comfortable to gather, where couples could find or rekindle romance, where the occasional business traveler could find a home away from home.

This was her moment to seize control of her life and make a new future for herself and her children. She couldn't let Taft ruin that for her.

All she had to do was remind herself that she hadn't loved him for ten years and she should be able to handle his presence here at the inn with calm aplomb.

No big deal whatsoever. Right?

If some part of him had hoped Laura might fall all over him with gratitude for stepping up to help with the inn renovations, Taft would have been doomed to disappointment.

Over the next few days, as he settled into his surprisingly comfortable room in the wing overlooking the creek, a few doors down from the fire-damaged room, he helped Mrs. Pendleton with the occasional carpentry job. A bathroom cabinet repair here, a countertop fix there. In that time, he barely saw Laura. Somehow she was always mysteriously absent whenever he stopped at the front desk.

The few times he did come close enough to talk to her, she would exchange a quick, stiff word with him and then manufacture some excuse to take off at the earliest opportunity, as if she didn't want to risk some kind of contagion.

She had dumped *him,* not the other way around, but she was acting as if he was the biggest heel in the county. Still, he found her prickly, standoffish attitude more a challenge than an annoyance.

Truth was, he wasn't used to women ignoring him—and he certainly wasn't accustomed to *Laura* ignoring him.

They had been friends forever, even before that momentous summer after her freshman year of college when he finally woke up and realized how much he had come to care about her as much more than simply a friend. After she left, he had missed the woman he loved with a hollow ache he had never quite been able to fill, but he sometimes thought he missed his best friend just as much.

After three nights at the hotel with these frustrating, fleeting encounters, he was finally able to run her to ground early one morning. He had an early meeting at the fire station, and when he walked out of the side entrance near where he parked the vehicle he drove as fire chief—which was as much a mobile office as a mode of transportation— he spotted someone working in the scraggly flower beds that surrounded the inn.

The beds were mostly just a few tulips and some stubbly, rough-looking shrubs but it looked as if somebody was trying to make it more. Several flats of colorful blooms had been spaced with careful efficiency along the curvy sidewalk, ready to be transplanted into the flower beds.

At first, he assumed the gardener under the straw hat was someone from a landscaping service until he caught a glimpse of honey-blond hair.

He instantly switched direction. "Good morning," he called as he approached. She jumped and whirled around. When she spotted him, her instinctive look of surprise twisted into something that looked like dismay before she tucked it away and instead gave him a polite, impersonal smile.

"Oh. Hello."

If it didn't sting somewhere deep inside, he might have been amused at her cool tone.

"You do remember this is eastern Idaho, not Madrid, right? It's only April. We could have snow for another six weeks yet, easy."

"I remember," she answered stiffly. "These are all hardy early bloomers. They should be fine."

What he knew about gardening was, well, *nothing,* except how much he used to hate it when his mom would wake him and his brothers and Caidy up early to go out and weed her vegetable patch on summer mornings.

"If you say so. I would just hate to see you spend all this money on flowers and then wake up one morning to find a hard freeze has wiped them out overnight."

"I appreciate your concern for my wallet, but I've learned in thirty-one years on the earth that if you want to beautify the world around you a little bit, sometimes you have to take a few risks."

He could appreciate the wisdom in that, whether he was a gardener or not.

"I'm only working on the east-and south-facing beds for now, where there's less chance of frost kill. I might have been gone a few years, but I haven't quite forgotten the capricious weather we can see here in the Rockies."

What *had* she forgotten? She didn't seem to have too many warm memories of their time together, not if she could continue treating him with this annoyingly polite indifference.

He knew he needed to be heading to the station house for his meeting, but he couldn't resist lingering a moment with her to see if he could poke and prod more of a reaction out of her than this.

He looked around and had to point out the obvious. "No kids with you this morning?"

"They're inside fixing breakfast with my mother." She gestured to the small Craftsman-style cottage behind the inn where she had been raised. "I figured this was a good time to get something done before they come outside and my time will be spent trying to keep Alex from deciding he could dig a hole to China in the garden and Maya from picking every one of the pretty flowers."

He couldn't help smiling. Her kids were pretty darn cute—besides that, there was something so *right* about standing here with her while the morning sunlight glimmered in her hair and the cottonwood trees along the river sent out a few exploratory puffs on the sweet-smelling breeze.

"They're adorable kids."

She gave him a sidelong glance as if trying to gauge his sincerity. "When they're not starting fires, you mean?"

He laughed. "I'm going on the assumption that that was a fluke."

There. He saw it. The edges of her mouth quirked up and she almost smiled, but she turned her face away and he missed it.

He still considered it a huge victory. He always used to love making her smile.

Something stirred inside him as he watched her pick up a cheerful yellow flower and set it in the small hole she had just dug. Attraction, yes. Most definitely. He had forgotten how much he liked the way she looked, fresh and bright and as pretty as those flowers. Somehow he had also forgotten over the years that air of quiet grace and sweetness.

She was just as lovely as ever. No, that wasn't quite true. She was even more beautiful than she had been a decade ago. While he wasn't so sure how life in general had treated her, the years had been physically kind to her. With those big eyes and her high cheekbones and that silky hair he used to love burying his hands in, she was still beautiful. Actually, when he considered it, her beauty had more depth now than it did when she had been a young woman, and he found it even more appealing.

Yeah, he was every bit as attracted to her as he'd been in those days when thoughts of her had consumed him like the wildfires he used to fight every summer. But he'd been attracted to plenty of women in the past decade. What he felt right now, standing in the morning sunshine with Laura, ran much more deeply through him.

Unsettled and more than a little rattled by the sudden hot ache in his gut, he took the coward's way out and opted for the one topic he knew she wouldn't want to discuss. "What happened to the kids' father?"

She dumped a trowel full of dirt on the seedling with enough force to make him wince. "Remind me again why that's any of your business," she bit out.

"It's not. Only idle curiosity. You married him just a few years after you were going to marry me. You can't blame me for wondering about him."

She raised an eyebrow as if she didn't agree with that particular statement. "I'm sure you've heard the gory details," she answered, her voice terse. "Javier died six months ago. A boating accident off the coast of Barcelona. He and his mistress du jour were both killed. It was a great tragedy for everyone concerned."

Ah, hell. He knew her husband had died, but he hadn't heard the rest of it. He doubted anyone else in Pine Gulch had or the rumor would have certainly slithered its way toward him, given their history together.

She studiously refused to look at him. He knew her well enough to be certain she regretted saying anything and he couldn't help wondering why she had.

He also couldn't think of a proper response. How much pain did those simple words conceal?

"I'm sorry," he finally said, although it sounded lame and trite.

"About what? His death or the mistress?"

"Both."

Still avoiding his gaze, she picked up another flower start from the colorful flat. "He was a good father. Whatever else I could say about Javier, he loved his children. They both miss him very much."

"You don't?"

"Again, why is this your business?"

He sighed. "It's not. You're right. But we were best friends once, even before, well, everything, and I would still like to know about your life after you left here. I never stopped caring about you just because you dumped me."

Again, she refused to look at him. "Don't go there, Taft. We both know I only broke our engagement because you didn't have the guts to do it."

Oh. Ouch. Direct hit. He almost took a step back, but he managed to catch himself just in time. "Jeez, Laura, why don't you say what you really mean?" he managed to get out past the guilt and pain.

She rose to her feet, spots of color on her high cheekbones. "Oh, don't pretend you don't know what I'm talking about. You completely checked out of our relationship after your parents were murdered. Every time I tried to talk to you, you brushed me off, told me you were fine, then merrily headed to the Bandito for another drink and to flirt with some hot young thing there. I suppose it shouldn't have come as a surprise to anyone that I married a man who was unfaithful. You know what they say about old patterns being hard to break."

Well, she was talking to him. *Be careful what you wish for, Bowman.*

"I was *never* unfaithful to you."

She made a disbelieving sound. "Maybe you didn't actually go that far with another woman, but you sure seemed to enjoy being with all the Bandito bar babes much more than you did me."

This wasn't going at all the way he had planned when he stopped to talk to her. Moving into the inn and taking the temporary carpenter job had been one of his craziest ideas. Really, he had only wanted to test the waters and see if there was any chance of finding their way past the ugliness and anger to regain the friendship they had once shared, the friendship that had once meant everything to him.

Those waters were still pretty damn frigid.

She let out a long breath and looked as if she regretted bringing up the past. "I knew you wanted out, Taft. *Everyone* knew you wanted out. You just didn't want to hurt me. I understand and appreciate that."

"That's not how it happened."

"I was there. I remember it well. You were grieving and angry about your parents' murder. Anyone would be. It's completely understandable, which is why, if you'll remember, I wanted to postpone the wedding until you were in a better place. You wouldn't hear of it. Every time I brought it up, you literally walked away from me. How could I have married you under those circumstances? We both would have ended up hating each other."

"You're right. This way is much better, with only you hating me."

Un-freaking-believable. She actually looked hurt at that. "Who said I hated you?"

"*Hate* might be too big a word. *Despise* might be a little more appropriate."

She drew in a sharp breath. "I don't feel either of those

things. The truth is, Taft, what we had together was a long time ago. I don't feel anything at all for you other than maybe a little fond nostalgia for what we once shared."

Oh. Double ouch. Pain sliced through him, raw and sharp. That was certainly clear enough. He was very much afraid it wouldn't take long for him to discover he was just as crazy about her as he had always been and all she felt in return was "fond nostalgia."

Or so she said anyway.

He couldn't help searching her expression for any hint that she wasn't being completely truthful, but she only gazed back at him with that same cool look, her mouth set in that frustratingly polite smile.

Damn, but he hated that smile. He suddenly wanted to lean forward, yank her against him and kiss away that smile until it never showed up there again.

Just for the sake of fond nostalgia.

Instead, he forced himself to give her a polite smile of his own and took a step in the direction of his truck. He had a meeting and didn't want to be later than he already was.

"Good to know," he murmured. "I guess I had better let you get back to your gardening. My shift ends tonight at six and then I'm only on call for the next few days, so I should have a little more time to work on the rooms you're renovating. Leave me a list of jobs you would like me to do at the front desk. I'll try my best to stay out of your way."

There. That sounded cool and uninvolved.

If he slammed his truck door a little harder than strictly necessary, well, so what?

Chapter 4

When would she ever learn to keep her big mouth shut?

Long after Taft climbed into his pickup truck and drove away, Laura continued to yank weeds out of the sadly neglected garden beds with hands that shook while silently castigating herself for saying anything.

The moment she turned and found him walking toward her, she should have thrown down her trowel and headed back to the cottage.

Their conversation replayed over and over in her head. If her gardening gloves hadn't been covered in dirt, she would have groaned and buried her face in her hands.

First of all, why on earth had she told him about Javier and his infidelities? Taft was the *last* person in Pine Gulch with whom she should have shared that particular tidbit of juicy information.

Even her mother didn't know how difficult the last few years of her marriage had become, how she would have left in an instant if not for the children and their adoration for Javier. Yet she had blurted the gory details right out to Taft, gushing her private heartache like a leaky sprinkler pipe.

So much for wanting him to think she had moved on-ward and upward after she left Pine Gulch. All she had accomplished was to make herself an object of pity in his eyes—as if she hadn't done that a decade ago by throwing all her love at someone who wasn't willing or capable at the time of catching it.

And then she had been stupid enough to dredge up the past, something she vowed she wouldn't do. Talking about it again had to have made him wonder if she were *thinking* about it, which basically sabotaged her whole plan to ap-pear cool and uninterested in Taft.

He could always manage to get her to confide things she shouldn't. She had often thought he should have been the police officer, not his twin brother, Trace.

When she was younger, she used to tell him everything. They had talked about the pressure her parents placed on her to excel in school. About a few of the mean girls in her grade who had excluded her from their social circle because of those grades, about her first crush—on a boy other than him, of course. She didn't tell him that until much later.

They had probably known each other clear back in grade school, but she didn't remember much about him other than maybe seeing him around in the lunchroom, this big, kind of tough-looking kid who had an identical twin and who always smiled at everyone. He had been two whole grades ahead of her after all, in an entirely different social stratosphere.

Her first real memory of him was middle school, which in Pine Gulch encompassed seventh through ninth grades. She had been in seventh grade, Taft in ninth. He had been an athletic kid and well-liked, always able to make any-one laugh. She, on the other hand, had been quiet and shy, much happier with a book in her hand than standing by her locker with her friends between classes, giggling over the cute boys.

She and Taft had ended up both taking a Spanish elective and had been seated next to each other on Señora Baker's incomprehensible seating chart.

Typically, guys that age—especially jocks—didn't want to have much to do with younger girls. Gawky, insecure, bookish girls might as well just forget it. But somehow while struggling over past participles and conjugating verbs, they had become friends. She had loved his sense of humor and he seemed to appreciate how easily she picked up Spanish.

They had arranged study groups together for every test, often before school because Taft couldn't do it afterward most of the time due to practice sessions for whatever school sport he was currently playing.

She could remember exactly the first moment she knew she was in love with him. She had been in the library wait-ing for him early one morning. Because she lived in town and could easily walk to school, she was often there first. He and his twin brother usually caught a ride with their older brother, Ridge, who was a senior in high school at the time and had a very cool pickup truck with big tires and a roll bar.

While she waited for him, she had been fine-tuning a history paper due in a few weeks when Ronnie Lowery showed up. Ronnie was a jerk and a bully in her grade who had seemed to have it in for her for the past few years.

She didn't understand it but thought his dislike might have something to do with the fact that Ronnie's single mother worked as a housekeeper at the inn. Why that should bother Ronnie, she had no idea. His mom wasn't a very good maid and often missed work because of her drinking, but she had overheard her mom and dad talking once in the office. Her mom had wanted to fire Mrs. Lowery, but her dad wouldn't allow it.

"She's got a kid at home. She needs the job," her dad had said, which was exactly what she would have expected her dad to say. He had a soft spot for people down on their luck and often opened the inn to people he knew could never pay their tab.

She suspected Ronnie's mom must have complained about her job at home, which was likely the reason Ronnie didn't like her. He had tripped her a couple of times going up the stairs at school and once he had cornered her in the girls' bathroom and tried to kiss her and touch her chest— what little chest she had—until she had smacked him upside the head with her heavy advanced-algebra textbook and told him to keep his filthy hands off her, with melodramatic but firm effectiveness.

She usually did her best to avoid him whenever she could, but that particular morning in seventh grade, she had been the only one in the school library. Even Mrs. Pitt, the plump and kind librarian who introduced her to Georgette Heyer books, seemed to have disappeared, she saw with great alarm.

Ronnie sat down. "Hey, Laura the whore-a."

"Shut up," she had said, very maturely, no doubt.

"Who's gonna make me?" he asked, looking around with exaggerated care. "I don't see anybody here at all."

"Leave me alone, Ronnie. I'm trying to study."

"Yeah, I don't think I will. Is that your history paper? You've got Mr. Olsen, right? Isn't that a coin-ki-dink? So do I. I bet we have the same assignment. I haven't started mine. Good thing, too, because now I don't have to."

He grabbed her paper, the one she had been working on every night for two weeks, and held it over his head.

"Give it back." She did her best not to cry.

"Forget it. You owe me for this. I had a bruise for two weeks after you hit me last month. I had to tell my mom I ran into the bleachers going after a foul ball in P.E."

"Want me to do it again?" she asked with much more bravado than true courage.

His beady gaze narrowed. "Try it, you little bitch, and I'll take more from you than just your freaking history paper."

"This history paper?"

At Taft's hard voice, all the tension coiled in her stomach like a rattlesnake immediately disappeared. Ronnie was big for a seventh grader, but compared to Taft, big and tough and menacing, he looked like just what he was—a punk who enjoyed preying on people smaller than he was.

"Yes, it's mine," she blurted out. "I would like it back."

Taft had smiled at her, plucked the paper out of Ronnie's greasy fingers and handed it back to Laura.

"Thanks," she had mumbled.

"You're Lowery, right?" he said to Ronnie. "I think you've got P.E. with my twin brother, Trace."

"Yeah," the kid had muttered, though with a tinge of defiance in his voice.

"I'm sorry, Lowery, but you're going to have to move. We're studying for a Spanish test here. Laura is my tutor and I don't know what I would do if something happened to her. All I can say is, I would *not* be happy. I doubt my brother would be, either."

Faced with the possibility of the combined wrath of the

formidable Bowman brothers, Ronnie had slunk away like the coward he was, and in that moment, Laura had known she would love Taft for the rest of her life.

He had moved on to high school the next year, of course, while she had been left behind in middle school to pine for him. Over the next two years, she remembered going to J.V. football games at the high school to watch him, sitting on the sidelines and keeping her fingers crossed that he would see her and smile.

Oh, yes. She had been plenty stupid when it came to Taft Bowman.

Finally, she had been in tenth grade and they would once more be in the same school as he finished his senior year. She couldn't wait, that endless summer. To her eternal delight, when she showed up at her first hour, Spanish again, she had found Taft seated across the room.

She would never forget walking into the room and watching Taft's broad smile take over his face and how he had pulled his backpack off the chair next to him, as if he had been waiting just for her.

They hadn't dated that year. She had been too young and still in her awkward phase, and anyway, he had senior girls flocking around him all the time, but their friendship had picked up where it left off two years earlier.

He had confided his girl troubles to her and how he was trying to figure out whether to join the military like his brother planned to do, or go to college. Even though she had ached inside to tell him how she felt about him, she hadn't dared. Instead, she had listened and offered advice whenever he needed it.

He had ended up doing both, enrolling in college and joining the Army Reserve, and in the summers, he had left Pine Gulch to fight woodland fires. They maintained an email correspondence through it all and every time he came home, they would head to The Gulch to share a meal and catch up and it was as if they had never been apart.

And then everything changed.

Although a painfully late bloomer, she had finally developed breasts somewhere around the time she turned sixteen, and by the time she went to college, she had forced herself to reach outside her instinctive shyness. The summer after her freshman year of college when she had finally decided to go into hotel management, Taft had been fighting a fire in Oregon when he had been caught in a flare-up.

Everyone in town had been talking about it, how he had barely escaped with his life and had saved two other firefighters from certain death. The whole time, she had been consumed with worry for him.

Finally, he came back for a few weeks to catch up with his twin, who was back in Pine Gulch between military assignments, and she and Taft had gone for a late-evening horseback ride at the River Bow Ranch and he finally spilled out the story of the flare-up and how it was a miracle he was alive.

One minute he was talking to her about the fire, something she was quite certain he hadn't done with anyone else. The next—she still wasn't sure how it happened—he was kissing her like a starving man and she was a giant frosted cupcake.

They kissed for maybe ten minutes. She wasn't sure exactly how long, but she only knew they were the most glorious moments of her life. When he finally eased away from her, he had looked as horrified as if he had just accidentally stomped on a couple of kittens.

"I'm sorry, Laura. That was... Wow. I'm so sorry."

She remembered shaking her head, smiling at him, her

heart aching with love. "What took you so blasted long, Taft Bowman?" she had murmured and reached out to kiss him again.

From that point on, they had been inseparable. She had been there to celebrate with him when he passed his EMT training, then paramedic training. He had visited her at school in Bozeman and made all her roommates swoon. When she came home for summers, they would spend every possible moment together.

On her twenty-first birthday, he proposed to her. Even though they were both crazy-young, she couldn't have imagined a future without him and had finally agreed. She missed those times, that wild flutter in her stomach every time he kissed her.

She sighed now and realized with a little start of surprise that while she had been woolgathering, she had weeded all the way around to the front of the building that lined Main Street.

Her mom would probably be more than ready for her to come back and take care of the children. She stood and stretched, rubbing her cramped back, when she heard the rumble of a pickup truck pulling alongside her.

Oh, she hoped it wasn't Taft coming back. She was already off-balance enough from their encounter earlier and from remembering all those things she had purposely kept buried for years. When she turned, she saw a woman climbing out of the pickup and realized it was indeed a Bowman—his younger sister, Caidy.

"Hi, Laura! Remember me? Caidy Bowman."

"Of course I remember you," she exclaimed. Caidy rushed toward her, arms outstretched, and Laura just had time to shuck off her gardening gloves before she returned the other woman's embrace.

"How are you?" she asked.

Despite the six-year difference in their ages, they had been close friends and she had loved the idea of having Caidy for a sister when she married Taft.

Until their parents died, Caidy had been a fun, bright, openly loving teenager, secure in her position as the adored younger sister of the three older Bowman brothers. Everything changed after Caidy witnessed her parents' murder, Laura thought sadly.

"I'm good," Caidy finally answered. Laura hoped so. Those months after the murders had been rough on the girl. The trauma of witnessing the brutal deaths and being unable to do anything to stop them had left Caidy frightened to the point of helplessness. For several weeks, she refused to leave the ranch and had insisted on having one of her brothers present twenty-four hours a day.

Caidy and her grief had been another reason Laura had tried to convince Taft to postpone their June wedding, just six months after the murders, but he had insisted his parents wouldn't have wanted them to change their plans.

Not that any of that mattered now. Caidy had become a beautiful woman, with dark hair like her brothers' and the same Bowman green eyes.

"You look fantastic," Laura exclaimed.

Caidy made a face but hugged her again. "Same to you. Gosh, I can't believe it's been so long."

"What are you up to these days? Did you ever make it to vet school?"

Something flickered in the depths of her eyes but Caidy only shrugged. "No, I went to a couple semesters of school but decided college wasn't really for me. Since then, I've mostly just stuck around the ranch, helping Ridge with his daughter. I do a little training on the side. Horses and dogs."

"That's terrific," she said, although some part of her felt a little sad for missed opportunities. Caidy had always adored animals and had an almost uncanny rapport with them. All she used to talk about as a teenager was becoming a veterinarian someday and coming back to Pine Gulch to work.

One pivotal moment had changed so many lives, she thought. The violent murder of the Bowmans in a daring robbery of their extensive American West art collection had shaken everyone in town really. That sort of thing just didn't happen in Pine Gulch. The last murder the town had seen prior to that had been clear back in the 1930s when two ranch hands had fought it out over a girl.

Each of the Bowman siblings had reacted in different ways, she remembered. Ridge had thrown himself into the ranch and overseeing his younger siblings. Trace had grown even more serious and solemn. Caidy had withdrawn into herself, struggling with a completely natural fear of the world.

As for Taft, his answer had been to hide away his emotions and pretend everything was fine while inside he seethed with grief and anger and pushed away any of her attempts to comfort him.

"I'm looking for Taft," Caidy said now. "I had to make a run to the feed store this morning and thought I would stop and see if he wanted to head over to The Gulch for coffee and an omelet."

Oh, she loved The Gulch, the town's favorite diner. Why hadn't she been there since she returned to town? An image of the place formed clearly in her head—the tin-stamped ceiling, the round red swivel seats at the old-fashioned counter, the smell of frying bacon and coffee that had probably oozed into the paneling.

One of these mornings, she would have to take her children there.

"Taft isn't here. I'm sorry. He left about a half hour ago. I think he was heading to the fire station. He did say something about his shift ending at six."

"Oh. Okay. Thanks." Caidy paused a moment, tilting her head and giving Laura a long, inscrutable look very much like her brother would do. "I don't suppose you would like to go over to The Gulch with me and have breakfast, would you?"

She gazed at the other woman, as touched by the invitation as she was surprised. In all these years, Taft hadn't told his family that she had been the one to break their engagement? She knew he couldn't have. If Caidy knew, Laura had a feeling the other woman wouldn't be nearly as friendly.

The Bowmans tended to circle the wagons around their own.

That had been one of the hardest things about walking away from him. Her breakup with Taft had meant not only the loss of all her childish dreams but also the big, boisterous family she had always wanted as an only child of older parents who seemed absorbed with each other and their business.

For a moment, she was tempted to go to The Gulch with Caidy. Her mouth watered at the thought of Lou Archuleta's famous sweet rolls. Besides that, she would love the chance to catch up with Caidy. But before she could answer, her children came barreling out of the cottage, Maya in the lead for once but Alex close behind.

"Ma-ma! Gram made cakes. So good," Maya declared.

Alexandro caught up to his sister. "Pancakes, not cakes. You don't have cakes for breakfast, Maya. We're supposed to tell you to come in so you can wash up. Hurry! Grandma says I can flip the next one."

"Oh."

Caidy smiled at the children, clearly entranced by them.

"Caidy, this is my daughter, Maya, and my son, Alexandro. Children, this is my friend Caidy. She's Chief Bowman's sister."

"I like Chief Bowman," Alex declared. "He said if I start another fire, he's going to arrest me. Do you think he will?"

Caidy nodded solemnly. "Trust me, my brother never says anything he doesn't mean. You'll have to be certain not to start any more fires, then, won't you?"

"I know. I know. I already heard it about a million times. Hey, Mom, can I go so I can turn the pancakes with Grandma?"

She nodded and Alex raced back for the cottage with his sister in close pursuit.

"They're beautiful, Laura. Truly."

"I think so." She smiled and thought she saw a hint of something like envy in the other woman's eyes. Why didn't Caidy have a family of her own? she wondered. Was she still living in fear?

On impulse, she gestured toward the cottage. "Unless you have your heart set on cinnamon rolls down at The Gulch, why don't you stay and have breakfast here? I'm sure my mother wouldn't mind setting another plate for you."

Caidy blinked. "Oh, I couldn't."

"Why not? My mother's pancakes are truly delicious. In fact, a week from now, we're going to start offering breakfast at the inn to our guests. The plan is to start with some of Mom's specialties like pancakes and French toast but also to begin ordering some things from outside sources to showcase local businesses. I've already talked to the

Java Hut about serving their coffee here and the Archuletas about offering some of The Gulch pastries to our guests."

"What a great idea."

"You can be our guinea pig. Come and have breakfast with us. I'm sure my mother will enjoy the company."

She would, too, she thought. She missed having a friend besides her mother. Her best friend in high school, besides Taft, had moved to Texas for her husband's job and Laura hadn't had a chance to connect with anyone else.

Even though she still emailed back and forth with her dearest friends and support system in Madrid, it wasn't the same as sharing coffee and pancakes and stories with someone who had known her for so long.

"I would love that," Caidy exclaimed. "Thank you. I'm sure Taft can find his own breakfast partner if he's so inclined."

From the rumors Laura had heard about the man in the years since their engagement, she didn't doubt that for a moment.

Chapter 5

To her relief, her children were charming and sweet with Caidy over breakfast. As soon as he found out their guest lived on a real-life cattle ranch, Alex peppered her with questions about cowboys and horses and whether she had ever seen a real-life Indian.

Apparently she had to have a talk with her son about political correctness and how reality compared to the American Westerns he used to watch avidly with their gnarled old housekeeper in Madrid.

Maya had apparently decided Caidy was someone she could trust, which was something of a unique occurrence. She sat beside her and gifted Taft's sister with her sweet smile and half of the orange Laura peeled for her.

"Thank you, sweetheart," Caidy said, looking touched by the gesture.

Whenever someone new interacted with Maya, Laura

couldn't help a little clutch in her stomach, worry at how her daughter would be accepted.

She supposed that stemmed from Javier's initial reaction after her birth when the solemn-faced doctors told them Maya showed certain markers for Down syndrome and they were running genetic testing to be sure.

Her husband had been in denial for a long time and had pretended nothing was wrong. After all, how could he possibly have a child who wasn't perfect—by the world's standards anyway? Even after the testing revealed what Laura had already known in her heart, Javier has refused to discuss Maya's condition or possible outcomes.

Denial or not, he had still loved his daughter, though. She couldn't fault him for that. He was sometimes the only one who could calm the baby's crankiness and he had been infinitely calm with her.

Maya didn't quite understand that Javier was dead. She still had days when she asked over and over again where her papa was. During those rough patches, Laura would have to fight down deep-seated fury at her late husband.

Her children needed him and he had traded his future with them for the momentary pleasure he had found with his latest honey. Mingled with the anger and hurt was no small amount of guilt. If she had tried a little harder to open her heart to him and truly love him, maybe he wouldn't have needed to seek out other women.

She was doing her best, she reminded herself. Hadn't she traveled across the world to give them a home with family and stability?

"This was fun," Caidy said, drawing her back to the conversation. "Thank you so much for inviting me, but I probably better start heading back to the ranch. I've got a buyer coming today to look at one of the border collies I've been training."

"You're going to sell your dog?" Alex, who dearly wanted a puppy, looked horrified at the very idea.

"Sue isn't really my dog," Caidy explained with a smile. "I rescued her when she was a puppy and I've been training her to help someone else at their ranch. We have plenty of dogs at the River Bow."

Alex didn't seem to quite understand the concept of breeding and training dogs. "Doesn't it make you sad to give away your dog?"

Caidy blinked a little, but after a pause she nodded. "Yes, I guess it does a little. She's a good dog and I'll miss her. But I promise I'll make sure whoever buys her will give her a really good home."

"We have a good home, don't we, Grandma?" Alex appealed to Jan, who smiled.

"Why, yes, I believe we do, son."

"We can't have a dog right now, Alex."

Laura tried to head him off before he started extolling the virtues of their family like a used-car salesman trying to close a deal. "We've talked about this. While we're settling in here in Pine Gulch and living with Grandma here at the inn, it's just not practical."

He stuck out his lower lip, looking very much like his father when he couldn't get his way. "That's what you always say. I still really, really, really want a dog."

"Not now, Alexandro. We're not getting a dog. Maybe in a year or so when things here are a little more settled."

"But I want one now!"

"I'm sorry," Caidy said quickly, "but I'm afraid Sue wouldn't be very happy here. You see, she's a working dog and her very favorite thing is telling the cattle on our ranch which way we want them to go. You don't look very much like a steer. Where are your horns?"

Alex looked as if he wanted to ramp up to a full-fledged tantrum, something new since his father died, but he allowed himself to be teased out of it. "I'm not a steer," he said, rolling his eyes. Then a moment later he asked, "What's a steer?"

Caidy laughed. "It's another name for the male version of cow."

"I thought that was a bull."

"Uh." Caidy gave Laura a helpless sort of look.

While Jan snickered, Laura shook her head. "You're right. There are two kinds of male bovines, which is another word for cow. One's a bull and one is a steer."

"What's the difference?" he asked.

"Steers sing soprano," Caidy said. "And on that lovely note, I'd better get back to the bulls *and* steers of the River Bow. Thanks for a great breakfast. Next time it's my turn."

"Alex, will you and Maya help Gram with clearing the table while I walk Caidy out? I'll do the dishes when I come back inside."

To her relief, her son allowed himself to be distracted when Jan asked him if he and Maya would like to go to the park later in the day.

"I'm sorry about the near-tantrum there," she said as they headed outside to Caidy's pickup truck. "We're working on them, but my son still likes his own way."

"Most kids do. My niece is almost ten and she still thinks she should be crowned queen of the universe. I didn't mean to start something by talking about dogs."

"We've been having this argument for about three years now. His best friend in Madrid had this mangy old mutt, but Alex adored him and wanted one so badly. My husband would never allow it and for some reason Alex got it in his head after his father died that now there was no reason we couldn't get a dog."

"You're welcome to bring your kids out to the ranch sometime to enjoy my dogs vicariously. The kids might enjoy taking a ride, as well. We've got some pretty gentle ponies that would be perfect for them."

"That sounds fun. I'm sure they would both love it." She was quite certain this was one of those vague invitations that people said just to be polite, but to her surprise, Caidy didn't let the matter rest.

"How about next weekend?" she pressed. "I'm sure Ridge would be delighted to have you out."

Ridge was the Bowman sibling she had interacted with the least. At the time she was engaged to Taft, he and his parents weren't getting along, so he avoided the River Bow as much as possible. The few times she had met him, she had always thought him a little stern and humorless.

Still, he'd been nice enough to her—though the same couldn't have been said about his ex-wife, who had been rude and overbearing to just about everyone on the ranch.

"That's a lovely invitation, but I'm sure the last thing you need is to entertain a bunch of greenhorns."

"I would love it," Caidy assured her. "Your kids are just plain adorable and I can't tell you how thrilled I am that you're back in town. To tell you the truth, I'm a little desperate for some female conversation. At least something that doesn't revolve around cattle."

She should refuse. Her history with Taft had to make any interaction with the rest of the Bowmans more than a little awkward. But like Caidy, she welcomed any chance to resurrect their old friendship—and Alex and Maya *would* love the chance to ride horses and play with the ranch dogs.

"Yes, all right. The weekend would be lovely. Thank you."

"I'll call you Wednesday or Thursday to make some firm arrangements. This will be great!" Caidy beamed at her, looking fresh and pretty with her dark ponytail and sprinkling of freckles across the bridge of her nose.

The other woman climbed into her pickup truck and drove away with a wave and a smile and Laura watched after her for a moment, feeling much better about the morning than she had when the previous Bowman sibling had driven away from the inn.

Taft had visitors.

The whir of the belt sander didn't quite mask the giggles and little scurrying sounds from the doorway. He made a show of focusing on the window he was framing while still maintaining a careful eye on the little creatures who would occasionally peek around the corner of the doorway and then hide out of sight again.

He didn't want to let his guard down, not with all the power equipment in here. He could just imagine Laura's diatribe if one of her kids somehow got hurt. She would probably accuse him of letting her rambunctious older kid cut off his finger on purpose.

The game of peekaboo lasted for a few more minutes until he shut off the belt sander. He ran a finger over the wood to be sure the frame was smooth before he headed over to the window to hold it up for size, keeping an eye on the door the whole time.

"Go on," he heard a whispered voice say, then giggles, and a moment later he was joined by Laura's daughter.

Maya. She was adorable, with that dusky skin, curly dark hair in pigtails and Laura's huge blue eyes, almond-shaped on Maya.

"Hola," she whispered with a shy smile.

"Hola, señorita," he answered. Apparently he still remembered a *little* of the high-school Spanish he had struggled so hard to master.

"What doing?" she asked.

"I'm going to put some new wood up around this window. See?" He held the board into the intended place to demonstrate, then returned it to the worktable.

"Why?" she asked, scratching her ear.

He glanced at the doorway where the boy peeked around, then hid again like a shadow.

"The old wood was rotting away. This way it will look much nicer. More like the rest of the room."

That face peeked around the doorway again and this time Taft caught him with an encouraging smile. After a pause, the boy sidled into the room.

"Loud," Maya said, pointing to the belt sander with fascination.

"It can be. I've got things to block your ears if you want them."

He wasn't sure she would understand, but she nodded vigorously, so he reached for his ear protectors on top of his toolbox. The adult-size red ear guards were huge on her—the bottom of the cups hit her at about shoulder height. He reached out to work the slide adjustment on top. They were still too big but at least they covered most of her ears.

She beamed at him, pleased as punch, and he had to chuckle. "Nice. You look great."

"I see," she said, and headed unerringly for the mirror hanging on the back of the bathroom door, where she turned her head this way and that, admiring her headgear as if he had given her a diamond tiara.

Oh, she was a heartbreaker, this one.

"Can I use some?" Alexandro asked, from about two feet away, apparently coaxed all the way into the room by what his sister was wearing.

"I'm afraid I've got only the one pair. I wasn't expecting company. Sorry. Next time I'll remember to pack a spare. I probably have regular earplugs in my toolbox."

Alex shrugged. "That's okay. I don't mind the noise. Maya freaks at loud noises, but I don't care."

"Why is that? Maya, I mean, and loud noises?"

The girl was wandering around the room, humming to herself loudly, apparently trying to hear herself through the ear protection.

The kid looked fairly protective himself, watching over his sister as she moved from window to window. "She just does. Mom says it's because she has so much going on inside her head she sometimes forgets the rest of us and loud noises startle her into remembering. Or something like that."

"You love your sister a lot, don't you?"

"She's my sister." He shrugged, looking suddenly much older than his six years. "I have to watch out for her and Mama now that our papa is gone."

Taft wanted to hug him, too, and he had to fight down a lump in his throat. He thought about his struggle when his parents had died. He had been twenty-four years old. Alex was just a kid and had already lost his father, but he seemed to be handling it with stoic grace. "I bet you do a great job, protecting them both."

The boy looked guilty. "Sometimes. I didn't on the day of the fire."

"We've decided that was an accident, right? It's over and you're not going to do it again. Take it from me, kid. Don't beat yourself up over past mistakes. Just move on and try to do better next time."

Alex didn't look as if he quite understood. Why should he? Taft rolled his eyes at himself. Philosophy and six-year-old boys didn't mix all that well.

"Want to try your hand with the sander?" he asked.

Alex's blue eyes lit up. "Really? Is it okay?"

"Sure. Why not? Every guy needs to know how to run a belt sander."

Before beginning the lesson, Taft thought it wise to move toward Maya, who was sitting on the floor some distance away, drawing her finger through the sawdust mess he hadn't had time to clear up yet. Her mom would probably love that, but because she was already covered, he decided he would clean her up when they were done.

He lifted one of the ear protectors away from her ear so he could talk to her. "Maya, we're going to turn on the sander, okay?"

"Loud."

"It won't be when you have this on. I promise."

She narrowed her gaze as if she were trying to figure out whether to believe him, then she nodded and returned to the sawdust. He gazed at the back of her head, tiny compared to the big ear guards, and was completely bowled over by her ready trust.

Now he had to live up to it.

He turned on the sander, hoping the too-big ear protectors would still do their job. Maya looked up, a look of complete astonishment on her cute little face. She pulled one ear cup away, testing to see if the sander was on, but quickly returned it to the original position. After a minute, she pulled it away again and then replaced it, a look of wonder on her face at the magic of safety wear.

He chuckled and turned back to Alex, waiting eagerly by the belt sander.

"Okay, the most important thing here is that we don't sand your fingers off. I'm not sure your mom would appreciate that."

"She wouldn't," Alex assured him with a solemn expression.

Taft had to fight his grin. "We'll have to be careful, then. Okay. Now you always start up the belt sander before you touch it to the wood so you don't leave gouges. Right here is the switch. Now keep your hands on top of mine and we can do it together. That's it."

For the next few minutes, they worked the piece of wood until he was happy with the way it looked and felt. He always preferred to finish sanding his jobs the old-fashioned way, by hand, but a belt sander was a handy tool for covering a large surface quickly and efficiently.

When they finished, he carefully turned off the belt sander and set it aside, then returned to the board and the boy. "Okay, now here's the second most important part, after not cutting your fingers off. We have to blow off the sawdust. Like this."

He demonstrated with a puff of air, then handed the board to the boy, who puckered up and blew as if he were the big, bad wolf after the three little pigs.

"Perfect," Taft said with a grin. "Feel how smooth that is now?"

The boy ran his finger along the wood grain. "Wow! I did that?"

"Absolutely. Good job. Now every time you come into this room, you can look out through the window and remember you helped frame it up."

"Cool! Why do you have to sand the wood?"

"When the wood is smooth, it looks better and you get better results with whatever paint or varnish you want to use on it."

"How does the sander thingy work?"

"The belt is made of sandpaper. See? Because it's rough, when you rub it on the wood, it works away the uneven surface."

"Can you sand other things besides wood?" he asked.

Taft had to laugh at the third degree. "You probably can but it's made for wood. It would ruin other things. Most tools have a specific purpose and when you use them for something else, you can cause more problems."

"Me," an abnormally loud voice interrupted before Alex could ask any more questions. With the ear protectors, Maya obviously couldn't judge the decibel level of her own voice. "I go now."

"Okay, okay. You don't need to yell about it," Alex said, rolling his eyes in a conspiratorial way toward Taft.

Just like that, both of these kids slid their way under his skin, straight to his heart, partly because they were Laura's, but mostly because they were just plain adorable.

"Can I?" she asked, still speaking loudly.

He lifted one of the ear protectors so she could hear him. "Sure thing, sweetheart. I've got another board that needs sanding. Come on."

Alex looked disgruntled, but he backed away to give his sister room. Taft was even more careful with Maya, keeping his hands firmly wrapped around hers on the belt sander as they worked the wood.

When they finished, he removed her earwear completely. "Okay, now, like I told your brother, this is the most important part. I need you to blow off the sawdust."

She puckered comically and puffed for all she was worth and he helped her along. "There. Now feel what we did."

"Ooh. Soft." She smiled broadly at him and he returned her smile, just as he heard their names.

"Alex? Maya? Where are you?"

Laura's voice rang out from down the hall, sounding harried and a little hoarse, as if she had been calling for a while.

The two children exchanged looks, as if they were bracing themselves for trouble.

"That's our mama," Alex said unnecessarily.

"Yeah, I heard."

"Alex? Maya? Come out this instant."

"They're in here," he called out, although some part of him really didn't want to take on more trouble. He thought of their encounter a few days earlier when she had looked so fresh and pretty while she worked on the inn's flower gardens—and had cut into his heart more effectively than if she had used her trowel.

She charged into the room, every inch the concerned mother. "What's going on? Why didn't you two answer me? I've been calling through the whole hotel."

Taft decided to take one for the team. "I'm afraid that's my fault. We had the sander going. We couldn't hear much up here."

"Look, Mama. Soft." Maya held up the piece of wood she had helped him sand. "Feel!"

Laura stepped closer, reluctance in her gaze. He was immediately assailed by the scent of her, of flowers and springtime.

She ran a hand along the wood, much as her daughter had. "Wow. That's great."

"I did it," Maya declared.

Laura arched an eyebrow. She managed to look huffy and disapproving at him for just a moment before turning back to her daughter with what she quickly transformed into an interested expression. "Did you, now? With the power sander and everything?"

"I figured I would let them run the circular saw next," he said. "Really, what's the worst that can happen?"

She narrowed her gaze at him as if trying to figure out if he was teasing. Whatever happened to her sense of humor? he wondered. Had he robbed her of that or had it been her philandering jackass of a husband?

"I'm kidding," he said. "I was helping them the whole way. Maya even wore ear protection, didn't you? Show your mom."

The girl put on her headgear and started singing some made-up song loudly, pulling the ear guards away at random intervals.

"Oh, that looks like great fun," Laura said, taking the ear protectors off her daughter and handing them to Taft. Their hands brushed as he took them from her and a little charge of electricity arced between them, sizzling right to his gut.

She pulled her hands away quickly and didn't meet his gaze. "You shouldn't be up here bothering Chief Bowman. I told you to stay away when he's working."

And why would she think she had to do that? he wondered, annoyed. Did she think he couldn't be trusted with her kids? He was the Pine Gulch fire chief, for heaven's sake, and a trained paramedic to boot. Public safety was sort of his thing.

"It was fun," Alex declared. "I got to use the sander first. Feel my board now, Mama."

She appeared to have no choice but to comply. "Nice

job. But next time you need to listen to me and not bother Chief Bowman while he's working."

"I didn't mind," Taft said. "They're fun company."

"You're busy. I wouldn't want them to be a bother."

"What if they're not?"

She didn't look convinced. "Come on, you two. Tell Chief Bowman thank-you for letting you try out the dangerous power tools, after you promise him you'll never touch any of them on your own."

"We promise," Alex said dutifully.

"Promise," his sister echoed.

"Thanks for showing me how to use a sander," Alex said. "I need one of those."

Now *there* was a disaster in the making. But because the kid wasn't his responsibility, as his mother had made quite clear, he would let Laura deal with it.

"Thanks for helping me," he said. "I couldn't have finished without you two lending a hand."

"Can I help you again sometime?" the boy asked eagerly.

Laura tensed beside him and he knew she wanted him to say no. It annoyed the heck out of him and he wanted to agree, just to be contrary, but he couldn't bring himself to blatantly go against her wishes.

Instead, he offered the standard adult cop-out even though it grated. "We'll have to see, kiddo," he answered.

"Okay, now that you've had a chance with the power tools, take your sister and go straight down to the front desk to your grandmother. No detours, Alex. Got it?"

His stubborn little chin jutted out. "But we were having fun."

"Chief Bowman is trying to get some work done. He's not here to babysit."

"I'm not a baby," Alex grumbled.

Laura bit back what Taft was almost certain was a smile. "I know you're not. It's just a word, *mi hijo*. Either way, you need to take your sister straight down to the lobby to find your grandmother."

With extreme reluctance in every step, Alex took his little sister's hand and led her out the door and down the hall, leaving Laura alone with him.

Even though he could tell she wasn't thrilled to have found her children there with him and some part of him braced himself to deal with her displeasure, another, louder part of him was just so damn happy to see her again.

Ridiculous, he knew, but he couldn't seem to help it.

How had he forgotten that little spark of happiness that always seemed to jump in his chest when he saw her after an absence of just about any duration?

Even with her hair in a ponytail and an oversize shirt and faded jeans, she was beautiful, and he wanted to stand here amid the sawdust and clutter and just savor the sight of her.

As he might have expected, she didn't give him much of a chance. "Sorry about the children," she said stiffly. "I thought they were watching *SpongeBob* in the bedroom of Room Twelve while I cleaned the bathroom grout. I came out of the bathroom and they were gone, which is, unfortunately, not all that uncommon with my particular kids."

"Next time maybe you should use the security chain to keep them contained," he suggested, only half-serious.

Even as he spoke, he was aware of a completely inappropriate urge to wrap her in his arms and absorb all her cares and worries about wandering children and tile grout and anything else weighing on her.

"A great idea, but unfortunately I've already tried that. Within about a half hour, Alex figured out how to lift his sister up and have her work the chain free. They figured out the dead bolt in about half that time. I just have to re-member I can't take my eyes off them for a second. I'll try to do a better job of keeping them out of your way."

"I told you, I don't mind them. Why would I? They're great kids." He meant the words, even though his previous experience with kids, other than the annual fire-safety lecture he gave at the elementary school, was mostly his niece, Destry, Ridge's daughter.

"I think they're pretty great," she answered.

"That Alex is a curious little guy with a million questions."

She gave a rueful sigh and tucked a strand of hair behind her delicate ear. She used to love it when he kissed her neck, just there, he remembered, then wished the memory had stayed hidden as heat suddenly surged through him.

"Yes, I'm quite familiar with my son's interrogation technique," Laura said, oblivious to his reaction, thank heavens. "He's had six years to hone them well."

"I don't mind the questions. Trace and I were both the same way when we were kids. My mom used to say that between the two of us, we didn't give her a second to even catch a breath between questions."

She trailed her fingers along the wood trim and he remembered how she used to trail them across his stomach....

"I remember some of the stories your mother used to tell me about you and Trace and the trouble you could get into. To be honest with you, I have great sympathy with your mother. I can't imagine having two of Alex."

He dragged his mind away from these unfortunate memories that suddenly crowded out rational thought. "He's a good boy, just has a lot of energy. And that Maya. She's a heartbreaker."

She pulled her hand away from the wood, her expression suddenly cold. "Don't you dare pity her."

"Why on earth would I do that?" he asked, genuinely shocked.

She frowned. "Because of her Down syndrome. Many people do."

"Then you shouldn't waste your time with them. Down syndrome or not, she's about the sweetest thing I've ever seen. You should have seen her work the belt sander, all serious and determined, chewing on her lip in concentration—just like you used to do when you were studying."

"Don't."

He blinked, startled at her low, vehement tone. "Don't what?"

"Try to charm me by acting all sweet and concerned. It might work on your average bimbo down at the Bandito, but I'm not that stupid."

Where did *that* come from? "Are you kidding? You're about the smartest person I know. I never thought you were stupid."

"That makes one of us," she muttered, then looked as if she regretted the words.

More than anything, he wanted to go back in time ten years and make things right again with her. He had hurt her by closing her out of his pain, trying to deal with the grief and guilt in his own way.

But then, she had hurt him, too. If only she had given him a little more time and trusted that he would work things through, he would have figured everything out eventually. Instead, she had gone away to Spain and met her jerk of a husband—and had two of the cutest kids he had ever met.

"Laura—" he began, not sure what he intended to say, but she shook her head briskly.

"I'm sorry my children bothered you. I won't let it happen again."

"I told you, I don't mind them."

"I mind. I don't want them getting attached to you when you'll be in their lives for only a brief moment."

He hadn't even known her kids a week ago. So why did the idea of not seeing them again make his chest ache? Uneasy with the reaction, he gave her a long look.

"For someone who claims not to hate me, you do a pretty good impression of it. You don't even want me around your kids, like I'll contaminate them somehow."

"You're exaggerating. You're virtually a stranger to me after all this time. I don't hate you. I feel nothing at all for you. Less than nothing."

He moved closer to her, inhaling the springtime scent of her shampoo. "Liar."

The single word was a low hush in the room and he saw her shiver as if he had trailed his finger down her cheek.

She started to take a step back, then checked the motion. "Oh, get over yourself," she snapped. "Yes, you broke my heart. I was young and foolish enough to think you meant what you said, that you loved me and wanted forever with me. We were supposed to take vows about being with each other in good times and bad, but you wouldn't share the bad with me. Instead, you started drinking and hanging out at the Bandito and pretending nothing was wrong. I was devastated. I won't make a secret of that. I thought I wouldn't survive the pain."

"I'm sorry," he said.

She made a dismissive gesture. "I should really thank you, Taft. If not for that heartbreak, I would have been only a weak, silly girl who would probably have become a weak, silly woman. Instead, I became stronger. I took my broken heart and turned it into a grand adventure in Europe, where I matured and experienced the world a little bit instead of just Pine Gulch, and now I have two beautiful children to show for it."

"Why did you give up on us so easily?"

Her mouth tightened with anger. "You know, you're right. I should have gone ahead with the wedding and then just waited around wringing my hands until you decided to pull your head out of whatever crevice you jammed it into. Although from the sound of it, I might still have been waiting, ten years later."

"I'm sorry for hurting you," he said, wishing again that he could go back and change everything. "More sorry than I can ever say."

"Ten years too late," she said tersely. "I told you, it doesn't matter."

"It obviously does or you wouldn't bristle like a porcupine every time you're near me."

"I don't—" she started to say, but he cut her off.

"I don't blame you. I was an ass to you. I'll be the first to admit it."

"The second," she said tartly.

If this conversation didn't seem so very pivotal, he might have smiled, but he had the feeling he had the chance to turn things around between them right here and now, and he wanted that with a fierce and powerful need.

"Probably. For what it's worth, my family would fill out the rest of the top five there, waiting in line to call me names."

She almost smiled but she hid it quickly. What would it take for him to squeeze a real smile out of her and keep it there? he wondered.

"I know we can't go back and change things," he said

slowly. "But what are the chances that we can at least be civil to each other? We were good friends once, before we became more. I miss that."

She was quiet for several moments and he was aware of the random sounds of the old inn. The shifting of old wood, the creak of a floorboard somewhere, a tree branch that needed to be pruned back rattling against the thin glass of the window.

When she spoke, her voice was low. "I miss it, too," she said, in the tone of someone confessing a rather shameful secret.

Something inside him seemed to uncoil at her words. He gazed at her so-familiar features that he had once known as well as his own.

The high cheekbones, the cute little nose, those blue eyes that always reminded him of his favorite columbines that grew above the ranch. He wanted to kiss her, with a raw ferocity that shocked him to his toes. To sink into her and not climb out again.

He managed, just barely, to restrain himself and was grateful for it when she spoke again, her voice just above a whisper.

"We can't go back, Taft."

"No, but we can go forward. That's better anyway, isn't it? The reality is, we're both living in the same small town. Right now we're living at the same address, for Pete's sake. We can't avoid each other. But that doesn't mean we need to go on with this awkwardness between us, does it? I would really like to see if together we can find some way to move past it. What do you say?"

She gazed at him for a long moment, uncertainty in those eyes he loved so much. Finally she seemed to come to some internal decision.

"Sure. We can try to be friends again." She gave him a tentative smile. A real one this time, not that polite thing he had come to hate, and his chest felt tight and achy all over again.

"I need to get back to work. I'll see you later."

"Goodbye, Laura," he said.

She gave him one more little smile before hurrying out of the room. He watched her go, more off-balance by the encounter with Laura and her children than he wanted to admit. As he turned back to his work, he was also aware of a vague sense of melancholy that made no sense. This was progress, right? Friendship was a good place to start— hadn't their relationship begun out of friendship from the beginning?

He picked up another board from the pile. He knew the source of his discontent. He wanted more than friendship with Laura. He wanted what they used to have, laughter and joy and that contentment that seemed to seep through him every time he was with her.

Baby steps, he told himself. He could start with friendship and then gradually build on that, see how things progressed. Nothing wrong with a little patience once in a while.

Her hands were still shaking as Laura walked out of the room and down the hall. She headed for the lobby, with the curving old stairs and the classic light fixtures that had probably been installed when Pine Gulch finally hit the electrical grid.

Only when she was certain she was completely out of sight of Taft did she lean against the delicately flowered wallpaper and press a hand to her stomach.

What an idiot she was, as weak as a baby lamb around

him. She always had been. Even if she had hours of other more urgent homework, if Taft called her and needed help with Spanish, she would drop everything to rush to his aid.

It didn't help matters that the man was positively dangerous when he decided to throw out the charm.

Oh, it would be so easy to give in, to let all that seductive charm slide around and through her until she forgot all the reasons she needed to resist him.

He asked if they could find a way to friendship again. She didn't have the first idea how to answer that. She wanted to believe her heart had scarred over from the disappointment and heartache, the loss of those dreams for the future, but she was more than a little afraid to peek past the scars to see if it had truly healed.

She was tough and resilient. Hadn't she survived a bad marriage and then losing the husband she had tried to love? She could surely carry on a civil conversation with Taft on the rare occasions they met in Pine Gulch.

What was the harm in it? For heaven's sake, reestablishing a friendly relationship with the man didn't mean she was automatically destined to tumble headlong back into love with him.

Life in Pine Gulch would be much easier all the way around if she didn't feel jumpy and off-balance every time she was around him.

She eased away from the wallpaper and straightened her shirt that had bunched up. This was all ridiculous anyway. What did it matter if she was weak around him? She likely wouldn't ever have the opportunity to test out her willpower. From the rumors she heard, Taft probably had enough young, hot bar babes at the Bandito that he probably couldn't be bothered with a thirty-two-year-old widow with two children, one of whom with a disability that would require lifelong care.

She wasn't the same woman she had been ten years ago. She had given birth to two kids and had the body to show for it. Her hair was always messy and falling out of whatever clip she had shoved it in that morning, half the time she didn't have time to put on makeup until she had been up for hours and, between the kids and the inn, she was perpetually stressed.

Why on earth would a man like Taft, gorgeous and masculine, want anything *but* friendship with her these days?

She wasn't quite sure why that thought depressed her and made her feel like that gawky seventh grader with braces crushing on a ninth-grade athlete who was nice to her.

Surely she didn't *want* to have to resist Taft Bowman. It was better all around if he saw her merely as that frumpy mother.

She knew that was probably true, even as some secret, silly little part of her wanted to at least have the *chance* to test her willpower around him.

Chapter 6

"Hurry, Mama." Alex practically jumped out of his booster seat the moment she turned off the engine at the River Bow Ranch on Saturday. "I want to see the dogs!"

"Dogs!" Maya squealed after him, wiggling and tugging against the car-seat straps. The only reason she didn't rush to join her brother outside the car was her inability to undo the straps on her own, much to her constant frustration.

"Hang on, you two." Their excitement made her smile, despite the host of emotions churning through her at visiting the River Bow again for the first time in a decade. "The way you're acting, somebody might think you'd never seen a dog before."

"I have, too, seen a dog before," Alex said. "But this isn't just *one* dog. Miss Bowman said she had a *lot* of dogs. And horses, too. Can I really ride one?"

"That's the plan for now, but we'll have to see how things go." She was loath to make promises about things that were out of her control. Probably a fallback to her marriage, those frequent times when the children would be so disappointed if their father missed dinner or a school performance or some special outing.

"I hope I *can* ride a horse. Oh, I hope so." Alex practically danced around the used SUV she had purchased with the last of her savings when she arrived back in the States. She had to smile at his enthusiasm as she unstrapped Maya and lifted her out of the vehicle.

Maya threw her chubby little arms around Laura's neck before she could set her on the ground.

"Love you," her daughter said.

The spontaneously affectionate gesture turned her insides to warm mush, something her sweet Maya so often did. "Oh, I love you, too, darling. More than the moon and the stars and the sea."

"Me, too," Alex said.

She hugged him with the arm not holding Maya. "I love you both. Aren't I the luckiest mom in the world to have two wonderful kiddos to love?"

"Yes, you are," he said, with a total lack of vanity that made her smile.

She supposed she couldn't be a completely terrible mother if she was raising her children with such solid assurance of their place in her heart.

At the sound of scrabbling paws and panting breaths, she raised her head from her children. "Guess what? Here come the dogs."

Alex whirled around in time to see Caidy approaching them with three dogs shadowing her. Laura identified two of them as border collies, mostly black with white patches on their faces and necks, quizzical ears and eerily intelligent expressions. The third was either a breed she didn't recognize or some kind of mutt of undetermined origin, with reddish fur and a German shepherd–like face.

Maya stiffened nervously, not at all experienced around dogs, and tightened her arms around Laura's neck. Alex, on the other hand, started to rush toward the dogs, but Laura checked him with a hand on his shoulder.

"Wait until Caidy says it's safe," she ordered her son, who would run directly into a lion's enclosure if he thought he might have a chance of petting the creature.

"Perfectly safe," Caidy assured them.

Taft's sister wore jeans and a bright yellow T-shirt along with boots and a straw cowboy hat, her dark hair braided down her back. She looked fresh and pretty as she gave them all a welcoming smile. "The only danger from my dogs is being licked to death—or maybe getting knocked over by a wagging tail."

Alex giggled and Caidy looked delighted at the sound.

"Your mother is right, though," she said. "You should never approach any strange animal without permission until you know it's safe."

"Can I pet one?"

"Sure thing. King. Forward."

One of the lean black-and-white border collies obeyed and sidled toward them, sniffing eagerly at Alex's legs. The boy giggled and began to pet the dog with sheer joy.

"This was such a great idea," Laura said, smiling as she watched her son. "Thank you so much for the invitation, Caidy."

"You're welcome. Believe me, it will be a fun break for me from normal ranch stuff. Spring is always crazy on the ranch and I've been looking forward to this all week as a great respite."

She paused. "I have to tell you, I'm really glad you're

still willing to have anything to do with the Bowmans after the way things ended with Taft."

She really didn't want to talk about Taft. This was what she had worried about after Caidy extended the invitation, that things might be awkward between them because of the past.

"Why wouldn't I? Taft and I are still friendly." And that's all they ever *would* be, she reminded herself. "Just because he and I didn't end up the way we thought we would doesn't mean I should shun his family. I loved your family. I'm only sorry I haven't stayed in touch all these years. I see no reason we can't be friends now, unless you're too uncomfortable because of…everything?"

"Not at all!" Caidy exclaimed. Laura had the impression she wanted to say something else, but Alex interrupted before she could.

"He licked me. It tickles!"

Caidy grinned down at the boy's obvious enjoyment of the dogs. He now had all three dogs clustered around him and was petting them in turns.

"We've got puppies. Would you like to see them?" Caidy asked.

"Puppies!" Maya squealed, still in her arms, while Alex clasped his hands together, a reverential look on his face.

"Puppies! Oh, Mama, can we?"

She had to laugh at his flair for drama. "Sure. Why not? As long as it's all right with Caidy."

"They're in the barn. I was just checking on the little family a few minutes ago and it looks like a few of the pups are awake and might just be in the mood to play."

"Oh, yay!" Alex exclaimed and Caidy grinned at him.

They followed her into the barn. For Laura, it was like walking back in time. The barn smelled of hay and leather and animals, and the familiar scent mix seemed to trigger an avalanche of memories. They tumbled free of whatever place she'd stowed them after she walked away from Pine Gulch, jostling and shoving their way through her mind before she had a chance to block them out.

She used to come out to the ranch often to ride horses with Taft and their rides always started here, in the barn, where he would teach her about the different kinds of tack and how each was used, then patiently give her lessons on how to tack up a horse.

One wintry January afternoon, she suddenly remembered, she had helped him and his father deliver a foal. She could still vividly picture her astonishment at the gangly, awkward miracle of the creature.

Unbidden, she also remembered that the relative privacy of the barn compared to other places on the ranch had been one of their favorite places to kiss. Sultry, long, intense kisses that would leave them both hungry for more....

She absolutely did not need to remember *those* particular memories, full of heat and discovery and that all-consuming love that used to burn inside her for Taft. With great effort, she struggled to wrestle them back into the corner of her mind and slam the door to them so she could focus on her children and Caidy and new puppies.

The puppies' home was an empty stall at the end of the row. An old russet saddle blanket took up one corner and the mother dog, a lovely black-and-white heeler, was lying on her side taking a rest and watching her puppies wrestle around the straw-covered floor of the stall. She looked up when Caidy approached and her tail slapped a greeting.

"Hey, Betsy, here I am again. How's my best girl? I brought some company to entertain your pups for a while."

Laura could swear she saw understanding and even relief

in the dog's brown eyes as Caidy unlatched the door of the stall and swung it out. She could relate to that look—every night when her children finally closed their eyes, she would collapse onto the sofa with probably that same sort of look.

"Are you sure it's okay?" Alex asked, standing outside the stall, barely containing his nervous energy.

"Perfectly sure," Caidy answered. "I promise, they love company."

He headed inside and—just as she might have predicted—Maya wriggled to get down. "Me, too," she insisted.

"Of course, darling," Laura said. She set her on her feet and the girl headed inside the stall to stand beside her brother.

"Here, sit down and I'll bring you a puppy each," Caidy said, gesturing to a low bench inside the stall, really just a plank stretched across a couple of overturned oats buckets.

She picked up a fat, waddling black-and-white puppy from the writhing, yipping mass and set it on Alex's lap, then reached into the pile again for a smaller one, mostly black this time.

Now she had some very different but infinitely precious memories of this barn to add to her collection, Laura thought a few moments later. The children were enthralled with the puppies. Children and puppies just seemed to go together like peanut butter and jelly. Alex and Maya giggled as the puppies squirmed around on their laps, licking and sniffing. Maya hugged hers as enthusiastically as she had hugged her mother a few minutes earlier.

"Thank you for this," she said to Caidy as the two of them smiled at the children and puppies. "You've thrilled them to their socks."

"I'm afraid the pups are a little dirty and don't smell the greatest. They're a little young for baths yet."

"I don't worry about a little dirt," Laura said. "I've always figured if my kids don't get dirty sometimes, I'm doing something wrong."

"I don't think you're doing *anything* wrong," Caidy assured her. "They seem like great kids."

"Thank you."

"It can't be easy, especially now that you're on your own."

As much as Javier had loved the children, she had always felt very much on her own in Madrid. He was always busy with the hotel and his friends and, of course, his other women. Bad enough she had shared that with Taft. She certainly wasn't about to share that information with his sister.

"I have my mother to help me now. She's been a lifesaver."

Coming home had been the right decision. As much as she had struggled with taking her children away from half of their heritage probably forever, Javier's family had never been very welcoming to her. They had become even less so after Maya was born, as if Laura were to blame somehow for the genetic abnormality.

"I'm just going to come out and say this, okay?" Caidy said after a moment. "I really wish you had married Taft so we could have been sisters."

"Thank you," she said, touched by the words.

"I mean it. You were the best thing that ever happened to him. We all thought so. Compared to the women he... Well, compared to anybody else he's dated, you're a million times better. I still can't believe any brother of mine was stupid enough to let you slip through his fingers. Don't think I haven't told him so, too."

She didn't know quite how to answer—or why she had this sudden urge to protect him. Taft hadn't been stupid, only hurt and lost and not at all ready for marriage.

She hadn't been ready, either, although it had taken her a few years to admit that to herself. At twenty-one, she had been foolish enough to think her love should have been enough to help him heal from the pain and anger of losing his parents in such a violent way, when he hadn't even had the resolution of the murderers being caught and brought to justice.

An idealistic, romantic young woman and an angry, bitter young man would have made a terrible combination, she thought as she sat here in this quiet barn while the puppies wriggled around with her children and a horse stamped and snorted somewhere nearby.

"I also have a confession." Caidy shifted beside her at the stall door.

She raised an eyebrow. "Do I really want to hear this?"

"Please don't be mad, okay?"

For some reason, Laura was strongly reminded of Caidy as she had known her a decade ago, the lighthearted, mischievous teenager who thought she could tease and cajole her way out of any situation.

"Tell me. What did you do?" she asked, amusement fighting the sudden apprehension curling through her.

Before the other woman could answer, a male voice rang out through the barn. "Caidy? Are you in here?"

Her stomach dropped and the little flutters of apprehension became wild-winged flaps of anxiety.

Caidy winced. "Um, I may have casually mentioned to Taft that you and the children were coming out to the ranch today and that we might be going up on the Aspen Leaf Trail, if he wanted to tag along."

So much for her master plan of escaping the inn today so she could keep her children—and herself—out from underfoot while he was working on the other renovations.

"Are you mad?" Caidy asked.

She forced a smile when she really wanted to sit right down on the straw-covered floor of the stall and cry.

Yes, when she decided to return to Pine Gulch, she had known seeing him again was inevitable. She just hadn't expected to bump into the dratted man every flipping time she turned around.

"Why would I be mad? Your brother and I are friends." Or at least she was working hard at pretending they could be. Anyway, this was his family's ranch. Some part of her had known when she accepted Caidy's invitation to come out for a visit that there was a chance he might be here.

"Oh, good. I was worried things might be weird between the two of you."

But you invited him along anyway? she wanted to ask, but decided that sounded rude. "No. It's perfectly fine," she lied.

"I thought he could lend a hand with the children. He's really patient with them. In fact, he's the one who taught Gabi to ride. Gabi is the daughter of Becca, Trace's fiancée. Anyway, it's always good to have another experienced rider on hand when you've got kids who haven't been on a horse before."

"Caidy?" he called again.

"Back here, with the puppies," she returned.

A moment later, Taft rounded the corner of a support beam. At the sight of him, everything inside her seemed to shiver.

Okay, really? This was getting ridiculous. She huffed. So far since she had been back in town, she had seen the man in full firefighter turnout gear when he and his crew responded to the inn fire, wearing a low-slung construction belt while he worked on the renovations at the inn, and now he was dressed in worn jeans, cowboy boots and a tan Stetson that made him look dark and dangerous.

Was he purposely trying to look as if he just stepped off every single page of a beefcake calendar?

Taft Bowman—doing his part to fulfill any woman's fantasy.

"Here you are," he said with that irresistible smile.

She couldn't breathe suddenly as the dust motes floating on the air inside the barn seemed to choke her lungs. This wasn't really fair. Why hadn't his hair started to thin a little in the past decade or his gut started to paunch?

He was so blasted gorgeous and she was completely weak around him.

He leaned in to kiss his sister on the cheek. After a little awkward hesitation, much to her dismay he leaned in to kiss her on the cheek, as well. She could do nothing but endure the brush of his mouth on her skin as the familiar scent of him, outdoorsy and male, filled her senses, unleashing another flood of memories.

Before she could make her brain cooperate and think of something to say, her children noticed him for the first time.

"Hi!" Maya beamed with delight.

"Hey, pumpkin. How are things?"

"Look! Puppies!"

She thrust the endlessly patient black puppy at him and Taft graciously accepted the dog. "He's a cute one. What's his name, Caid?"

"Puppy Number Five," she answered. "I don't name them when I sell them as pups without training. I let their new owners do it."

"Look at this one." Alex pushed past his sister to hold up his own chubby little canine friend.

"Nice," Taft said. He knelt right there in the straw and

was soon covered in puppies and kids. Even the tired-looking mother dog came over to him for affection.

"Hey, Betsy. How are you holding up with this brood?" he asked, rubbing the dog between the ears and earning a besotted look that Laura found completely exasperating.

"Thanks for coming out," Caidy said.

"Not a problem. I can think of few things I enjoy more than going on a spring ride into the mountains."

"Not too far into the mountains," she assured Laura. "We can't go very far this time of year anyway. Too much snow, at least for a good month or so."

"Aspen Leaf is open, though, isn't it?"

"Yes. Destry and I checked it the other day. She was disappointed to miss the ride today, by the way," Caidy told Laura. "Becca was taking her and Gabi into Idaho Falls for fittings for their flower-girl dresses."

"And you missed out on all that girly fun?" Taft asked, climbing to his feet and coming to stand beside his sister and Laura. Suddenly she felt crowded by his heat and size and…maleness.

"Are you kidding? This will be much more enjoyable. If you haven't heard, Trace is getting hitched in June," she said to Laura.

"To Pine Gulch's newest attorney, if you can believe that," Taft added.

She *had* heard and she was happy for Trace. He had always been very kind to her. Trace, the Pine Gulch police chief, had always struck her as much more serious than Taft, the kind of person who liked to think things through before he spoke.

For being identical twins, Taft and Trace had two very unique personalities, and even though they were closer than most brothers, they had also actively cultivated friendships beyond each other, probably because of their mother's wise influence.

She did find it interesting that both of them had chosen professions in the public-safety sector, although Trace had taken a route through the military to becoming a policeman while Taft had gravitated toward fire safety and becoming a paramedic.

"Why don't we give the kids another few minutes with the puppies?" Caidy said. "I've already saddled a couple of horses I thought would be a good fit."

"Do I need to saddle Joe?"

"Nope. He's ready for you."

Taft grinned. "You mean all I had to do today was show up?"

"That's the story of your life, isn't it?" Caidy said with a disgruntled sort of affection. "If you want to, I'll let you unsaddle everybody when we're done and groom all the horses. Will that make you feel better?"

"Much. Thanks."

The puppy on Maya's lap wriggled through her fingers and waddled over to squat in the straw.

"Look," she exclaimed with an inordinate degree of delight. "Puppy pee!"

Taft chuckled at that. "I think all the puppies are ready for a snack and a nap. Why don't we go see if the horses are ready for us?"

"Yes!" Maya beamed and scampered eagerly toward Taft, where she reached up to grab his hand. After a stunned sort of moment, he smiled at her and folded her hand more securely in his much bigger one.

Alex rose reluctantly and set the puppy he had been playing with down in the straw. "Bye," he whispered, a look of naked longing clear for all to see.

"I hear the kid wants a dog. You know you're going to have to cave, don't you?" Taft spoke in a low voice.

Laura sighed through her own dismay. "You don't think I'm tough enough to resist a six-year-old?"

"I'm not sure a hardened criminal could resist *that* particular six-year-old."

He was right, darn it. She was pretty sure she would have to give in and let her son have a dog. Not a border collie, certainly, because they were active dogs and needed work to do, but she would find something.

As they walked outside the barn toward the horse pasture, she saw Alex's eyes light up at the sight of four horses saddled and waiting. Great. Now he would probably start begging her for a horse, too.

She had to admit, a little burst of excitement kicked through her, too, as they approached the animals. She loved horses and she actually had Taft to thank for that. Unlike many of her schoolmates in the sprawling Pine Gulch school district, which encompassed miles of ranch land, she was a city girl who walked or rode her bike to school instead of taking the bus. Even though she had loved horses from the time she was young—didn't most girls?—her parents had patiently explained they didn't have room for one of their own at their home adjacent to the inn.

She had enjoyed riding with friends who lived outside of town, but had very much considered herself a greenhorn until she became friends with Taft. Even before they started dating, she would often come out to the ranch and ride with him and sometimes Caidy into the mountains.

This would be rather like old times—which, come to think of it, wasn't necessarily a good thing.

Since moving away from Pine Gulch, she hadn't been

on a horse one single time, she realized with shock. Even more reason for this little thrum of anticipation.

"Wow, they're really big," Alex said in a soft voice. Maya seemed nervous as well, clinging tightly to Taft's hand.

"Big doesn't have to mean scary," Taft assured him. "These are really gentle horses. None of them will hurt you. I promise. Old Pete, the horse you're going to ride, is so lazy, you'll be lucky to make it around the barn before he decides to stop and take a nap."

Alex giggled but it had a nervous edge to it and Taft gave him a closer look.

"Do you want to meet him?"

Her son toed the dirt with the shiny new cowboy boots she had picked up at the farm-implement store before they drove out to the ranch. "I guess. You sure they don't bite?"

"Some horses do. Not any of the River Bow horses. I swear it."

He picked Maya up in his arms and reached for Alex's hand, leading them both over to the smallest of the horses, a gray with a calm, rather sweet face.

"This is Pete," Taft said. "He's just about the gentlest horse we've ever had here at River Bow. He'll treat you right, kid."

As she watched from the sidelines, the horse bent his head down and lipped Alex's shoulder. Alex froze, eyes wide and slightly terrified, but Taft set a reassuring hand on his other shoulder. "Don't worry. He's just looking for a treat."

"I don't have a treat." Alex's voice quavered a bit. These uncharacteristic moments of fear from her usually bold, mischievous son always seemed to take her by surprise, although she knew they were perfectly normal from a developmental standpoint.

Taft reached into his pocket and pulled out a handful of small red apples. "You're in luck. I always carry a supply of crab apples for old Pete. They're his favorite, probably because I can let him have only a few at a time. It's probably like you eating pizza. A little is great, but too much would make you sick. Same for Pete and crab apples."

"Where on earth do you find crab apples in April?" Laura couldn't resist asking.

"That's my secret."

Caidy snorted. "Not much of a secret," she said. "Every year, my crazy brother gathers up two or three bushels from the tree on the side of the house and stores them down in the root cellar. Nobody else will touch the things—they're too bitter even for pies unless you pour in cup after cup of sugar—but old Pete loves them. Every year Taft puts up a supply so he's got something to bring the old codger."

She shouldn't find it so endearing to imagine him picking crab apples to give to an old, worn-out horse—or to watch his ears turn as red as the apples under his cowboy hat.

He handed one of the pieces of sour fruit to her son and showed him the correct way to feed the horse. Alex held his hand out flat and old Pete lapped it up.

"It tickles like the dog," Alex exclaimed.

"But it doesn't hurt, right?" Taft asked.

The boy shook his head with a grin. "Nope. Just tickles. Hi, Pete."

The horse seemed quite pleased to make his acquaintance, especially after he produced a few more crab apples for the horse, handed to him by Taft.

"Ready to hop up there now?" Taft asked. When the boy nodded, Caidy stepped up with a pair of riding helmets waiting on the fence.

"We're going to swap that fancy cowboy hat for a helmet, okay?"

"I like my cowboy hat, though. I just got it."

"And you can wear it again when we get back. But when you're just learning to ride, wearing a helmet is safer."

"Just like at home when you have to wear your bicycle helmet," Laura told him.

"No helmet, no horse," Taft said sternly.

Her son gave them all a grudging look, but he removed his cowboy hat and handed it to his mother, then allowed Caidy to fasten on the safety helmet. Caidy took Maya from Taft and put one on her, as well, which eased Laura's safety worries considerably.

Finally Taft picked up Alex and hefted him easily into the saddle. The glee on her son's face filled her with a funny mix of happiness and apprehension. He was growing up, embracing risks, and she wasn't sure she was ready for that.

Caidy stepped up to adjust the stirrups to the boy's height. "There you go, cowboy. That should be better."

"What do I do now?" Alex asked with an eager look up into the mountains as if he were ready to go join a posse and hunt for outlaws right this minute.

"Well, the great thing about Pete is how easygoing he is," Taft assured him. "He's happy to just follow along behind the other horses. That's kind of his specialty and what makes him a perfect horse for somebody just beginning. I'll hold his lead line so you won't even have to worry about turning him or making him slow down or anything. Next time you come out to the ranch we'll work on those other things, but this time is just for fun."

Next time? She frowned, annoyed that he would give Alex the impression there would be another time—and that Taft would be part of it, if she ever did bring the kids out to River Bow again. Children didn't forget things like that. Alex would hold him to it and be gravely disappointed if a return trip never materialized.

This was not going at all like she'd planned. She and Caidy were supposed to be taking the children for an easy ride. Instead Taft seemed to have taken over, in typical fashion, while Caidy answered her cell phone a short distance away from the group.

After a moment, Maya grew impatient and tugged on his jeans. "My horse?" she asked, looking around at the animals. She looked so earnest and adorable that it was tough for Laura to stay annoyed at anything.

He smiled down at her with such gentleness that her chest ached. "I was thinking you could just ride with me on my old friend Joe. What do you say, pumpkin? We'll try a pony for you another day, okay?"

She appeared to consider this, looking first at the big black gelding he pointed at, then back at Taft. Finally she gave him that brilliant, wide heartbreaker of a smile. "Okay."

Taft Bowman may have met his match for sheer charm, she thought.

"I guess that just leaves me," she said, eyeing the two remaining horses. Something told her the dappled gray-and-black mare was Caidy's, which left the bay for her.

"Do you need a crab apple to break the ice, too?" Taft asked with a teasing smile so appealing she had to turn away.

"I think I'll manage," she said more tersely than she intended. She modified her tone to be a little warmer. "What's her name?"

"Lacey," he answered.

"Hi, Lacey." She stroked the horse's neck and was rewarded with an equine raspberry sound that made Alex laugh.

"That sounded like her mouth farted!" he exclaimed.

"That's just her way of saying hi." Taft's gaze met hers, laughter brimming in his green eyes, and Laura wanted to sink into those eyes.

Darn the man.

She stiffened her shoulders and resolve and shoved her boot in the stirrup, then swung into the saddle and tried not to groan at the pull of muscles she hadn't used in a long time.

Taft pulled the horse's reins off the tether and handed them to her. Their hands brushed again, a slight touch of skin against skin, and she quickly pulled the reins to the other side and jerked her attention away from her reaction to Taft and back to the thousand-pound animal beneath her.

Oh, she had missed this, she thought, loosely holding the reins and reacquainting herself to the unique feel of being on a horse. She had missed all of it. The stretch of her muscles, the heat of the sun on her bare head, the vast peaks of the Tetons in the distance.

"You ready, sweetie?" he asked Maya, who nodded, although the girl suddenly looked a little shy.

"Everything will be just fine," he assured her. "I won't let go. I promise."

He loosed his horse's reins from the hitch as well as the lead line for old Pete before setting Maya in the saddle. Her daughter looked small and vulnerable at such a height, even under her safety helmet, but she had to trust that Taft would take care of her.

"While I mount up, you hold on right there. It's called the saddle horn. Got it?"

"Got it," she mimicked. "Horn."

"Excellent. Hang on, now. I'll keep one hand on you."

Laura watched anxiously, afraid Maya would slide off at the inevitable jostling of the saddle, but she needn't have worried. He swung effortlessly into the saddle, then scooped an arm around the girl.

"Caid? You coming?" Taft called.

She glanced over and saw Caidy finish her phone conversation and tuck her cell into her pocket, then walk toward them, her features tight with concern. "We've got a problem."

"What's wrong?"

"That was Ridge. A speeder just hit a dog a quarter mile or so from the front ranch gates. Ridge was right behind the idiot and saw the whole thing happen."

"One of yours?" Taft asked.

Her braid swung as she shook her head. "No. I think it's a little stray I've seen around the last few weeks. I've been trying to coax him to come closer to the house but he's pretty skittish. Looks like he's got a broken leg and Ridge isn't sure what to do with him."

"Can't he take him to the vet?"

"He can't reach Doc Harris. I guess he's been trying to find the backup vet but he's in the middle of equine surgery up at Cold Creek Ranch. I should go help. Poor guy."

"Ridge or the stray?"

"Both. Ridge is a little out of his element with dogs. He can handle horses and cattle, but anything smaller than a calf throws him off his game." She paused and sent a guilty look toward Laura. "I'm sorry to do this after I invited you out and all, but do you think you'll be okay with only my brother as a guide while I go help with this injured dog?"

If not for the look in Caidy's eyes, Laura might have thought she had manufactured the whole thing as an elaborate ruse to throw her and Taft together. But either Caidy was an excellent actress or her distress was genuine.

"Of course. Don't worry about a thing. Do you need our help?"

The other woman shook her head again. "I doubt it. To be honest, I'm not sure there's anything *I* can do, but I have to try, right? I'm just sorry to invite you out here and then ditch you."

"No worries. We should be fine. We're not going far, are we?"

Taft shook his head. "Up the hill about a mile. There's a nice place to stop and have the picnic Caidy packed."

She did *not* feel like having a picnic with him but could think of no graceful way to extricate herself and her children from it, especially when Alex and Maya appeared to be having the time of their lives.

"Thanks for being understanding," Caidy said, with a harried look, unsaddling the other horse at lightning speed. "I'll make it up to you."

"No need," Laura said as her horse took a step or two sideways, anxious to go. "Take care of the stray for us."

"I'll do my best. Maybe I'll try to catch up with you. If I don't make it, though, I'll probably see you later after you come back down."

She glanced up at the sky. "Looks like a few clouds gathering up on the mountain peaks. I hope it doesn't rain on you."

"They're pretty high. We should be fine for a few hours," Taft said. "Good luck with the dog. Shall we, guys?"

Leaving Caidy behind to deal with a crisis felt rude and selfish, but Laura didn't know what else to do. The children would be terribly disappointed if she backed out of the ride, and Caidy was right. What could they do to help her with the injured dog?

She sighed. And of course this also meant she and the children would have to be alone with Taft.

She supposed it was a very good thing Taft had no reason to be romantically interested in her anymore. She had a feeling she would be even more weak than normal on a horseback ride with him into the mountains, especially when she had so many memories of other times and other rides that usually ended with them making out somewhere on the ranch.

"Yes," she finally said. "Let's go."

The sooner they could be on their way, the quicker they could return and she and her children could go back to the way things were before Taft burst so insistently back into her life.

Chapter 7

With Maya perched in front of him, Taft led the way and held the lead line for Alex's horse while Laura brought up the rear. A light breeze danced in her hair as they traveled through verdant pastureland on their way to a trailhead just above the ranch.

The afternoon seemed eerily familiar, a definite déjà vu moment. It took her a moment to realize why—she used to fantasize about a day exactly like this when she had been young and full of dreams. She used to imagine the two of them spending a lovely spring afternoon together on horseback along with their children, laughing and talking, pausing here and there for some of those kisses she had once been so addicted to.

Okay, they had the horses and the kids here and definitely the lovely spring afternoon, but the rest of it wasn't going to happen. Not on her watch.

She focused on the trail, listening to Alex jabber a mile

a minute about everything he saw, from the double-trunked pine tree alongside the trail, to one of Caidy's dogs that had come along with them, to about how much he loved old Pete. The gist, as she fully expected, was that he now wanted a horse *and* a dog of his own.

The air here smelled delicious: sharp, citrusy pine, the tart, evocative scent of sagebrush, woodsy earth and new growth.

She had missed the scent of the mountains. Madrid had its own distinctive smells, flowers and spices and baking bread, but this, this was home.

They rode for perhaps forty minutes until Alex's chatter started to die away. It was hard work staying atop a horse. Even if the rest of him wasn't sore, she imagined his jaw muscles must be aching.

The deceptively easy grade led one to think they weren't gaining much in altitude, but finally they reached a clearing where the pines and aspens opened up and she could look down on the ranch and see its eponymous river bow, a spot where the river's course made a horseshoe bend, almost folding in on itself. The water glimmered in the afternoon sunlight, reflecting the mountains and trees around it.

She admired the sight from atop her horse, grateful that Taft had stopped, then realized he was dismounting with Maya still in his arms.

"I imagine your rear end could use a little rest," he said to Alex, earning a giggle.

"Sí," he said, reverting to the Spanish he sometimes still used. "My bum hurts and I need to pee," he said.

"We can take care of that. Maya, you sit here while I help your brother." He set the girl atop a couch-size boulder, then returned to the horses and lifted Alex down, then turned to Laura again. "What about you? Need a hand?"

"I've got it," she answered, quite certain it wouldn't be a good idea for him to help her dismount.

Her muscles were stiff, even after such a short time on the horse, and she welcomed the chance to stretch her legs a little. "Come on, Alex. I'll take you over to the bushes. Maya, do you need to go?"

She shook her head, busy picking flowers.

"I'll keep an eye on her," Taft said. "Unless you need me on tree duty?"

She shook her head, amused despite herself, at the term. "I've got it."

As she walked away, she didn't want to think about what a good team they made or how very similar this was to those fantasies she used to weave.

Alex thought it was quite a novel thing to take care of his business against a tree and didn't even complain when she whipped the hand sanitizer out of her pocket and made him use it afterward.

The moment they returned to the others, Caidy's dog King brought a stick over and dropped it at Alex's feet, apparently knowing an easy mark when he saw one. Alex picked up the stick and chucked it for the dog as far as his little arm could go and the dog bounded after it while Maya clapped her hands with excitement.

"Me next," she said.

The two were perfectly content to play with the dog and Laura was just as content to lean against a sun-warmed granite boulder and watch them while she listened to a meadowlark's familiar song.

Idaho is a pretty little place. That's what her mother always used to say the birds were trilling. The memory made her smile.

"I can picture you just like that when you were younger. Your hair was longer, but you haven't changed much at all."

He had leaned his hip against the boulder where she sat and her body responded instantly to his proximity, to the familiar scent of him. She edged away so their shoulders wouldn't brush and wondered if he noticed.

"I'm afraid that's where you're wrong. I'm a very different person. Who doesn't change in ten years?"

"Yeah, you're right. I'm not the same man I was a decade ago. I like to think I'm smarter these days about holding on to what's important."

"Do you ride often?" she asked.

A glint in his eye told her he knew very well she didn't want to tug on that particular conversational line, but he went along with the obvious change of topic. "Not as much as I would like. My niece, Destry, loves to ride and now Gabi has caught the bug. As often as they can manage it, they do their best to persuade one of us to take them for a ride. I haven't been up for a few months, though."

He obviously loved his niece. She had already noticed that soft note in his voice when he talked about the girl. She would have expected it. The Bowmans had always been a close, loving family before their parents' brutal murder. She expected they would welcome Becca and her sister into the family's embrace, as well.

"Too busy with your social life?"

The little niggle of envy under her skin turned her tone more caustic than she intended, but he didn't seem offended.

He even chuckled. "Sure. If by *social life* you mean the house I'm building on the edge of town that's filled all my waking hours for the last six months. I haven't had much room for other things."

"You're building it yourself?"

"Most of it. I've had help here and there. Plumbing. HVAC. That sort of thing. I don't have the patience for good drywall work, so I paid somebody else to do that, too. But I've done all the carpentry and most of the electrical. I can give you some good names of subcontractors I trust if you decide to do more on the inn."

"Why a house?"

He appeared to be giving her question serious thought as he watched the children playing with the dog, with the grand sprawl of the ranch below them. "I guess I was tired of throwing away rent money and living in a little apartment where I didn't have room to stretch out. I've had this land for a long time. I don't know. Seemed like it was time."

"You're building a house. That's pretty permanent. Does that mean you're planning to stay in Pine Gulch?"

He shrugged, and despite her efforts to keep as much distance as possible between them, his big shoulder still brushed hers. "Where else would I go? Maybe I should have taken off for somewhere exotic when I had the chance. What do they pay firefighters in Madrid?"

"I'm afraid I have no idea. I have friends I can ask, though." He would fit in well there, she thought, and the *madrileñas*—the women of Madrid—would go crazy for his green eyes and teasing smile.

Which he utilized to full effect on her now. "That eager to get rid of me?"

She had no answer to that, so she again changed the subject. "Where did you say your house was?"

"A couple of miles from here, near the mouth of Cold Creek Canyon. I've got about five acres there in the trees. Enough room to move over some of my own horses eventually."

He paused, an oddly intent look in his green eyes. "You ought to come see it sometime. I would even let Alex pound a couple of nails if he wanted."

She couldn't afford to spend more time with him, not when he seemed already to be sneaking past all her careful defenses. "I'm sure we've got all the nails Alex could wish to pound at the inn."

"Sure. Yeah. Of course." He nodded, appearing nonchalant, but she had the impression she had hurt him somehow.

She wanted to make it right, tell him she would love to come see his house under construction anytime he wanted them to, but she caught the ridiculous words before she could blurt them out.

Taft picked up an early-spring wildflower—she thought it might be some kind of phlox—and twirled it between his fingers, his gaze on the children playing with the dog. This time he was the one who picked another subject. "How are the kids settling into Pine Gulch?"

"So far they're loving it, especially having their grandmother around."

"What about you?"

She looked out over the ranch and at the mountains in the distance. "It's good. There are a lot of things I love about being home, things I missed more than I realized while I was in Spain. Those mountains, for instance. I had forgotten how truly quiet and peaceful it could be here."

"This is one of my favorite places on the ranch."

"I remember."

Her soft words hung between them and she heartily wished she could yank them back. Tension suddenly seethed between them and she saw that he also remembered the significance of this place.

Right here in this flower-strewn meadow was where

they had kissed that first time when he had returned after the dangerous flashover. She had always considered it their place, and every time she came here after that, she remembered the sheer joy bursting through her as he finally—finally!—saw her as more than just his friend.

They had come here often after that. He had proposed, right here, while they were stretched out on a blanket in the meadow grass.

She suddenly knew it was no accident he had stopped the horses here. Anger pumped through her, hot and fierce, that he would dredge up all these hopes and dreams and emotions she had buried after she left Pine Gulch.

With jerky motions, she climbed off the boulder. "We should probably be heading back."

His mouth tightened and he looked as if he wanted to say something else but he seemed to change his mind. "Yeah, you're right. That sky is looking a little ominous."

She looked up to find dark clouds smearing the sky, a perfect match to her mood, as if she had conjured them. "Where did those come from? A minute ago it was perfectly sunny."

"It's springtime in Idaho, where you can enjoy all four seasons in a single afternoon. Caidy warned us about possible rain. I should have been paying more attention. You ready, kids?" he called. "We've got to go."

Alex frowned from where he and Maya were flopped in the dirt petting the dog. "Do we have to?"

"Unless you want to get drenched and have to ride down on a mud slide all the way to the ranch."

"Can we?" Alex asked eagerly.

Taft laughed, although it sounded strained around the edges. "Not this time. It's up to us to make sure the ladies make it back in one piece. Think you're up to it?"

If she hadn't been so annoyed with Taft, she might have laughed at the way Alex puffed out his little chest. "Yes, sir," he answered.

"Up you go, then, son." He lifted the boy up onto the saddle and adjusted his helmet before he turned back to Maya.

"What about you, Maya, my girl? Are you ready?"

Her daughter beamed and scampered toward him. Watching them all only hardened Laura's intention to fortify her defenses around Taft.

One person in her family needed to resist the man. By the looks of things, she was the only one up for the job.

Maybe.

They nearly made it.

About a quarter mile from the ranch, the clouds finally let loose, unleashing a torrent of rain in one of those spring showers that come on so fast, so cold and merciless that they had no time to really prepare themselves.

By the time they reached the barn, Alex was shivering, Laura's hair was bedraggled and Taft was kicking himself for not hurrying them down the hill a little faster. At least Maya stayed warm and dry, wrapped in the spare raincoat he pulled out of his saddlebag.

He took them straight to the house instead of the barn. After he climbed quickly down from his horse, he set Laura's little girl on the porch, then quickly returned to the horses to help Alex dismount.

"Head on up to the porch with your sister," he ordered. After making sure the boy complied, he reached up without waiting for permission and lifted Laura down, as well. He winced as her slight frame trembled when he set her onto solid ground again.

"I'm sorry," he said. "I should have been paying better attention to the weather. That storm took me by surprise."

Her teeth chattered and her lips had a blue tinge to them he didn't like at all. "It's okay. My SUV has a good heater. We'll warm up soon enough."

"Forget it. You're not going home in wet clothes. Come inside and we'll find something you and the kids can change into."

"It's fine. We'll be home in fifteen minutes."

"If I let you go home cold and wet, I would never hear the end of it from Caidy. Trust me—the wrath of Caidy is a fearful thing and she would shoot me if I let you get sick. Come on. The horses can wait out here for a minute."

He scooped both kids into his arms, much to their giggly enjoyment, and carried them into the ranch house to cut off any further argument. That they could still laugh under such cold and miserable conditions touched something deep inside him.

He loved these kids already. How had that happened? Alex, with his million questions, Maya with her loving spirit and eager smile. Somehow when he wasn't looking, they had tiptoed straight into his heart and he had a powerful feeling he wasn't going to be able to shoo them out again anytime soon.

He wanted more afternoons like this one, full of fun and laughter and this sense of belonging. Hell, he wasn't picky. He would take mornings or evenings or any time he could have with Laura and her kids.

Yet Laura seemed quite determined to keep adding bricks to the wall between them. Every time he felt as if he was maybe making a little progress, she built up another layer and he didn't know what the hell to do about it.

"Here's the plan," he said when she trailed reluctantly

inside after him. "You get the kids out of their wet clothes and wrapped in warm blankets. We've got a gas fireplace in the TV room that will warm you up in a second. Meanwhile, I'll see what I can do about finding something for you to wear."

"This is ridiculous. Honestly, Taft, we can be home and changed into our own clothes in the time it's going to take you to find something here."

He aimed a stern look at her. "Forget it. I'm not letting you leave this ranch until you're dry, and that's the end of it. I'm a paramedic, trained in public safety. How would it look if the Pine Gulch fire chief stood around twiddling his thumbs while his town's newest citizens got hypothermia?"

"Oh, stop exaggerating. We're not going to get hypothermia," she muttered, but she still followed him to the media room of the ranch house, a big, comfortable space with multiple sofas and recliners.

This happened to be one of his favorite rooms at River Bow Ranch, a place where he and his brothers often gathered to watch college football and NBA basketball.

He flipped the switch for the fireplace. The blower immediately came on, throwing welcome heat into the room while he grabbed a couple of blankets from behind one of the leather sofas for the kids.

"Here you go. You guys shuck your duds and wrap up in these blankets."

"Really?" Alex looked wide-eyed. "Can we, Mama?"

"Just for a few minutes, while we throw our clothes in the dryer."

"I'll be back in a second with something of Caidy's for you," he told her.

He headed into his sister's room and quickly found a pair

of sweats and a hooded sweatshirt in the immaculately or-
ganized walk-in closet.

By the time he returned to the TV room, the children
were bundled in blankets and cuddled up on the couch. He
set the small pile of clothes on the edge of the sofa.

"Here you go. I know Caidy won't mind if you borrow
them. The only thing in this situation that would make her
angry would be if I *didn't* give you dry clothes."

Even though her mouth tightened as if she wanted to
argue, she only nodded. The wet locks of hair hanging
loosely around her face somehow made her even more beautiful to him. She seemed delicate and vulnerable here in the
flickering firelight, and he wanted to tuck her up against
him and keep her safe forever.

Yeah, he probably should keep that particular desire to
himself for the moment.

"Give me a few minutes to take care of the horses and
then I can throw your clothes in the dryer."

"I think I can probably manage to find the laundry room
by myself," she murmured. "I'll just toss everything in there
together after I change."

"Okay. I'll be back in a few minutes."

Caring for the horses took longer than he'd hoped. He
was out of practice, he guessed, plus he had three horses
to unsaddle.

When he finally finished up in the barn about half an
hour later, the rain was still pouring in sheets that slanted
sideways from the wind. Harsh, punishing drops cut into
him as he headed back up the porch steps and into the entryway.

Caidy wouldn't be happy about him dripping all over her
floor but she would probably forgive him, especially because he had done his best to take good care of the horses—

and her guests. That would go a long way toward keeping him out of the doghouse.

He headed into Ridge's room to swipe a dry pair of jeans and a soft green henley. After quickly changing, he walked through the house in his bare feet to the TV room to check on Laura and her kids.

When he opened the door, she pressed a finger to her mouth and gestured to one of the sofas. He followed her gaze and found both Alex and Maya asleep, wrapped in blankets and nestled together like Caidy's puppies while a cartoon on the television murmured softly in the background.

"Wow, that was fast," he whispered. "How did *that* happen?"

She rose with a sidelong look at her sleeping children and led the way back into the hall. She had changed into Caidy's clothes, he could see, and pulled her damp hair back into a ponytail. In the too-big hoodie, she looked young and sweet and very much like the girl he had fallen in love with.

"It's been a big afternoon for them, full of much more excitement than they're used to, and Maya, at least, missed her nap. Of course, Alex insists he's too old for a nap, but every once in a while he still falls asleep in front of the TV."

"Yeah, I have that problem, too, sometimes."

"Really? With all that company I've heard you keep? That must be so disappointing for them."

He frowned. "I don't know what you've heard, but the rumors about my social life are greatly exaggerated."

"Are they?"

He didn't want to talk about this now. What he wanted to do was wrap his arms around her, press her up against that wall and kiss her for the next five or six hours. Because he couldn't do that, he figured he should at least try to set the record straight.

"After you broke things off and left for Spain, I…went a little crazy, I'll admit." He had mostly been trying to forget her and the aching emptiness she left behind, but he wasn't quite ready to confess that much to her. A few years later when he found out she had married another man in Madrid and was expecting a baby, he hadn't seen any reason for restraint.

"I did a lot more drinking and partying than I should have. I'm not particularly proud of who I was back then. The thing is, a guy gets a reputation around Pine Gulch and that's how people tend to see him forever. I haven't been that wild in a long time."

"You don't have to explain yourself to me, Taft," she said, rather stiffly.

"I don't want you to think I'm the Cold Creek Casanova people seem to think."

"What does it matter what I think?"

"It matters," he said simply and couldn't resist taking her hand. Her fingers were still cold and he wrapped his bigger hands around hers. "Brrr. Let me warm up your hands. I'm sorry I didn't keep a better eye on the weather. I should have at least provided gloves for you."

"It's fine. I'm not really cold anymore." She met his gaze, then quickly looked away, and her fingers trembled slightly inside his. "Anyway, I don't think the children minded the rain that much. To them, it was all part of the adventure. Alex already told me he pretended he was a Texas marshal trying to track a bad guy. Rain and all, the whole day will be a cherished memory for them both."

Tenderness for this woman—and her children—washed through him just like that rain, carving rivulets and channels through all the places inside him that had been parched for far too long. "You're amazing at that."

A faint blush soaked her cheeks. "At what?"

"Finding the good in every situation. You always used to do that. Somehow I'd forgotten it. If you had a flat tire, you would say you appreciated the chance to slow down for a minute and enjoy your surroundings. If you broke a nail, you would just say you now had a good excuse to give yourself a manicure."

"Annoying, isn't it? How do people stand me?"

Her laugh sounded embarrassed and she tried to tug her hands away, but he held them fast, squeezing her fingers.

"No, I think it's wonderful. I didn't realize until right this moment how much I've missed that about you."

She gazed up at him, her eyes that lovely columbine-blue and her mouth slightly parted. Her fingers trembled again in his and he was aware of the scent of her, flowery and sweet, and of the sudden tension tightening between them.

He wanted to kiss her as he couldn't remember wanting anything in his life, except maybe the first time he had kissed her on the mountainside so many years ago.

If he followed through on the fierce hunger curling through him, she would just think he was being the player the whole town seemed to think he was, taking advantage of a situation just because he could.

Right now she didn't even like him very much. Better to just bide his time, give her a chance to come to know him again and trust him.

Yeah, that would be the wise, cautious thing to do. But as her hands trembled in his, he knew with a grim sort of resignation that he couldn't be wise or cautious. Not when it came to Laura.

As everything inside him tightened with anticipation, he tugged her toward him and lowered his mouth to hers.

Magic. Simply delicious. She had the softest, sweetest mouth and he couldn't believe he had forgotten how perfectly she fit against him.

Oh, he had missed her, missed this.

For about ten seconds, she didn't move anything except her fingers, now curled in his, while his mouth touched and tasted hers. For those ten seconds, he waited for her to push him away. She remained still except for her hands, and then, as if she had come to some internal decision—or maybe just resisted as long as she could—she returned the kiss, her mouth warm and soft and willing.

That was all the signal he needed to deepen the kiss. In an instant, need thundered through him and he released her hands and wrapped his arms around her, pulling her closer, intoxicated by her body pressed against him.

She felt wonderfully familiar but not quite the same, perhaps a little curvier than she'd been back when she had been his. He supposed two children and a decade could do that. He tightened his arms around her, very much appreciating the difference as her curves brushed against his chest.

She made a low sound in her throat and her arms slipped around his neck and he did what he had imagined earlier, pressed her back against the wall.

She kissed him back and he knew he didn't imagine the hitch in her breathing, the rapid heartbeat he could feel beneath his fingers.

This. This was what he wanted. Laura, right here.

All the aimless wandering of the past ten years had finally found a purpose, here in the arms of this woman. He wanted her and her children in his life. No, it was more than just a whim. He *needed* them. He pictured laughter and joy, rides into the mountains, winter nights spent cuddling by the fireplace of the log home he was building.

For her. He was building it for her and he had never realized it until this moment. Every fixture, every detail had been aimed at creating the home they had always talked about building together.

That didn't make sense. It was completely crazy. Yeah, he'd heard her husband died some months back and had grieved for the pain she must have been feeling, but he hadn't even known she was coming home until he showed up to fight the fire at the inn and found her there.

He had thought he was just building the house he wanted, but now he could see just how perfectly she and her children would fit there.

Okay, slow down, Bowman, he told himself. One kiss did not equal happy ever after. He had hurt her deeply by pushing her away so readily after his parents died and it was going take more than just a few heated embraces to work past that.

He didn't care. He had always craved a challenge, whether that was climbing a mountain, kayaking rapids or conquering an out-of-control wildfire. He had been stupid enough to let her go once. He damn well wasn't going to do it again.

She made another low sound in her throat and he remembered how very sexy he used to find those little noises she made. Her tongue slid along his, erotic and inviting, and heat scorched through him, raw and hungry.

He was just trying to figure out how to move this somewhere a little more comfortable than against the wall of the hallway when the sound of the door opening suddenly pierced his subconscious.

A moment later, he heard his sister's voice from the entry at the other side of the house.

"We've got to go look for them." Caidy sounded stressed and almost frantic. "I can't believe Taft didn't make it back before the rain hit. What if something's happened to them?"

"He'll take care of them. Don't worry about it," Ridge replied in that calm way of his.

They would be here any second, he realized. Even though it was just about the toughest thing he'd ever done— besides standing by and letting her walk out of his life ten years ago—he eased away from her.

She looked flustered, pink, aroused. Beautiful.

He cleared his throat. "Laura," he started to say, but whatever thoughts jumbled around in his head didn't make it to words before his siblings walked down the hall and the moment was gone.

"Oh!" Caidy pedaled to a stop when she saw them. Her gaze swiveled between him and Laura and then back to him. Her eyes narrowed and he squirmed at the accusatory look in them, as if he was some sort of feudal lord having his way with the prettiest peasant. Yeah, he had kissed her, but she hadn't exactly put up any objections.

"You made it back safely."

"Yes."

Laura's voice came out husky, thready. She cleared it. Her cheeks were rosy and she refused to meet his gaze. "Yes. Safe but not quite dry. On our way down, we were caught in the first few minutes of the rainstorm. Taft loaned me some of your clothes. I hope you don't mind."

"Oh, of course! You can keep them, for heaven's sake. What about the kids? Are they okay?"

"More than okay." Her smile seemed strained, but he wasn't sure anyone but him could tell. "This was the most exciting thing that has happened to them since we've been back in Pine Gulch—and that's saying something, considering Alex started a fire that had four ladder trucks responding. They were so thrilled by the whole day that they were both exhausted and fell asleep watching cartoons while we have been waiting for our clothes to run through the dryer—which is silly, by the way. We could have been home in fifteen minutes, but Taft wouldn't let us leave in our wet gear."

"Wise man." Ridge spoke up for the first time. His brother gave him a searching look very much like Caidy's before turning back to her. "Great to see you again, Laura."

Ridge stepped forward and pulled her into a hug, and she responded with a warm smile she still hadn't given *Taft*.

"Welcome back to Pine Gulch. How are you settling in?"

"Good. Being home again is…an adventure."

"How's the dog?" Taft asked.

"Lucky. Looks like only a broken leg," Caidy said. "Doc Harris hurried back from a meeting in Pocatello so he could set it. He's keeping him overnight for observation."

"Good man, that Doc Harris."

"I know. I don't know what we're all going to do when he finally retires."

"You'll have to find another vet to keep on speed dial," Taft teased.

Caidy made a face at him, then turned back to Laura. "You and the kids will stay for dinner, won't you? I can throw soup and biscuits on and have it ready in half an hour."

As much as he wanted her to agree, he knew—even before she said the words—exactly how she would answer.

"Thank you for the invitation, but I'm afraid I'm covering the front-desk shift this evening. I'm sorry. In fact,

I should really be going. I'm sure our clothes are dry by now. Perhaps another time?"

"Yes, definitely. Let me go check on your clothes."

"I can do it," Laura protested, but Caidy was faster, probably because she had grown up in a family of boys where you had to move quick if you wanted the last piece of pie or a second helping of potato salad.

Ridge and Laura talked about the inn and her plans for renovating it for the few moments it took for Caidy to return from the laundry room off the kitchen with her arms full of clothing.

"Here you go. Nice and dry."

"Great. I'll go wake up my kids and then we can get out of your way."

"You're not in our way. I promise. I'm so glad you could come out to the ranch. I'm only sorry I wasn't here for the ride, since I was the one who invited you. I'm not usually so rude."

"It wasn't rude," Laura protested. "You were helping a wounded dog. That's more important than a little ride we could have done anytime."

Caidy opened the door to the media room. Laura gave him one more emotion-charged look before following his sister, leaving Taft alone with Ridge.

His brother studied him for a long moment, reminding Taft uncomfortably of their father when he and Trace found themselves in some scrape or other.

"Be careful there, brother," Ridge finally said.

He was thirty-four years old and wasn't at all in the mood for a lecture from an older brother who tended to think he was the boss of the world. "About?"

"I've got eyes. I can tell when a woman's just been kissed."

He was *really* not in the mood to talk about Laura with

Ridge. As much as he respected his brother for stepping up and taking care of both Caidy and the ranch after their parents died, Ridge was *not* their father and he didn't have to answer to the man.

"What's your point?" he asked, more belligerently than he probably should have.

Ridge frowned. "You sure you know what you're doing, dredging everything up again with Laura?"

If I figure that out, I'll be sure to let you know. "All I did was take her and her kids for a horseback ride."

Ridge was silent for a long moment. "I don't know what happened between the two of you all those years ago, why you didn't end up walking down the aisle when everybody could tell the two of you were crazy in love."

"Does it matter? It's ancient history."

"Not that ancient. Ten years. And take it from an expert, the choices we make in the past can haunt us for the rest of our lives."

Ridge should definitely know that. He had married a woman completely unsuitable for ranch life who had ended up making everybody around her miserable, too.

"Given your track record with women in the years since," Ridge went on, "I'm willing to bet you're the one who ended things. You didn't waste much time being heartbroken over the end of your engagement."

That shows what you know, he thought. "It was a mutual decision," he lied for the umpteenth time.

"If I remember right, you picked up with that Turner woman just a week or two after Laura left town. And then Sonia Gallegos a few weeks after that."

Yeah, he remembered those bleak days after she left, the gaping emptiness he had tried—and failed—to fill, when he had wanted nothing but to chase after her, drag her home and keep her where she belonged, with him.

"What's your point, Ridge?"

"This goes without saying—"

"Yet you're going to say it anyway."

"Damn straight. Laura isn't one of your Bandito bimbos. She's a decent person with a couple of kids, including one with challenges. Keep in mind she lost her husband recently. The last thing she probably needs is you messing with her head and heart again when she's trying to build a life here."

Like his favorite fishing knife, his brother's words seemed to slice right to the bone.

He wanted her fiercely—but just because he wanted something didn't mean he automatically deserved it. He'd learned that lesson young when his mother used to make him and Trace take out the garbage or change out a load of laundry if they wanted an extra cookie before dinner.

If he wanted another chance with her after the way he had treated her—and damn it, he *did*—he was going to have to earn his way back. He didn't know how yet. He only knew he planned to work like hell to become the kind of man he should have been ten years ago.

Chapter 8

Laura was going to kill him. Severely.

Five days after going riding with her and her kids above River Bow, Taft set down the big bag of supplies his sister had given him onto the concrete, then shifted the bundle into his left arm so he could use his right arm to wield his key card, the only way after hours to enter the side door of the inn closest to his room.

"Almost there, buddy," he said when the bundle whimpered.

He swiped the card, waiting for the little light to turn green, but it stayed stubbornly red. Too fast? Too slow? He hated these things. He tried it again, but the blasted light still didn't budge off red.

Apparently either the key code wasn't working anymore or his card had somehow become demagnetized.

Shoot. Of all the nights to have trouble, when he literally had his hands full.

"Sorry, buddy. Hang on a bit more and we'll get you settled inside. I promise."

The little brown-and-black corgi-beagle mix perked his ginormous ears at him and gave him a quizzical look.

He tried a couple more times in the vain hope that five or six times was the charm, then gave up, accepting the inevitable trip to the lobby. He glanced at his watch. Eleven thirty-five. The front desk closed at midnight. Barring an unforeseen catastrophe between here and the front door, he should be okay.

He shoved the dog food and mat away from the door in case somebody else had better luck with their key card and needed to get through, then carried the dog around the side of the darkened inn.

The night was cool, as spring nights tended to be in the mountains, and he tucked the little dog under his jacket. The air was sweet with the scent of the flowers Laura had planted and new growth on the trees that lined the Cold Creek here.

On the way, he passed the sign he had noticed before that said Pets Welcome.

Yeah. He really, really hoped they meant it.

The property was quiet, as he might have expected. Judging by the few cars behind him in the parking lot, only about half the rooms at the inn were occupied. He hadn't seen any other guests for a couple of days in his wing of the hotel, which he could only consider a good thing, given the circumstances—though he doubted Laura would agree.

At least his room was close to the side door in case he had to make any emergency trips outside with the injured dog his sister had somehow conned him into babysitting. He had to consider that another thing to add to the win column.

Was Laura working the front desk? She did sometimes,

probably after her children were asleep. In the few weeks he'd been living at the inn, most of the time one of the college students Mrs. Pendleton hired was working the front desk on the late shift, usually a flirtatious coed he tried really hard to discourage.

He wasn't sure whether he hoped to find Laura working or would prefer to avoid her a little longer. Not that he'd been avoiding her on purpose. He had been working crazy hours the past few days and hadn't been around the inn much.

He hadn't seen her since the other afternoon, when she had melted in his arms, although she hadn't been far from his mind. Discovering he wanted her back in his life had been more than a little unsettling.

The lobby of the inn had seen major changes in the few weeks since Laura arrived. Through the front windows he could see that the froufrou couches and chairs that used to form a conversation pit of sorts had been replaced by a half-dozen tables and chairs, probably for the breakfast service he'd been hearing about.

Fresh flower arrangements gave a bright, springlike feeling to the place—probably Laura's doing, as well.

When he opened the front door, he immediately spotted a honey-blond head bent over a computer and warmth seeped through him. He had missed her. Silly, when it had been only four days, but there it was.

The dog in his arms whimpered a little. Deciding discretion was the better part of valor and all that, he wrapped his coat a little more snugly around the dog. No sense riling her before she needed to be riled.

He wasn't technically doing anything wrong—pets *were* welcome after all, at least according to the sign, but somehow he had a feeling normal inn rules didn't apply to him.

He warily approached her and as she sensed him, she looked up from the computer with a ready smile. At the sight of him, her smile slid away and he felt a pang in his gut.

"Oh. Hi."

He shifted Lucky Lou a little lower in his arm. "Uh, hi. Sorry to bug you, but either my key card isn't working or the side door lock is having trouble. I tried to come in that way, but I couldn't get the green light."

"No problem. I can reprogram your card."

Her voice was stiff, formal. Had that stunning kiss ruined even the friendship he had been trying to rekindle?

"I like the furniture," he said.

"Thanks. It was just delivered today. I'm pleased with the colors. We should be ready to start serving breakfast by early next week."

"That will be a nice touch for your guests."

"I think so."

He hated that they had reverted back to polite small talk. They used to share everything with each other and he missed it.

The bundle under his jacket squirmed a little and she eyed him with curiosity.

"Uh, here's my key," he said, handing it over.

She slid it across the little doohickey card reader and handed it back to him. "That should work now, but let me know if you have more trouble."

"Okay. Thanks. Good night."

"Same to you," she answered. He started to turn and leave just as Lou gave a small, polite yip and peeked his head out of the jacket, his mega-size ears cocked with interest.

She blinked, clearly startled. "Is that…"

"Oh, this? Oh. Yeah. You probably need to add him to your list of guests. This is Lucky Lou."

At his newly christened name, the dog peeked all the way out. With those big corgi ears, he looked like a cross between a lemur and some kind of alien creature.

"Oh, he's adorable."

He blinked. Okay, she wasn't yelling. That was a good sign. "Yeah, pretty cute, I guess. Not exactly the most manly of dogs, but he's okay."

"Is this the dog that was hit by a car the other day?"

"This is the one."

To his great surprise, she walked around the side of the lobby desk for a closer look. He obliged by unwrapping the blanket, revealing the cast on the dog's leg.

"Oh, he's darling," she exclaimed and reached out to run a hand down the animal's fur. The dog responded just as Taft wanted to do, by nudging his head closer to her hand. So far, so good. Maybe she wasn't going to kill him after all.

"How is he?" she asked.

"Lucky. Hence the name."

She laughed softly and the sound curled through him, sweet and appealing.

He cleared his throat. "Somehow he came through with just a broken leg. It should heal up in a few weeks, but he needs to be watched closely during that time to make sure he doesn't reinjure himself. He especially can't be around the other dogs at the ranch because they tend to play rough, which poses a bit of a problem."

"What kind of problem?"

"It's a crazy-busy time at the ranch, with spring planting and all, not to mention Trace's wedding. Caidy was looking for somebody who could keep an eye on Lou here and I sort of got roped into it."

He didn't add that his sister basically blackmailed him to take on the responsibility, claiming he owed her this because she told him about the planned horseback ride with Laura and her children in the first place.

"I guess I should ask whether you mind if I keep him here at the inn with me. Most of the time he'll be at the station house or in my truck with me, but he'll be here on the nights I'm not working there."

She cupped the dog's face in her hand. "I would have to be the most hardhearted woman on the planet to say no to that face."

Okay, now he owed his sister big-time. Who knew the way to reach Laura's heart was through an injured mongrel?

As if she suddenly realized how close she was standing, Laura eased away from him. The dog whimpered a little and Taft wanted to join him.

"Our policy does allow for pets," she said. "Usually we charge a hundred-dollar deposit in case of damages, but given the circumstances I'm sure we can waive that."

"I'll try to keep him quiet. He seems to be a well-behaved little guy. Makes me wonder what happened. How he ended up homeless."

"Maybe he ran away."

"Yeah, that's the logical explanation, but he didn't have a collar. Caidy checked with animal control and the vet and everybody else she could think of. Nobody in the county has reported a lost pet matching his description. I wonder if somebody just dropped him off and abandoned him."

"What's going to happen to him? Eventually, I mean, after he heals?" she asked.

"Caidy has a reputation for taking in strays. Her plan is to nurse him back to health and then look for a good placement somewhere for the little guy. Meantime I'm just the dogsitter for a few days."

"And you can take him to the fire station with you?"

"I'm the fire chief, remember? Who's going to tell me I can't?"

She raised an eyebrow. "Oh, I don't know. Maybe the mayor or the city council."

He laughed, trying to imagine any of the local politicians making a big deal about a dog at the fire station. "This is Pine Gulch," he answered. "We're pretty casual about things like that. Anyway, it's only for a few days. We can always call him our unofficial mascot. Lucky Lou, Fire Dog."

The dog's big ears perked forward, as if eager to take on the new challenge.

"You like the sound of that, do you?" He scratched the dog's ears and earned an adoring look from his new best friend. He looked up to find Laura watching him, an arrested look in her eyes. When his gaze collided with hers, she turned a delicate shade of pink and looked away from him.

"Like I said, he doesn't seem to be much of a barker. I'll try to keep him quiet when I'm here so he doesn't disturb the other guests."

"Thank you, I appreciate that. Not that you have that many guests around you to be disturbed."

The discouragement in her voice made him want to hold her close, dog and all, and take away her worries. "Things will pick up come summer," he assured her.

"I hope so. The inn hasn't had the greatest reputation over the years. My mom did her best after my dad died, but I'm afraid things went downhill."

He knew this to be an unfortunate fact. Most people in town steered their relatives and friends to other establishments. A couple new B and Bs had sprung up recently and there were some nice guest ranches in the canyon. None had the advantage of Cold Creek Inn's location and beautiful setting, though, and with Laura spearheading changes, he didn't doubt the inn would be back on track in no time.

"Give it time. You've been home only a few weeks."

She sighed. "I know. But when I think about all the work it's going to require to counteract that reputation, I just want to cry."

He could certainly relate to that. He knew just how tough it was to convince people to look beyond the past. "If anybody can do it, you're perfect for the job. A degree in hotel management, all those years of international hotel experience. This will be a snap for you."

She gave him a rueful smile—but a smile nonetheless. He drew in a breath, wishing he could set the dog down and pull Laura into his arms instead. He might have considered it, but Lucky made a sound as if warning him against that particular course of action.

"What you need is a dog," he said suddenly. "A *lucky* dog."

"Oh, no, you don't," she exclaimed on a laugh. "Forget that right now, Taft Bowman. I'm too smart to let myself be swayed by an adorable face."

"Mine or the dog's?" he teased.

This smile looked definitely genuine, but she shook her head. "Go to bed, Taft. And take your lucky dog with you."

I'd rather take you.

The words simmered between them, unsaid, but she blushed anyway, as if she sensed the thoughts in his head.

"Good night, then," he said with great reluctance. "I really don't mind paying the security deposit for the dog."

"No need. Consider it my way of helping in Lucky Lou's recovery."

"Thanks, then. I'll try to be sure you don't regret it."

He hitched the dog into a better position, picked up the key card from the counter and headed down the hall.

He had enough regrets for the both of them.

Her children were in love.

"He's the cutest dog *ever*," Alex gushed, his dark eyes bright with excitement. "And so nice, too. I petted him and petted him and all he did was lick me."

"Lou tickles," Maya added, her face earnest and sweet.

"Lucky Lou. That's his name, Chief Bowman says."

Alex was perched on the counter, pulling items out of grocery bags, theoretically "helping" her put them away, but mostly just jumbling them up on the counter. Still, she wasn't about to discourage any act of spontaneous help from her children.

"And where was your grandmother while Chief Bowman was letting you play with his dog?" she asked.

The plan had been for Jan to watch the children while Laura went to the grocery store for her mother, but it sounded very much as if they had been wandering through the hotel, bothering Taft.

"She had a phone call in the office. We were coloring at a new table in the lobby, just like Grandma told us to. I promise we didn't go anywhere like upstairs. I was coloring a picture of a horse and Maya was just scribbling. She's not a very good colorer."

"She's working on it, aren't you, *mi hija?*"

Maya giggled at the favorite words and the everyday tension and stress of grocery shopping and counting coupons and loading bags into her car in a rainstorm seemed to fade away.

She was working hard to give her family a good life here.

Maybe it wasn't perfect yet, but it was definitely better than what they would have known if she'd stayed in Madrid.

"So you were coloring and…" she prompted.

"And Chief Bowman came in and he was carrying the dog. He has great big ears. They're like donkey ears!"

She had to smile at the exaggeration. The dog had big ears but nothing that unusual for a corgi.

"Really?" she teased. "I've never noticed that about Chief Bowman."

Alex giggled. "The dog, silly! The *dog* has big ears. His name is Lucky Lou and he has a broken leg. Did you know that? He got hit by a car! That's sad, huh?"

"Terribly sad," she agreed.

"Chief Bowman says he has to wear a cast for another week and he can't run around with the other dogs."

"That's too bad."

"I know, huh? He can only sit quiet and be petted, but Chief Bowman says I can do it anytime I want to."

"That's very kind of Chief Bowman," she answered, quite sure her six-year-old probably wouldn't notice the caustic edge to her tone. She knew just what Taft was after—a sucker who would take the dog off his hands.

"He's super nice."

"The dog?"

"No! Chief Bowman! He says I can come visit Lou whenever I want, and when his cast comes off, I can maybe take him for a walk."

The decided note of hero-worship she heard in Alex's voice greatly worried her. Her son was desperate for a strong male influence in his life. She understood that.

But Taft wasn't going to be staying at the inn forever. Eventually his house would be finished and he would move out, taking his little dog with him.

The thought depressed her, although she knew darn well it was dangerous to allow herself to care what Taft Bowman did.

"And guess what else?" Alex pressed, his tone suddenly cagey.

"What?"

"Chief Bowman said Lucky Lou is going to need a new home once he recovers!"

Oh, here we go, she thought. It didn't take a child-behavior specialist to guess what would be coming next.

Sure enough, Alex tilted his head and gave her a deceptively casual look. "So I was thinking maybe *we* could give him a new home."

You're always thinking, aren't you, kiddo? she thought with resignation, gearing up for the arguments she could sense would follow that declaration.

"He's a super-nice dog and he didn't bark one single time. I know I could take care of him, Mama. I just *know* it."

"I know it," Maya said in stout agreement, although Laura had doubts as to whether her daughter had even been paying attention to the conversation she played with a stack of plastic cups at the kitchen table.

How was she going to get out of this one without seeming like the meanest mom in the world? The dog *was* adorable. She couldn't deny it. With those big ears and the beagle coloring and his inquisitive little face, he was a definite charmer.

Maybe in a few months she would be in a better position to get a pet, but she was barely holding on here, working eighteen-hour days around caring for her children so she could help her mother rehabilitate this crumbling old inn and bring it back to the graceful accommodations it once had been.

She had to make the inn a success no matter how hard she had to work to do it. She couldn't stomach another failure. First her engagement to Taft, then her marriage. Seeing the inn deteriorate further would be the last straw.

A dog, especially a somewhat fragile one, would complicate *everything*.

"I would really, really love a dog," Alex persisted.

"Dog. Me, too," Maya said.

Drat Taft for placing her in this position. He had to have known her children would come back brimming over with enthusiasm for the dog, pressing her to add him to her family.

Movement outside the kitchen window caught her gaze and through the rain she saw Taft walking toward the little grassy area set aside for dogs. He was wearing a hooded raincoat and carrying an umbrella. At the dog-walking area, he set Lucky Lou down onto the grass and she saw the dog's cast had been wrapped in plastic.

She watched as Taft held the umbrella over the little corgi-beagle mix while the dog took care of business.

The sight of this big, tough firefighter showing such care for a little injured dog touched something deep inside her. Tenderness rippled and swelled inside her and she drew in a sharp breath. She didn't want to let him inside her heart again. She couldn't do it.

This was Taft Bowman. He was a womanizer, just as Javier had been. The more the merrier. That was apparently his mantra when it came to women. She had been through this before and she refused to do it again.

From his vantage point on top of the counter, Alex had a clear view out the window. "See?" he said with a pleading look. "Isn't he a great dog? Chief Bowman says he doesn't even poop in the house or anything."

She sighed and took her son's small hand in hers, trying to soften the difficulty of her words. "Honey, I don't know if this is the best time for us to get a dog. I'm sorry. I can't tell you yes or no right now. I'm going to have to think hard about this before I can make any decision. Don't get your hopes up, okay?"

Even as she said the words, she knew they were useless. By the adoration on his face as he looked out the rain-streaked window at the little dog, she could plainly tell Alex already had his heart set on making a home for Lou.

She supposed things could be worse. The dog was apparently potty-trained, friendly and not likely to grow much bigger. It wasn't as if he was an English sheepdog, the kind of pet who shed enough fur it could be knitted into a sweater.

But then, this was Taft Bowman's specialty, convincing people to do things they otherwise wouldn't even consider.

She was too smart to fall for it all over again. Or at least that's what she told herself.

Chapter 9

Nearly a week later, Laura spread the new duvet across the bed in the once-fire-damaged room, then stepped back to survey her work.

Not bad, if she did say so herself. She was especially proud of the new walls, which she had painted herself, glazing with a darker earth tone over the tan to create a textured, layered effect, almost like a Tuscan farmhouse.

Hiring someone else to paint would have saved a great deal of time and trouble, of course. The idea of all the rooms yet to paint daunted her, made her back ache just thinking about it. On the other hand, this renovation had been *her* idea to breathe life into the old hotel, and the budget was sparse, even with the in-kind labor Taft had done for them over the past few weeks.

It might take her a month to finish all the other rooms, but she would still save several thousand dollars that could be put into upgrading the amenities offered by the inn.

She intended to make each room at the inn charming and unique. This was a brilliant start. The room looked warm and inviting and she couldn't wait to start renting it out. She smoothed a hand over the wood trim around the windows, noting the tightness of the joints and the fine grain that showed beautifully through the finish.

"Wow, it looks fantastic in here."

She turned at the voice from the open doorway and found Taft leaning against the doorjamb. He looked tired, she thought, with a day's growth of whiskers on his cheeks and new smudges under his eyes. Not tired, precisely. Weary and worn, as if he had stopped here because he couldn't move another step down the hall toward his own room.

"Amazing the difference a coat of paint and a little love can do, isn't it?" she answered, worried for him.

"Absolutely. I would stay here in a heartbeat."

"You *are* staying here. Okay, not *here* precisely, in this particular room, but at the inn."

"If this room is any indication, the rest of this place will be beautiful by the time you're finished. People will be fighting over themselves to get a room."

"I hope so," she answered with a smile. This was what she wanted. The chance to make this historic property come to life.

"Do you ever sleep?" he asked.

"I could ask the same question. You look tired."

"Yeah, it's been a rough one."

She found the weary darkness in his gaze disconcerting. Taft was teasing and fun, with a smile and a lighthearted comment for everyone. She rarely saw him serious and quiet. "What's happened?"

He sank down onto the new sofa, messing up the throw pillows she had only just arranged. She didn't mind. He looked like a man who needed somewhere comfortable to rest for a moment.

"Car accident on High Creek Road. Idiot tourist took one of those sharp turns up there too fast. The car went off the road and rolled about thirty feet down the slope."

"Is he okay?"

"The driver just had scrapes and bruises and a broken arm." He scratched at a spot at the knee of his jeans. "His ten-year-old kid wasn't so lucky. We did CPR for about twenty minutes while we waited for the medevac helicopter and were able to bring him back. Last I heard, he survived the flight to the children's hospital in Salt Lake City, but he's in for a long, hard fight."

Her heart ached for the child and for his parents. "Oh, no."

"I hate incidents with kids involved." His mouth was tight. "Makes me want to tell every parent I know to hug their children and not let go. You just never know what could happen on any given day. If I didn't know Ridge would shoot me for it, I'd drive over to the ranch and wake up Destry right now, just so I could give her a big hug and tell her I love her."

His love for his niece warmed her heart. He was a man with a huge capacity to love and he must have deep compassion if he could be so upset by the day's events. Hadn't he learned how to keep a safe distance between his emotions and the emergency calls he had to respond to as a firefighter and paramedic?

"I'm sorry you had to go through that today."

He shrugged. "It's part of the job description, I guess. Sometimes I think my life would have been a hell of a lot easier if I'd stuck to raising cattle with Ridge."

These moments always took her by surprise when she

realized anew that Taft was more than just the lighthearted, laughing guy he pretended to be. He felt things deeply. She had always known that, she supposed, but it was sometimes easy to forget when he worked so hard to be a charming flirt.

After weighing the wisdom of being in too close proximity to him against her need to offer comfort, she finally sank onto the sofa beside him.

"I'm sure you did everything you could."

"That's what we tell ourselves to help us sleep at night. Yet we always wonder."

He had been driving back to the ranch after being with her that terrible December night his parents were killed, when a terrified Caidy had called 9-1-1, she remembered now. Taft had heard the report go out on the radio in his truck just as he'd been turning into the gates of the ranch and had rushed inside to find his father shot dead and his mother bleeding out on the floor.

Not that he ever talked about this with her, but one of the responding paramedics had told her about finding a blood-covered Taft desperately trying to do CPR on his mother. He wouldn't stop, even after the rescue crews arrived.

His failure to revive his mother had eaten away at him, she was quite certain. If he had arrived five minutes earlier, he might have been able to save her.

She suspected, though of course he blocked this part of his life from her, that some part of him had even blamed Caidy for not calling for rescue earlier. Caidy had been home, as well, and had hidden in a closet in terror for several moments after her parents were shot, not sure whether the thieves—who had come to what they thought was an empty ranch to steal the Bowmans' art collection and been surprised into murder—might still actually be in the house.

After Laura left Pine Gulch, she had wondered if he blocked out his emotions after the murders in an effort to protect himself from that guilt at not being able to do enough to save his parents.

Even though he pretended he was fine, the grief and loss had simmered inside him. If only he had agreed to postpone the wedding, perhaps time would have helped him reach a better place so they could have married without that cloud over them.

None of that mattered now. He was hurting and she was compelled by her very nature to help ease that pain if she could. "What you do is important, Taft, no matter how hard it sometimes must feel. Think of it this way—if not for you and the other rescuers, that boy wouldn't have any chance at all. He wouldn't have made it long enough for the medical helicopter. And he's only one of hundreds, maybe thousands, of people you've helped. You make a real difference here in Pine Gulch. How many people can say that about their vocation?"

He didn't say anything for a long time and she couldn't read the emotion in his gaze. "There you go again. Always looking for the good in a situation."

"It seems better than focusing on all the misery and despair around me."

"Yeah, but sometimes life sucks and you can't gloss over the smoke damage with a coat of paint and a couple new pictures on the wall."

His words stung more than they should have, piercing unerringly under an old, half-healed scar.

Javier used to call her *dulce y inocente*. Sweet and innocent. He treated her like a silly girl, keeping away all their financial troubles, his difficulties with the hotel, the other women he slept with, as if she were too fragile to deal with the harsh realities of life.

"I'm not a child, Taft. Believe me, I know just how harsh and ugly the world can be. I don't think it makes me silly or naive simply because I prefer to focus on the hope that with a little effort, people can make a difference in each other's lives. We can always make tomorrow a little better than today, can't we? What's the point of life if you focus only on the negative, on what's dark or difficult instead of all the joy waiting to be embraced with each new day?"

She probably sounded like a soppy greeting card, but at that moment she didn't care.

"I never said you were silly." He gave her a probing look that made her flush. "Who did?"

She wanted to ignore the question. What business was it of his? But the old inn was quiet around them and there was an odd sort of intimacy in this pretty, comfortable room.

"My husband. He treated me like I was too delicate to cope with the realities of life. It was one of the many points of contention between us. He wanted to put a nice shiny gloss over everything, pretend all was fine."

He studied her for a long moment, then sighed. "I suppose that's not so different from what I did to you after my parents died."

"Yes," she answered through her surprise that he would actually bring up this subject and admit to his behavior. "If not for our…history, I guess you could say, it might not have bothered me so much when Javier insisted on that shiny gloss. But I had been through it all before. I didn't want to be that fragile child."

Before she realized what he intended, he covered her hand with his there on the sofa between them. His hand was large and warm, his fingers rough from years of both working on the ranch and putting his life on the line to help the residents of Pine Gulch, and for one crazy moment, she wanted to turn her hand over, grab tightly to his strength and never let go.

"I'm so sorry I hurt you, Laura. It was selfish and wrong of me. I should have postponed the wedding until I was in a better place."

"Why didn't you? A few months—that might have made all the difference, Taft."

"Then I would have had to admit I was still struggling to cope, six months later, when I thought I should have been fine and over things. I was a tough firefighter, Laura. I faced wildfires. I ran into burning buildings. I did whatever I had to. I guess I didn't want to show any signs of weakness. It was…tough for me to accept that my parents' murders threw me for a loop, so I pretended I was fine, too selfish and immature a decade ago to consider that you might have been right, that I needed more time."

She closed her eyes, wondering how her life might have been different if she had gone ahead with the wedding, despite all her misgivings. If she had been a little more certain he would come through his anger and grief, if she had married him anyway, perhaps they could have worked through it.

On the other hand, even though she had loved him with all her heart, she would have been miserable in a marriage where he refused to share important pieces of himself with her. They probably would have ended up divorced, hating each other, with a couple of messed-up kids trapped in the middle.

He squeezed her fingers and his gaze met hers. Something glimmered in the depths of those green eyes, emotions she couldn't identify and wasn't sure she wanted to see.

"For the record," he murmured, "nothing was right after you left. It hasn't been right all this time. I've missed you, Laura."

She stared at him, blood suddenly pulsing through her. She didn't want to hear this. All her protective instincts were urging her to jump up from this sofa and escape, but she couldn't seem to make herself move.

"I should have come after you," he said. "But by the time I straightened out my head enough to do it, you were married and expecting a baby and I figured I had lost my chance."

"Taft—" Her voice sounded husky and low and she couldn't seem to collect her thoughts enough to add anything more. It wouldn't have mattered if she had. He didn't give her a chance to say a word before he leaned in, his eyes an intense, rich green, and lowered his mouth to hers.

His mouth was warm and tasted of coffee and something else she couldn't identify. Some part of her knew she should move now, while she still had the will, but she couldn't seem to make any of her limbs cooperate, too lost in the sheer, familiar joy of being in his arms again.

He kissed her softly, not demanding anything, only tasting, savoring, as if her mouth were some sort of rare and precious wine. She was helpless to do anything but try to remember to breathe while her insides twisted and curled with longing.

"I missed you, Laura," he murmured once more, this time against her mouth.

I missed you, too. So much.

The words echoed through her mind but she couldn't say them. Not now. Not yet.

She could do nothing now but soak in the stunning tenderness of his kiss and let it drift around and through her, resurrecting all those feelings she had shoved so deeply down inside her psyche.

Finally, when she couldn't think or feel past the thick flow of emotions, he deepened the kiss. Now. Now was the time she should pull away, before things progressed too far. Her mind knew it, but again, the rest of her was weak and she responded instinctively, as she had done to him so many times before, and pressed her mouth to his.

For long moments, nothing else existed but his strength and his heat, his mouth firm and determined on hers, his arms holding her tightly, his muscles surrounding her. She wasn't sure exactly how he managed it without her realizing, but he shifted and turned her so she was resting back against the armrest of the sofa while he half covered her with his body until she was lost in memories of making love with him, tangled bodies and hearts.

She was still in love with him.

The realization slowly seeped through her consciousness, like water finding a weakness in a seam and dripping through.

She was still in love with Taft and probably had been all this time.

The discovery left her reeling, disoriented. She had loved her husband. *Of course* she had. She never would have married him if she hadn't believed they could make a happy life together. Yes, she had discovered she was unexpectedly pregnant after their brief affair, but she hadn't married him for that, despite the intense pressure he applied to make their relationship legal.

Her love for Javier hadn't been the deep, rich, consuming love she had known with Taft, but she had cared deeply for the man—at first anyway, until his repeated betrayals and his casual attitude about them had eaten away most of her affection for him.

Even so, she realized now, throughout the seven years of her marriage, some part of her heart had always belonged to Taft.

"We were always so good together. Do you remember?"

The low words thrummed through her and images of exactly how things had been between them flashing through her head. From the very first, they had been perfectly compatible. He had always known just how to kiss, just where to touch.

"Yes, I remember," she said hoarsely. All the passion, all the heat, all the heartbreak. She remembered all of it. The memories of her despair and abject loneliness after leaving Pine Gulch washed over her like a cold surf, dousing her hunger with cruel effectiveness.

She couldn't do this. Not again. Not with Taft.

She might still love him, but that was even more reason she shouldn't be here on this sofa with him with their mouths entwined. She froze, needing distance and space to breathe and think, to remind herself of all the many reasons she couldn't go through this all over again.

"I remember everything," she said coldly. "I'm not the one whose memory might have been blurred by the scores of other people I've been with in the meantime."

He jerked his head back as if she had just slapped him. "I told you, reputation isn't necessarily the truth."

"But it has some basis in truth. You can't deny that."

Even as she snapped the words, she knew this wasn't the core of the problem. She was afraid. That was the bare truth.

She still loved him as much as she ever had, maybe more now that she was coming to know the man he had become over the past decade, but she had given her heart to him once and he had chosen his grief and anger over all she had wanted to give him.

If she only had herself to consider, she might be willing to take the risk. But she had two children to think about. Alex and Maya were already coming to care for Taft. What if he decided he preferred his partying life again and chose that over her and the children? He had done it once before.

Her late husband had done the same thing, chosen his own selfish pursuits over his family, time and again, and she had to remember she wouldn't be the only one devastated if Taft decided he didn't want a family. Her children had already been through the pain of losing their father. At all costs, she had to protect them and the life she was trying to create for them.

"I don't want this. I don't want *you,*" she said firmly, sliding away from him. Despite her resolve, her hands trembled and she shoved them into the pocket of her sweater and drew a deep breath for strength as she stood.

"Like apparently half the women in town, I'm weak when it comes to you, so I'm appealing to your better nature. Don't kiss me again. I mean it, Taft. Leave me and my children alone. We can be polite and friendly when we see each other in town, but I can't go through this again. I won't. The children and I are finally in a good place, somewhere we can be happy and build a future. I can't bear it if you bounce in and out again and break our hearts all over again. Please, Taft, don't make me beg. Go back to the life you had before and leave us alone."

Her words seemed to gouge and claw at his heart.
I don't want this. I don't want you.

That was clear enough. He couldn't possibly misunderstand.

The children and I are finally in a good place, somewhere we can be happy and build a future. I can't bear it if you bounce in and out again and break our hearts all over again.

As she had done mere days before their wedding, she had looked at him and found him somehow wanting. Again.

He sucked in a ragged breath, everything inside him achy and sore. This was too much after the misery of the day he had just been through, and left him feeling as battered as if he'd free-floated down several miles of level-five rapids.

In that moment, as he gazed at her standing slim and lovely in this graceful, comfortable room, he realized the truth. He loved her. Laura and her family were his life, his heart. He wanted forever with them—while *she* only wanted him gone.

The loss raced over him like a firestorm, like the sudden flashover he had once experienced as a wildlands firefighter in his early twenties. The pain was just like that fire, hot and raw and wild. He couldn't outrun it; he could only hunker down in his shelter and wait for it to pass over.

He wanted to yell at her—to argue and curse and tell her she was being completely unreasonable. He wasn't the same man he'd been a decade ago. Couldn't she see that? He had been twenty-four years old, just a stupid kid, when she left.

Yeah, it might have taken ten years to figure things out, but now he finally knew what he wanted out of life. He was ready to commit everything to her and her children. He wanted what Trace had found with Becca. Once he had held exactly that gift in his hands and he had let it slip away and the loss of it had never hurt as keenly as it did right in this moment.

What did it matter that he might have changed? She didn't want to risk being hurt again by him and he didn't know how to argue with that.

She was right, he had turned away from the warmth of her love at a time in his life when he had needed it most. He couldn't argue with that and he couldn't change things.

He didn't know how to demonstrate to her that *he* had changed, though, that he needed her now to help him become the kind of man he wanted to be. He would be willing to sacrifice anything to take care of her and her children now, and he had no idea how to prove that to her.

"Laura—" he began, but she shook her head.

"I'm sorry. I'm just… I'm not strong enough to go through this all over again."

The misery in her features broke his heart, especially because he knew he had put it there—now and ten years ago.

She gave him one last searching look, then rushed out of this bright, cheerily decorated room, leaving him alone.

He stood there for a long time in the middle of the floor, trying to absorb the loss of her all over again in this room that now seemed cold and lifeless.

What now? He couldn't stay here at the inn anymore. She obviously didn't want him here and he wasn't sure he could linger on the edges of her life, having to content himself with polite greetings at the front desk and the occasional wave in the hallway.

He had finished the carpentry work Jan asked of him in this room and the other six in this wing that had needed the most repair. Because his house was ready for occupancy, with only a few minor things left to finish, he had no real excuse for hanging around.

She hadn't wanted him here in the first place, had only tolerated his presence because her mother had arranged things. He would give her what she wanted. He needed to move out, although the thought of leaving her and Alex and Maya left him feeling grimly empty.

Losing her ten years ago had devastated him. He had a very strong suspicion the pain of their broken engagement would pale compared to the loss of her now.

Chapter 10

"So how's the house?"

Taft barely heard his brother's question, too busy watching a little kid about Alex's age eating one of The Gulch's famous hamburgers and chattering away a mile a minute while his parents listened with slightly glazed expressions on their faces.

Tourists, he figured, because he didn't recognize them and he knew most of the people in his town, at least by sight. It was a little early for the full tourism season to hit—still only mid-May, with springtime in full bloom— but maybe they were visiting family for the Mother's Day weekend.

Where were they staying? he wondered. Would it be weird if he dropped over at their booth and casually mentioned Cold Creek Inn and the new breakfast service people were raving about? Yeah, probably. Trace, at least, would never let him hear the end of it.

Anyway, if they asked him about the quality of the food, he would have to admit he had no idea. He had moved out of his room at the inn and into his new house the day before Laura started the breakfast service.

But then, he wasn't going to think about Laura right now. He had already met his self-imposed daily limit about ten minutes after midnight while he had been answering a call for a minor fender bender, a couple of kids who wouldn't be borrowing their dad's new sedan again anytime soon.

And then exceeded his thinking-about-Laura quota about 1:00 a.m. and 2:00 a.m. and 3:00 a.m. And so on and so on.

He was a cute kid, Taft thought now as he watched the kid take a sip of his soda. Not as adorable as Alex, of course, but then, he was a little biased.

"The house?" Trace asked again and Taft had to jerk his attention back to his brother.

"It's been okay," he answered.

"Just okay? Can't you drum up a little more excitement than that? You've been working on this all winter long."

"I'm happy to be done," he answered, not in the mood for an interrogation.

If his brother kept this up, he was going to think twice next time about inviting Trace for a late lunch after a long shift. It had been a crazy idea anyway. He and his twin used to get together often for meals at The Gulch, but since Trace's engagement, his brother's free time away from Becca and Gabi had become sparse, as it should be.

He hadn't been quite ready to go home for a solitary TV dinner after work, so had persuaded Trace to take a break and meet him. They could usually manage to talk enough about the general public safety of Pine Gulch for it to technically be considered a working lunch.

Except now, when the police chief appeared to have other things on his mind.

"I can tell when somebody's lying to me," Trace said with a solemn look. "I'm a trained officer of the law, remember? Besides that, I'm your brother. I know you pretty well after sharing this world for thirty-four years. You're not happy and you haven't been for a couple of weeks now. Even Becca commented on it. What's going on?"

He couldn't very well tell his brother he felt as if Laura had made beef jerky out of his heart. He ached with loneliness for her and for Maya and Alex. Right now, he would give anything to be sitting across the table from them while Maya grinned at him and Alex jabbered his ear off. Even if he could find the words to explain away his lousy mood, he wasn't sure he was ready to share all of that with Trace.

"Maybe I'm tired of the same-old, same-old," he finally said, when Trace continued to give him the Bowman interrogation look: *Talk or you* will *be sorry.*

"I've been doing the same job for nearly six years, with years fighting wildland fires and doing EMT work before I made chief. Maybe it's time for me to think about taking a job somewhere else."

"Where?"

He shrugged. "Don't know. I've had offers here and there. Nevada. Oregon. Alaska, even. A change could be good. Get out of Pine Gulch, you know?"

Trace lifted an eyebrow and looked at him skeptically. "You just finished your new house a week ago. And now you're thinking about leaving it? After all that work you put into it?"

He had come to the grim realization some nights ago during another sleepless episode that it would be torture continuing to live here in Pine Gulch, knowing she was so close but forever out of reach. He missed her. A hundred times a day he wanted to run over to the hotel claiming fire-code enforcement checks or something ridiculous like that just for the chance to see her and the children again.

Being without her had been far easier when she was half a world away in Spain. He was afraid the idea of weeks and months—and possibly *years*—of having her this close but always just out of his reach was more than he could endure.

Maybe it was his turn to leave this time.

"It's just an idea. Something I'm kicking around. I haven't actually *done* anything about it."

Before Trace could answer, Donna Archuleta, who owned The Gulch with her husband, brought over their order.

"Here you go, Chief Bowman." She set down Trace's plate, his favorite roast-beef sandwich with green peppers and onions. "And for the other Chief Bowman," she said in her gravelly ex-smoker voice, delivering Taft's lunch of meat loaf and mashed potatoes, a particular specialty of Lou's.

"Thanks, Donna."

"You're welcome. How are the wedding plans coming along?" she asked Trace.

His brother scratched his cheek. "Well, I'll admit I'm mostly staying out of it. You'll have to ask Becca that one."

"I would if she would ever come around. I guess now she's opened that fancy attorney-at-law office and doesn't have to wait tables anymore, she must be too busy for us these days."

Trace shook his head with a smile at the cantankerous old woman. "I'll bring her and Gabi in for breakfast over the weekend. How would that be?"

"I guess that'll do. You two enjoy your lunch."

She headed away amid the familiar diner sounds of rattling plates and conversation.

He had hoped the distraction would derail Trace's train of thought but apparently not. "If you think taking a job somewhere and moving away from Pine Gulch is what you want and need right now, I say go for it," his brother said, picking up right where he had left off. "You know the family will support you in whatever you decide. We'll miss you but we will all understand."

"Thank you, I appreciate that."

He considered it one of his life's greatest blessings that he had three siblings who loved him and would back him up whenever he needed it.

"We'll understand," Trace repeated. "As long as you leave for the right reasons. Be damn careful you're running *to* something and not just running away."

Lou must be having an off day. The meat loaf suddenly tasted like fire-extinguisher chemicals. "Running away from *what?*"

Trace took a bite of his sandwich and chewed and swallowed before he answered, leaving Taft plenty of time to squirm under the sympathy in his gaze. "Maybe a certain innkeeper and her kids, who shall remain nameless."

How did his brother do that? He hadn't said a single word to him about Laura, but Trace had guessed the depth of his feelings anyway, maybe before he did. It was one of those weird twin things, he supposed. He had known the first time he met Becca, here in this diner, that Trace was already crazy about her.

The only thing he could do was fake his way out of it. "What? Laura? We were done with each other ten years ago."

"You sure about that?"

He forced a laugh. "Yeah, pretty darn sure. You might have noticed we didn't actually get married a decade ago."

"Yeah, I did pick up on that. I'm a fairly observant guy." Trace gave him a probing look. "And speaking of observant, I've also got an active network of confidential informants. Word is you haven't been to the Bandito for the greater part of a month, which coincidentally happens to be right around the time Laura Santiago showed up back in town with her kids."

"Checking up on me?"

"Nope. More like vetting questions from certain segments of the female society in Pine Gulch about where the hell you've been lately. Inquiring minds and all that."

He took a forkful of mashed potatoes, but found them every bit as unappealing as the meat loaf. "I've been busy."

"So I hear. Working on renovations at the inn, from what I understand."

"Not anymore. That's done now."

He had no more excuses to hang around Cold Creek Inn. No more reason to help Alex learn how to use power tools, to listen to Maya jabber at him, half in a language he didn't understand, or to watch Laura make the inn blossom as she had dreamed about doing most of her life.

Yeah, he wasn't sure he could stick around town and watch as Laura settled happily into Pine Gulch, working on the inn, making friends, moving on.

All without him.

"When I heard from Caidy that you'd moved into the inn and were helping Laura and her mother with some carpentry work, I thought for sure you and she were starting something up again. Guess I was wrong, huh?"

Another reason he should leave town. His family and half the town were probably watching and waiting for just that, to see if the two of them would pick up where they left off a decade and an almost-wedding later.

"Laura isn't interested in rekindling anything. Give her a break, Trace. I mean, it hasn't even been a year since she lost her husband. She and the kids are trying to settle into Pine Gulch again. She's got big plans for the inn, and right now that and her children are where her focus needs to be."

Some of his despair, the things he thought he had been so careful not to say, must have filtered through his voice anyway. His brother studied him for a long moment, compassion in his green eyes Taft didn't want to see.

He opened his mouth to deflect that terrible sympathy with some kind of stupid joke, but before he could come up with one, his radio and Trace's both squawked at the same moment.

"All officers in the vicinity. I've got a report of a Ten Fifty-Seven. Two missing juveniles in the area of Cold Creek Inn. Possible drowning."

Everything inside him froze to ice, crackly and fragile. *Missing juveniles. Cold Creek Inn. Possible drowning. Alex and Maya.*

He didn't know how he knew so completely, but his heart cramped with agony and bile rose in his throat for a split second before he shoved everything aside. Not now. There would be time later, but right now he needed to focus on what was important.

He and Trace didn't even look at each other. They both raced out of the restaurant to their vehicles parked beside each other and squealed out of the parking lot.

He picked up his radio. "Maria, this is Fire Chief Bowman. I want every single damn man on the fire department to start combing the river."

"Yes, sir," she answered.

His heart pounding in his chest, he sped through the short three blocks to Cold Creek Inn, every light flashing and every siren blaring away as he drove with a cold ball of dread in his gut. He couldn't go through this. Not with her. Everything inside him wanted to run away from what he knew would be deep, wrenching pain, but he forced himself to push it all out of his head.

He beat Trace to the scene by a heartbeat and didn't even bother to turn off his truck, just raced to where he saw a group of people standing beside the fast-moving creek.

Laura was being restrained by two people, her mother and a stranger, he realized. She was crying and fighting them in a wild effort to jump into the water herself.

"Laura, what's happened?"

She gazed blankly at him for a moment, her eyes wide and shocky, then her features collapsed with raw relief.

"Taft, my children," she sobbed and it was the most heartrending sound he had ever heard. "I have to go after them. Why won't anyone let me go after them?"

Jan, still holding her, was also in tears and appeared even more hysterical, her face blotchy and red. He wouldn't be able to get much information out of either of them.

Beyond them, he could see the water running fast and high and Lucky Lou running back and forth along the bank, barking frantically.

"Laura, honey, I need you to calm down for just a moment." While everything inside him was screaming urgency, he forced himself to use a soothing, measured tone, aware it might be his only chance to get through to her.

"Please, sweetheart, this is important. Why do you think they're in the river? What happened?"

She inhaled a ragged breath, visibly struggling to calm

herself down to answer his question—and he had never loved her more than in that single moment of stark courage.

"They were just here. Right here. Playing with Lucky. They know they're not to go near the creek. I've told them a hundred times. I was out here with them, planting flowers, and kept my eye on them the whole time. I walked around the corner of the inn for another flat and was gone maybe thirty seconds. That's all. When I came back Lucky was running along the bank and they were g-gone." She said the last word on a wailing sob that made everything inside him ache.

"How long ago?"

The stranger, who must have restrained her from jumping in after them, spoke. "Three minutes. Maybe four. Not long. I pulled into the parking lot just in time to see her running down the bank screaming something about her kids. I stopped her from jumping in after them and called 9-1-1. I don't know if that was right."

He would shake the guy's hand later and pay for his whole damn stay, but right now he didn't have even a second to spare.

"You did exactly right. Laura, stay here. Promise me," he ordered. "You won't find them by jumping in and you'll just complicate everything. The water is moving too fast for you to catch up. Stay here and I will bring them back to you. Promise me."

Her eyes were filled with a terrified anguish. He wanted to comfort her, but damn it, he didn't have time.

"Promise me," he ordered again.

She sagged against the stranger and Jan and nodded, then collapsed to her knees in the dirt, holding on to her mother.

He raced back to his truck, shouting orders into his radio the whole time as he set up a search perimeter and called in the technical rescue team. Even as one part of his mind was busy dealing with the logistics of the search and setting up his second in command to run the grid, the other part was gauging the depth of the water, velocity of the current, the creek's route.

Given that the incident happened five minutes ago now, he tried to calculate how far the children might have floated. It was all guesswork without a meter to give him exact stream flow, but he had lived along Cold Creek all his life and knew its moods and its whims. He and Trace and their friends used to spend summers fishing for native rainbows, and as he grew older, he had kayaked the waters innumerable times, even during high runoff.

Something urged him to head toward Saddleback Road. Inspiration? Some kind of guardian angel? Just a semi-educated guess? He didn't know, but a picture formed itself clearly in his head, of a certain spot where the creek slowed slightly at another natural bow and split into two channels before rejoining. Somehow he knew *that* was the spot where he needed to be right now.

He could be totally off the mark but he could only hope and pray he wasn't.

"Battalion Twenty, what's your status?" he heard over the radio. Trace.

"Almost to Saddleback," he said, his voice hoarse. "I'm starting here. Send a team to the road a quarter mile past that. What is that? Barrelwood?"

"Copy. Don't be stupid, Chief."

One of the hazards of working with his brother—but he didn't care about that now, when he had reached the spot that seemed imprinted in his mind, for all those reasons he couldn't have logically explained.

He jerked the wheel to the side of the road and jumped

out, stopping only long enough to grab the water-rescue line in its throw bag in one of the compartments in the back of his truck. He raced to the water's edge, scanning up and down for any sign of movement. This time of year, mid-May, the runoff was fast and cold coming out of the mountains, but he thanked God the peak flow, when it was a churning, furious mess, was still another few weeks away as the weather warmed further.

Had he overshot them or had they already moved past him? Damn it, he had no way of knowing. Go down or up? He screwed his eyes shut and again that picture formed in his head of the side channel that was upstream about twenty yards. He was crazy to follow such a vague impression but it was all he had right now.

He raced up the bank, listening to the reports of the search on his radio as he ran.

Finally he saw the marshy island in the middle of the two channels. A couple of sturdy pine trees grew there, blocking a good part of his view, but he strained his eyes.

There!

Was that a flash of pink?

He moved a little farther upstream for a different vantage point. The instant he could see around the pines, everything inside him turned to that crackly ice again.

Two small dark heads bobbed and jerked, snagged in the deadfall of a tree that was half-submerged in the water. The tree was caught between two boulders in the side channel. From here, he couldn't tell if the kids were actually actively holding on or had just been caught there by the current.

He grabbed his radio, talking as he moved as close as he could. "Battalion Twenty. I've got a sighting twenty yards east of where my truck is parked on Saddleback Road. I need the tech team and Ambulance Thirty-Six here now."

He knew, even as he issued the order, that no way in hell was he going to stand here and do nothing during the ten minutes or so it might take to assemble the team and get them here. Ten minutes was the difference between life and death. Anything could happen in those ten minutes. He didn't know if the children were breathing—and didn't even want to think about any other alternative—but if they weren't, ten minutes could be critical to starting CPR.

Besides that, the water could be a capricious, vengeful thing. The relentless current could tug them farther downstream and away from him. He wasn't about to take that chance.

This was totally against protocol, everything he had trained his own people *not* to do. Single-man water rescues were potentially fatal and significantly increased the dangers for everybody concerned.

Screw protocol.

He needed to reach Laura's children. Now.

This would be much more comfortable in a wet suit but he wasn't about to take the time to pull his on. He raced upstream another ten yards to a small bridge formed by another fallen tree. On the other side of the creek, the children were only a dozen feet away. He called out and thought he saw one of the dark heads move.

"Alex! Maya! Can you hear me?"

He thought he saw the head move again but he couldn't be sure. No way could they catch the throw bag. He was going to have to go after them, which he had known from the moment he spotted that flash of pink.

If he calculated just right and entered at the correct place upstream, the current would float him right to them, but he would have to aim just right so the first boulder blocked his movement and his weight didn't dislodge the logjam, sending the children farther downstream.

He knew the swift-water safety algorithm. Talk. Reach. Wade. Throw. Helo. Go. Row. Tow. The only thing he could do here was reach them and get them the hell out.

He tied the rescue rope around the sturdy trunk of a cottonwood, then around his waist, then plunged into the water that came up to his chest. The icy water was agony and he felt his muscles cramp instantly, but he waded his way toward the deadfall, fighting the current as hard as he could. It was useless. After only a few steps, the rushing water swept his feet out from under him, as he expected.

It took every ounce of strength he could muster to keep his feet pointed downstream so they could take the brunt of any impact with any boulders or snags in the water. The last thing he needed here was a head injury.

He must have misjudged the current because he ended up slightly to the left of the boulder. He jammed his numb feet on the second boulder to stop his momentum. A branch of the dead tree gouged the skin of his forehead like a bony claw, but he ignored it, fighting his way hand over hand toward the children, praying the whole time he wouldn't dislodge the trunk.

"Alex, Maya. It's Chief Bowman. Come on, you guys." He kept up a nonstop dialogue with them but was grimly aware that only Alex stirred. The boy opened one eye as Taft approached, then closed it again, looking as if he were utterly exhausted.

The boy's arm was around his sister, but Maya was face-down in the water. He used all his strength to fight the current as he turned her and his gut clenched when he saw her eyes staring blankly and her sweet features still and lifeless.

He gave her a quick rescue breath. She didn't respond,

but he kept up the rescue breaths to her and Alex while he worked as quickly as he could, tying them both to him with hands that he could barely feel, wondering as he worked and breathed for all three of them how much time had passed and what the hell was taking his tech rescue crew so long.

This was going to be the toughest part, getting them all out of the water safely, but with sheer muscle, determination—and probably some help from those guardian angels he was quite certain had to be looking after these two kids—he fought the current and began pulling himself hand over hand along the tree trunk, wet and slippery with moss and algae, pausing every ten seconds to give them both rudimentary rescue breaths.

Just as he reached the bank, completely exhausted by the effort of fighting the current, he heard shouts and cries and felt arms lifting him out and untying the kids.

"Chief! How the hell did you find them clear over here?" Luke Orosco, his second in command, looked stunned as he took in the scene.

He had no idea how to explain the process that had led him here. Miracle or intuition, it didn't matter, not when both children were now unresponsive, although it appeared Alex was at least breathing on his own.

Satisfied that his crew was working with Alex, he immediately turned to the boy's sister and took command. He was the only trained paramedic in this group, though everyone else had basic EMT training. "Maya? Come on, Maya, honey. You've got to breathe, sweetheart."

He bent over the girl and turned her into recovery position, on her side, nearly on her stomach, her knee up to drain as much water from her lungs as he could. He could hear Alex coughing up water, but Maya remained still.

"Come on, Maya."

He turned her and started doing CPR, forcing himself to lock away his emotions, the knowledge that Laura would be destroyed if he couldn't bring back her daughter. He continued, shaking off other crew members who wanted to take over.

Some part of him was afraid all this work was for nothing—she had been in the water too long—but then, when despair began to grip him colder than the water, he felt something change. A stirring, a movement, a heartbeat. And then she gave a choking cough and he turned her to her side just in time as she vomited what seemed like gallons of Cold Creek all over the place.

Pink color began to spread through her, another miracle, then she gave a hoarse, raspy cry. He turned her again to let more water drain, then wrapped her in a blanket one of his crew handed over.

"Oxygen," he called. Maya continued to cry softly and he couldn't bring himself to let her go.

"Good job, Chief!"

He was vaguely aware of the guys clapping him and themselves on the back and the air of exultation that always followed a successful rescue, but right now he couldn't focus on anything but Maya.

"You ready for us to load her up?" Ron asked.

He didn't want to let her go, but he knew she needed more than the triage treatment they could offer here. There was still a chance she had been without oxygen long enough for brain damage, but he had to hope the cold water might help ease that possibility.

"Yeah, we'd better get her into the ambulance," he answered. When the EMTs loaded her onto the stretcher, he finally turned to find Alex being loaded onto another stretcher nearby. The boy was conscious and watching the activity around him. When Taft approached, his mouth twisted into a weary smile.

"Chief." The kid's voice sounded hoarse, raw. "You saved us. I knew you would."

He gripped the boy's hand, humbled and overwhelmed at that steady trust. "What happened, Alex? You know you're not supposed to be near the water."

"I know. We always stay away from it. *Always*. But Lucky ran that way and Maya followed him. I chased after her to take her back to Mama and she thought it was a game. She laughed and ran and then slipped and went in the creek. I didn't know what to do. I thought... I thought I could get her. I had swimming lessons last year. But the water was so *fast*."

The boy started to cry and he gathered him up there on the stretcher as he had done Maya. What a great kid he was, desperately trying to protect his little sister. Taft felt tears threaten, too, from emotion or delayed reaction, he didn't know, but he was deeply grateful for any guardian angels who had been on his rescue squad for this one.

"You're safe now. You'll be okay."

"Is Maya gonna be okay?" Alex asked.

He still wasn't sure he knew the answer to that. "My best guys are just about to put her in the ambulance. You get to take a ride, too."

Before Alex could respond to that, Taft saw a Pine Gulch P.D. SUV pull up to the scene. His brother's vehicle. The thought barely registered before the passenger door was shoved open and a figure climbed out.

Laura.

She stood outside the patrol vehicle for just a moment as if not quite believing this could be real and then she rushed toward them. In a second she scooped Alex into her arms and hugged him.

"Oh, baby. Sweetheart," she sobbed. "You're okay. You're really okay? And Maya?" Still carrying Alex, she rushed over to Maya and pulled her into her other arm.

"I'm sorry, ma'am, but we need to transport both of the children to the clinic in town." Ron looked compassionate but determined. "They're in shock and need to be treated for possible hypothermia."

"Oh. Of course." Her strained features paled a little at this further evidence that while the children were out of the water, they still required treatment.

"They're going to be okay, Laura," Taft said. He hoped anyway, though he knew Maya wasn't out of the woods.

She glanced over at him and seemed to have noticed him for the first time. "You're bleeding."

Was he? Probably from that branch that had caught him just as he was reaching the children. He hadn't even noticed it in the rush of adrenaline but now he could feel the sting. "Just a little cut. No big deal."

"And you're soaking wet."

"Chief Bowman pulled us out of the water, Mama," Alex announced, his voice still hoarse. "He tied a rope to a tree and jumped in and got us both. That's what *I* should have done to get Maya."

She gazed at her son and then at Taft, then at the roaring current and the rope still tied to the tree.

"You saved them."

"I told you I would find them."

"You did."

He flushed, embarrassed by the shock and gratitude in her eyes. Did she really think he would let the kids drown?

He loved them. He would have gone after them no matter what the circumstances.

"And broke about a dozen rules for safe rescue in the process," Luke Orosco chimed in, and he wanted to pound the guy for opening his big mouth.

"I don't care," she said. "Oh, thank you. Taft, thank you!"

She grabbed him and hugged him, Alex still in her arms, and his arms came around her with a deep shudder. He couldn't bear thinking about what might have happened. If he had overshot the river and missed them. If he hadn't been so close, just at The Gulch, when the call came in. A hundred small tender mercies had combined to make this moment possible.

Finally Luke cleared his throat. "Uh, Doc Dalton is waiting for us at the clinic."

She stepped away from him and he saw her eyes were bright with tears, her cheeks flushed. "Yes, we should go."

"We should be able to take you and both kids all in one ambulance," Luke offered.

"Perfect. Thank you so much."

She didn't look at him again as the crews loaded the two kids into their biggest ambulance. There wasn't room for him in there, although he supposed as battalion chief he could have pulled rank and insisted he wanted to be one of the EMTs assisting them on the way to the hospital.

But Laura and her children were a family unit that didn't have room for him. She had made that plain enough. He would have to remain forever on the outside of their lives. That was the way Laura wanted things and he didn't know how to change her mind.

He watched the doors close on the ambulance with finality, then Cody Shepherd climb behind the wheel and pull away from the scene. As he watched them drive away, he was vaguely aware of Trace moving to stand beside him. His brother placed a hand on his shoulder, offering understanding without words.

Another one of those twin things, he supposed. Trace must have picked up on his yearning as he watched the family he wanted drive away from him.

"Good save," Trace said quietly. "But it's a damn miracle all three of you didn't go under."

"I know." The adrenaline rush of the rescue was fading fast, leaving him battered and embarrassingly weak-kneed.

"For the record, you ever pull a stunt like that again, trying a single-man water rescue, Ridge and I will drag what's left of you behind one of the River Bow horses."

"What choice did I have? I knew the deadfall wasn't going to hold them for long, the way the current was pushing at them. Any minute, they were going to break free and float downstream and I wouldn't have had a second chance. Think if it was Destry or Gabi out there. You would have done the same thing."

Taft was silent for a moment. "Yeah, probably. That still doesn't make it right."

Terry McNeil, one of his more seasoned EMTs, approached the two of them with his emergency kit. "Chief, your turn."

He probably needed a stitch or two, judging by the amount of blood, but he wasn't in the mood to go to the clinic and face Laura again, to be reminded once more of everything he couldn't have. "I'll take care of it myself."

"You sure? That cut looks deep."

He gave Terry a long look, not saying anything, and the guy finally shrugged. "Your call. You'll need to clean it well. Who knows what kind of bacteria is floating in that water."

"I'm heading home to change anyway. I'll clean it up there."

He knew he should be jubilant after a successful rescue. Some part of him was, of course. The alternative didn't bear thinking about, but he was also crashing now after an all-nighter at the fire station combined with exhaustion from the rescue. Right now, all he wanted to do was go home and sleep.

"Don't be an idiot," Terry advised him, an echo of what his brother had said earlier.

He wanted to tell both of them it was too late for that. He had been nothing short of an idiot ten years ago when he let Laura walk away from him. Once, he had held happiness in his hands and had blown it away just like those cottonwood puffs floating on the breeze.

She might be back but she wouldn't ever be his, and the pain of that hurt far worse than being battered by the boulders and snags and raging current of Cold Creek.

Chapter 11

So close. She had been a heartbeat away from losing everything.

Hours after the miracle of her children's rescue, Laura still felt jittery, her insides achy and tight with reaction. She couldn't bear to contemplate what might have been.

If not for Taft and his insane heroics, she might have been preparing for two funerals right now instead of sitting at the side of her bed, watching her children sleep. Maya was sucking her thumb, something she hadn't done in a long time, while Alex slept with his arm around his beloved dog, who slept on his side with his short little legs sticking straight out.

So much for her one hard-and-fast rule when she had given in to Alex's determined campaign and allowed the adoption of Lucky Lou.

No dogs on the bed, she had told her son firmly, again

and again, but she decided this was a night that warranted exceptions.

She hadn't wanted to let either of them out of her sight, even at bedtime. Because she couldn't watch them both in their separate beds, she had decided to lump everyone together in here, just this once. She wasn't sure where she would sleep, perhaps stretched across the foot of the bed, but she knew sleep would be a long time coming anyway.

She should be exhausted. The day had been draining. Even after the rescue, they had spent several hours at the clinic, until Dr. Dalton and his wife, Maggie, had been confident the children appeared healthy enough to return home.

Dr. Dalton had actually wanted to send them to the hospital in Idaho Falls for overnight observation, but after a few hours, Maya was bouncing around the bed in her room like a wild monkey and Alex had been jabbering a mile a minute with his still-raspy voice.

"You can take them home," Dr. Dalton had reluctantly agreed, his handsome features concerned but kind, "as long as they remain under strict observation. Call me at once if you notice any change in breathing pattern or behavior."

She was so grateful to have her children with her safe and sound that she would have agreed to anything by that point. Every time she thought about what might have happened if Taft hadn't been able to find the children, her stomach rolled with remembered fear and she had to fold her arms around it and huddle for a few moments until she regained control.

She would never forget that moment she climbed out of his brother's patrol vehicle and had seen Taft there, bloodied and soaking wet, holding her son close. Something significant had shifted inside her in that moment, something so profound and vital that she shied away from examining it yet.

She was almost relieved when a crack of light through the doorway heralded her mother's approach. Jan pushed the door open and joined her beside the bed. Her mother looked older than she had that morning, Laura reflected. The lines fanning out from her eyes and bracketing her mouth seemed to have been etched a little deeper by the events of the day.

"They look so peaceful when they're sleeping, don't they?" Jan murmured, gazing down at her only grandchildren.

Laura was suddenly awash with love for her mother, as well. Jan had been a source of steady support during her marriage. Even though Laura hadn't revealed any of the tumult of living with Javier—she still couldn't—she had always known she could call or email her mother and her spirits would lift.

Her mother hadn't had an easy life. She had suffered three miscarriages before Laura was born and two after. When Laura was a teenager, she had often felt the pressure of that keenly, knowing she was the only one of six potential siblings who had survived. She could only hope she was the kind of daughter her mother wanted.

"They do look peaceful," she finally answered, pitching her voice low so she didn't wake the children, although she had a feeling even the high-school marching band would have a tough time rousing them after their exhausting day. "Hard to believe, looking at them now, what kind of trouble they can get into during daylight hours, isn't it?"

"I should have fenced off the river a long time ago." Weary guilt dragged down the edges of her mother's mouth.

Laura shook her head. "Mom, none of this was your

fault. I should have remembered not to take my eyes off them for a second. They're just too good at finding their way to trouble."

"If Taft hadn't been there…"

She reached out and squeezed her mother's hand, still strong and capable at seventy. "I know. But he *was* there." And showed incredible bravery to climb into the water by himself instead of waiting for a support team. The EMTs couldn't seem to stop talking about the rescue during the ambulance ride to the clinic.

"Everyone is okay," she went on. "No lasting effects, Dr. Dalton said, except possibly intestinal bugs from swallowing all that creek water. We'll have to keep an eye out for stomachaches, that sort of thing."

"That's a small thing. They're here. That's all that matters." Her mother gazed at the children for a long moment, then back at Laura, her eyes troubled. "You're probably wondering why you ever came home. With all the trouble we've had since you arrived—fires and near-drownings and everything—I bet you're thinking you would have been better off to have stayed in Madrid."

"I wouldn't want to be anywhere else right now, Mom. I still think coming home was the right thing for us."

"Even though it's meant you've had to deal with Taft again?"

She squirmed under her mother's probing look. "Why should that bother me?"

"I don't know. Your history together, I guess."

"That history didn't seem to stop you from inviting the man to live at the inn for weeks!"

"Don't think I didn't notice during that time how you went out of your way to avoid him whenever you could. You told me things ended amicably between you, but I'm not so sure about that. You still have feelings for him, don't you?"

She started to give her standard answer. *The past was a long time ago. We're different people now and have both moved on.*

Perhaps because the day had been so very monumental, so very profound, she couldn't bring herself to lie to her mother.

"Yes," she murmured. "I've loved him since I was a silly girl. It's hard to shut that off."

"Why do you need to? That man still cares about you, my dear. I could tell that first day when he came to talk to me about helping with the inn renovations. He jumped into the river and risked his life to save your children. That ought to tell you something about the depth of his feelings."

She thought of the dozens of reasons she had employed to convince herself not to let Taft into her life again. None of them seemed very important right now—or anything she wanted to share with her mother. "It's complicated."

"Life is complicated, honey, and hard and stressful and exhausting. And *wonderful*. More so if you have a good man to share it with."

Laura thought of her father, one of the best men she had ever known. He had been kind and compassionate, funny and generous. The kind of man who often opened the doors of his inn for a pittance—or sometimes nothing—to people who had nowhere else to go.

In that moment, she would have given anything if he could be there with them, watching over her children with them.

Perhaps he had been, she thought with a little shiver. By rights, her children should have died today in the swollen waters of Cold Creek. That they survived was nothing short of a miracle and she had to think they had help somehow.

She missed her father deeply in that moment. He had loved Taft and had considered him the son he had always wanted. Both of her parents had been crushed by the end of her engagement, but her father had never pressed her to know the reasons.

"While you were busy at the clinic this afternoon," Jan said after a moment, "I was feeling restless and at loose ends and needed to stay busy while I waited for you. I had to do something so I made a caramel-apple pie. You might not remember but that was always Taft's favorite."

He did have a sweet tooth for pastries, she remembered.

"It's small enough payment for giving me back my grandchildren, but it will have to do for now, until I can think of something better. I was just about to take it to him…unless you would like to."

Laura gazed at her sleeping children and then at her mother, who was trying her best to be casual and nonchalant instead of eagerly coy. She knew just what Jan was trying to do—push her and Taft back together, which was probably exactly the reason she agreed to let him move into the inn under the guise of trading carpentry work for a room.

Jan was sneaky that way. Laura couldn't guess at her motives—perhaps her mother was looking for any way she could to bind Laura and her children to Pine Gulch. Or perhaps she was matchmaking simply because she had guessed, despite Laura's attempts to put on a bright facade, that her marriage had not been a happy one and she wanted to see a different future for her daughter.

Or perhaps Jan simply adored Taft, because most mothers did.

Whatever the reason, Laura had a pivotal decision to make: Take the pie to him herself as a small token of their vast gratitude or thwart her mother's matchmaking plans and insist on staying here with the children?

Her instincts urged her to avoid seeing him again just now. With these heavy emotions churning inside her, she was afraid seeing him now would be too dangerous. Her defenses were probably at the lowest point they had been since coming home to Pine Gulch. If he kissed her again, she wasn't at all certain she would have the strength to resist him.

But that was cowardly. She needed to see him again, if for no other reason than to express, now that she was more calm and rational than she had been on that riverbank, her deep and endless gratitude to him for giving her back these two dear children.

"I'll go, Mom."

"Are you sure? I don't mind."

"I need to do this. You're right. Will you watch the children for me?"

"I won't budge," her mother promised. "I'll sit right here and work on my crocheting the entire time. I promise."

"You don't have to literally watch them. You may certainly sit in the living room and check on them at various intervals."

"I'm not moving from this spot," Jan said. "Between Lou and me, we should be able to keep them safe."

The evening was lovely, unusually warm for mid-May. She drove through town with her window down, savoring the sights and sounds of Pine Gulch settling down for the night. Because it was Friday, the drive-in on the edge of the business district was crowded with cars. Teenagers hanging out, anxious for the end of the school year, young families grabbing a burger on payday, senior citizens treating their grandchildren to an ice-cream cone.

The flowers were beginning to bloom in some of the sidewalk planters along Main Street and everything was greening up beautifully. May was a beautiful time of year in eastern Idaho after the inevitable harshness of winter, brimming with life, rebirth, hope.

As she was right now.

She had heard about people suffering near-death encounters who claimed the experience gave them a new respect and appreciation for their life and the beauty of the world around them. That's how she felt right now. Even though it was her children who had nearly died, Laura knew she would have died right along with them if they hadn't been rescued.

She had Alex and Maya back now, along with a new appreciation for those flowers in carefully tended gardens, the mountains looming strong and steady over the town, the sense of home that permeated this place.

She drove toward those mountains now, to Cold Creek Canyon, where the creek flowed out of the high country and down through the valley. Her mother had given her directions to Taft's new house and she followed them, turning onto Cold Creek Road.

She found it no surprise that Jan knew Taft's address. Jan and her wide circle of friends somehow managed to keep their collective finger on the pulse of everything going on in town.

The area here along the creek was heavily wooded with Douglas fir and aspen trees and it took her a moment to find the mailbox with his house number. She peered through the trees but couldn't see anything of his house except a dark green metal roof that just about matched the trees in the fading light.

A bridge spanned the creek here and as she drove over it, she couldn't resist looking down at the silvery ribbon of water, darting over boulders and around fallen logs. Her children had been in that icy water, she thought, chilled all over again at how close she had come to losing everything.

She couldn't let it paralyze her. When the runoff eased a little, she needed to take Alex and Maya fishing in the river to help all of them overcome their fear of the water.

She stayed on the bridge for several moments, watching lightning-fast dippers crisscross the water for insects and a belted kingfisher perching on a branch without moving for long moments before he swooped into the water and nabbed a hapless hatchling trout.

As much as she enjoyed the serenity of the place, she finally gathered her strength and started her SUV again, following the winding driveway through the pines. She had to admit, she was curious to see his house. He had asked her to come see it, she suddenly remembered, and she had deflected the question and changed the subject, not wanting to intertwine their lives any further. She was sorry now that she hadn't come out while it was under construction.

The trees finally opened up into a small clearing and she caught her breath. His house was gorgeous: two stories of honey-colored pine logs and river rock with windows dominating the front and a porch that wrapped around the entire house so that he could enjoy the view of mountains and creek in every direction.

She loved it instantly, from the river-rock chimney rising out of the center to the single Adirondack chair on the porch, angled to look out at the mountains. She couldn't have explained it but she sensed warmth and welcome here.

Her heart pounded strangely in her ears as she parked the SUV and climbed out. She saw a light inside the house but she also heard a rhythmic hammering coming from somewhere behind the structure.

That would be Taft. Somehow she knew it. She reached in for the pie her mother had made—why hadn't she thought of doing something like this for him?—and headed in the direction of the sound.

She found him in another clearing behind the house, framing up a building she assumed would be an outbuilding for the horses he had talked about. He had taken off his shirt to work the nail gun, and that leather tool belt he had used while he was working at the inn—not that she had noticed or anything—hung low over his hips. Muscles rippled in the gathering darkness and her stomach shivered.

Here was yet another image that could go in her own mental Taft Bowman beefcake calendar.

She huffed out a little breath, sternly reminding herself that standing and salivating over the man was *not* why she was here, and forced herself to move forward. Even though she wasn't trying to use stealth, he must not have heard her approach over the sound of the nail gun and the compressor used to power it, even when she was almost on top of him. He didn't turn around or respond in any way and she finally realized why when she saw white earbuds dangling down, tethered to a player in the back pocket of his jeans.

She had no idea what finally tipped him off to her presence, but the steady motion of the nail gun stopped, he paused for just a heartbeat and then he jerked his head around. In that instant, she saw myriad emotions cross his features—surprise, delight, resignation and something that looked very much like yearning before he shuttered his expression.

"Laura, hi."

"Hello."

"Just a second."

He pulled the earbuds out and tucked them away, then crossed to the compressor and turned off the low churning sound. The only sound to break the abrupt silence was the moaning of the wind in the treetops. Taft quickly grabbed a T-shirt slung over a nearby sawhorse and pulled it over his head, and she couldn't help the little pang of disappointment.

"I brought you a pie. My mother made it for you." She held out it, suddenly feeling slightly ridiculous at the meagerness of the offering.

"A pie?"

"I know, it's a small thing. Not at all commensurate with everything you did, but...well, it's something."

"Thank you. I love pie. And I haven't had anything to eat yet, so this should be great. I might just have pie for dinner."

He had a square bandage just under his hairline that made him look rather rakish, a startling white contrast to his dark hair and sun-warmed features.

"Your head. You were hurt during the rescue, weren't you?"

He shrugged. "No big deal. Just a little cut."

Out of nowhere, she felt the hot sting of tears threaten. "I'm sorry."

"Are you kidding? This is nothing. I would have gladly broken every limb, as long as it meant I could still get to the kids."

She stared at him there in the twilight, looking big and solid and dearly familiar, and a huge wave of love washed over her. This was Taft. Her best friend. The man she had loved forever, who could always make her laugh, who made her feel strong and powerful and able to accomplish anything she wanted.

Everything she had been trying to block out since she arrived back in Pine Gulch seemed to break through some invisible dam and she was filled, consumed, by her love for him.

Those tears burned harder and she knew she had to leave or she would completely embarrass herself by losing her slippery hold on control and sobbing all over him.

She drew in a shuddering breath. "I… I just wanted to say thank-you. Again, I mean. It's not enough. It will never be enough, but thank you. I owe you…everything."

"No, you don't. You owe me nothing. I was only doing my job."

"Only your job? Really?"

He gazed at her for a long moment and she prayed he couldn't see the emotions she could feel nearly choking her. "Okay, no," he finally said. "If I had been doing my job and following procedure, I would have waited for the swift-water tech team to come help me extricate them. I would have done everything by the book. I spend seventy percent of my time training my volunteers in the fire department *not* to do what I did today. This wasn't a job. It was much, much more."

A tear slipped free but she ignored it. She could barely make out his expression now in the twilight and had to hope the reverse was also true. She had to leave. Now, before she made a complete fool of herself.

"Well… I'm in your debt. You've got a room anytime you want at the inn."

"Thanks, I appreciate that."

She released a breath and nodded. "Well, thank you again. Enjoy the pie. I'll, uh, see you later."

She turned so swiftly that she nearly stumbled but caught herself and began to hurry back to her SUV while the tears she had struggled to contain broke free and trickled down her cheeks. She didn't know exactly why she was crying. Probably not a single reason. The stress of nearly losing her children, the joy of having them returned to her. And the sudden knowledge that she loved Taft Bowman far more than she ever had as a silly twenty-one-year-old girl.

"Laura, wait."

She shook her head, unable to turn around and reveal so much of her heart to him. As she should have expected, she only made it a few more steps before he caught up with her and turned her to face him.

He gazed down at her and she knew she must look horrible, blotchy-faced and red, with tears dripping everywhere.

"Laura," he murmured. Just that. And then with a groan he folded her into his arms, wrapping her in his heat and his strength. She shuddered again and could no longer stop the deluge. He held her as she sobbed out everything that suddenly seemed too huge and heavy for her to contain.

"I could have lost them."

"I know. I know." His arms tightened and his cheek rested on her hair, and she realized this was exactly where she belonged. Nothing else mattered. She loved Taft Bowman, had always loved him, and more than that, she trusted him.

He was her hero in every possible way.

"And you." She sniffled. "You risked your life to go after them. You could have been carried away just as easily."

"I wasn't, though. All three of us made it through."

She tightened her arms around him and they stood that way for a long time with the creek rumbling over rocks nearby while the wind sighed in the trees and an owl hooted softly somewhere close and the crickets chirped for their mates.

Something changed between them in those moments. It reminded her very much of the first time he had kissed her, on that boulder overlooking River Bow Ranch, when she somehow knew that the world had shifted in some fundamental way and nothing would ever be the same.

After several moments, he moved his hands from around her and framed her face, his eyes reflecting the stars, then he kissed her with a tenderness that made her want to weep all over again.

It was a perfect moment, standing here with him as night descended, and she never wanted it to end. She wanted to savor everything—the soft cotton of his shirt, the leashed muscles beneath, his mouth, so firm and determined on hers.

She spread her palms on his back, pressing him closer, and he made a low sound in his throat, tightening his arms around her and deepening the kiss. She opened her mouth for him and slid her tongue out to dance with his while she pressed against those solid muscles, needing more.

His hand slipped beneath her shirt to the bare skin at her waist and she remembered just how he had always known how to touch her and taste her until she was crazy with need. She shivered, just a slight motion, but it was enough that he pulled his mouth away from hers, his breathing ragged and his eyes dazed.

He gazed down at her and she watched awareness return to his features like storm clouds crossing the moon, then he slid his hands away and took a step back.

"You asked me not to kiss you again. I'm sorry, Laura. I tried. I swear I tried."

She blinked, trying to force her brain to work. After a

moment, she remembered the last time he had kissed her, in the room she had just finished decorating. She remembered her confusion and fear, remembered being so certain he would hurt her all over again if she let him.

That all seemed another lifetime ago. Had she really let her fears rule her common sense?

This was Taft, the man she had loved since she was twelve years old. He loved her and he loved her children. When she had climbed out of his brother's police vehicle and seen him there by the stretcher with his arms around Alex—and more, when she had seen that rope still tied to the tree and the churning, dangerous waters he had risked to save both of her children—she had known he was a man she could count on. He had been willing to break any rule, to give up everything to save her children.

I would have gladly broken every limb, as long as it meant I could still get to the kids.

He had risked his life. How much was she willing to risk?

Everything.

She gave him a solemn look, her heart jumping inside her chest, feeling very much as if *she* was the one about to leap into Cold Creek. "Technically, *I* could still kiss you, though, right?"

He stared at her and she saw his eyes darken with confusion and a wary sort of hope. That little glimmer was all she needed to step forward into the space between them and grab his strong, wonderful hands. She tugged him toward her and stood on tiptoe and pressed her mouth to the corner of his mouth.

He didn't seem to know how to respond for a moment and then he angled his mouth and she kissed him fully, with all the joy and love in her heart.

Much to her shock, he eased away again, his expression raw and almost despairing. "I can't do this back-and-forth thing, Laura. You have to decide. I love you. I never stopped, all this time. I think some part of me has just been biding my time, waiting for you to come home."

He pulled his hands away. "I know I hurt you ten years ago. I can't change that. If I could figure out how, I would in a heartbeat."

At that, she had to shake her head. "I wouldn't change anything," she said. "If things had been different, I wouldn't have Alex and Maya."

He released a breath. "I can tell you, I realized right after you left what a fool I had been, too stubborn and proud to admit I was hurting and not dealing with it well. And then I compounded my stupidity by not coming after you like I wanted to."

"I waited for you. I didn't date anyone for two years, even though I heard all the stories about…well, the Bandito and everything. If you had called or emailed or anything, I would have come home in an instant."

"I'm a different man than I was then. I want to think I've become a *better* man, but I've still probably picked up a few more nicks and bruises than I had then."

"Haven't we all?" she murmured.

"I need to tell you, I want everything, Laura. I want a home, family. I want those things with you, the same things I wanted a decade ago."

Joy burst through her. When he reached for her hand, she curled her fingers inside his, wondering how it was possible to go from the depths of hell to this brilliant happiness in the course of one day.

"I hope you know I love your children, too. Alex is such a great kid. I can think of a hundred things I would love to show him. How to ride a two-wheeler, how to throw a spitball, how to saddle his own horse. I think I could be a good father to him."

He brought their intertwined fingers to his heart. "And Maya. She's a priceless gift, Laura. I don't know exactly what she's going to need out of life, but I can promise you, right now, that I would spend the rest of my life doing whatever it takes to give it to her. I swear to you, I would watch over her, keep her safe, give her every chance she has to stretch her wings as far as she can. I want to give her a place she can grow. A place where she knows, every single minute, that she's loved."

If she hadn't already been crazy in love with this man, his words alone and his love for her fragile, vulnerable daughter would have done the trick. She gazed up at him and felt tears of joy trickle out.

"I didn't mean to make you cry," he murmured, his own eyes wet. The significance of that did not escape her. The old Taft never would have allowed that sign of emotion.

"I love you, Taft. I love you so very much."

Words seemed wholly inadequate, like offering a caramel-apple pie in exchange for saving two precious lives, so she did the only thing she could. She kissed him again, holding him tightly to her. Could he feel the joy pulsing through her, powerful, strong, delicious?

After long, wonderful moments, he eased away again and she saw that he had been as moved as she by the embrace.

"Will you come see the house now?" he asked.

Was this his subtle way of taking her inside to make love? She wasn't quite sure she was ready to add one more earthshaking experience on this most tumultuous of days, but she did want to see his house. Besides that, she trusted him completely. If she asked him to wait, he would do it without question.

"Yes," she answered. He grinned and grabbed her hand and together they walked through the trees toward his house. He guided her up the stairs at the side of the house that led first to the wide uncovered porch and then inside to the great room with the huge windows.

She saw some similarities to the River Bow ranch house in the size of the two-story great room and the wall of windows, but there were differences, too. A balcony ringed the great room and she could see rooms leading off it.

How many bedrooms were in this place? she wondered. And why would a bachelor build this house that seemed made for a family?

The layout seemed oddly familiar to her and some of the details, as well. The smooth river-rock fireplace, the open floor plan, the random use of knobby, bulging, uniquely shaped logs as accents.

Only after he took her into the kitchen and she looked around at the gleaming appliances did all the details come together in her head.

"This is my house," she exclaimed.

"Our house," he corrected. "Remember how you used to buy log-home books and magazines and pore over them? I started building this house six months ago. It wasn't until you came back to Pine Gulch that I realized how I must have absorbed all those dreams inside me. I guess when I was planning the house, some of them must have soaked through my subconscious and onto the blueprints. I didn't even think about it until I saw you again."

It was a house that seemed built for love, for laughter, for children to climb over the furniture and dangle toys off the balcony.

"Do you like it?" he asked, and she saw that wariness in his eyes again that never failed to charm her far more than a teasing grin and lighthearted comment.

"I love everything about it, Taft. It's perfect. Beyond perfect."

He pulled her close again and as he held her there in the house he had built, she realized that love wasn't always a linear journey. Sometimes it took unexpected dips and curves and occasional sheer dropoffs. Yet somehow, despite the pain of their past, she and Taft had found their way together again.

This time, she knew, they were here to stay.

Epilogue

His bride was late.

Taft stood in the entryway of the little Pine Gulch chapel under one of the many archways decorated with ribbons and flowers of red and bronze and deep green, greeting a few latecomers and trying his best not to fidget. He glanced at his watch. Ten minutes and counting when he was supposed to be tying the knot, and so far Laura was a no-show.

"She'll go through with it this time. The woman is crazy about you. Relax."

He glanced over at Trace, dressed in his best-man's Western-cut tuxedo. His brother looked disgustingly calm and Taft wanted to punch him.

"I know," he answered. For all his nerves, he didn't doubt that for a moment. Over the past six months, their love had only deepened, become more rich and beautiful like the autumn colors around them. He had no worries about her pulling out of the wedding at the last minute.

He glanced through the doors of the chapel as if he could make her appear there. "I'm just hoping she's not having trouble somewhere. You don't have your radio on you, do you?"

Trace raised an eyebrow. "Uh, no. It's a wedding, in case you forgot. I don't need to have my radio squawking in the middle of the ceremony. I figured I could do without it for a few hours."

"Probably a good idea. You don't think she's been in an accident or something?"

Trace gave him a compassionate look. One of the hazards of working in public safety was this constant awareness of all the things that could go wrong in a person's life, but usually didn't. He was sure Trace worried about Becca and Gabi just as much as he fretted for Laura and the children.

"No. I'm sure there's a reasonable explanation. Why don't we check in with Caidy?"

That would probably be the logical course of action before he went off in a panic, since as maid of honor, she should be with Laura. "Yeah. Right. Good idea. Give me your phone."

"I can do it. That's what a best man is for, right?"

"Just give me your phone. Please?" he added, when Trace looked reluctant.

Trace reached into the inside pocket of his black suit jacket for his phone. "Hold on. I'll have to turn it back on. Wouldn't want any phones going off as you're taking your vows, either."

He waited impatiently, and after an eternity, his brother handed the activated phone over. Before he could find Caidy's number in the address book, the phone buzzed.

"Where are you?" he answered when he saw her name on the display.

"Taft? Why do you have Trace's phone?"

"I was just about to call you. What's wrong? Is Laura okay?"

"We're just pulling up to the church. I was calling to give you the heads-up that we might need a few more minutes. Maya woke up with a stomachache, apparently. She threw up before we left the cottage and then again on our way, all over her dress. We had to run back to the inn to find something else for her to wear."

"Is she all right now?"

"Eh. Okay, but not great. She's still pretty fretful. Laura's trying to soothe her. Have the organist keep playing, and as soon as we get there, we'll try to fix Maya up and calm her down a little more, then we can get this show on the road. Here we are now."

He saw the limo he had hired from Jackson Hole pulling up to the side door of the church, near the room set aside for the bridal party. "I see you. Thanks for calling."

He hung up the phone and handed it back to Trace. Ridge had joined them, he saw, and wore a little furrow of concern between his eyes.

"The girls okay?" Ridge asked.

"Maya's got a stomachache. Can you stall for a few more minutes?"

"Sure. How about a roping demonstration or something? I think I've got a lasso in the pickup."

He had to look closely at his older brother to see that Ridge was teasing, probably trying to ease the tension. Yeah, it wasn't really working. "I think a few more songs should be sufficient. I'm going to go check on Maya."

"What about the whole superstition about not seeing the

bride before the wedding?" Trace asked. "As I recall, you and Ridge practically hog-tied me to keep me away from Becca before ours."

"These are special circumstances. You want to try to stop me, you're more than welcome. Good luck with that."

Neither brother seemed inclined to interfere, so Taft made his way through the church to the bridal-party room. Outside the door, he could hear the low hush of women's voices and then a little whimper. That tiny sound took away any remaining hesitation and he pushed open the door.

His gaze instinctively went to Laura. She was stunning in a cream-colored mid-length lace confection, her silky golden hair pulled up in an intricate style that made her look elegant and vulnerable at the same time. Maya huddled in her lap, wearing only a white slip. Caidy and Jan stood by, looking helpless.

When Maya spotted him, she sniffed loudly. "Chief," she whimpered.

He headed over to the two females he loved with everything inside him and picked her up, heedless of his rented tux.

"What's the matter, little bug?"

"Tummy hurts."

She didn't seem to have a fever, from what he could tell.

"Do you think it's the giardiasis?" Jan asked.

He thought of the girl's abdominal troubles after her near-drowning, the parasite she had picked up from swallowing half the Cold Creek. "I wouldn't think so. She's been healthy for three months. Doc Dalton said she didn't need any more medicine."

His knees still felt weak whenever he thought of the miraculous rescue of the children. He knew he had been guided to them somehow. He found it equally miraculous that Alex had emerged unscathed from the ordeal and Maya's only lingering effect was the giardia bug she'd picked up.

She sure didn't look very happy right now, though. He wondered if he ought to call in Jake Dalton from the congregation to check on her, when he suddenly remembered a little tidbit of information that had slipped his mind in the joy-filled chaos leading up to the wedding.

"Maya, how many pieces of cake did you have last night at the rehearsal dinner?"

Two separate times he'd seen her with a plate of dessert but hadn't thought much about it until right now.

She shrugged, though he thought she looked a little guilty as she held up two fingers.

"Are you sure?"

She looked at her mother, then back at him, then used her other hand to lift up two more fingers.

Laura groaned. "No wonder she's sick this morning. I should have thought of that. We were all so distracted, I guess we must not have realized she made so many trips to the dessert table."

"I like cake," Maya announced.

He had to smile. "I do too, bug, but you should probably go easy on the wedding cake at the reception later."

"Okay."

He hugged her. "Feel better now?"

She nodded and wiped a fist at a few stray tears on her cheeks. She was completely adorable, and he still couldn't believe he had been handed this other miraculous gift, the chance to step in and be the father figure to this precious child and her equally precious brother.

"My dress is icky."

"You won't be able to wear your flower-girl dress with the fluffy skirt," Jan agreed. "We're going to have to wash it. It will probably be dry by the reception tonight, though. And look! I bought this red one for you for Christmas. We'll use that one at the wedding now and you'll look beautiful."

"You're a genius, Mom," Laura murmured.

"I have my moments," Jan said. She took her grand-daughter from his arms to help her into the dress and fix her hair again.

"Crisis averted?" he asked Laura while Jan and Caidy fussed around Maya.

"I think so." She gave him a grateful smile and his heart wanted to burst with love for her, especially when she stepped closer to him and slipped her arms around his waist. "Are you sure you're ready to take on all this fun and excitement?"

He wrapped his arms around her, thinking how perfectly she fit there, how she filled up all the empty places that had been waiting all these years just for her. He kissed her forehead, careful not to mess up her pretty curls. "I've never been more sure of anything. I hope you know that."

"I do," she murmured.

He desperately wanted to kiss her, but had a feeling his sister and her mother wouldn't appreciate it in the middle of their crisis.

The door behind them opened and Alex burst through, simmering with the energy field that always seemed to surround him except when he was sleeping. "When is the wedding going to start? I'm tired of waiting."

"I know what you mean, kid," Taft said with a grin, stepping away from Laura a little so he could pull Alex over for a quick hug.

His family. He had waited more than ten years for this, and he didn't know if he had the patience to stand another minute's delay before all his half-buried dreams became reality.

"Okay. I think we're good here," Caidy said, as Jan adjusted the ribbon in the girl's brown hair.

"Doesn't she look great?"

"Stunning," he claimed.

Maya beamed at him and slipped her hand in his. "Marry now."

"That's a great idea, sweetheart." He turned to Laura. "Are you ready?"

She smiled at him, and as he gazed at this woman he had known for half his life and loved for most of that time, he saw the rest of their lives ahead of them, bright and beautiful, and filled with joy and laughter and love.

"I finally am," she said, reaching for his hand, and together they walked toward their future.

* * * * *

WE HOPE YOU ENJOYED THIS BOOK FROM

HARLEQUIN
SPECIAL
EDITION

Believe in love. Overcome obstacles. Find happiness.

Relate to finding comfort and strength in the
support of loved ones and enjoy the journey
no matter what life throws your way.

6 NEW BOOKS AVAILABLE EVERY MONTH!

SPECIAL EXCERPT FROM

(H) HARLEQUIN

SPECIAL EDITION

*Skylar Davis is grateful to have her late husband's dog.
But the struggling widow can barely keep her three daughters
fed, much less a hungry canine. Kyle Mitchell was her
husband's best friend and he can't stop himself from rescuing
them. But will his exposed secrets ruin any chance they
have at building a family?*

Read on for a sneak peek at
Their Rancher Protector,
*the latest book in the Texas Cowboys & K-9s miniseries
by* USA TODAY *bestselling author Sasha Summers!*

"Even the strongest people need a break now and then. It's not a sign of being weak—it's part of being human," he murmured against her temple. "As far as I'm concerned, you're a badass."

She shook her head but didn't say anything.

"Look at your girls," he insisted. "You put those smiles on their faces. You found a way to keep them entertained and positive and with enough imagination to turn that leaning wooden shack into a playhouse—"

"Hey," she interrupted, peering up at him with red-rimmed eyes.

"I was teasing." He smiled. "You're missing the point here."

"Oh?" She didn't seem fazed by the fact that she was still holding on to him—or that there was barely any space between them.

But he was. And it had him reeling. The moment her gaze met his, the tightness and pressure in his chest gave way. And having Skylar in his arms, soft and warm and all woman, was something he hadn't prepared himself for.

Focus. Not on the unnerving reaction Skylar was causing, but on being here for Skylar and the girls. *Focus on honoring Chad's last request.* Chad—who'd expected him to take care of the family he'd left behind, not get blindsided and want more than he should. How could he not? Skylar was a strong, beautiful woman who had his heart thumping in a way he didn't recognize.

"Thank you, again." Her gaze swept over his face before she rose on tiptoe and kissed his cheek. "You're a good man, Kyle Mitchell."

Don't miss
Their Rancher Protector *by Sasha Summers,*
available August 2021 wherever
Harlequin Special Edition books and ebooks are sold.

Harlequin.com

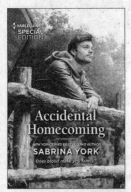

HARLEQUIN
SPECIAL EDITION

Believe in love. Overcome obstacles.
Find happiness.

Save **$1.00**

on the purchase of **ANY**
Harlequin Special Edition book.

Available wherever books are sold,
including most bookstores, supermarkets,
drugstores and discount stores.

Save $1.00

on the purchase of ANY Harlequin Special Edition book.

Coupon valid until September 27, 2021. Redeemable at participating outlets in the U.S. and Canada
only. Not redeemable at Barnes & Noble stores. Limit one coupon per customer.

52617238

Canadian Retailers: Harlequin Enterprises ULC will pay the face value of this coupon plus
10.25¢ if submitted by customer for this product only. Any other use constitutes fraud. Coupon is
nonassignable. Void if taxed, prohibited or restricted by law. Consumer must pay any government taxes.
Void if copied. Inmar Promotional Services ("IPS") customers submit coupons and proof of sales to
Harlequin Enterprises ULC, P.O. Box 31000, Scarborough, ON M1R 0E7, Canada. Non-IPS retailer—
for reimbursement submit coupons and proof of sales directly to Harlequin Enterprises ULC, Retail
Marketing Department, Bay Adelaide Centre, East Tower, 22 Adelaide Street West, 40th Floor, Toronto,
Ontario M5H 4E3, Canada.

5 65373 00076 2   (8100)0 12512

U.S. Retailers: Harlequin Enterprises ULC will pay the face
value of this coupon plus 8¢ if submitted by customer for
this product only. Any other use constitutes fraud. Coupon is
nonassignable. Void if taxed, prohibited or restricted by law.
Consumer must pay any government taxes. Void if copied.
For reimbursement submit coupons and proof of sales directly
to Harlequin Enterprises ULC 482, NCH Marketing Services,
P.O. Box 880001, El Paso, TX 88588-0001, U.S.A. Cash value
1/100 cents.

® and ™ are trademarks owned by Harlequin Enterprises ULC.

© 2021 Harlequin Enterprises ULC

HSECOUP91778MAX

Get 4 FREE REWARDS!

We'll send you 2 FREE Books plus 2 FREE Mystery Gifts.

FREE
Value Over
$20

Both the **Romance** and **Suspense** collections feature compelling novels written by many of today's bestselling authors.